SPRING BLIGHT

SEASON'S WAR BOOK THREE

OLENA NIKITIN

Content Warning

Season's War Series

AUTUMN CHAOS
WINTER DRAGON
SPRING BLIGHT
SUMMER VEIL coming in July 2023

A free prequel (short story) available upon subscription to the
newsletter: A LITTLE ACCIDENT
Other books, series page, snippets and more: HERE
For free books, ARCs, giveaways and more, sign up to :
NEWSLETTER
Don't want to commit - follow us on Amazon to get updates
about new releases.

Contents

AUTUMN CHAOS

Lady Inanuan of Thorn, Ina to her friends, is a former royal mage exiled from the court ten years ago and has been living a peaceful, if slightly unorthodox, life in the mystical Black Forest because of her sharp tongue and uncensored opinion. Still, she grew to love the magical forest until, one day, the local villagers deposited a half-dead warrior on her doorstep. With no other means to heal his mortal injuries, she resorted to performing her variation of a forbidden spell called the Sacrifice, linking his life energy to her in the process.

After awakening in a strange woman's bed, her patient reacted with an unchivalrous lack of gratitude. To make matters worse, Ina's property is overrun by a gaggle of nobles accusing her of killing Marcach of Liath, Captain of the King's Guards. With the supposedly dead captain standing alive and well beside her broken door, an officious judicial mage decided to take our hapless mage into custody, suspecting her of being a person of interest in a slew of recent monster attacks. The same monsters that Marcach or Mar, as we learn he is referred to, had come to investigate.

On the way to the capital, Ina is forced to heal the captain's best friend, Sa'Ren, an exotic Yanwo man and skilled swordsman whose troubles brought him to the Kingdom of Cornovii. The spell she performed now connects her with him as well, awakening dark desires and creating an intense rivalry between the brothers-in-arms. After an intense confrontation with the Magical Council, Ina is allowed to go free. However, her conscience is weighed down by the possibility that the mutagen she developed during her university years is now being used to turn ordinary citizens of all races into flesh-eating monsters.

Mar can't stop thinking about Ina and sends Ren to investigate and guard her secretly, finding, as time goes on, that not only does he think she isn't involved, but that he is drawn to her passionate soul. Despite their differences and fighting their mutual attraction, Mar and Ina team up to investigate the citizen's disappearances and find the mastermind behind the attacks.

Trying to reacclimatise to city living, Ina drags her friend to their old haunt, The Drunken Wizard, a dive of a pub run by a loveable, suspicious troll called Gruff, but this attempt at a normal life signals an increase in monster attacks and Ina herself is attacked in her new home by a giant spider-like creature. Once Ina and a frustrated Mar defeat the creature, the warrior realises his feelings for this fiery spitfire have grown.

Ina realises she needs help and asks her long-time friend, tavern owner Gruff, to find her a gem able to store significant amounts of magical energy, only to be unknowingly given one of the Chaos Regalia. Forced to crawl through the sewers of Osterad to find answers, Mar has to fight for his life, and the witch finds out her chaos magic is not as useless as she was taught. Ina soon learns that she has some fighting skills, and much to her displeasure, she realises she cares for this brute that the fates partnered her with. Their progress is disrupted by the king's death, which comes conveniently during Ina's convalescence, as the two men supposed to guard the king are fighting for her attention.

The grand coronation ball reveals the identity of our villains, but not their plans. While Mar makes headway with the investigation, Ina explores a different path, resulting in her capture by her former boyfriend, a mind mage called Liander. She learns an extra dimension to her magic, saving herself from Liander as Ren comes to her rescue, killing several mercenaries in a hypnotic dance of death. However, her moment of triumph is disturbed by the ominous sound of bells ringing in the city. The battle of Osterad had begun.

The battlefield reveals the true and terrifying potential of her chaos magic and the destruction it can bring. Unable to hold herself back, seeing her friends hurt and the mindless slaughter of innocent victims, she resorts to the ultimate measure and calls to the very thread of reality, dismantling the transformed monsters. Her command, "Bring them back to what they truly are," has unexpected consequences. The golden spark she'd discovered during Mar's healing is the long-buried secret of Liath, which responds to her command and transforms him into his true self, a beautiful, terrifying dragon.

Even though the battle is won, Ina feels she lost the war. She learns that whilst the king's older sister, her former friend, had orchestrated the attacks, seducing Mar's lieutenant Senad to carry out her plans, the young king knew about it and did nothing to prevent the carnage. Instead, he used his sister's greed for power and gambled on Ina's magic to secure the full support of his subjects. Rejecting the position of the court mage once more, Ina prepares to search for Mar in the Grey Mountains, the last known location of Dragons in Cornovii.

WINTER DRAGON

Ina and Ren travel to Liath in their search for Mar, encountering a blizzard on the way. Ina uses her magic to create a protective dome, saving herself and the dwarves they met during the storm, receiving a promise of help in exchange. Still, the amount of magic used makes her ill, and together with Ren, she is forced to rest in a nearby village.

Meanwhile, Mar flies away from the Osterad to prevent further bloodshed after the battle, heading to Liath thanks to a memory of his grandmother's stories, but as he gets injured by a ballista, he is forced to seek refuge in the ruins of a temple. The next day, while recovering, he meets Ayni, who teaches him to speak in dragon form and feeds him, revealing her true form.

Under the mountains, Tar'eth, a drow prince, has enslaved a local kobold tribe, searching their mines for the tomb of the last drow empress, Sowenna, the World Breaker, to retrieve a piece of her magical regalia. Already possesses the ring, given to him by a necromancer, he craves to gather a full set of regalia. After encountering Ina in Osterad, he knows she has the necklace. Now, Tar'eth wants both Ina's magic and the gem she carries.

Unaware of his plans, while recovering, Ina trains with Ren in swordsmanship, letting him teach her his Jian-kata style. In the meantime, with no other choice, Mar is healing in the dragon temple while Ayni teaches him about being a dragon. They begin forming an emotional bond thanks to the strange situation. Unfortunately, the dragoness mistakes his friendly curiosity for romantic affection. The next day Ayni takes him flying. Unaware of the custom, Mar unwittingly begins the mating dance with her.

After defending the village of Stary Brod from bandits, Ina and Ren arrive at the castle, receiving a frosty reception from Mar's parents. Her story leads to the revelation of the hidden dragon heritage of Liath. The next day, two dragons arrive, and an overjoyed witch runs to welcome Mar, but to her shock, Ayni separates them, claiming that Mar is her husband after they've completed the mating dance.

The feeling of betrayal makes her reject any voice of reason despite Mar vehemently denying being married, she later announces her plans to leave Liath, but during a tense supper, Alleron uses her new court position and forces Ina to investigate some unusual kobolds' attacks. Mar is so focused on Ina that he is oblivious to Ayni's flirting with him, which causes further discord between him and the witch, encouraging Ren, who loved her from the moment she healed him, to act on his feelings.

After retreating to her room, Ina is visited by Ren, and the Chaos mage confesses she knows how the warrior feels about her and, still feeling hurt, embraces him. Despite her determination and his desire, Ina cannot move past her love for Mar, and Ren accepts they will always be close but only as friends.

It takes more than a few bruises to clear the misunderstanding between the men. Still, it allows Mar to explain what happened with Ayni and convince Ina how he feels. Ina reflects on the conversation with Mar while his father takes her on a journey. On the road, they meet a strange man that Ina insists on helping, and in exchange, she receives a blessing from the mountain in the shape of a horse-like mountain spirit called an orein.

After some planning, Ina, Mar, Ren and Ayni head further into the mountains to investigate the attacks. During the night, they get attacked, with Ina forced to use her Chaos magic, and the situation gets out of hand. The soldiers they capture inform them that the drow prince is preparing to attack Liath. After a short debate, they split, Ren and Ayni heading back to Liath to prepare for the war with the drow while Mar and Ina continue the expedition.

Arriving at a beautiful protected glade, Ina makes an important choice and reconciles fully with Mar, renewing their relationship before, at the sign of pursuit, they head into a cave to hide, becoming trapped when the ceiling collapses.

With the entrance blocked, Mar and Ina have no choice but to continue further underground, with Ina feeling a strange pull towards something in the direction they are travelling. They find a peculiar cavern filled with crystals and gemstones. While they are resting, an old man appears, and Ina recognises the guardian of the mountains. He offers to take her to Sowenna's crypt.

On arriving, Ina discovers what is causing the alluring attraction, Sowenna's diadem - the remaining piece of the legendary Chaos regalia, which the guardian offers to the witch. Ina refuses to take the circlet, afraid of its power, which seems to amuse the powerful god.

After leaving the cave, they decide to fly to Liath, but Ina discovers a fear of flying, and they are forced to land. While recovering from her shock, she meets Tar'eth, who finds her thanks to his ring's connection to the witch's necklace. Tar'eth uses his affiliation with mind magic to take control of Ina's Chaos and fight Mar with her power. Mar is forced to retreat to Liath. Kidnapped by the drow, Ina fights to regain control over her magic, and Mar has to stay and prepare Liath's defences.

During the attack, Tar'eth tries using Ina's Chaos to break Liath's wall, only to learn she has regained control. They fight and, fuelled by the immense wave of Chaos, Ina kills him. Feeling overwhelmed by the sheer amount of raw magic, she notices the drow mages performing blood sacrifices to help their forces.

Shocked by the sheer atrocity of it and feeling her control will slip any moment, Ina sacrifices herself, opening a chasm that kills drow mages She falls into the abyss with them, unaware that Mar witnessed this and transformed into a dragon, diving in to save her. Later in the battle, Ina uses a vast amount of Chaos magic to force both armies to their knees, creating a spell with a single word. She gives them a choice: to surrender or die.

During the peace negotiations, Ina persuades the kobolds to become a part of Cornovii, gives the shifters citizenship rights, forces the capitulation of the drow, and returns, triumphant, to Osterad.

CHAPTER ONE

Gruff looked at the charred remains on the chair and huffed in irritation. The last thing he'd expected when Kaian asked him for an interrogation space was a magical fire engulfing the room. The only thing that saved the master assassin from painful contact with the troll's fist was his dumbfounded expression as he watched the suspect's immolation. The small rat-faced man they'd dragged in hadn't looked like a mage, with no garish robes or gem-encrusted jewellery, but the magical fire that had engulfed the poor soul's body was unmistakable. Looking at Kaian's face, it appeared they'd stumbled upon a more complex issue than he'd expected.

'Care to tell me what this is about, now that you've almost burned down my tavern?' Gruff asked.

'Do you really want me to?' The assassin tried to mask his concern with flippancy, but his attitude didn't fool the troll.

'No, it would be best to ask about it at the official meeting of the royal council for the king to explain it,' Gruff said with a smile that not even a mountain troll would call pleasant, and Kaian winced before sighing and leaning against the least charred wall.

'Fine. The king already knows, but we're trying to keep a lid on this, and it was his idea to interrogate the suspect away from the palace. You know about the unrest in the South?' Kaian asked, and Gruff realised he expected him to confirm his knowledge. When he nodded, the assassin continued. 'Last month, we noticed increased activity between the southern nobles and the capital. The correspondence we intercepted was in some unknown code, always stamped with a sheaf of three golden ears of wheat. This man carried one of those letters, and I was hoping for some answers.'

Gruff silently folded his massive arms and looked at the assassin until Kaian until he shifted under his gaze. 'So, you have a traitor in the palace who works for the South. What are you not telling me?'

The question seemed simple, but Kaian shook his head before answering. 'I'm not hiding things from you. We don't have much information ourselves. From what little Rewan deciphered, the southern border provinces want to separate and join the Southern March Union, and we are pretty sure Verdante's council is involved somehow. I was hoping to get more from this unhelpful piece of coal.' Kaian stood up, visibly irritated, and paced the small space until he stopped before the charred corpse. 'This makes no sense. He wasn't a mage, I'm sure of it. My people searched him before bringing his worthless arse here, yet this still happened. Do you know how he managed it?'

'Why are you asking me?' Gruff's eyebrows shot high at this sudden question. 'Ask the mages or bring the issue to Arun himself. He will be available after the council meeting.'

'I don't trust them, and Rewan can't afford to confide in anyone. First Liath, and now the South? It's just too big a

2

coincidence. Do you think Ina would know this magic?' Kaian was talking to himself, and suddenly added, 'Ha, no. Too sneaky for our little witch, but I think this situation would suit her perfectly. If anyone can flush out trouble, it's her.'

A sudden thud shook the wall when Gruff's fist crushed the plaster next to Kaian's head. 'Will you two stop pushing her from one catastrophe to another? She saved Liath for you, and now you want her to drive out the traitors when she just returned home? Find yourself some other bait and leave that girl alone.'

It was Kaian's turn to raise an eyebrow at the rare display of the troll's affection. He pushed off from the wall and shrugged before replying curtly. 'I would if I could, but we don't have many options where magic is involved. I can promise you this, Rewan will ask nicely and not push her to agree.'

Gruff's laugh shook soot from the rafters. 'Just give me a ring-side seat if he ever tries. However, I know you and your king, and I respect how he manipulates people to do his bidding. If you tell her the truth and she agrees, that's fine, but I will know if any of you try to fool her into doing this, and I will make sure Rewan loses this city if he tries.'

Kaian approached the troll and raised his head, examining his craggy features. 'Why do you care about her so much? Hmm. Believe it or not, Rewan likes his royal witch and would never ask for something she couldn't accomplish.'

Gruff turned from the assassin's gaze, tensing his massive shoulders. 'Ina is my friend, one who offers her heart honestly without demanding payment,' he said, as though that simple sentence contained all the answers, and his challenging glare made Kaian smile.

'I will be on my way and update you on the situation once we know more. Keep our incorrigible Ina safe, especially now they've asked her to teach at the university. We don't want any more frog incidents.' The stunned look on Gruff's face starkly contrasted Kaian's gleeful expression. The troll had the fleeting impression that the assassin master had just congratulated himself on this small victory.

'Are they out of their minds? Which dimwit came up with that inspired idea?' The troll's loud voice chased him through the underground corridors, but Kaian was already deep in thought. The patrons moved out of his way promptly; no one wanted to disturb a man who looked like he planned on killing his next victim.

Ina woke up and stretched, the first light of a spring day warming her face. Since returning from Liath, Mar had been staying in her home; he went as far as giving Ren and Ayni his townhouse, and while it took some getting used to having various pieces of armour and weapons around the place, she didn't regret allowing him to stay. It had taken Marika chasing him around the yard a few times, but now the Lord Marshal was especially careful to clean and store his armoury neatly and discretely in an annexe he'd paid to have built in the yard.

Ina couldn't help smiling, thinking about how he found more and more ridiculous reasons to stay in her house each day and how she pretended to believe them. They both knew he was lying, but it made them happy to keep the pretence going.

It was all fun and games till one day, Mar had to stay in the camp and forgot to send a message home, and she sat the whole night by the fire, worried he was dead in a ditch or had found somewhere else to live after she repeatedly told him to move out. When Mar finally came home in the morning, she threw him on his back with her magic and told him she wanted him to stay for good.

'About time. I've run out of excuses,' he had answered, kissing her fiercely, making them both laugh.

Turning to the side, Ina looked at the sleeping warrior. She couldn't resist reaching out and stroking the thick hair on his chest, smiling as Mar moaned, but didn't wake. The witch shivered at the sound, taking it as a challenge, and slowly slid her hand down, trailing her fingertips over the narrowing band of hair till it reached his manhood. The mischievous smile on her lips widened as Ina discovered Mar's less-than-little soldier was ready for inspection. With practised ease, she straddled his body, gently stroking herself with his cock. The growl her dragon made surprised her almost as much as the sudden grip on her hips, but her moan of satisfaction as he pushed inside stole that thought, and Ina rocked her hips to meet his passionate thrusts.

Mar's breath quickened, and when his eyes flashed gold, Ina reached down, stroking herself as her dragon took charge of their pace. When his roar shook the room, Ina tightened her muscles, riding him till her own pleasure peaked, then slowly collapsed onto his chest. She was ready to drift back to sleep when she felt the tickle of his beard on her cheek.

'If there were ever a perfect morning, it is this one. Did you just use me to pleasure yourself, my spitfire?' Mar stroked her back, but the amusement and contentment in his voice were unmistakable. 'I should be offended by such liberties done to my sleeping body, but if you promise me a hearty breakfast, I'm willing to forgive your transgressions,' he added as he stretched out on the bed. Ina realised she could smell fried bacon cooking downstairs. She could only roll her eyes. Having three—well, four if you count the orein—carnivorous beasts in the house, meant she spent a small fortune on meat, despite hardly eating any herself.

'Should I promise I will never do it again?'

'Don't you dare! I have to keep my beautiful chaos away from the madness, and I'm ready for any sacrifice it takes. Besides, how could you resist this glorious beast? I'm so bloody adorable.' He stretched even further, allowing the covers to fall on the floor, and Ina burst out laughing.

He was impossible, cute, and so easy to be with in his indecently grumpy way, disarming her completely. Ina stood up from the bed, inhaling deeply, pulling her shoulders back till she felt her bones creak.

'Are you heading to the training grounds again today?' she asked, already knowing the answer. Mar had been tasked with building Cornovii's new army, and he'd embraced this responsibility with an enthusiasm she hadn't expected.

'Yes, Ren has some recruits he thinks have potential, and we are still trying to incorporate the mages into the army, but neither side trusts the other, and that's causing accidents to soldiers and mages alike.'

The laugh Ina almost snorted was full of disdain. 'Good luck with that. Battle mages are the most arrogant bastards you'll ever meet. My advice? Find a way to cut them off from magic mid-fight. A nullifying field should help. If they are confronted with their mortality, it might help them see the soldiers as equals if they have to rely on others a few times.'

Mar nodded and kissed the top of Ina's head before he helped her to the dressing table as she grumbled about a large something causing weak knees. 'I will try. And what are your plans? Will I see you at home this evening, or will I have to carry you home from the *Drunken Wizard*? Or is it Daro's turn to chase our women across the city?'

Ina playfully elbowed him and shook her head, looking up. 'Not tonight. Velka is not in the mood recently, and I have things to do. I'm going to the university. I'm teaching a new class, remember? Then I have to see Jorge, as he's requested a meeting. The old stick probably wants a pound of flesh for another prediction spell.'

Mar groaned and looked at her. 'Can't you sit back and enjoy the spring or something? I want some time at home to get cosy with my little witch instead of digging for another monster in the sewers.'

The punch in the shoulder only made him laugh, but Ina looked at him with a serious expression. 'Mar, I'm not a housewife or a king's trophy. You have your toy soldiers to play with, and I have a job to do. So far, all I've done is traipse back and forth to the palace, sitting on my butt through all those boring council meetings. I can't be what you want me to be. I'm sorry.'

Mar's eyes widened, and he leaned over, crushing her cheek to his chest. 'No, I'm sorry. I know you're not someone who'd be content with sitting at home embroidering silk handkerchiefs. You are perfect the way you are, and I should think before I show you just how big a fool I really am.'

Ina nodded and was about to say something when a loud meow and scratching at the door interrupted their conversation, making Ina chuckle.

'Come, Boruta is hungry, and you don't want to annoy our dark overlord. He still blames you for losing his place in my bed.'

Mar smiled and helped lace her dress. 'And yet he fell asleep on my lap the other day. Perhaps I earned my blessing from the forest after all,' he said. Despite the smile on his face, his eyes darkened, giving her a pause. Mar hid something from her, and she intended to explore this later.

After a breakfast full of interruptions from the demanding cat, with his desire for the best of the meat, Ina kissed her dragon goodbye and went to Magical University. With no clue what to expect, the chaos mage wondered how they saw her teaching a class about the one type of magic they had spent decades attempting to eradicate. Since receiving the invitation from the new archmage, Arun, to demonstrate her magic, Ina had been feeling a maelstrom of emotions. While it felt good to be finally acknowledged, she felt completely out of her depth at the thought of teaching a type of magic she didn't fully understand herself.

Distracted by those thoughts, Ina missed the chance to stop Zjawa from stealing a ham hock hanging from a butcher's stall as they passed. The cursing of the stall owner was soon replaced with generous thanks as the witch threw him enough coin to buy a whole pig and turned her attention to the now happy mare, patting her neck with a good-natured insult. Frankly, she had more money than she needed, with Rewan showering her with gifts and the wages from her new position of Royal Witch, or Royal Deterrent as Daro called it, so she didn't mind handing out a few extra coins to the local traders.

The traffic thinned, and Ina's shoulders tensed as the university gates loomed ahead. She sighed at the effort to remind herself she was no longer a bungling student and forced her shoulders to relax. As she looked around, conversations stopped, heads turned towards her, and urgent whispering filled the sudden silence before a horde of eager students rushed over to gawk at her strange mount.

'You're the crimson witch,' one brave soul called out with palpable disdain, only flinching a little when Ina turned to face him.

'I am Lady Inanuan of Thorn, *the* Royal Witch, Chaos Mage or Master Alchemist. Any of those titles will do. If you haven't learnt the manners befitting a student of this illustrious institution, perhaps you should be taught respect for your instructors. So if you wouldn't mind providing me with your name?' The smile that followed her answer and the shimmer of magic made them gasp. However, the young oaf standing in front of her was too stupid to back down in his desire to impress the young ladies of the academy, and he stepped forward, the sneer on his lips growing.

'I'm Raleigh Caven, a fifth-year necromancer, and I'm sure everyone here would love to see a demonstration of the weakest magical discipline. I'm sure a *witch* of your sort is almost comparable to a first-year mage of the university.' The look he shared with the crowd received far too many cheers for Ina's temper.

'Oh well, then...' Ina feigned disinterest, but the necromancer's attitude reminded her of the years of humiliation at the hands of ignorant mages demeaning her magic. It was clear the indoctrination of the students was still thriving.

She almost didn't blame the young mage for his attitude, but Ina was there to teach, and he was about to learn not to patronise the one mage capable of unravelling his existence. The gathered students gasped as tendrils of chaos wove themselves around her arms, and Ina was pleased to see the uncertainty in her opponent's eyes. The crackling of leashed power built up, but before Ina could release her intent, a panicked voice interrupted the proceedings as Arun, provost of the university and head of battle magic, pushed in front of the now cowering necromancer.

'Ina! I mean, Lady Inanuan. I'm so happy to see you've arrived safely. I would be grateful if you refrained from disciplining students here in the yard, as magical duels frighten the servants and take too long to wash away the blood. Would you follow me to meet with the rest of our faculty?'

The nervous look Arun gave her came with a smirk, and Ina sighed before allowing her magic to dissipate. After dismounting from Zjawa, she tossed the reins to the annoying necromancer and nodded to the battle mage.

'Then please lead on. Speaking of student discipline, I will allow Master Raleigh to care for my mount. If he still lacks manners by the time he joins my class, I am sure we can remedy his attitude there.'

Arun led her to his office, and Ina barely restrained her glee. Since becoming the head of the university, the hot-headed battle mage spent more time behind a desk than he did flinging fireballs at his enemies, but right now, it looked like he wished to be throwing a few in her direction.

'Ina, would you care to explain that display outside? With your age and status, you still allowed some pissant lord's son to rile you up?' Arun's sigh was more groan than breath as he sat down, shaking his head.

'You're calling me, a chaos mage, old?'

'I'm saying the king's advisor should know better than getting into a magical brawl with a fifth-year know-it-all student.' By the end of the sentence, Arun was half out of his seat shouting, his face more purple than was healthy for a man his age.

'Arun, you'll make yourself ill if you don't calm down. It wasn't a duel, and the only thing that would happen was some little boy losing his splendid clothes in front of the pretty ladies. I'm sure they would've appreciated seeing his little wand.' Ina shrugged, wiggling her pinkie as she sat on the edge of the archmage's desk, carelessly pushing his paperwork aside.

'You will be teaching here, so perhaps behave with a little decorum?' Arun gathered his scattered documents and added, 'I scheduled you for several classes on chaos magic. I want you to show our students what it is, how it works, and what happens when they use it without sigils and diagrams. I am not asking you to scare them off, or maybe I am? I don't know what will work best, but since your antics in Liath, they started experimenting with it themselves, and I don't want any more incidents.'

'What does my time in Liath have to do with it?' Ina was genuinely surprised and frowned when Arun's lips tightened to a mere slit.

'You made two bloody armies kneel on command. The mind mages nearly wet themselves when they found out, so, of course, they all tried to replicate it. There are three idiots in the infirmary. There is also the one who did… something, and now he can't access magic at all.' He stood up and paced the room as Ina watched, mouth wide open in surprise. 'Oh, and don't get me started on the nitwits trying to bespell every man they find attractive in case they have a hint of dragon bloodline. The poor fellows are still getting over being stuck on all fours while the faculty searched for a counter-spell. So fix your mess before it gets worse.'

Finally getting her voice back, Ina pointed a shaking finger at Arun. 'What do you mean, *fix your mess?* Who was it that suppressed knowledge of this magic in the first place? If you hadn't hidden the information, these idiots would already know how dangerous it is. Oh, and let's not forget, I have no idea what I'm doing, either, because all books that contain any knowledge of chaos are in the forbidden section. I'm making it up as I go along, and neither of us has forgotten the frog incident, so scheduling me to teach a class was not your best idea.'

Arun sighed heavily. 'As long as you agree to be a teacher, you will be granted special privileges. You now have access to every book in the library, including the restricted section. Research everything you need to learn about your talent, but you must put an end to their curiosity. The one thing I am certain of is your talent to scare the stupid, so until you have the knowledge you need, just give them a demonstration to prevent further experimentation. And Ina, it is not a charity. For as long as you teach, all doors are open for you. Quit, and they will close right in front of your face.'

Ina couldn't stop looking at his face, his agitated expression showing how every word pained him, and at the end of his long speech, she shrugged.

'I knew your offer was too good to be true. Still, I can show them a few things I've learned in exchange for library privileges. So where is my class?' Ina was already halfway to the exit when she heard Arun.

'The northern wing, next to your old alchemy classroom. And Ina, please don't destroy anything.'

The small, round building separated from the northern wing didn't have enough space for the gathered crowd. When the witch arrived at the auditorium, every seat was taken, and the bruises on the faces of those still standing revealed fierce competition for the seats. Ina tapped on the nearest shoulder, nodding at the scowling male who turned towards her.

'What is going on here?'

'The royal witch is here to demonstrate chaos magic, and everyone came to watch.'

She smiled at the man. 'Well, in that case, you should let her pass.'

The young man, clearly a new arrival to Osterad, snorted, looking her over with disdain. 'As if you're the royal witch, shortie. Wait your turn like everybody else.'

Ina briefly considered adding to the collection of bruises on his face but sighed, turned around and left the building, heading towards the empty training field behind it that was conveniently overseen by the auditorium's large windows. Ina wished Mar or Ren were there to illustrate the effectiveness of her fighting technique, but for now, she needed something awe-inspiring to get the student's attention.

The witch focused on her magic, feeling the chaos of nature's rebirth calling to her senses. Gathering small amounts from the surrounding vegetation to avoid killing the plants, Ina formed the power into a spell and released it into the ground towards the sturdy building before her, smiling in satisfaction at how easy it had become to manipulate chaos. The more she used it, the more natural it became, and the witch finally absolved herself of the sense of failure that had plagued her life.

A slow, rumbling tremor shook the stones of the auditorium. As panicking students fled the shuddering building, Ina closed her hand into a fist and drew more power from the peridot on her finger. With a mocking smile, she whipped her hand towards the panicked mages and projected a web of magic that hung in the air, quickly capturing them. In a flash of inspiration, Ina linked the spell to any other magic used in the courtyard. As their training finally began kicking in, necromancers, battle, and mind mages wove their spells, only to look at their hands in disbelief as their power disappeared, fuelling her net. Ina walked towards her helpless prey and snapped out fiery vipers, the crack of the whip focusing all attention on her.

Their attempt to fight widened Ina's smile. When the whimpering stopped, Ina let the silence stretch out as she casually looked each student in the eye, finally speaking when each helpless mage looked down.

'That is your first lesson about chaos mages. We are versatile and unpredictable and… well, often insane. We are not limited to a single domain, and we are vicious. Chaos is not just magic. It is life itself. A primal force that will tear you apart if you use it without spell constructs. If you are lucky enough to be born with the spark, then congratulations, you can use chaos as easily as breathing. All you need to worry about is losing your mind, destroying everything and everyone you love before finally tearing out the magic inside you to feed your addiction, killing yourself in the process. Remember this, and never dare taunt me again or touch chaos magic without permission. Class dismissed.'

With a wave of her hand, Ina allowed her magical net to dissipate, but when the students didn't move, she whipped the ground in front of them with her vipers, laughing openly at their scrambling escape.

Ina smiled in triumph at the disappearing students. *That was perfect. Arun's mission is fulfilled, and now I can go to the library,* she thought, feeling she had accomplished all her goals. There wouldn't be many candidates for her class, and if Arun still forced her to take on students, she was more than ready to torment those who did. Especially if it meant she gained unlimited library access. So little effort and the witch could finally learn more about her chaos magic. Her time in Liath showed how little she knew and how dangerous it could be.

That looming pit of darkness deep inside her grew every time she harnessed death to fuel her spells. Soon, even the bright light anchoring her to Mar and Ren might fail to ward off the impending madness. *I have to find another way to use chaos. Royal witch, my ass. I'm useless if I can only shake some bricks unless thrown into the middle of a slaughter.* The peridot on her finger shimmered in response to her mood, reminding her of the circlet she left behind under Skarbnik's care, and Ina shook her head. Mar had the golden eyes of his dragon betraying his mood. She had the ring that twinkled like some damned fairy. *Enough brooding for today, woman. Get yourself together. There is an entire library to plunder.*

CHAPTER TWO

The clash of swords frightened the songbirds into silence and Ina sighed deeply, grateful for a little fresh air and a respite after spending several days between dusted volumes of the university library. Still, she had to admit it was worth it, and what she had learned changed her outlook on her bond with both men. Velka sprawled on her chair by her side, holding onto a potted plant for dear life, trying to coax the poor thing to grow. The mage seemed oblivious to the fighting men, and Ina was about to leave her to her efforts when Velka said, 'Tell them if they trample my flower bed, I will skewer them and use their corpses as fertiliser.'

Ina snorted and, picking up her weapon, strolled over to the grass to join the fighters. The three men were happily engaged in a melee fight, and Ina noticed Ren and Daro picking on her dragon. Mar was laughing, fending off his attackers, but the sweat was already beading on his forehead as he did his best to match Ren's speed and Daro's strength.

This will be fun, she thought, calling forth chaos and conjuring her fire vipers to life.

'Kneel, weaklings. The Lady of the Crimson Veil is coming!' she shouted, jumping between them and taking Mar's side. The men roared in mock anger, and then laughter scared the remaining birds away as they adjusted their stance to accommodate another fighter. Since the battle of Liath and her unconventional way of subduing the army, those words had become running jokes in the barracks, with veterans threatening the recruits that if they didn't work harder, the Lady of the Crimson Veil would come for their souls.

Ina had initially felt offended by the moniker, but that didn't mean she couldn't use it as banter between friends. From the day she'd started practising with Ren after stabbing the wardrobe with a fire poker, her skills had improved, and she took genuine pleasure in this daily exercise. Now fighting beside them in the garden full of colourful flowers, Ina felt carefree. They continued for a while until Mar called for a stop, and, panting, Ina threw herself onto the ground.

Her life was good, the sky was blue, and the earth suspiciously smelled of oranges.

'Velka, stop messing around.' Ina laughed. She didn't need to look at the nature mage to know her rose lips were now pursed in an adorable pout that would send Daro to the palace kitchen to get oranges for his demanding wife.

'But I want an orange….' The mage's pitiful voice and the creaking of leather told her she was correct in her suspicions, and Daro was already on citrus duty.

'I wish you were like him,' Ina said, placing her head on Mar's thigh when he sat close by, seeing his eyebrows rise.

'I thought I was. Big, burly and in love, what else could my lady desire?' he asked, laughing, then started cleaning his sword above her head.

'First off, you could stop waving that smelly rag over my face, and second, you could fulfil my every wish without question.' She grinned and snapped her fingers, incinerating the dirty cloth.

'For this, you must marry me, as I could never refuse my wife.' Mar's eyes lit up, and Ina felt like choking him. Since she let him stay in her house, the new marshal had made more and more of these little slips about further commitment. Their bumpy relationship had evolved, and she grudgingly admitted to being happy with the situation, but didn't want it to change any further. However, their carefree life was clearly not enough for Mar, but Ina was too pragmatic to be annoyed.

'You wish,' she said and slowly stood up. Ina kissed Mar's cheek and decided she needed a walk before her muscles got stiff. When her eyes met Ren's, Ina made a flash decision.

'Come, I need the company of a man who doesn't want to marry me,' she said, reaching out and smiling when she heard Mar's soft grumble, but Ren had already given her his arm. Ina led them through the garden, the springtime barely waking the somnolent plant life before she sat down on a rock and gazed upon the river. She felt his arm embracing her, and Ina supported her head on his shoulder.

'What troubles you?' he asked, as usual, unmistakably detecting her mood change.

'Mar, the peace and whether it will last, how good I feel now. It is too good to be true, Ren, and good things never last long around me. What if I'm going to lose it all?' She knew one word about her genuine worries, and both men would shelter her from anything that could fuel her magic. *If I don't want to spend my life in a beautiful padded box guarded by a dragon, I will have to figure it out somehow*, she thought.

'It is difficult to answer this, but maybe I can help. Do you want me to talk to Mar? He is blinded by happiness living with you, and if I know what he is doing wrong, I can beat some sense into his thick dragon skull.' Ren stroked her hair, and when she looked up, she saw concern in his eyes.

'He is not doing anything wrong. He makes me happy, Ren. Far too happy for my own good. Still, at some point, he will want to settle down, have kids and take over Liath. I can't give him this.' Ina felt giving voice to her worry had finally lifted the heavy weight she'd been carrying since Mar's proposal, but Ren tugged her braid and laughed at her words.

'Ina, he earned your love, and it is far more than that pugnacious lizard deserves, and he knows it. Stop worrying about problems that don't exist.'

'Maybe. You're probably right. Now, tell me, where is Ayni? I haven't seen her in days,' Ina said, feeling the need to change the subject.

'All around town, mostly making new friends and shopping. I think she is trying to figure out how to fit in with ordinary humans, and I even heard a rumour that my dragoness is thinking of opening a dressmaking shop. She keeps saying the ladies here have no taste, and it is her mission to fix it,' Ren answered with a smile. It appeared her friend had settled in at Mar's old townhouse. Each time she mentioned Ayni, Ren's eyes lit up, and his face softened.

Seeing the happiness in his eyes as he talked about Ayni's plans, Ina dared to ask, 'Are you happy, Ren? Do you love her?' But before he could answer, a young messenger appeared before them.

'My lady, the king awaits…' he said, panting heavily, causing Ina to curse under her breath. The sun was high in the sky, and

20

she had completely forgotten Rewan wanted to talk to her this morning.

'Was Lord Marcach summoned as well?' She recalled Rewan wanted to see them both this time.

'Yes, he asked—erm…' answered the boy before blushing like a peony. 'The captain said, "Tell her if she doesn't shift her pretty arse, I will spank it".' At the end of the message, the boy's stutter was so apparent that Ina laughed and jumped off the rock.

'Well, we must preserve a lady's virtue. I'll see you later, my friend.' She kissed Ren's cheek and walked towards the palace.

After the palace battle, Rewan used the opportunity to change the current decor, and Ina had to admit she liked it. Opulence was replaced by simple elegance and light colours. It gave the palace an elusively airy and soft feeling. Still, the heavy layer of protective spells and magical reinforcement was slightly oppressive to mages. After several assassination attempts, Kaian took it upon himself to remove every weak point. He'd spent several days with Mar discussing defensive strategies in case of external attacks and internal struggles. As a result, the palace was turned into a gorgeous fortress, beautiful but deadly, just like the good king's mind.

Everyone was already there when she entered Rewan's office, but to her surprise, the king looked anxious. It was rather odd, as he usually maintained a straight face, even in the direst of circumstances. Mar and Kaian had already dived into another military strategy, evaluating it from every angle, and she couldn't help but smile, seeing how their minds synchronised regarding military matters. Mar wanted to incorporate shifters into the king's guards, especially after their pivotal role in sensing the drow army during the Winter War. Ina had to admit it was an excellent idea. Their heightened senses could provide invaluable intel and additional protection, but Kaian didn't seem convinced. Was that the reason she had been called?

'Ina, I'm glad you're here.' Rewan noticed her first. She smiled and settled on the windowsill's pillow, looking at the gathering. She saw Kaian stop his conversation and move to Rewan, placing a hand on his shoulder in a reassuring gesture.

'So, what catastrophe are we dealing with now?'

Her light tone and playful wink were meant to relieve the tension, but she saw Rewan's pale fingers tighten, much like his advisor's on his shoulder.

'Oh, for fuck's sake, just tell me,' Ina said, jumping down and approaching the king. 'You're not dying or something, are you?' She grabbed Rewan's chin and tilted his head, looking for concerning signs. The tension burst, and Rewan pulled back with a brief chuckle.

'No, I'm not dying. I'm thinking of getting married.'

Ina rolled her eyes and moved away, standing behind Mar, who had listened silently to this exchange. She placed her hand on the dragon's shoulder, mimicking Kaian's gesture, and shrugged.

'You're thinking? Well, congratulations, Your Majesty. Who is the lucky lady? One of the spring chicks from the South that have been flocking to the palace lately?'

Rewan's lips tightened, and he gripped the edge of the desk, sending her a challenging stare. 'We both know you know it is not a lady. I will marry Kaian,' he said, and his voice rang with determination.

'I keep telling him it is a stupid idea. He needs a proper bride and an heir. I love him too much to make Rewan face the wrath of the nobles or comparison to his father, but our righteous king won't listen. The only thing stopping this disaster is me saying no.' Kaian's voice was calm, but she still could hear the underlying grief of a selfless man who preferred to live in the shadow of a future queen over harming his lover.

She looked at them standing next to each other, as different as night and day, and smiled. 'Rewan, if you're asking for my blessing, you have it, but I still don't understand what I have to do with it.'

The king went to answer, but Kaian got there first. 'We have a problem with the South. We recently discovered that Rewan's drunkard father, King Roda, promised the next queen to the South. The spring chicks flocking to the palace are maidens hopeful of catching His Majesty's eye, while their fathers are scrambling for the power a marriage would grant them. The southern provinces are already on the brink of rebellion, and announcing this unusual betrothal will destroy whatever support we still have.'

Ina looked at Rewan, who sat there, crumpled in his chair. She felt sorry for the man who had even less ability to control his life than she did. Still, when she looked closer, something in this heart-touching story wasn't right. 'You're not one to make political mistakes, so what aren't you telling me?' She didn't expect what would happen next. Rewan stood up, and with an angry gesture, he threw a pile of papers to the floor.

'What happened? For once, I want to do something for myself.' He turned to Kaian, who studied his lover with a worried expression. 'I love you. That should not be too difficult to understand. I spend all my time keeping this kingdom together without a word of complaint. All I want is to be with you instead of stealing time like thieves in the night.'

'So you are keeping the southern lords' daughters as a guarantee of peace, but this guarantee will expire as soon as you choose your bride. Your declaration will lead to rebellion when a few hesitant nobles join those who already oppose your rule.' Mar, quiet so far, summarised the problem.

Kaian nodded and smiled at Mar. 'And that is why I asked you two here. I can stop this silly man from making trouble for himself, but I can't stop him forever.' Kaian looked at Ina and bowed slightly. 'I'm asking for your help, my lady. If anyone could solve the trouble with the southern lands, it's you.'

Ina slowly clapped her hands, shaking her head, and looked at Rewan with amusement. 'You really overdid it, my king. I almost bought it, but throwing your papers and bowing? You both need to work on your acting. I know you can take whatever southern maiden you choose to your bed, and her father won't protest Kaian's presence as long as his daughter is queen. This kingdom is used to such arrangements. Can we stop insulting my intelligence now and tell me what in Nawia is going on?' She was about to march back to her windowsill when Rewan approached her and placed a hand on her shoulder.

'I'm sorry. I was trying to test a theory. We need to stall for time, and I thought if I could convince you, I could convince everyone else. The South will rebel, and we have a spy in the palace who allows them to counter our every move, but I was truthful about my desire to marry Kaian, and it will happen.'

He gave her a coy smile and returned to his chair, letting the master assassin detail the recent troubles on the southern border, including ominous letters and the messenger's immolation in the *Drunken Wizard's* basement. When he finished, Ina took a deep breath.

'Fine!' she said, shaking her head, 'I will investigate what is going on there, and you can stay here, keep quiet and play attentive gallant to the noble daughters. If I can suggest something, spread the rumour that they must find their way into Kaian's good graces to get to your bed. That way, you can scrutinise the most cunning and desperate. I need you to buy me some time, so please be as charming as Kaian is cunning.'

'I'm not just cunning. I'm charming too when I want to be, but that is a good idea and can reduce the danger to Rewan. If they consider me an obstacle to conquer, I will be the focal point for attacks.'

'I'm not putting you in danger.' Rewan's anger sounded genuine this time, and Ina turned to face him.

'But you can endanger me? We all do what we must do, and Kaian is more than capable of defending himself. We can't choose who we are, Rewan, but by sheer luck, those we love can fight their own battles. If you want me to fight for Cornovii, you must also fight for it, my friend.'

Rewan's gaze softened, and Ina noticed shame flash over his expression when he looked at her, but Mar interjected before the king could say something more.

'I can't go right now. We need an army, even if just on standby, and I need at least three weeks to finish training the latest recruits and delegate command to Ren. Besides, you can't just "go and see", Ina. Everybody will know that you are acting on Rewan's order. You would have to go there as a judicial mage to investigate the problem, and we both know that's how you end up getting your pretty little arse deep in trouble.'

The king and Kaian exchanged uncertain glances at hearing this statement, and Ina bit her lip. 'No, if I go there trumpeting my arrival, whatever I'm attempting to investigate will retreat into the deepest burrow. We can spend some time here, and you can teach me everything you know about the southern provinces, the known alliances and any suddenly popular names. Or, better yet, not talked about at all and find some convenient excuse to go there. Maybe you and I can argue somewhere visible, and I could throw a tantrum, leaving the Osterad to visit the southern provinces.'

Mar looked at her, and Ina felt foolish under his judgemental stare. 'No one will buy this, my love. Yes, they will believe in your tantrum, but everybody knows you are not fond of the South, so why would you suddenly go to your family's home? We need something that could force you to go to Castle Thorn.'

Rewan looked at the couple and smirked. 'How about Nerissa? Your great aunt announced yesterday during the council meeting, the same one you didn't grace with your attendance, that she is going to Thorn to visit her brother.'

'What?! She hates that old goat and wouldn't even go to spit on his grave. What did she say?' Ina asked, instantly snapping her back straight, which only made all the men in the room laugh.

'No, she just mentioned the health of the head of her house had deteriorated recently. Isn't this a good reason to go to Thorn?' the king said. Ina looked at him, dumbfounded, before shaking her head. It was easy to forget how cunning the monarch was, but she had to admit his plan was sound.

'Rewan, it's complicated. I don't want to go to Thorn unless I really must, but I will go to the South somehow. Just give me a couple of days to devise a compelling reason.'

Mar raised from the chair and paced like a caged animal. 'You are not going alone. I know you can defend yourself, but we don't know what you are facing.'

'Well, you can join me later. My possessive dragon, chasing me around the southern towns.' Ina laughed before she placed her palm on his cheek. 'Mar, that's the best way. My absence can be easily explained, as I already attend the council meetings as I please. You have an army to command, so gossip will spread like hellfire once you are gone.'

Mar, with tightened lips, grabbed her elbow and gave a quick bow to Rewan. 'Well, in that case, I have to plan some training manoeuvres out in the countryside far away from prying eyes. If you allow, my king, I will take my woman home. We need to discuss her insane plan in more detail.'

Rewan didn't even wave them off as Mar dragged her out of the office. When the door closed behind them, he pushed her against the wall and locked her between his body and the stone surface.

'We just came back from Liath. Why did you agree to this? I will give Rewan his army to send if the barons rebel. Why does it have to be you with your "go-and-see" attitude that, may I remind you, gets you in trouble all the time? For fuck's sake, Ina, you are not here to solve his every problem.'

His worry softened her heart, and Ina reached up, cupping his face with her hands, bringing him down for a kiss. Mar tried to pull away but calmed under her touch, reciprocating her caress with his own possessive kiss, but before they lost themselves in it, he shook his head.

'Stop distracting me. Whatever you do won't change my mind.'

Ina reached for him again, wrapping her arms around his torso. She placed her head on his chest, listening to his frantic heartbeat. The sound that lulled her to sleep now brought a smile to her face.

'It is a few grumpy rebels using coded letters, and I'm the royal witch. I didn't like it initially, but I thought about it. I wanted my life to be free and for my magic to have a purpose, and Rewan gave me both with this stupid title. I can protect those people. If there was a war and you were the most capable of commanding the army, what would you do? Because I don't see you staying behind to warm my bed.'

'That's not what the problem is, Ina. I have an army if we go to war, but you are heading there alone,' he said, and she noticed him frantically searched her face for understanding while pressing her to his body.

'And I have my chaos. I must have been given it for a reason, not just to cause trouble, and you and Ren trained me to fight. If I can solve this problem, there'll be no need for violence, and I don't want to be part of another war. If not… well, at least I can buy us the time to bring trained soldiers instead of frightened children into the battlefield. We both knew the South would have to be confronted eventually,' Ina said, trying to reason with him while stroking the small of his back. And now, with the words spoken out loud, the plan she'd had in her head for days was laid bare.

Since they returned from Liath, Ina's days were more or less stagnant. She travelled to the palace daily for endless council meetings, growing increasingly bored by the mundane issues of running the kingdom. Most of the time, Mar was absent, working with Ren to create a new army for the king. It was impressive how quickly they'd formed a military camp outside the city. Initially, it was nothing more than a few barracks and stables. Before long, the Magical Council sent battle mages, healers and artefact masters, which now accounted for a quarter of the army. Much to her surprise, some shifter clans and non-human races volunteered when the word spread that skill and effort were more important than birthright or race for the Lord Marshal. Now, the camp was a true representation of Cornovii: a melting pot of all races, trades and crafts led by the dragon of Liath.

Ina laughed at her thoughts, startling Mar. 'We are the shield of this kingdom and its people, so let's be heroes again, my brave dragon. And don't worry about me. I have you as my lucky charm, so nothing bad will happen.' She jumped on his hips, kissing his cheek, and the warrior instinctively grabbed her rear. A loud gasp behind them made him turn, and Ina saw the shocked stares of several young maidens, undoubtedly the daughters whose goal was to lure the king to their beds. Ina felt her mischievous nature get the better of her, and, pressing her cheek to Mar's ear, she pointed to women.

'Maybe we should take one home. I could use some help in dealing with your insatiable appetite. It is so hard to satisfy my heroic dragon.'

The panicked squeal and drumming of running feet echoed in the hallway as the noble daughters turned, running away in panic, leaving Ina helplessly laughing and Mar shaking his head in disbelief.

'Maybe this trip will do you some good. Too much time in Rewan's court has given you the strangest ideas. I will not share you with anyone, ever. You are mine, and mine alone. Stop pretending you're pouting, you evil minx. We both know you love it.' His hand drifted to her nape and, tilting her head to the side, whispered in her ear. 'Let's go home now, and later I will prove you need no help to satisfy your dragon.'

'I don't know. There is so much to learn before leaving for the South. I definitely need instruction on how to escape restraints. Do you think you can teach me tonight? Just in case?'

'You are killing me, woman.' Mar groaned, shaking his head when his tease backfired and, after easing her to the ground, offered Ina his arm, gallantly leading her from the palace. She could feel the stares of the nobles drilling holes in her back, but she could hardly blame them. They were an eccentric couple who held the king's ear and trust, and the court still wondered what they would do with it. At least the Magical Council had taken their return home in better graces. The faculty of Mythical Creatures had constantly been pestering Mar for demonstrations, while Arun and the rest of the council insisted on Ina lecturing students about the dangers of chaos magic. At least she'd delivered that yesterday.

Slowly trotting through the streets and alleys of Osterad, Ina pondered over the events leading them here. Then it hit her. She'd forgotten about her new position at the university when offering her services to the king. *I'll have to talk to Arun and somehow arrange an absence. Or maybe my little demonstration was enough. I'm not made to be a teacher.* The pitiful moan that escaped her lips at the thought of teaching a hellion like herself instantly grabbed Mar's attention.

'Did something happen?' he asked, stopping Woron to look around, hand on the hilt of his sword. Zjawa instantly used this opportunity to snatch a juicy chicken hanging close to the street. Ina gave the merchant an apologetic smile and threw a small silver coin. There was no point in arguing.

'Nothing happened. I just thought I would have to teach at the university, and if the students are anything like me, I would prefer to fight the drow.'

Mar chuckled and encouraged his stallion to move off. 'Well, I'm sure you will do well on both occasions. Speaking of opportunities, you know the merchants put their best goods within the orein's reach on purpose? Your mount dines better than many nobles.'

'I know, but what can I do?' Ina said, smiling when the gates to their house appeared at the end of the street. The mouthwatering smell of chicken soup and mushroom sauce reached her nose. She looked at Mar, and when her stomach grumbled with appreciation, she kicked Zjawa to a gallop, shouting, 'Race you! The winner gets the pot of gold and magic mushrooms.' Her laugh echoed in the street long after the thunder of Woron's hooves told her Mar was in pursuit of his brazen prey.

CHAPTER THREE

Two weeks after that fateful conversation in the palace, Mar woke up with a thumping heart and the overwhelming urge to make sure Ina was there. For the last two days, he'd constantly deliberated over how to keep her with him, away from the turmoil in the southern march and far from danger. He instinctively looked at the other side of the bed, and there she was, copper hair tussled on the pillow and an open mouth that was so enticing to kiss. The loud purr from the end of the bed made him realise they were not alone, and, looking at the reflection in Boruta's eyes, Mar recalled the night terror that woke him up.

'It was you again? What is it this time?' he asked quietly, to avoid waking the sleeping woman. The black cat held his gaze and approached, placing his front paws on Mar's chest. His dream returned as if on command, and once more, he was standing in front of the ancient tree.

'She must journey south. Don't hinder her, no matter what your heart tells you.' A deep voice, dry like autumn leaves, filled the air, and Mar turned around, looking for its source. A wild-looking man *emerged from the massive trunk, and for a moment, both men eyed each other in silence.*

'Will she be safe?' Mar asked, hoping for a reassuring answer, but Leshy shook his head.

'No, she is the harbinger of chaos. Her fate is not to be safe, but to bring change.'

'Why must she go south alone? That makes no sense. It is just the nobles fighting over scraps. Nothing the old gods should be concerned about,' Mar said, disturbed by the sudden visitation.

'Oh, we are not concerned with people, but chains of foul magic constrict the land, poisoning the earth. She is needed, and you, dragon lord, can only help her. So remember, this will always be my Ina's journey.'

Leshy's voice faded, and Mar became aware of his surroundings as the overgrown cat released its hold on his mind. Ina stirred in her sleep, and wanting to be close to the woman he loved, Mar lay beside her, gently stroking her, wondering why gods threw such a burden onto her shoulders. She never complained, but he struggled to comprehend how she wasn't disturbed by such a difficult calling.

Slowly, Ina opened her eyes and yawned before her sight focused on his face.

'Did I miss something? You look like you walked through Nawia,' she said, and Mar promptly smiled, masking his foul mood.

'Maybe, or maybe I just saw a striga in the bed,' he answered cheerily, hiding his feelings and observing her pouty expression.

'Well, you're not exactly looking like some Elven stallion yourself,' she said, and he could hear the grumpy undertones in her voice. She was about to say more, but a commotion outside caught their attention. Seconds later, Mar's squire burst inside, blushing heavily upon seeing them together in the bed.

'My lady, I'm sorry. My lord, there is trouble in the garrison. The king called for you to attend immediately,' he said, quaking, as Mar and Ina exchanged a look.

'Wait downstairs. I will be there shortly,' he said to the young lad, and when the door closed, he turned towards Ina. 'Please don't do anything rash while I'm gone. I should be back in a day or two.' His last hope dissipated when Ina rolled her eyes.

'You always assume the worst. I know I've packed my bags, but I don't have a good reason to go yet,' she said, and Mar sighed, kissing her forehead.

'I know, love, but I also know how quickly circumstances change around you. That's why I put the communication crystal from Jorge in your bag. Just in case, of course.'

Mar knew they didn't have time for a long goodbye, and he already felt tense about leaving her. Ina had her own ideas on how to do things, and he could only hope she hadn't schemed with Rewan to get him out of the picture before she left, but maybe he was being paranoid. There was nothing to suggest she would depart before his return, so he swallowed his paranoia. Mar bent over her curvy frame for the last time, placing a long, possessive kiss on her lips.

'See you soon, my love. Don't get yourself in too much trouble, and give Rewan my warmest regards at the council meeting.'

Mar dressed and left while Ina relaxed on the bed. She knew Mar didn't like Rewan's plan, and asking to send his regards held a hidden warning. Mar's disapproval had become even more palpable in the last few days, hanging like a thundercloud over their lives. Still, he'd helped her identify the problem nobles and their positions on the map, as well as political affiliations and family feuds. Together with Ren, they'd trained mercilessly, and Ina could feel every bone and muscle in her body wince at the memory.

She needed to learn what happened in the military camp. That meant today she would have to attend the boring council meeting. She'd barely put on something decent when a tense Ren walked into the house, grabbing Ina by her shoulders.

'What is going on here? Why is Mar racing to the barracks like we're going to war, and why have you barely talked to me in the last few days?'

Ina stiffened. She had been ignoring Ren, mainly because she hoped to avoid telling him about the plan and her role in it. She knew he wouldn't want to stay behind, but she'd have to convince him, nonetheless. Avoiding him over the last few days had only made that more difficult.

'If I tell you, I need you to promise you will trust my judgment,' she said, noticing his eyes narrow and his grip tighten on her arms. 'Ren, please.' She untangled herself from his grasp and walked towards the window. At a safe distance, she detailed the conversation with the king and the task given to her. The more she talked, the more Ghost's expression grew thunderous. He wasn't exactly surprised, and Ina knew he often worked with Kaian. Still, the plan for her southern investigation was news to him.

'I know about all this, but why did you keep your trip secret, my lady? I will go with you. Just tell me when and I will be ready in the blink of an eye. At least this time, we won't be surprised by a blizzard.' His reassuring smile and warm voice were why she'd procrastinated on breaking the news to him.

'You can't go, Ren. You and Mar are the face of the army, and your disappearance will be noticed. Stay and prepare the soldiers, just in case we need them.'

Her words made Ren snap out a curse and start pacing the room.

'I don't like it. It is not safe, not even with your magic. Why do you insist on going alone?'

'Who would I take except you or Mar? I can't arrive with an entourage because I want to carry out my investigation without the southern lords knowing and finding out what's truly going on, not what they want the royal witch to see. Jorge is working on making my departure look like a family affair or one of my trifles, or at least nothing that would look like an official inspection carried by a royal witch. I will be gone as soon as we can mislead the palace spies. Mar doesn't know because he would try to go with me against common sense, and he is needed here. Going alone is the best option.'

'Ina, that is insane. If whoever is behind it learns you are on the road and by yourself, what stops them from killing you and blaming some random brigands? What if you get lost on the road? My lady, you are excellent in many things, but your sense of direction is dubious at best. It is a long way to the southern marches, and we both know you hate maps,' Ren said, and Ina clenched her fists, trying to control her temper.

'Then you can shake hands with Mar and congratulate each other on how you men knew best. It isn't like I need to travel alone. If need be, I can join a caravan or hitch a ride with a farmer. I was born in the South, and if this poor stupid witch can't manage, she can always beg for help at Castle Thorn. Will you please give me the benefit of the doubt because, clearly, despite all my magic and sword fighting lessons, I'm still a fragile little flower?' Her voice rose on the last sentence, and Ren stopped before her.

'You became my family, and, after all we've been through, I know you better than anyone except Mar. In some ways, you are a fragile little flower, my lady. Your magic and skills only carry you so far, then your heart takes over and tells you to rescue some unworthy scum or injured soldier just because you pity them. I promised to always keep you safe, but how can I do that when you don't include me in your plans?'

Ina sighed and embraced him before tentatively placing a hand on his cheek. 'You worry too much. You and Mar were the exceptions, and I've learned my lesson regarding saving overprotective men. I will be fine. Please let me do it my way and look after Mar in my absence,' she said, and when Ren looked down at her, she added, 'Besides, you have Ayni now, and you can't build your happiness strolling with me all over Cornovii. You are needed here. She needs you here.'

Ren didn't protest. He leaned down, pressing his forehead to hers, but she could feel the soft tremble of his fingers when he pressed her to his frame.

'I love Ayni, and thanks to you, I have found a happiness I thought lost after my exile from Yanwo. The bond you created allowed me to experience being part of a family again. Something precious like that should be treasured, and if you think I'd let you ignore me so that you can escape the capital, then you're dead wrong. The bond will never be a burden to me, but a blessing that helped me find myself when I expected nothing but loneliness, so accept my help and let me keep you safe.'

'I'm sorry, I'm not trying to take that from you. You, Mar, and even Ayni are my family now, better than what's left of mine, at least, and I still need my moonlight guardian to keep me away from trouble.' Ina noticed he smiled when she called him by the monicker she had given him long ago. 'Ren, our bond is a beacon that will always bring me home, so I ask that you stay here and guide me back from my mission to the South this time.' Ina looked down, biting her lip and hoped the quiet warrior accepted her words as her voice cracked.

After a moment of silence, Ren walked out of the room. The tension in his posture told her neither Mar nor the trainee soldiers would have an easy day today, but she was determined to stand by her choice. The winter love that blossomed between Ren and Ayni was still fragile. She would not forgive herself for taking Ren away, even if she could, when Ayni was here and needed him.

'I'm such a bloody kind soul.' Ina's sarcastic words bounced off the empty room as she dressed in simple clothes. It was time to head for the palace, but she didn't intend to dress for the occasion.

Ina shifted on the ornamental chair, feeling an uncomfortable pressure on her hips. These decorative monstrosities were not designed for long audiences. Rewan seemed to make a point of prolonging today's debate about tax rebates beyond the witch's tolerance, especially now when she was worried about her friend.

When she arrived at the palace, Ina had been pleasantly surprised to see Velka in the garden. Still, the usually cheerful mage was quiet and distant. She'd become restless with worry and had planned to at least steal a moment for a chat before going home. She hoped Velka would still be around after the audience ended. Deep in her thoughts, she missed when the grand door opened, and a messenger walked in, apologising to the king.

'Lady Inanuan—Ina. There is a letter for you.' She heard the king's voice and looked behind her, noticing the messenger standing there with an unreadable expression, holding a tray with the letter.

'Yes, Your Majesty, I apologise. Taxes always put me to sleep.' The witch smirked when a displeased murmur followed her answer. Despite all she'd done, many nobles still didn't like her unconventional relationship with the king. Ina took the letter and opened it with a blasé expression. She quickly skimmed through the contents, and a shiver ran through her body. The magical seal of the house of Thorn shimmered in front of her, undeniable proof that a member of House Thorn sent this message.

Rewan sat there, feigning indifference, waiting for her to finish reading, impatiently drumming his fingers on the table. He was acutely aware that Ina glanced at him occasionally, but although they discussed creating a letter, this one was not a part of the plan, and he had no idea of the missive's contents.

Ina slammed her hands on the table, clenching her teeth to tame the vortex of Chaos swirling around her fingers as it threatened to seep through her self-imposed barriers, making him curse quietly, seeing how she struggled with her power.

'Soft-hearted, empty-headed old biddy,' she said through clenched teeth. 'Bloody fucking idiot. Rewan, debate your taxes without me. I have to sort this mess out.' She waved the letter, and the nearest council members pushed their chairs backwards, ready to leap to cover in case the witch lost her temper.

'You can't just leave... Ina! Stop! I'm bloody talking to you!' Rewan shouted when she sprinted towards the doors.

Throwing the heavy parchment to the floor at some nameless lord's feet, Ina left the room shouting over her shoulder, 'Read the letter, then tell me how important your pennies are.'

The noble picked up the crumpled message and delivered it to the king, who, in a dismissive gesture, ordered, 'Just read the relevant part.'

The noble looked at it for a moment, then read. '"You are disgracing yourself and our ducal house. You shall no longer live with a man under your roof unless you are married. I expect you in Thorn in no more than two weeks. Make no mistake, Inanuan, your aunt is here to guarantee your arrival. We both know I have the means to ensure her stay will last till I see your shameful face...."'

The nobles exchanged concerned looks, and Rewan looked at the messenger. 'Find the Royal Witch. Tell her to join me in my office later.' Then, he turned to the nobles and said, 'Let's continue. Despite this turmoil, we need to reach an agreement today.'

With disappointed expressions, the council returned to their duties. As they were nearing the end of their discussion, the messenger returned, looking troubled.

'Your Majesty, Lady Inanuan has left the city. I'm sorry I could not stop her. The Lady asked me to tell you, "I will be back when I am back, and I don't have time for any more meetings".'

Rewan sighed and rubbed his temples before addressing no one in particular. 'Now we have a witch on the run, and I'm sure the raging dragon will follow her. Council is dismissed. I need to think about how to tackle this disaster before she wipes out the Thorn clan.'

Ina rushed through the palace corridors. She was fuming and trying not to worry. It was the perfect opportunity for the witch to leave the capital, but the reason behind it made her blood boil. Even with his bored expression, the anxious drumming revealed Rewan's anxiety, making it clear this letter was not part of his machination. How had Nerissa allowed herself to be dragged into such a mess? Neither of them should ever set foot into that misbegotten den of poisonous vipers for as long as the old duke lived, and yet her aunt ran there as soon as she heard her brother was unwell.

Her grandfather's seal was clear evidence the cantankerous old man had stepped in to tame the unruly chaos mage, using her to gain power in the current political struggle. Or, even worse, her grandfather would use her notoriety to take out his anger and shame on Nerissa. Both options were equally unacceptable.

'Ina, where are you going?' The voice behind her, filled with soft, sad tones, could only belong to Velka. The witch turned around and looked at the nature mage heading towards her. Guilt swept over her. She completely forgot about Velka, and stewing in her anger, she almost left Osterad without even saying goodbye.

'I'm sorry. I'm in a bit of a rush. I need to leave Osterad for a while.' Ina hoped Velka would accept this simple explanation, but looking at her friend's pale face, she saw a sudden frown before the valkyrie's lips tightened in determination.

'I'm going with you,' Velka stated, determination seeping from her, taking Ina aback. She looked deep into her friend's eyes before replying.

'I'm going to Thorn. My grandfather has gone completely insane and imprisoned Nerissa. It won't be a pleasant conversation or a pleasant journey. There are other things I have to do while I'm there. I don't need to remind him why I was kicked out in the first place, so dragging you into this mess wouldn't be the best idea. Things may turn nasty. I'm sorry, Velka.'

'I don't care. You're not leaving me behind. I'm going with you, or you aren't going anywhere. I'm your friend, and if you think I will let you jump into that pit of vipers alone, you are sorely mistaken.'

Suddenly, vine branches spread over the wall, growing so rapidly that they'd wrapped themselves around Ina's legs before she could react. Ina looked at those green shackles in disbelief and raised her eyes to the usually docile mage. Velka stood there with an unyielding expression, and it hit her. Her friend, the babbling bundle of joy, had been quiet and withdrawn lately, and Ina hadn't even asked what was wrong. First Ren, now Velka; it seemed as though she had been neglecting her friends recently. She gestured to the vines, and when Velka removed the overgrown plants, Ina approached her, embracing the much taller woman.

'What's wrong? Who has hurt you? Tell me, and when I return, I will make their lives so miserable they will pray to Veles to take them. Or, better yet, I will tell Daro, and he will chop their head off.' Ina tried to cheer her up using the old moniker, but one mention of Daro and Velka's lips tightened into a thin line. Ina looked up, searching for confirmation of her suspicions, and, seeing Velka avoid her eyes, cursed, struggling to control her magic.

'It was Daro, wasn't it?' Ina asked, the silence enough for an answer for the angry witch. 'I'll kill him. I'll chop his balls off and feed them to the cat, I promise you, but I can't right now. There's trouble with my family. The letter was sent a week ago, and I don't have much time left,' Ina said, and the air shimmered from her magic, but Velka placed her hand on Ina's shoulder.

'Don't change the subject, Striga. I'm going with you, and if I want to punish my husband's sorry arse, I will do it myself. Now, can we go?'

This new forceful Velka sent a shiver down Ina's spine. Whatever happened, Ina would rip the orc's head off and stick it where the sun never shone, but right now, she had too much to worry about, and Nerissa had too little time for her to stand there and dawdle, so rubbing her temples, she tried to focus on one problem at a time.

'I need to go now. Are you ready to go as you stand? We can stop by your house to get some necessary things, but I don't have much more time to spare.'

The abrupt laugh that followed her question was disconcerting, but Velka seemed pleased by this hasty departure. 'My horse is here, and I need very little, so we can go right now.'

Ina nodded, and they headed towards the stables. It was an unexpected turn of events, but the witch had learned long ago to take things as they came. Now saddled with a travel companion and a more than convenient excuse to leave Osterad, she didn't dwell on the implications of this sudden change in plans. Her orein also seemed pleased with the company and sniffed Velka's hand diligently before stealing the apple that appeared out of nowhere.

As they rode through the town, Ina purchased a few more supplies to make the journey more comfortable. She asked Velka if she wanted to leave a message with her household or royal gardeners about her journey, but the mage declined, and without further discussion, they arrived at the main gates. Ina suspected whoever spied for the South already knew about the council meeting drama and the sudden reason for her departure. Now, she had to make a big enough scene to ensure no one thought it was just a decoy. She'd be remembered as an angry woman rushing from the city to sort out some family affairs. For a brief moment, Velka frowned, confused about her grumbling. Ina raised her eyebrow minutely, and with an understanding born from years of friendship and unspoken communication, Velka joined in with the loud complaints until the annoyed town guard gave in and awarded them priority passage out of Osterad.

They rode in silence as the city walls fell behind them until Velka turned to Ina with an all-knowing smile.

'This isn't just a simple trip to teach your grandfather a lesson, is it?'

Ina sighed, wondering how much she could reveal without endangering her friend's safety. 'Partially, yes. The letter is a convenient, if infuriating, excuse. The southern march is planning a rebellion, and I've been tasked with the investigation. Thanks to my less-than-wonderful grandfather, I can travel there without alerting the rebels to any hint of royal interference.'

Velka gazed at her for a long time; her light-blue eyes were shining with excitement as she leant back with a small smile on her lips. 'I'll help you the best I can. I promise not to be a burden. No one will notice my absence, anyway. This could be my opportunity to prove I'm not just a glorified gardener.'

'You will never be a burden. Just promise me you will do as I say. My grandfather is old, likely insane, but he is still a terrifyingly powerful mind mage. We will need to tread lightly there. As for the rest, that's our little secret. There's a spy watching the court right now, and I'm sure someone is also keeping a close eye on me.'

Velka nodded with a serious expression that didn't last long before Ina saw her curiosity take over, and biting her lower lip, the mage asked, 'Ina… what exactly was in this letter?'

'Some idiocy about not living with a man while unmarried and that he will hold Nerissa hostage until I arrive. I hope she gives him boils for that.'

Velka's lip trembled when she tried to contain a laugh. 'And your dragon? Does he know about your grandfather's objections?'

'No, and it will stay that way. Mar would fly to Thorn and, in one breath, renounce my dowry and promise to marry me that day if he got my family's blessing.'

Ina's outrage was so palpable that Velka burst out laughing. 'But I want you to wed. I can be your bridesmaid, and I want to celebrate this sour expression when you're forced to pledge yourself to a man.'

Ina huffed, provoking more laughter, and pushed the orein into a trot. 'Not going to happen, my sweet flower. My life has enough complications already.'

CHAPTER FOUR

After discussing her hypothetical wedding, Ina and Velka lapsed into a comfortable silence. Ina enjoyed this peaceful moment, using it to build a plan in her head. Despite her best efforts, no matter how she tried to picture the situation and her options, nothing constructive came out of it. She wished Mar was there. His military approach to problems always helped to centre her chaotic, let's *"go and see"* attitude.

Now, she had nothing except the plan to go to Castle Thorn, make sure Nerissa was safe, and take it from there. Ina felt tingles of uncertainty and even fear when thinking about revisiting her birthplace. The Duke of Thorn was, as his title said, thorny. Her last memory of him was of a man with an unyielding face sitting proudly on his ornate chair when her mother, Nessa, begged him for shelter after Ina's father passed away.

She clenched her teeth, trying to dissipate her memories. Young and impulsive, she'd lashed out after seeing her mother humiliated for loving a commoner. Ina hadn't intended to hurt anyone, but when she shouted in her grandfather's face that he was a disgrace for abandoning his daughter, a maelstrom of unrestrained chaos broke free. The last thing she remembered was her mother's scream and his disgust as he cast a magical shield, hammering her mind with his will.

The rest of her memory was dull and blurred. Some people were shouting, her grandfather's voice issuing orders before she blacked out. When Ina woke up, she was in the room with Nerissa. Her great aunt's irises were so lifeless that Ina worried someone had died during her outburst, and when the old healer noticed Ina's stare, she turned her head, avoiding looking the grand niece in the eyes. Ina shuddered when her grandfather entered the room with her mother hanging off his sleeve.

'Please, you already took so much from her,' she'd pleaded. Ina still hated the begging tone in her mother's voice.

'Nessa! That's for the best. I shouldn't have ever allowed you to marry into the family of the forest. Look what your tryst did. She is an abomination.'

As soon as he'd said those words, her temper flared again, and with it, her chaos, but before she could say or do anything more, Nerissa's icy fingers locked around her wrist, forcing Ina into a magic-induced sleep and the next day dawned as if nothing had happened. Her mother was granted a pension, and Nerissa took them to Osterad. There was a rumour that the arch healer's goodbye to her brother was not a peaceful one, and Nerissa hadn't set foot in Castle Thorn again—until now. And Ina was heading there to talk to the man who had treated *her* like a monster.

Her heavy sigh drew Velka's attention. 'Is everything all right? You looked like your thoughts were far away from here. Are you thinking of Mar… or maybe Ren?' she asked, and Ina smiled at the teasing tone in her voice.

'No, I was thinking about my grandfather and how much he hated my father.'

'You've never really talked much about your father, except that he was a weak nature mage. Was that the reason the old duke despised him so much?'

'Possibly, this and the fact my father was the last lord of House Willow. My grandfather was repulsed that any noble family could fall so low to become, as he said, "*an unwashed commoner from the forest*".' Ina's answer made Velka gasp.

'You never said your father was from the House of Willow. That changes everything!' Velka's excitement took Ina aback.

'It changes nothing. There is no House of Willow anymore, and the only proof they ever existed is the sad ruins of the castle on the outskirts of the Black Forest. It looks even worse than my hovel here.' Ina's brief laugh reverberated in the air, but Velka was serious.

'Ina, the House of Willow had the most potent line of nature mages in the kingdom, and the House of Thorn is affiliated with elements and chaos magic. Maybe that's why you're blessed with the ability to access pure, raw chaos, and now you are with Mar and his dragon blood. Just imagine what your child would be!' Velka clapped her hands so loud she spooked the horse, but Ina only smiled.

'As interesting as it is to think about, I won't have a child.'

'Why? You love Mar, admit it. I've known you for a long time, and you've never been so head over heels for any man. You even let him live with you. So why not?'

Ina knew her friend's curiosity came from a good place. She also knew Velka wouldn't stop asking till she told her the real reason behind her objections.

'The main reason is that I don't want a child. There's a high chance they'd inherit my chaos, which I wouldn't wish on anyone, let alone my own kin.' Ina paused, taking a deep breath before continuing. 'And the second reason is much more straightforward. I'm barren.'

Velka reared back at the revelation, but Ina kept her expression calm as her friend frowned. 'How long have you known?'

'Since university. Remember, I had a bit of a scare with Liander. I went to the healing house, and they told me I didn't have to worry. Not now, not ever.'

'And you just… took it? Ina, you never give up without the fight.'

Velka's anger surprised her, but Ina only smiled and shrugged. 'What can I say? I never wanted children, so it was a blessing in disguise, but now you know. It doesn't matter how much I love Mar. He is the scion of Liath, and I can't take his future, locking him in marriage, when I lack the essential attribute to be Lady of Liath.'

'Does he know?'

'No,' Ina admitted, biting her lip. 'I didn't think we'd be together long enough for it to be an issue. I know I'm being selfish, but I just want a little happiness in my life before the sky comes crashing down on top of me again.' Ina bit her lip. She could only hope Velka understood and supported her through heartache when Mar finally decided to fulfil his obligations to the ducal house.

'I'm so sorry, Ina.' Velka's quiet words brushed dangerously close to the soft spot in her heart the witch tried to deny. Looking at her friend's eyes with tears glistening, Ina felt grateful that the gods sent her such a pure soul for a friend. Velka's understanding and acceptance meant more to Ina than she cared to admit, and that left the witch feeling dangerously close to tears too, but she squared her shoulders and pushed her orein into a trot.

'Enough about my sad maiden life. Let's move; otherwise, we will spend the night on the road. There is a village ahead of us, somewhere.' Or at least she hoped there would be one. She'd spent hours with Mar and Jorge over the maps of Cornovii, and she still lost her bearings. Or maybe she felt slightly lost because she was still on the wide, well-paved road. They should arrive in Thorn if they kept to the main thoroughfare. After spending the first night in the cheap tavern swarming with bedbugs, Ina was adamant about choosing a better establishment for her next stay, no matter how long it took.

They rode for another couple of hours, passing a few road crossings where Ina almost tossed a coin to choose the direction. When the sun began to set, they were truly lost. The witch looked at Velka swaying on her horse in a half-sleep stupor and regretted not stopping in one of the halfway inns, or even the tiny villages they passed, but she'd wanted to cover as much ground as she could during the day.

Ina stopped the horse and turned to Velka, hoping her friend could help her with the dilemma. She looked around, instantly knowing it would be an interesting night. The surrounding forest was not as dense as the Black Forest, but it was thick enough to shelter night predators, so moving forward in the dark was also the wrong solution.

'We need to stay here for the night. Soon we'll barely be able to see the road, and I don't want to miss anything. I'm so sorry. I thought we would reach Madron earlier.'

Velka looked at her and shrugged. 'If we must, then we will stay here.' She was already dismounting, with tiredness visible in her every movement. The dark circles under the mage's eyes worried Ina a lot; they were visible, even in the low light of dusk, but she busied herself with the horses while Velka coaxed trees and shrubs into making a comfortable bed. The roots and branches formed a solid frame, and soft spring twigs provided a lining for their makeshift invention. Ina whistled with appreciation, throwing a blanket over it.

'You are a hidden talent, oh mighty mage. I should bring you along for every trip,' Ina teased. As she started setting up a few warning spells around the camp, a sudden voice spooked her.

'Oh, I agree. Not only talented, but beautiful, too. She'll fetch a good price.' The women turned as if choreographed to face a group of scruffy individuals looking at them with interest. The men looked like someone had taken everything wrong about soldiering, thrown it into a pit of avarice and resentment, and then picked out the worst pieces. Their mismatched armour and crude, battered weapons didn't look very intimidating, but Ina had learned to appreciate the resilience of men that had fought their battles and survived to tell the tale. Their gazes lingered on Velka, who hadn't had the chance to change into less formal attire for the journey, while Ina still wore her simple garb from that morning.

'And who are you?' Ina asked, moving forward in front of her friend. She hadn't realised her hand lingered on the sword handle.

'Oh, look, the mage brought a bodyguard with her.'

'Aren't you too small for a guardian, sweetie?'

The roar of laughter shook the forest when the men mocked her.

'Maybe she's feisty in bed.'

'Look at her tits.'

'Drop the toy sword, and we'll show you how to be a woman.'

The taunting continued, and all except one man encircled them, expecting easy prey. Ina felt Velka's hand on her shoulder, and her soft, amused voice filled the air.

'I think we met the gods' stupidest creations. Do you know who you're talking to?' Her carefree attitude seemed to disconcert them, but only for a moment. The leader stepped forward and drew his axe.

'I don't care, so shut up. You're coming with us. Your family will pay a hefty price for their precious mage, and this one will fetch us some money. Madron brothel is always looking for fresh faces.' His smirk, so full of pride, made the women look at each other and burst into laughter. When Ina contained herself, she pulled the Falchion Mar had commissioned for her and took a stance.

'Well, come and get these titties, big boy,' she said with a bright smile. Not one to look a gift horse in the mouth, Ina welcomed the chance to test her fighting skills before she placed herself in Duke Thorn's clutches, and this time, she didn't have Mar or Ren getting in her way and trying to protect her. Ina didn't want to resort to siphoning chaos from death and destruction, reserving her magic in case things went wrong, but she was confident it wouldn't come to that. *Poor bastards don't know what's coming for them*, she thought with a hint of pity, soon replaced by a shiver of anticipation.

'Ina... no.' Velka's voice behind her was so scornful that Ina knew her friend was rolling her eyes at her eagerness to headbutt these mongrels, but it was too late to change her mind. The leader charged; the rest of the pack quickly following his example.

Ina danced as Ren had taught her, gliding effortlessly between the clumsy attackers. Her cuts were light and precise, aiming to disable, not kill, and the witch revelled in it. Soon, most of the goons were on the floor, bleeding from torn muscles and cut tendons, and the remaining ones withdrew with new respect in their eyes.

Chaos swirled around her, but Ina didn't reach for it, enjoying her hard-earned victory. That wouldn't be fair if her magic brought them to heel. But now? Now the witch felt all those painful lessons and hours of training finally pay off. If only Mar and Ren could see it, maybe they would stop treating her as a fragile glass flower in constant need of protection.

The only man who didn't take part in this skirmish barked a quick command, ordering his companions to step away before he approached slowly, raising his hands in a gesture of surrender. When he kneeled in front of her, Ina frowned in surprise.

'My lady, I beg for forgiveness. I was in Liath. I beg you, spare my life.' His forehead hit the dirt road with such force that dust rose into the air.

'Ina, you won't hurt him, right?' Velka's hand on her shoulder made the witch sigh.

'I don't hurt people for no reason. Still, this is the messy reality of life, and I won't hesitate if he forces my hand. We're not in a soppy ballade, but I won't hurt him if he behaves.' Ina pointed to the kneeling man. 'You will show us the way to the nearest village as soon as the sun rises. Then you will be free to go.'

'Yes, my lady,' he said, withdrawing to the side of the road, overseeing the rest of his group as they gathered up their wounded before leaving for shelter.

When they'd all left, Ina went back to her disrupted work. It took her some time to set up the warding spell and then light a fire under the watchful eye of their new guide. Before long, Ina became annoyed by his worried looks and constant flinching. As Velka drifted off to sleep in the bower, Ina could take it no longer. She marched over to where he cowered, standing before him with her hands on her hips.

'What is wrong with you?'

'Nothing, my lady. I apologise if I caused any offence.'

'So why are you afraid of me? If you were in Liath, you know I'm not the enemy.' Ina felt the need to defend herself yet again. The fact that this man was lying prostrate in front of her, trembling in fear, did not sit well with the freedom-loving witch. Since that last battle, everyone, with the exception of a few friends, treated her with a god-like reverence, tiptoeing around her, careful not to hurt her precious feelings.

'You broke my leg on the battlefield with your spell. Many were injured when they tried to resist you. After this, our company was disbanded.' There was no bitterness in the man's voice, he was simply stating a fact, but Ina found her curiosity piqued.

'Which was your company? I know the king hired several of them to support the regular army.' They say curiosity killed the cat, and Ina gasped when the man gave her the name.

'I was in Janik's. So yeah, I know you, and the veteran said his luck ran dry when he took on the crimson witch. They voted to strip him of command, but in the end, the company was disbanded, and that's why I'm here strolling on this road like a stray cat.'

'Janik was in Liath, and this son of a bitch didn't show himself to me? And where is he now?' Ina's voice rose to a pitch till she lowered her voice to avoid waking the sleeping Velka.

The warrior laughed shortly and shook his head. 'Do you blame him? You handed him his arse in front of the entire group. You and that Yanwo devil defeated a mind mage and a group of headstrong mercenaries like we were nothing. Things were not what they used to be after that.'

Ina stared into the flames of the small fire and bit her lip. Yes, Janik had betrayed her, but he was Janik, and after her anger cooled down, she realised she didn't harbour any bad feelings towards him. And upon hearing the mercenary's story, she had to admit he'd been punished enough, losing his company, his pride and joy he'd worked for since she'd known him.

'Where is he now?'

'Nobody knows. Maybe he went north to his home or south. I heard the southern march is gathering soldiers.' Pulling out his small supplies, the soldier shrugged, and Ina drifted into her thoughts. She'd already talked about it with Jorge. He'd even made one of his predictions and was adamant that the unrest at the southern borders would come to a head before too long. Rewan was convinced that it was just a few disgruntled barons who were trying to carve out independence for themselves, using the recent events and uncertain position of Cornovii as an excuse for their rebellion. Did Verdante have a role in this?

The question was, what could Verdante's goal be? Cornovii, even weakened, was still a sizable power in the region and should be taken seriously. The southern march, that loose conglomeration of nations led by Verdante, had long claimed ownership of the southern provinces of Cornovii, often citing a common heritage and ethnic origin, but they didn't have the men to take and hold the region.

The witch shook her head slightly to rid her mind of politics and looked at her sleeping friend, envying her peaceful countenance. Ina and the grubby mercenary eyed each other until, after flinching for some reason, he lost the staring contest and prepared his bed for the night.

Ina felt strangely unsettled. The news about Janik might have been partially responsible for this, but she could not shake the feeling that their little camp was observed by someone or *something* else in the forest. Slowly, she rose from her makeshift seat and started pacing the camp. Her protection spell was intact, but Ina still felt uneasy. She walked out of the circle and turned to face the forest. The years of exile had taught her how to listen to the night, and now with closed eyes, Ina dived into the slow and dark melody. The creaking of the trees mixed with the crunching noises of the bugs living their life on the forest floor, and she could hear night birds occasionally, revealing their presence, but one noise differed from the others. Quiet and raspy, like inhuman lungs expelling excess fluid. Her instinct told her to run away, but one look at her defenceless friend and a suddenly more aware mercenary was enough to stop her. After all, she *had* just proven she could hold her own when fighting.

'Show yourself.'

Her quiet and decisive voice surprised her almost as much as the creature that came out of the bushes. The revenant walked vigorously despite the rotten flesh and stood a few feet away. That was unexpected; those creatures usually attacked anything that stood in their way with mindless ferocity. Ina tilted her head, inspecting it—him. The remains of the peasant clothing still hung from the decomposing frame, but other than the offensive smell, he wasn't hostile. He repeated her gesture, and she presented something she could only describe as a toothy grin.

'What on Veles's arse is going on here?'

Ina's words provoked a wider grimace. *He must be piloted by a necromancer.* It was the only reasonable explanation she had for his bizarre behaviour. It irked her. She was worried sick, and some death-reeking idiot was playing tricks on her. She stalked closer and grabbed the monster by the chin, tilting it till she saw the fading light of the necromancer's magic in his eyes.

'One more trick like this, and I will find you and kick your arse back to the Dawn of the Magical Age,' she snarled. It jerked, leaving the whole of its mandible in her grasp. The magic faded completely, and the revenant collapsed into a heap of rotting flesh, leaving Ina cursing in annoyance before turning around to return to the fire.

'What were you doing?' Velka's sleepy voice rang out in the sudden silence, and Ina sighed, throwing the useless jaw into the bushes. Her unwilling guide, making the most of her distraction, had fled; she could hear him floundering through the bushes. Velka simply stared at her, waiting for an answer.

'Nothing much. I was just being an idiot who let herself get distracted. I suspect our guide had a mage as a friend, and I truly hope someone, or something, will use him as a snack in the forest.' She frowned before continuing. 'Anyway, I've lost my trust that we're safe here. It's still early, so we should leave.'

'But who were you talking to?'

Velka could be merciless in her questioning, and Ina relented as she plopped herself down beside her friend. 'Looks like a necromancer paid us a visit, or at least sent a revenant to get my attention. Don't worry, it's all sorted now. Still, it is time to move our perky rears. Those bandits are too lazy to live far from here. There must be a village nearby, and I don't want any more surprises.'

Velka smiled and laid her head on Ina's shoulder, yawning so widely the witch could count her teeth. 'If you say so. But why a necromancer? I'm glad you sorted him out because they are all treacherous bastards.'

Ina couldn't help but snort a short laugh. 'You still hold a grudge from our uni days? Oh, now I hope we meet one. I want to see how my favourite tree hugger will fight against death magic.'

Velka grumbled something under her breath and wrapped the cloak tighter around her frame while saddling her horse. 'Well, you'll have to wait and see, Striga. I truly hope this bloody village is somewhere nearby. I'm hungry and would like to sleep in a proper bed.'

CHAPTER FIVE
(THE DAY OF INA'S DEPARTURE)

Mar paced back and forth in his makeshift office, feeling trapped in the small space. He thought he could handle this mess when leaving Ina this morning, but now, each time the marshal faced the exit, he had to talk himself out of leaving the whole shambles behind and returning to Osterad. However, as time dragged by and a solution still hadn't presented itself, the marshal felt his sanity slowly unravelling. He knew it was just a matter of time before Ina's patience ran out, and she set off to investigate the troubles in the South. After spending so much time poring over maps and their discussions on southern politics, his spitfire was as prepared as she could be. Ren had also worked her mercilessly in his style of swordsmanship, to the point he'd actually smiled at her progress, but Mar was still worried.

When Kaian discovered someone was fomenting unrest in the barracks, Mar had been more than happy to bash a few heads. Still, despite the improvement in discipline, neither he nor Ren had discovered the troublemaker. It was leaving both men on edge. A short, decisive knock stopped his pacing.

'Enter.'

Ren appeared at the entrance and, without further formalities, walked in to pour himself a good measure of mead from Mar's supplies. It wasn't the first time, but everything immensely irritated him today, and Mar snapped. 'Anything else I can serve you with?'

'So, she left.'

Ren emptied the cup and put it on the table with a loud thud, with Mar looking at him, stunned. It was barely a day since he left Ina to come to the training grounds, and his stubborn woman left without even saying goodbye. 'How do you know?'

'A messenger was sent from the palace, saying Ina received a letter from Duke Thorn and left shortly after, but they didn't add any more detail. I assumed you knew about it, seeing the trail of bloodied noses and incapacitated soldiers you left in your wake today. You should take out your anger on someone who can defend themselves. That, or persuade her to take me along the moment you learned about her plans. How could you allow this insanity to happen?'

'As if either of us could influence Ina into doing anything against her will. Why didn't you chase after her? I can release you from service right now if you want to go.'

Mar smiled at the flash of anger in Ren's eyes before his friend answered. 'She wouldn't let me. Besides, she'd know if I attempted to shadow her. Even I'm not that stupid. I leave that to Daro, damn mooncalf.' His exasperated sigh broke the tension, and Mar's laughter erupted into the night.

'Well, let's drink. To Cornovii's bravest warriors, thoroughly cowed by a red-headed force of nature. I knew she would be going soon, but I hoped I would have time to change her mind or go with her. If the Leshy hadn't said….'

'Leshy?'

'Yes, whenever I thought of stopping Ina, I'd dream of the forest god. Why does that feel so normal to say? I was a simple soldier. Now I'm a dragon who dreams of gods.' Mar laughed with a hint of bitterness, and, to change the subject, he pointed to his empty cup. His gesture brought a half-smile to Ren's lips, who, taking pity on his friend, filled their mugs to the brim.

At first, they drank the first cup in silence, stewing in their thoughts, but the potent brew soon loosened their tongues, and Mar broke the silence, asking, 'Are you happy, Ren?'

His friend looked at him over the mug's rim, and Mar saw his eyebrows knit together in silent query.

'I'm not trying to pry into your life. I just want to know if you're happy. It's not like you want to hear more about my adventures.' The need to explain himself grew stronger the longer Ren looked at him, and his friend seemed to savour the moment.

'Are you jealous again?' the quiet warrior finally asked, and a slight twitch of his cheek told Mar what he thought of this idea.

'Forget I asked. Why would I care if my best friend and second-in-command is happy, especially when my relationship completely fucked up his life?' Sarcasm dripped from every word, but Ren spread himself more comfortably on the chair. Mar thought about how much the quiet and deadly Ghost had changed since he'd met Ina, his blind adherence to duty now softened by a cutting wit, and Mar realised how much closer they'd become since the changes caused by the chaotic witch.

What hadn't changed was his unwavering loyalty. However, his focus shifted from blind duty to devotion to those he loved. Ina had somehow found the key to Ren's soul, unlocking the best of him.

'I'm happy, Mar.'

Ren's voice broke through his stream of thoughts, and Mar smiled slightly, hearing the honesty in it.

'I'm happy too, but Ina is still holding back. Whatever it is in her mind, I can't shake the feeling she expects me to disappear at any moment and is just enjoying things while they last. Did she share anything with you?' Mar finally articulated his worry and looked at Ren, hoping his friend may have some answers.

'You know I wouldn't tell you if she confided in me, but no, she hasn't mentioned anything.'

Mar sagged on the chair and emptied his cup. 'You were my only hope for an answer.' He sighed, pulling his beard.

'Why don't you ask her?'

'I did, and guess what? I'm a stupid dragon imagining things. And maybe I am, but she is everything to me. I want her to believe it's not just a passionate fling.' Mar grabbed the jug and poured the mead straight down his throat, embarrassed at how he'd turned the conversation back to him and Ina.

'Save something for the man trying to convince a dragoness he has feelings for her, despite her knowing he will always share a soul-bond with someone else.'

Mar pushed the jug in his direction, 'Well, let's drink for this and our future offspring if our women finally decide we are worthy of their love,' he said, sharing the mead till the last dregs disappeared, calling out to his squire for more, as both men drunkenly set their romantic worlds to rights, then bemoaning womankind in general, until at long last, their words turned to rasping snores, forcing their disapproving squires to carry the two drunks back to their beds.

A series of bangs, followed by coarse curses, slowly penetrated the fog that was Mar's mind. With entirely too much effort, he looked up, seeing what appeared to be a strange red-faced berserker standing in the doorway. As the ability to think slowly returned, the marshal realised it was Daro, though why he was here and not cuddled up to his wife, he did not know. *She must have kicked him out again,* Mar thought, turning to the sluggishly moving Ren at his side.

'Where the fuck is my wife?'

The orc's hand grabbed a handful of Mar's shirt and lifted him from the cot, shaking the still befuddled marshal like a rag doll.

'Not here, you deranged pig-headed oaf. What the fuck is going on?' he asked, shaking his head till the world slowly settled into focus. 'You think we'd be hiding Velka in the barracks?'

Mar watched Daro tearing at his earring in frustration, ripping the skin till blood poured out of the deformed hole, and grabbed the orc by the arm before pushing him into the nearest chair. 'Soldier! Report!' he commanded, hoping to snap his friend out of his distress and get some answers.

'Velka didn't come home last night. Maybe she was with Ina, but your bloody witch didn't go home either. Where the fuck have they gone? I thought perhaps she was with you....' The orc hid his face in his hands. 'We had some stupid argument before she left for the palace yesterday, and I don't even know what I did wrong.'

The young orc looked desperate and clueless, and it didn't help when Ren, his voice husky from too much mead, commented. 'If you messed up with Velka, you'd better not see Ina for a while. Not if you value your balls, at least.' The warrior approached Mar's desk, grabbed the pitcher of wash water, gulped down its contents and added when he finished, 'Now, let's work out how to find your little flower.'

It only took a moment to realise that Daro didn't have a clue what prompted Velka's disappearance. He told them his usually cheerful, little ray of a sunshine wife had been subdued and withdrawn for some time. Daro couldn't recall any recent troubles or reasons for her to be in a bad mood, but Mar couldn't shake the feeling they were missing something important. He tried to reassure the orc that Velka must be in the city because she could not be with Ina. His certainty made Daro suspicious, and in the end, Mar had no choice but to tell him the truth.

'Velka is unlikely to be with Ina because our gracious king tasked his royal witch with investigating the rumours of a southern rebellion. Why do you think we are sitting here drowning our worries? There are spies in the palace, so we get to sit here as diversions as Ina heads off, gallivanting around her old stomping grounds. There's no way she'd want to drag Velka into this mess.'

His words had the opposite effect. Instead of calming the orc, Daro was growling in Mar's face. 'If your crazy witch causes any harm to my wife, I swear….'

'You swear what?' Ren's voice was bereft of emotion, but Daro growled, hearing the underlying threat. Ren approached him and placed a hand on the orc's shoulder. 'Where was she seen last?'

'She went to the palace for routine garden maintenance. I asked the guards. No one saw her after that.'

'Did you ask the servants? Many of them serve Kaian and see more than you realise.'

Daro shook his head and slumped like a schooled pupil. 'No, I went straight to Ina's house, but her servant told me she didn't come back for the night, so I came here.'

Mar looked at Ren, who nodded, and both men devised a plan while Daro waited impatiently.

'Ren, I'll go with our headstrong captain to the palace to see what we can learn of Velka and hopefully find someone to shed some light on the mysterious letter. I don't remember any plans for Ina's journey being finalised, but you never know with that woman. If you can stand in for me here, keeping order and ensuring training goes smoothly, that should keep any spies clueless to what we're doing.' Mar's speech was brushed off casually by Ren with a smile.

'I've been leading troops since I was old enough to wear armour, so go ahead, find Daro's errant bloom, and chase down that headstrong woman, or I'll do it for you.'

'You have?' Daro's surprised query made Ren look at the orc.

'Yes, albeit a long time ago.'

Before the orc could ask more questions, Mar and Ren clasped forearms in a warrior's farewell, and Ren left the tent, leaving Mar looking at Daro with a slight frown.

'Whatever happens, you will not disclose or mention Ina's mission or even that she left. Not to anyone, especially not in the palace.'

'Yes, Captain,' Daro said out of habit, and Mar could only shake his head.

'You're the captain now, you big lunk, so try to behave as such. Let's go to the palace.'

Mar tried to keep from galloping back to the city like some mother hen worried for its chick, playing his part as the unconcerned marshal, but tension thrummed through his body, leaving Woron confused and prancing at the mixed messages he was sensing. He had to behave as if nothing had happened, despite wanting to spread his wings and follow her trail. A glance at Daro showed the orc acting exactly the same, worry clearly etched on his features. While the idea of Ina taking Velka on such a perilous mission should be unthinkable, Mar couldn't help but speculate that his spitfire had done exactly that.

The sentry at the palace entrance saluted them with an eagerness born of profound relief. Daro must have scared the poor soul half to death while searching for Velka. With a brief nod, Mar acknowledged the salute and dismounted, taking his friend to the side.

'Ask the staff about Velka, and remember, they are servants, not soldiers, so be gentle. I will go to the king.' With a sombre expression, the orc nodded and headed towards the maid's quarters.

After taking a deep breath to calm his racing heart, Mar set off to find the king. From the frightened reactions of the passing nobles and officials, he hadn't managed as well as he'd thought, but instead of caring, the marshal used their fear, asking a sallow-faced aristocrat where the king was, which resulted in a shakily pointed finger towards the council chamber and a sudden flood of tears.

The chuckle that escaped Mar's lips didn't help as he set off again, bursting into the chamber, looking around at the shocked council, and slowly bowing to an exasperated monarch.

'Your Majesty, forgive me for the interruption, but I request a private audience to discuss an issue related to the army's training camp.' Mar again noticed the stench of fear that hung over the royal council. Worse still, the king also looked unsettled at his presence. The worry that had choked Mar all of yesterday resurfaced, and, struggling to restrain the urge to transform, the dragon stormed into the king's office without another word. The moment the door closed once Rewan walked in, Mar spun to face him, snarling out his anguish.

'Where is Ina?'

'I'm afraid Lady Inanuan received a rather concerning letter from her family and left for Castle Thorn in great haste.' Rewan's voice matched his concerned pose, and Mar grasped the end of a marble table, fighting to stay human.

'What did the letter say that made Ina rush off without bothering to send me a message?'

'Her grandfather berated her for living with you and ordered her to go to Thorn immediately.'

'We both know Ina never obeys an order. What else did it say?'

The King nodded to a servant who slipped out, returning shortly with a crumpled piece of parchment before handing it to the frustrated marshal.

Within seconds, the vellum was destroyed as Mar lost control of his transformation. Before he could collect his thoughts, a sudden collision from behind forced him to stumble further into the room, and as he turned to punch the offending person, he cursed, stopping himself as he saw a furious Daro attempting to bow to the king.

'Velka left to go south with Ina. I ask for leave from my post to retrieve my errant wife before that crazy witch gets her embroiled in any more ridiculous incidents.'

Mar grabbed the orc by the collar, cutting off his friend's words before he revealed more of Ina's plans in front of the servants.

'Sa'Ren and I have discussed the issue of Ina's family. As it appears that I'm the cause of the conflict, he has agreed to step in for me at the training grounds whilst I head off to see Lord Thorn. As this hot-headed captain wishes to join his wife, I shall accompany him on his journey.'

Rewan nodded with relief, calling for his chancellor, coughing pointedly in Daro's direction when the old lord arrived.

'Ah, Lord Chancellor, thank you for your prompt arrival. Due to the special circumstances of Lady Inanuan's departure, I am sending Marshal Marcach and Captain Daro to facilitate an early conclusion to the issue. In the meantime, Sa'Ren Gerel will take over the marshal's duties. I would prefer if this were kept as quiet as possible because of Marshal Marcach's status. We would like to avoid any controversy, after all.' Turning to Mar and Daro, he rolled his eyes. 'You both are free to journey to Castle Thorn, but I can't spare you forever. You have a month to sort this out, and if it's any consolation, this was also a surprise for me. Lord Marcach, I know you remember our discussion, but I want to assure you *this* was not something I planned.'

Mar muttered his thanks and left the room, dragging Daro by the grip he still held on his collar, ignoring the curses and complaints the guard captain shouted towards his friend.

Ina rarely talked about her childhood, always changing the subject whenever her family was mentioned, and after reading the disdain that coated every word of that damned letter, he finally began to realise why. He came to the palace hoping to find an explanation for why Ina was sent away, but the king was clear, saying it wasn't his doing. Revulsion for Ina's grandfather shivered through Mar as he wondered how any sane person could threaten both Ina and Nerissa.

After successfully dragging Daro away from the populated areas of the palace, Mar turned to his friend and asked. 'So, what did you learn?'

'Not much, only that Velka came to the gardens as usual, then met with Ina in the main corridor. However, despite the public setting, no one knows what was discussed, just that both women tore out of the palace as though chased by a horde of ghouls.'

Mar turned to leave, but Daro's hand on his forearm stopped him. He looked at the orc with a question in his eyes when Daro bared his fangs.

'Tell me, Captain. Tell me you and Ina aren't using Velka for whatever plans you've made. Mar, my wife is no warrior, and I won't stand by and let her be hurt.'

Mar's eyebrow lifted, and he held his friend's gaze till the captain released his grip. Only then did Mar answer. 'Do you really think Ina would knowingly put Velka in harm's way?'

Daro lowered his head and kicked a stray stone. 'Knowingly? Maybe not, but we both know trouble follows Ina's coattails like a faithful puppy. I doubt she even realises it half the time.'

Mar shook his head, gaping at Daro in disbelief. 'I'm not sure what is happening in your head, but this must stop now. That old bastard Thorn told Ina he was holding Nerissa hostage to ensure her prompt arrival. Those women share everything, which means Velka would have insisted on going with her friend as soon as she found out. Now, will you get your head out of your arse and help keep them safe, or keep standing there, throwing around accusations? If Velka heard this shit coming out of your mouth, you'd be sleeping in the doghouse for a year.'

Mar's speech seemed to take the wind out of Daro's sails as he lowered his head, looking defeated. 'I thought you would understand. What if it was Ina?' he said, and Mar put his hand on the orc's shoulder.

'It is about Ina. What didn't you understand? She rushed off to save her aunt. Ina couldn't give a rat's arse about the rest. I will wreck the world to keep her safe, but I would never suspect Velka of using her. Their friendship is stronger than the Grey Mountains, and if Ina let your wife come with her, there had to be a really good reason.'

When they left the palace, Daro seemed calmer, but a cloud of guilt hovered around him like a dismal fog. Mar wondered what could have happened between the two lovebirds that made his friend so sure someone was using his wife.

Ren sat at Mar's table and began sorting through the pile of reports. How had he ended up in charge of an army? After his voluntary exile from Yanwo, he'd never wanted to be in this position ever again, never wanted to decide the fates of his fellow warriors, but here he was, in charge of Cornovii's army. At least they weren't at war. The battle at Liath might have been brief, but people had died; people under his responsibility.

A soft knock at the door interrupted his thoughts, and expecting another soldier, Ren called for them to enter. Instead of the usual squire, Ayni stood hesitantly in the doorframe. With a genuine smile and welcoming gesture, he gestured for the beautiful dragoness to join him.

'You look tense, and you are in Mar's chair. Care to tell me what happened?' she asked as she came close, fingers stroking through his thick hair, making him sigh, close his eyes and surrender to her gentle touch.

'Ina went south, and I'm guessing Velka went with her, so Mar and Daro are probably chasing after them. That left me in charge of all... this,' he said, opening his eyes when her hands stilled.

Ayni's body tensed, and her face told him she was weighing something in her mind.

'She left... and you stayed? Even though it might be dangerous?'

Her words carried more meaning than simple questions, and they both knew it. Ren took the dragoness's hand and guided her to his lips.

'I tried to tell you before, but I will repeat it. Ina and I made our decisions in Castle Liath. I won't lie to you. I am bound to her and probably always will be. She is my friend, my family, my ward... It's not something I can or wish to reject, but I fell in love with you and am happy. I would go after her if I were truly needed, but Ina has grown in power and confidence. Mar is there to look after the rest.' He stroked Ayni's back, feeling the light tremble under his fingers. He didn't blame her, but he didn't want to lie to her and wondered how he could express his mixed feelings.

'Ina... I will always care for her, and I know that hurts you. You deserve better, a man who can give you all his heart. I promise you, though, Ayni, when I say I am happy for the first time since I left Yanwo, I can say it without a shadow of hurt or anger, all thanks to you. You became a part of my life, part of me. It may differ from the love you need, and I wouldn't blame you if—'

The dragoness stroked her fingers over his smooth chin and leaned down, silencing him with a fierce, passionate kiss. Her acceptance of his less-than-perfect feelings awakened something he thought he'd never have, and Ren's heart unclenched, opening up fully to the affection this wonderful woman gave him.

With a passion that surprised him, Ren returned Ayni's kiss, months of repressed desire pouring into it as the lovers gave in to their feelings.

'Life can be complicated, especially where magic is involved. Just love me the best you can,' she gasped between his kisses.

Until now, the careful couple had done little more than embrace each other, seeking comfort for their loneliness. It felt wrong to take advantage of Ayni when there was a woman he devoted himself to protecting, but now, after admitting his feelings for the wonderful woman in his arms, he gave in to the desire he'd held back for so long. The sound of the ripping fabric woke him from his ardour, and he looked down, only to realise he had torn open Ayni's clothing in his excitement.

'If you want me to stop?' he asked, attempting to control himself, but to his amusement, the dragoness rolled her eyes and grabbed the collar of his shirt.

'You're not backing off now.' She growled, tugging at his shirt, and Ren swiftly took it off, but it wasn't enough for her. When he felt her hands sliding down, trailing over his battle-hardened muscles, Ghost felt his self-control disappear. He lifted her onto the table, scattering the papers to the floor, and lost himself in kissing her soft, iridescent skin as Ayni's legs wrapped around his hips, pulling him closer.

'Ayni… your skin…' he whispered when he noticed the shimmering, soft scales under his fingertips.

'I'm sorry,' she said, embarrassed, focusing on her body and changing back, but Ren stopped her.

'No, it is beautiful, and deliciously enticing.'

The honest desire in his words brought a shy smile to her lips, and Ayni pulled him close and whispered in his ear. 'I want you to have my bond too. If you can share your heart, you can share my mind, Sa'Ren. I waited long enough for this. You are magnificent.'

Her consciousness opened like a beautiful flower, and Ren fell into her mind, linking their thoughts and feelings. Passion bloomed, and as one, they tore away the barriers between them, coming together instinctively; urging each other on, delighting in their union until pleasure overwhelmed them.

Later, resting on the chair with Ayni curled on his lap, Ren looked around at the mayhem and destruction their lovemaking had caused and burst into a hearty laugh. When he saw the question in her eyes, he explained. 'Well, so much for taking good care of Mar's office, but who cares? It was worth it.'

Ren's words made Ayni smile, basking in the perfect moment.

They may have come together in the worst circumstances, but now, fingertips trailing over the dragoness's warm, soft scales, nothing felt more right.

'Thank you, Minii Khair, for accepting me for who I am.'

CHAPTER SIX

Ina did not appreciate having to travel at night, having to keep a watch on their surroundings, unable to rely on magical protection with a fellow mage helping the local banditry. The belladonna collyrium she'd applied hardly helped her see any better in the sporadic moonlight and left her eyes stinging and teary. It took far too much effort to stay awake, with Zjawa's gentle gait, whilst usually appreciated, was not helping Ina remain alert in this potentially dangerous situation.

With a deep sigh that definitely wasn't a yawn, the witch wondered how Mar and Ren did this so effortlessly, then winced as she remembered that neither man knew she'd left already. If her dragon hadn't mortally offended the king over her disappearance, Ina would count herself lucky. Ren, she knew, would be the dangerous one. If he thought the king had tricked her, then even the best of Kaian's assassins wouldn't stop Ghost from exacting his retribution.

A quick scan of their surroundings and Ina glimpsed the swaying Velka. *Gods, what about Daro?* she thought, biting on an already tender lip as she realised who else would be upset.

This development didn't bode well. Daro was guaranteed to come after his wife, worried for her safety around such a chaotic influence, and that would mean Mar would follow if only to stop the hot-headed orc from punching her. Would that mean Ren following too? *Oh, fuck, all our plans.* Ina cursed herself. If all those men came south, they'd trigger the exact response the witch wanted to avoid.

'Oh bloody hell, now I've done it,' she said, much louder than she intended, and Velka glanced at her with a question in her eyes. Unwilling to disclose her thoughts, Ina lied. 'Nothing, it is just my butt hurting, and I feel sorry for myself.'

Her orein snorted at the comment, giving her a meaningful look, while Velka didn't look convinced, thankfully refraining from commenting. With a slow brightening of the moonlight, they emerged from the dense forest into a clearing, and between a few tangled shrubs, they could see the village's lights in front of them.

'Finally, I thought we'd have to spend the entire night in this forest.'

With a light kick into orein's side, Ina sped up, lured by the promise of a hot meal and a nap in an inn tavern. She could hear Velka cursing as she tried to keep up with the disappearing orein. However, Ina was already in the village before she could catch up.

The villagers didn't look hostile, even if the level of activity was uncommon for such a late hour. They also didn't offer a welcome, casting the pair nothing but suspicious, worried glances, causing Ina to stop, taking a moment to assess the situation.

'Why are they not sleeping? It must be past midnight,' Velka wondered aloud, expressing what had bothered Ina. The witched nodded slowly, looking around, but no one met their eyes except for an old lady spinning wool at the threshold of her house.

'Forgive me, Grandmother, what is going on so late at night? Do you have a tavern in the village?' Ina asked politely, leading Zjawa closer to the spinster's fence.

'The village idiots are going to the square to sacrifice a pig to Marzanna. We'll soon have nothing left at the rate they're killing livestock. You'll find the tavern next to it. You can't miss it; the headman and his cronies will be falling out of it soon.' The old woman waved them off, and Ina turned her mount to return to Velka, noting how uncomfortable her friend was with this new revelation.

Morana, or as people called her in the South, Marzanna, wasn't a popular goddess. Her cult, although not forbidden, was frowned upon and considered barbaric even amongst the gods-fearing citizens of Cornovii, but Ina suspected in poor, isolated villages, the deity of death and rebirth was still popular. The witch just hoped locals didn't follow the old ways. Otherwise, she would have another problem to hand to Rewan. Pigs or chicken offerings might be overlooked, but Marzanna's followers sometimes resorted to drowning maidens to bid farewell to the winter, which Ina would not allow.

'I don't like it, Ina.' Velka's deep frown mirrored her own when they arrived at the village square just in time for the religious ceremony, the squealing of the sacrificial pig cutting through the crowd's chanting as they rode into the tavern's yard.

A stable boy took their mounts as the women dismounted and entered the tavern. The room was empty but stank of freshly spilt ale, and Ina sighed with relief when she noticed the massive troll behind the counter. The barman noticed them, too, and nodded to the empty chairs next to the bar. Taking a seat, Ina couldn't shake the feeling they were being silently judged.

The sensation only intensified when the troll came closer and reached over with his gnarled hand in her direction. Ina reached out, intending to shake it as per the custom, but much to her surprise, the troll took her hand and sniffed it, smacking his lips like he was tasting the finest meal. Both women shifted on their chairs, and Ina instinctively reached for her magic, ready to strike if the troll tried to eat her, but he only flashed her a crooked grin and called forth a serving maid.

'Bring the letter and our best mead, then leave us alone.'

They sat silent till the tavern maiden delivered three tankards and a crumpled envelope. The troll pushed it in her direction, and the frowning witch opened it, only to find a scrap of fabric with the distinctive smell of winter apples, her favourite perfume.

'Gruff sends his regards and says if you need anything, you can ask my family, and we will provide it.'

Another grin followed his words, and Ina sighed with relief as she finally understood why the troll had sniffed her before. She reached for the tankard, feeling her mood improve after just one sip of the amber liquid, and nodded to Velka, who sat there looking at her mug with hungry eyes without drinking it.

'We would ask for food and a safe place to rest for what's left of the night. If I don't get some sleep, I will start killing people for simply breathing on me.' Ina grinned, knowing he would enjoy her sense of humour. She wasn't mistaken, and the troll's smile widened.

'We cannot let that happen, not with your talent for mayhem. I will have a room and food ready soon. Is there anything the special friend of my friend desires?'

As with Gruff, there was a sharp intelligence in this troll's eyes, and Ina couldn't help but think how humanity misjudged his species. They may look like village idiots, but they were more than happy to use that prejudice to trick the ignorant.

'Information, starting from what the hell is going on here. Why are people turning to Marzanna? And my apologies, but what is your name?'

'I'm Hem. As for the village, it is all because of war and greed,' he said before pulling up an oversized wooden chair to sit with them.

'When the King asked for provisions for the winter war, offering an amount of gold unseen in this region, those fools dragged everything they had from their granaries and sold it to the government.'

He paused when the food arrived at the table, and Velka, with an appetite of a hungry wolf, threw herself on the steaming beetroot soup before their host resumed his story.

'You see, spring comes earlier in the South, so the farmers thought they could survive on spring vegetables and a good lambing season, but spring came, and nothing grew in their fields, no grass to feed the animals, not even nettles grew to make tea. With just enough grain for a few loaves of bread, hunger led to desperation, and then two strangers appeared.'

Ina's hand, stretched out for the last piece of bread, stilled as she turned her gaze at the troll. 'Two men?'

'Yes. One was a typical volkhv, full of piss and vinegar, claiming to talk to the gods. The other? That one felt wrong, never showed his face, smelled like death gone bad, and answered every question with another. To cut a long story short, they sacrificed some pigs in Marzanna's name, though it was more like one of those plays from the capital. Folks were close to driving the fools away, but the next day, the grass was green, and lettuce was sprouting like a miracle. Since then, we've had this mummery every week without fail. There was talk of stopping the sacrifices now things were growing, but three weeks ago, a man claiming to be the new zrest appeared, supposedly sent here by the volkhv to ensure Marzanna continued blessing our crops, which may be difficult as we're running out of pigs.'

'I don't think our night encounter with the revenant was a coincidence,' Velka remarked, making Ina grimace.

'Yes, I should have gone after that mage and at least found out who he was. Instead, I let him slip away like a fool, thinking it was just some idiot playing a prank.' To distract herself from this mistake, Ina grunted before turning to Hem.

'What about Castle Thorn? My grandfather is supposed to protect this region. How can the cult of Marzanna flourish right under his nose?'

The troll snorted a short laugh and shook his head. 'The duke is old, but instead of giving up power to someone younger or even delegating some responsibility, he clutches it tight to his chest, ignoring anyone willing to advise him on the province. Your uncle tries his best, but without the dukedom's authority to back him, it's all meaningless. Now the family lives locked away in the castle, under siege from a delegation of the local yeomanry. I'm glad you're heading there, not for your sake, but I hope you can shake some sense into the old duke. The land is suffering, and its leader needs to step up and help.'

Ina bit her lip and reached for the troll's hand as she stood up.

'I will do my best. Thank you for your hospitality, but I have to think and get some rest, so could you please show us to our room?'

They were escorted upstairs by the same maid who had served them the food, and Ina, with relief, fell on the bed, too tired to even pull her boots off. Before she could dwell on the day's events, exhaustion overcame her, and Ina drifted into a deep sleep.

A loud banging on the door boomed inside her still tired brain like thunder, waking a groggy Ina, and for a moment, she felt utterly lost and confused. As soon as Velka opened the door, Hem barrelled into the room. With a start, Ina realised that the haze she'd initially assumed was the dawn was actually a sea of torches that surrounded the tavern. The unwelcome buzz of voices raised in a religious chant reached her ears.

'Get dressed. You have to run.'

The insistence in the troll's voice finally pushed her into action. Velka already stood ready with their small bags hung over her shoulder, but Ina needed to find out why.

'Hem, what's going on?' she asked, pulling on her boots, which Velka had compassionately removed while Ina slept.

'I don't know. The village had their usual ritual, and then suddenly, everyone was waving pitchforks and torches, chanting about capturing the witch. So please, run. I know what you can do, but they aren't bad people, just fearful, easily led ones, and they don't deserve to be killed or turned into monsters.'

When Ina snapped a hurt glare at the troll, it was Velka who responded, though, jumping to Ina's defence.

'Ina would never do such a thing. Tell us, how can we escape? They have surrounded the tavern.'

'There's a tunnel that leads from the tavern on the forest's edge. I've already told the servant to take your horses there, but you must hurry.'

Ina snuck a look through the window, taking in the faces of the hunger-stricken crowd outside, screaming their rage. Only one person stood out in the fervent crowd. The zhrest, dressed in his robes, face calm, looking directly at her with an easy, sinister smile. Ina gasped when she saw his expression. It was the same as the mad drow prince when he lost himself in tal-maladie. *What is going on? That shouldn't be possible for a human. Gods, I wish I could do mind magic. Is something else driving these men mad?* Ina thought, pulling back and grabbing Velka's hand.

'Let's go. There won't be any reasoning with those people. Hem, come with us. They'll blame you for whatever transgressions they've dreamed up.'

The troll simply grimaced, shaking his head as he answered. 'I will take you to the tunnel and hide there. This madness can't last forever, and this is my home, after all. Just try to fix it for all of us.'

With that, they set off down the stairs, following the towering troll to the dark basement, its walls cold and damp. Ina felt Velka's hand tremble in her grasp, but her gentle friend bravely pushed forward without a word of complaint. Before the trap door closed over their head, Ina asked again, 'Are you sure? I can take you to Thorn. I don't want to be the one who paid for your kindness with misfortune.'

'Yes, I'm sure. Now go, autumn girl. Remember my words, the peasants are just pawns in this game—stupid, greedy and gullible—but please spare them if you can.'

The thud that followed his last words plunged the tunnel into darkness before Ina conjured a tiny pulsar. The passage was crude and looked more like a giant mole had clawed its way through the ground than anything man-made, and Ina cursed the crowd when a cold droplet of water landed on her exposed neck.

'Welcome to my world, Velka. It seems my destiny is to crawl underground anytime someone tries to kill me.'

'It is still better than making the roses bloom day in and day out for a capricious princess.'

Ina laughed in reply, and Velka, in her practicality, put her hand on the tunnel's dirt walls, using her talent to clear away the stray roots from their path.

'Why did he call you the autumn girl?' she asked when they moved slowly, trying not to bang her head on the ceiling.

'I don't know. The Leshy called me that once, and since then, all the old races followed suit. Can you do something about this blockage?'

Ina pointed to the problem. A thick twisted root had broken through the tunnel walls, preventing their escape. Velka squeezed past her friend, reaching out to caress the living barrier lightly. A soft humming grew as Velka's magic merged with the root, influencing its form. Seconds later, their path now clear, the nature mage turned, frowning as she looked back at Ina.

'Something is wrong, Ina. I don't know what, but this tree felt twisted, warped by some strange influence, and it can't heal or be healed.'

The witch nodded and pushed her way forward. 'We'll talk about it later. I feel like I'm being crushed. Will this bloody tunnel ever end?'

They walked a while longer before feeling a breeze on their faces, and both women sped up. They had to climb a ladder to emerge from an overgrown hole in the ground. The night was still dark, with most of the sky covered with thick rain clouds telling them they hadn't slept long. Despite the darkness, Ina didn't dare keep her light in the open, not when she saw the glow of flames in the village. The witch brushed the dirt off her clothes and turned towards their quietly snorting mounts.

'I feel like a revenant rising from the grave. If those people hurt Hem, I will come back and turn this little shithole into a pile of rubble.'

The maliciousness in her voice didn't escape Velka's attention, and Ina felt the nature mage grab her sleeve.

'No, you won't. You saw their faces. Starving, cornered people do stupid things, and mages are easy to blame, but I promise you if you find the one who started this, I will be happy to assist you in hiding the corpse.'

Ina couldn't help but chuckle. Even in a bloodthirsty mood, all Velka could think of was to help her. 'You've changed, and this new fierce Velka is so different from my sweet, fragile flower. This streak of revenge and steel in you is very appealing. I must thank Daro for this.' She felt Velka still for a moment before resuming the walk.

'No, Ina. After the palace battle, I realised that life is not all leaf buds and roses, and sometimes you have to do what's needed to save those you love.'

Velka's words stung so much that Ina wished she could turn back time to preserve Velka's innocence. If there was someone who didn't deserve to face the harsh reality of life, it was her gentle friend. To make matters worse, she was now dragged into a problem with dying crops, poisoned land, weird necromancers and a southern rebellion that was more complicated than a few nobles taking issue with a new king. That anger firmed into resolve, and while placing her hand on orein's back, Ina turned to Velka.

'I will sort this out. You will have your leaf buds and roses back, and the South will have peace. I promise.'

Thunder shook the sky, following Ina's words, and moisture filled the air, threatening rain. Velka looked up at the sky, and the witch saw her shocked expression in a flash of lightning.

'Ina, what did you do?'

'Nothing, it's just a spring storm. We both saw the clouds when we climbed out of the tunnel.'

'This isn't an ordinary storm, Striga. I think the gods have accepted your promise.'

'Don't be silly. The gods have no time to listen to my words. Otherwise, I'd have been struck by lightning many times for cursing them. Let's move on before we get soaked and stuck in the mud.'

'Right, and that's why you have a forest spirit curled up on your bed and are riding an orein,' Velka muttered under her breath, and Ina, refusing to argue further, mounted her horse. She felt a cold sweat on the back of her neck and looked at the sky. The distant rumble of thunder echoed her tumultuous thoughts, especially the one that, despite her best efforts, constantly floated to the surface. What if the gods truly were listening?

The women turned their horses away from the hostile village and headed off, realising quickly how difficult riding in the forest at night was. After being hit in the face for the fifth time by yet another branch, Ina swore bloody vengeance on the next tree that attacked her and dismounted. As the first droplets of rain splashed against her face, the witch looked at the sky with concern. They had to find shelter before the thunderstorm caught up with them. Lightning and trees were Perun's personal invitation to Wyraj, and Ina wasn't ready to accept a trip to the afterlife just yet. There was only one problem. There was the forest or the village and no path to follow.

'What should I do?' Ina didn't realise she had spoken aloud until the last words left her mouth.

'Let's go forward. I know we're lost. We can't go back, so let's go forward.' Hearing the chattering of her friend's teeth gave Ina pause. Despite the mage's protests, she removed her cloak and threw it over Velka's shoulders.

'You need it more than I do. And you're right, let's go forward.'

They moved at a snail's pace through the dense foliage, fighting with plants that seemed determined to block the way. The moisture that had built up an oppressive atmosphere finally broke into a heavy rain that found its way into every gap in their clothing, turning the chilly night into frigid torture. The flickering of a distant light caught Ina's attention and renewed her strength. She pointed it out to Velka, and with one last effort, they pushed through the brushwood into another clearing.

The source of the light was a small and shabby hut, but it had a good roof and was more welcome than the finest palace at that moment. Even the rank swamp surrounding the place wasn't a deterrent. The witch marched forwards on the hardened dirt path towards the cabin.

'I will find a warm welcome here even if I have to scrub their hearth with my soaking wet bloomers.'

Velka didn't protest. Her hunched posture and drooping head spoke for themselves, making Ina even more determined to have a dry place to rest. She knocked on the doors and readied herself as best she could.

'I call on the law of hospitality. My friend and I are looking for shelter from the storm. Please open the door.'

Ina hoped calling upon the ancient custom would grant them access, but her request went unanswered so long that the witch considered blasting the door with chaos. When a bloodshot eye surrounded by matted grey hair appeared in a gap in the doorway, radiating hostility, Ina offered a tight smile.

'We mean no harm. We only want a few hours to rest and warm our bones, if you please.'

She moved to the side, showing Velka and their mounts to prove her good intentions. After a moment of silence, the doors opened wide, and a gnarled old woman gestured them in. 'Come in. You can leave the horses in the shed out back. They will be safe there. Come in.' The eagerness she invited them in brought a genuine smile to Ina's face, and she nodded to Velka.

'Go warm yourself. I will look after the horses and join you shortly.' Her words caused even more vigorous waving as Ina took hold of the reins, leaving Velka in the care of their unusual host.

The shed was small, but removing the tack took her longer than expected. Partly because of her icy, uncooperative fingers, partly because Zjawa blatantly refused to be stripped and danced around the small space, making her work more complicated than it needed to be.

'What the hell is wrong with you today? I know you're tired, but I'm tired too. Just let me...' Ina didn't finish as the orein cracked their heads together, and as soon as the witch stopped cursing, the unruly mare pushed her out of the shed. Hands on her hips, Ina looked at the orein. 'You don't like it here?' she asked, and when Zjawa nodded, Ina's eyebrows knitted together before she continued. 'Are we safe here?'

A distressed whinny and another push sent her running towards the cottage. Ina burst through the door expecting the worst, only to be surprised by Velka sleeping on their host's bed and the strange grandma stroking her face with unexpected tenderness. Ina opened her mouth to apologise when the old woman turned her gaze upon her, and the witch felt the world spin around as she fell into a deep, dark well of disappearing consciousness.

CHAPTER SEVEN

Ina woke to a blinding headache from whatever magic the old crone had used, and it took her a moment to get her bearings. The last thing she remembered was the hypnotic eyes of their host and then oblivion. With a groan that signalled how much she'd hurt her back in her graceless tumble, the witch closed her eyes, hoping she hadn't alerted the old woman.

Ina squinted her eyes while surreptitiously looking around till a low muttering drew her gaze to the corner of the hut. The hag crouched over Velka's unmoving body, stroking her tummy and muttering something in an unknown language. The woman was noticeably overjoyed, lost in whatever ritual she was performing.

Ina minced the curse as she analysed the situation. She had messed up, badly, missing the now obvious clues in her haste to get warm. A hut in the middle of the swamp, an old hag living alone and having hypnotic eyes, all this pointed to the woman being a mamuna, a child stealing hag and one of the most terrifying swamp demons. What she couldn't understand was why the creature took Velka as her victim.

Why must they be so close? With her friend in the hands of the demon, Ina couldn't attack using chaos without potentially hurting Velka. It was time to try something different, but what? Ina moved slightly, and as the hilt of her sword dug painfully into her side, a new plan came to mind. A mamuna was challenging to fight, but not invulnerable. They were also solitary beings, giving the tired witch the upper hand. Or it would have given her an upper hand if she wasn't exhausted from fighting, running, and the lack of sleep, but she didn't have the time to think about that while Velka was in danger.

Slowly rising, Ina created a shield in her mind. The mirror spell Skarbnik taught her in the Grey Mountains had already saved her life once before, and with her mind protected, Ina felt more confident about facing the malicious spirit in her own domain.

'Leave her,' the witch commanded, pulling out her sword. The mamuna turned her head, and two glowing eyes bore into Ina's mind, trying to reach the depths of her soul, but the mirror wall rebuffed the sinister will. The demon hissed at the failure of her attack and turned the rest of her body to face Ina.

'Leave her alone. I don't want to hurt you in your home, but if you cause my friend any harm, you will die.'

Ina tried to remain calm and reason with the creature, but the unnatural stillness of Velka's body didn't make it easy. The mamuna's throaty laugh echoed in the small chamber. 'Hurt? Oh no, she and the one she carries are precious and mine, but I will suck the marrow from your bones with pleasure, little witch.'

The demon leapt towards Ina so fast her body seemed to blur, claws erupting from her arthritic hands. Eyes widening in fear, the witch fell back, crashing into the filthy hearth as razor-sharp claws tore through her thigh. Blood splattered on her face, bringing clarity, and Ina lashed out wildly with her sword, missing as the mamuna dodged, attacking from a different angle.

There was no Mar or Ren to save her, and despite her gnarled body, this demon was faster and stronger than any human. Ina parried one clawed hand with her sword, cutting a few fingers, but the other tore into her forearm, drawing blood. Pain seared her mind, but the demon was close, creating the perfect opportunity. Magic came at her command, stripping the flames from the hearth, creating a deadly wreath of chaos that wrapped itself around the demon's arm. Inhuman shrieking battered Ina's senses as the mamuna fell back, her arm disintegrating when the magic tore apart her flesh. Fear widened the demon's eyes as she retreated, cradling the bloody remains of her limb.

'I curse you. You will watch one you love die and be the reason for it. You will feel the pain and the burden of your magic, just as I feel it now.'

Ina rushed towards her, but it was too late; the demon burst through the door and disappeared into the swamp.

'Oh, for fuck's sake. Robbers, angry peasants, a thunderstorm, and now a raging demon? What in the Abyss is wrong with this place?'

Before she could finish ranting against the fates, heavy rain forced her back inside the hovel. As Ina moved inside, the door barely hung on its hinges, reminding her of Mar's jokes about her relationships with the carpenters' creations. It took a little kicking and cursing to close it, but Ina did the best she could before turning back to her unconscious friend, who, despite the commotion, still hadn't woken up. The witch looked at Velka with worry plastered all over her face when she sat on the bed.

She winced when the fabric scratched her wounded thigh, but her concern for the nature mage forced the pain into the background as she grabbed Velka's shoulders and shook them vigorously.

'Wake up!' she shouted, with no success. Velka looked like a princess from the folk tales. They only needed a prince charming to wake her from this magical slumber. Unfortunately, her prince charming was far away, and after Velka's sudden departure from Osterad, Ina wasn't sure if he was still in good standing.

With a soft sigh, Ina kissed her friend's forehead. 'Please, wake up. I'm not Daro, but you know I love you from the depths of my rotten heart.'

Nothing happened, and Ina felt a cold sweat drench her body as she realised the old woman's curse might be coming true right now. Worst of all, there was no one she could turn to for help; no Nerissa, no healer, not even a village mage. All Velka had now was an undereducated mage with destructive magic and one powerful healing spell full of calamitous consequences.

Ina rolled her sleeves, looking with disdain at the dark puncture wounds where the mamuna's claws had pierced her forearm. She would have to sort that out, but later, once she fixed the bigger problem. *One small step at a time,* she thought while opening Velka's blouse, placing her hand over her friend's heart to perform the sacrifice spell. Yet something deep inside Ina protested at having another life linked so deeply to her soul.

I'm so bloody tired. Think, Ina. Check what's wrong first. Maybe there is a way around it, she thought, trying to focus through the exhaustion, sending a pulse of magic through Velka's body that lit up her meridians. Nothing seemed unusual until the witch looked down at her friend's stomach, gasped and pulled back her hands, looking at her friend in disbelief.

'Oh, my sweet, silly girl. You should have told me.'

Suddenly, the demon's words and obsessive interest all made sense. Velka's mood and impulsive behaviour finally added up, and, unable to resist, Ina reached out again, touching the spark of life growing in her friend's womb. When her magic made contact, the spark danced, attracted to it, alien and familiar at the same time, a little half-orc with a potent seed of power.

At the thought of the father, the joy singing in her heart washed away. *Did Daro know? Did Velka know? Velka wouldn't leave like this if she knew she was pregnant, would she? Had she argued with that hotheaded orc?* While the questions raced through her head, Ina looked at her sleeping friend. *I hope it is all a misunderstanding, but if he's the reason you embarked on this journey with me, not even a dragon will save him from my wrath,* she thought. It took a moment to calm the storm in her heart before Ina restarted her inspection. She found the residue of a sleep spell slowly degrading, and relief swept over her. By sheer luck and Velka's pregnancy, they hadn't ended up at the bottom of the swamp, drowned by an angry demon, all because the mamuna wanted to preserve the mother to steal her child.

Ina removed Velka's wet outer clothing and put more wood onto the fire. The house was shabby but warm, and they both needed some rest, Velka now more than ever, and this was the best opportunity they would get.

The witch inspected her leg, trying to ignore the pain that burned the damaged flesh. *I need to clean it,* she thought, reaching for the knife to widen the hole in the already torn fabric.

The milky white skin contrasted harshly with the exposed tissue. The wound itself looked dangerously unnatural. Whatever venom coated the demon's claws had entered the ragged injury, and greenish tendrils now spread outward. Even more concerning was the appalling smell that assaulted Ina's nose. She looked at it for a moment, biting her lip and wondering what to do. There was a small charge left in Nerissa's healing gem and a few potions in her bag, but they were lost, and the way to Thorn seemed to be neverending. *The wound looks awful, but is it bad enough to use the last of my resources? What if Velka needs them later? You never know what a pregnant woman may need.* That final thought won the argument, and the witch kept her last precious resources for a life-or-death situation.

The witch debated using chaos magic to purge the putrid injury, but the magic refused to affect her body, so she had to resort to old-fashioned methods. *Nerissa would be so bloody proud,* she thought, and with a determined expression, limped to their baggage and retrieved a minor healing potion, hoping it worked on demon venom. After a further look around and a lot of cursing, the witch gathered water and a ragged cloth to apply the potion to the wound, hissing quietly to ward off the pain as she liberally spread the concoction on her leg.

Within moments, the potion was burning through the mamuna's venom, forcing a sob from Ina's lips, even as she continued applying the tincture, but her efforts seemed to work, and in lieu of sewing, reluctantly placed the tip of her dagger into the fire.

'You can do it. It can't be worse than healing Mar,' Ina muttered, looking at the dancing flames till the blade shone from the heat. Afraid of losing her nerve, Ina grabbed the blade and pressed its tip to the bleeding injury.

'Motherfucker! Bastard demon, come back so I can kill you!' Her unsophisticated screaming didn't bring back the demon, but had one unexpected effect. Velka stirred on the bed and looked at her with a confused expression.

'Ina, what happened?'

'Nothing, go back to sleep,' the witch answered, holding back the tears from her *healing*, watching the confused Velka slowly lower herself to the bed.

As quietly as she could, Ina finished cleaning the wound and applied a generous amount of poultice before bandaging it and the one on her arm. After she finished, Ina approached the bed and sat on the edge. It looked like another sleepless night for her. Not that she suspected the mamuna of returning to her abode after being severely injured by fire, but Ina didn't want to risk it. She weaved the warning spell around the small space and put the sword on her lap. *Just like you taught me, Ren. Always have your weapon close.* The thought of the Ghost lightened up her mood, and Ina hummed the melody her friend played every time, injured or sad, she turned to him for consolation. It helped, and soon she drifted into a half-aware state, letting her tired body rest before facing another challenge.

Mar let Woron choose the speed when they left Osterad. Despite their measured pace annoying Daro immensely, the marshal used the time to think about what they should do next. He couldn't fly there, challenge Lord Thorn, a powerful mage, then wait for Ina's arrival. Not only would the sight of a gigantic dragon alert everyone who saw it, but he also didn't know how his spitfire wanted to deal with the rebellion.

It would be best if they caught up to the women on the road and offered whatever assistance the cunning witch needed. Still, it was easier said than done, as his woman had taken the most convoluted way to travel in a straight line. Mar rolled his eyes. His spitfire was hopeless with maps and directions, but at least that gave him a chance to catch up with her before she got lost and ended up in Liath. So far, each time he asked about her, whether in a village or passing travellers, the information they gave him suggested Ina had chosen yet another wrong turn.

So, giving his mount a little encouragement, he set off at a brisk pace and distracted the orc with questions related to his new position, suggesting interesting ideas whenever Daro seemed to struggle. It worked on the first day, but after they rode during the night and a tired Daro grew more snappy, he knew he'd have to ask him about Velka. It took him almost a whole day to find the right words, but Mar devised a plan.

Not that he was particularly interested in their love life and marriage quarrels, but if Daro crossed the nature mage, he would have to stop his spitfire from maiming his friend, and Mar liked to be prepared for such situations.

'Can you recall what happened in the last few days before Velka disappeared?' he asked, and was taken aback by the orc's outburst.

'Nothing happened. How many times do I have to tell you? Velka was moody, that's all. Before you ask, no, I didn't cheat on her. I haven't even looked at another woman since I met Velka. You and Ina can sleep well. I did nothing to my wife to deserve it, but how would you know what it's like to be with the one who compliments your soul?' Daro kicked his horse forward, leaving Mar blinking rapidly alone on the muddy road. Woron turned his head as if asking for direction, and Mar shrugged.

'Yes, go after him. I need to beat some reason into this blockheaded orc.' Woron snorted and jumped forward, rapidly closing in on the distance from the orc's heavy horse. The quick pace took them deeper into the forest. Before long, Mar found Daro standing in the middle of the road, a concerned expression on his face.

'Your witch was busy.' He pointed to the side, and Mar noticed a corpse in the trench. Before the marshal dismounted, he added, 'Don't bother. I've already checked the traces. They were both here, and some local low-lives took their chances. It didn't end well for the poor bastards.' Mar couldn't help but smile when Daro detailed what he had discovered about the skirmish.

'Let's not waste your wife's perfect invention. We won't get to the village today, and this bed is much better than sleeping on the bare ground.' Mar pointed to the living bed Velka left in their camping space. Soon the horses were looked after, and the small fire buzzed nicely next to the makeshift camp.

'I'm sorry.' Daro's apology surprised Mar, and he looked up at the orc. His gaze opened the floodgates, and Mar could only sit and listen as his friend continued.

'I shouldn't snap like this, but the truth is I'm scared, and I don't know what happened. I can't live without her. I know the world is full of eager women, but since you sent me to seduce her, there's not been a single day when I haven't thought I should bless you for giving me that mission. Now I'm terrified she could leave me forever.'

Mar placed his hand on the orc's shoulder and turned back to the fire. 'She hasn't. She wouldn't be Ina's friend if she were a fickle woman. And I believe you if you say you have done nothing wrong, but there must be a reason behind it.'

They sat silently for a moment, gazing at the dancing flames until the orc asked, 'Why didn't you marry her? People are talking, and she is of noble birth, you both are, but you should consider what they say about her. Ina may not wait forever till you make up your mind.'

Mar's roaring laugh reverberated through the clearing, one hand slapping his thigh in his merriment. Daro waited till Mar settled and asked, 'What was so bloody funny about marriage?'

'I'm afraid you misjudged the situation, my friend. I would marry her tomorrow, but I don't think it is what she wants. Ina is a peculiar woman regarding love, and I don't want to spook her with a premature proposal.'

'But what about Liath? You're the heir, and you need a wife.'

Mar shook his head, and Daro stopped, surprised by this sudden gesture. 'I'm a dragon. I know Liath needs an heir, but I know it can't be me. I don't know many things, but if my spitfire wants this, I will marry her the day she says yes. If she doesn't, I will be happy with things as they are.'

Daro laughed shortly, and Mar saw the careless old orc still there under his mask of concern. 'They domesticated us so much, my friend, and we are too happy about it to complain.'

They talked through most of the night as Mar struggled to fall asleep, feeling as though he were under threat. When they finally lay down, hoping for some rest, Mar's face twisted in a sudden spasm of pain, his shape blurring. Daro cursed, rubbing his eyes when the dragon gripped his thigh, hissing through the clenched teeth. The orc jumped to his feet with a dagger flashing in his hand, but Mar shook his head.

'It's Ina. She is injured. Get the horses. We need to go.' He tried to stand up but staggered and heavily sat back on the wooden frame.

'What about Velka? Is she injured too?'

'How do I know? I'm not chaos linked with your bloody wife?!' Mar tried to stand up and hobbled to the horses. The pain eased up, but not his worry. Their connection had never been so physical. He could feel her mood, especially since he'd moved in, but he had never felt Ina's pain before, and his imagination pictured the worst possible scenario.

Daro was already halfway to packing up their belongings when he asked, 'Do you know where they are?'

Mar looked at the dark road ahead, filled with the noises of night predators. Once the pain disappeared, he could jump on Woron in one smooth motion. 'We'll carry on in this direction. I don't know where they are, but someone on the way must have noticed two single women and a strange horse. We will ask.'

That was the best he could come up with. Feeling like a complete idiot, Mar set off at a blistering pace, racing their horses along the dark forest path.

They rode for hours, and the sun was peeking over the horizon when they arrived at the village. Mar cursed, seeing the wisps of smoke still lingering in the remains of a tavern with only its sign still intact. The people looked hostile but didn't dare to speak or attack two well-armed men, and Mar almost regretted it. The moan from the rubble got his attention, and he directed his horse towards the tavern ruins.

Under a partially burnt beam lay a troll, unconscious but still showing signs of life. Mar gestured to Daro, and the orc moved the heavy wood with a strength born of emotional distress. The tavern was the only place showing signs of recent damage, and Mar tried to bring the injured host back to the real world as gently as he could. Suddenly, Daro stepped in and slapped the unfortunate man's face, and the troll slowly opened his eyes. Seeing strange faces bent over him, Hem swung his fist, but Mar caught it easily, locking the massive troll's hand in his transformed claws.

'We are not your enemies. We only want to know if you saw two women from Osterad. One of them had a strange horse.' Mar released his hand when he saw the shadow of understanding in the troll's eyes.

'They escaped by the tunnel before the fire.'

Mar slowly released the breath he hadn't realised he was holding, hearing a raspy, smoke-damaged voice. He had to grab Daro's hands when the orc jumped in, ready to shake more information in less than polite methods.

'You are her dragon… yes?'

Mar involuntarily smiled, amused by his new title. 'Yes, I'm her dragon. Where is she? Where does your tunnel lead?'

The troll coughed and spat out coal-black sputum. 'Tunnel ends up in the forest. The autumn child will be safe there. The forest will never harm the blood of Leshy.'

Mar and Daro exchanged glances. Many old races called Ina autumn girl. It dawned on Mar that more than just her mane of copper tresses might have earned her that particular nickname. The troll coughed again, splattering blood on his chest. Mar cursed silently.

'He needs a healer,' Mar said, more to himself, but the voice behind him answered.

'Not here. This place is tainted by greed. They tried to capture the women, and this idiot stayed to delay them.'

Mar turned around to see the owner of the voice and came face to face with a prune-faced old woman, looking at him without fear. His eyebrows shot up when she commanded them.

'Take him to the next village. He helped your women. You owe him this. He is a good boy. Ugly… but good.'

As if nothing else was to be said, the old woman turned on her heel and walked down the dusty road, leaving Mar with a decision to make.

'We don't have time for this. We need to find Velka.'

Daro didn't share his concern, ready to hit the road, leaving the troll to his fate in the single-minded attempt to find his wife.

'No. How would you explain to Velka that you left the person who saved her life to die? Load him onto Woron. We leave him in the next village and continue to Castle Thorn.'

'Load him yourself. I'm going to find my wife.'

Daro bared his fangs and turned towards his horse when a clawed hand grabbed him by his shoulder and turned him around like a puppet. The orc's eyes widened when Mar's contours blurred, and an irritated dragon peeked through the embers of his golden eyes.

'Daro Vakmu Yargrat, you will do as you are told. Trust your wife, as I trust mine. They will go to Castle Thorn, and we will meet them there with a clear conscious rather than leaving this one to perish and chase ghosts in the forest.'

'Ina is not your wife!' Daro shouted in his face, and Mar felt something snap deep inside him.

'Not yet,' he said with a snarl, hammering the armoured fist straight into the orc's temple.

Soon leading two horses, both burdened with limp bodies, Mar left the village, praying he made the right decision.

CHAPTER EIGHT

A man in formal priest's robes stepped out from the crowd as the warriors entered the ruins of the tavern. His surprise when the troll was dragged alive from the rubble was quickly masked as he ducked down and hid again. Once the interlopers had finished their discussion, and the human began riding away with the unconscious bodies, the zhrets turned to one of the villagers.

'Follow them. I want to know where they are going. And send someone to Agatha's house. It is time to silence that old hag.'

He knew these orders would be followed. Since the day he'd arrived and scared the villagers to reinforce the volkhv's religious message, the peasants had treated him like the avatar of the gods, and as time passed, he had started believing they were right. But now, it seemed the capital had noticed the situation, and killing those interfering wenches hadn't put an end to it. No, it would be best to inform his master of this recent development. It was a shame Hem hadn't also died in the fire. He and that old hag, Agatha, were the last dissenters to his rule of this area. With the troll's survival, the zhrets worried his misdeeds would come to light, and he knew Hem would seek him out if he survived.

He hurried to the old temple that served as his home and the source of his borrowed magic, locking the door behind him. Symbols on the wall lit up when he uncovered a hidden runic diagram, and looking at it, the zhrets hesitated. But the desire to communicate with the master overcame his repulsion. He dragged out the mummified corpse of his predecessor and placed it in the middle of the symbol, wondering why there wasn't an easier way to send a message. It took him a moment to find one of the magic storage gems, and he had to toss most of his belongings onto the floor before he pulled it from the chest and pressed it into the corpse's mouth. Sweat beaded on his forehead when he activated the runes using the little magic he had. All he needed to do now was to sit and wait until a portal opened to the underworld, connecting him with the other side. Minutes passed slowly before the last rune lit up, and the cadaver rose from the floor, making the zhrets exhale with relief.

'My lord, your servant, Slavo, has news.'

The dead man's mouth opened, and a voice, distorted by the dry vocal cords, rasped like rotten wood falling apart. 'Yes?'

The zhrets sat outside the circle, separated from the body by only a thin veil of flickering magic. He tried to relax, letting his thoughts flow freely as he made his report. 'Two mages came to the village last night. I suspected they were conspiring with the troll, so I ordered the peasants to burn down the tavern—'

He hadn't finished his sentence before a skeletal hand shot through the barrier and locked itself to his throat. 'What gave you the right to be violent towards mages?' The anger of his master was palpable, and the pressure on his throat intensified, squeezing more and more painfully and cutting off the air. The zhrets choked, scrambling to escape as the corpse, with terrifying, inhuman strength, lifted him off the ground and shook him like a rag doll. 'Are they alive?'

The question shouted into his face caused the bile to rise in his throat at the putrid stench of rotten flesh filling his nostrils. 'Yes... I think so, Master.'

His body could barely force the words past the pressure on his neck as the priest begged for his life, positive death was staring him in the face.

'*Think?* Then think harder. If anything befalls my guests before I welcome them, you will die... everyone will die. Remember this and tell the others.'

Eyes wide in fear, the desperate priest gasped again, forcing out more words. 'No, my lord, I know. The troll survived, and no bodies were left behind. Even their horses were gone. Please, lord, spare me.' Whatever words he managed in his panic seemed to placate his furious master, and he was thrown to the floor, discarded. The zhrets lay there catching his breath, afraid to move, the light in the room fading as the magic slowly dissipated.

The corpse sagged to the floor, and the zhrets realised he'd forgotten to mention the two warriors who'd taken the troll away with them, but, looking down at the rotting body of his predecessor, decided the information wasn't significant enough to bother his busy master. Slavo waited a moment longer, ensuring the spell was exhausted, then jumped to his feet, erased all signs of magical sigils from his small room, and packed his meagre belongings. When the old volkhv promised a comfortable life and full belly, he hadn't mentioned dealing with dead bodies and necromancers. There had definitely been no mention of losing your life because some damn mages died.

Slavo waited until the village had gone to sleep, ensuring the obedient peasants couldn't see their shepherd sneaking out and abandoning his flock. The zhrets had decided that no power in the world was worth dealing with living corpses and fled the small village without a backward glance.

On the other side of the spell, a man with raven hair lightly dusted with grey looked at the remains of a communication crystal shattered on the ground. He shouldn't have lashed out, but hearing of the zhrets' attack on the women integral to the plan made him lose his temper, and the sudden surge of magic in the necromancy spell destroyed the delicate device.

Rurik turned and sat at his desk, only to stare at his spies' reports and the letters from those lords hoping to use his talents for their own gain. The mage's lips curled in a scornful smile as he thought about just how wrong they were. Not for the first time, those who believed themselves superior to everyone else underestimated his influence, and he'd long ago learned how to use that to his advantage. He worried briefly as he thought about the zhrets' actions, hoping the fool had been right about Ina escaping the fire. His spies had already told him she was travelling with Velka, as both women had become inseparable since their autumn reunion, and he hoped neither mage had been harmed. It hadn't been easy to coax Ina out of Osterad, but he had no influence there anymore. Gruff and Kaian had thoroughly destroyed his network, earning Rurik's grudging respect, but that made it much harder to conceal his activities.

Velka's presence provided additional leverage over Ina, but if he could, he wanted to avoid hurting her. Rurik wanted to repay the kindness shown to him in their youth. The talented nature mage had been the first not to reject the death master. Her gentle, giving soul had saved the necromancer at the lowest point of his life, hands stained with the blood of innocents, and the truth of his birth fresh in his mind. And with that love, Rurik's vision had been born.

'I should have done things differently, my sweet girl. I hope, one day, you can forgive me.' The words were a sad reminder of past mistakes.

A shudder rippled over Rurik at the memories of the pain from the slaver's whips, the moment magic had blossomed in his soul, and how, in blind fury, he had raised the corpse of the friend killed by an over-enthusiast overseer. He still recalled savouring the terror of that man as he begged for his life, revealing the identity of the necromancer's mother to save his miserable hide, then snuffing out the maggot's existence before escaping to the South.

The rage in Rurik's soul had seemed impossible to tame, not even after he met his mother. Still, a chance meeting at a seedy tavern in Osterad had changed his life. Velka's touch, her kind, soothing words, brought peace and clarity, planting the seeds for his great endeavour, and that ultimately led to the end of their brief interlude.

Rurik ran a hand carelessly through his hair, leaving a ragged mess behind, thinking about the trick he'd played on Ina during her journey through the forest. It had taken a lot of power, but leaving a crystal with the local brigand leader had made it possible to project his magic so far. Ina hadn't changed over the years, a few laughter lines maybe, a little less arrogant, but on the whole, she was still the infamous striga who ruled over the common room of the *Drunken Wizard*. Only her magic had changed. Now chaos cloaked her with the power of the old gods, visible only to the ancient races and those who made a pact with Veles. But for the ones who could see? She was magnificent; a shining beacon, reminiscent of times long gone, when the world was forming, and the gods themselves were young.

I will find a way for you to claim the circlet so you can ascend to what you're meant to be, he thought, dressing in a dark robe and looking in the mirror. His handsome face and tall, muscular frame didn't match his current disguise, so he took a moment to adjust his posture, rounding his shoulders and back till his appearance corresponded to the impression of a reverential devotee of the gods. It had taken some good acting and unusual applications of his necromancy to convince the old volkhv of his connection to the goddess of death, but once convinced, the priests followed his every order, and now they had an army of worshippers at their disposal.

Thanks to his manipulation of the princess, and the battles at the capital and Liath, it had been easy to show how volatile King Rewan's rule would be and to guide them into accepting his plan to create their own country. Add in a few assassination attempts, both here and in Verdante, and the entire region was ripe for the picking.

It was time to move his plan forward again. Rurik picked up a time-worn scroll from his desk and headed out. This scroll was another reason he was beyond redemption. Its curse, recovered by his mother from Castle Thorn, would cause the deaths of those the necromancer wanted free from tyranny, but fulfilling his vision was worth the sacrifice. The intention now was to use the old volkhv to plant the evidence for Ina to find. Once she realised the blight was caused by such powerful magic, there'd be no choice but to claim the last piece of the regalia to destroy the spell, and once she had, Rurik would be there, a friend from the good old days, offering his knowledge and helping to guide her in the right direction.

With the scroll in hand, the necromancer walked to the centre of the temple and approached the old volkhv. 'Our Lady Marzanna revisited my dreams and has sent me north. People are still sinning, rejecting her worship, delaying the coming of spring, so prepare a sacrificial pyre to prove our devotion. There are two mages travelling through this region that are not to be harmed, as they are the chosen ones who will awaken her with their magic. Spread the message and start the preparations.'

His low melodic voice, full of terror and foreboding, shook the old man's body, and the volkhv turned his dull eyes up to his. 'Blessed be the Winter Death, mother of rebirth. Her humble servants will fulfil her wish.'

'Good. I will see to the sanctuaries and temples on my journey, but I urge you to keep the flames high and look for her words in the sacrificial pyre.' Rurik nodded and bowed deeply in front of Marzanna's statue, avoiding looking at the victims of his sacrifice shackled to the goddess by magic. *Forgive me, Winter Death. I do what I must, so no other child will suffer my fate.*

Deep in his heart, the necromancer hoped his words reached the deity, and she understood, but as he walked away, something inside his mind howled in protest. As he read from the scroll, the old volkhv's words were repeated by his acolytes, and the spell rolled outwards in waves; the prayer they were told would appease their goddess poisoning the land. Rurik looked towards the smoke that rose over the offered sacrifice, and for a moment, sadness and shame overcame him before he turned and walked into the darkness, making sure no one saw him heading south towards Alesia. As the mage walked away, he could feel the corruption in the soil, even without being a nature mage, and smiled ruefully. Only the power of a chaos archmage could undo the damage now, and only if she used every tool she had.

Rurik shook his head, nails digging into the flesh of his tightly clenched fists. *Everybody dies; that is the nature of things.* He repeated it like a mantra, calming his doubts until iron conviction replaced his conscience. He needed to ensure the southern barons' coup would bear fruit and create unrest that further weakened the king's rule over these lands.

Kaian stood in silence, watching the blood drip from his dagger. In the darkness of the king's bedroom, a young man slowly choked out his last breath. His raven hair and tanned skin were a clear testament to his origins, but the master assassin hadn't let him die easily, not after the scum had attacked the man he loved. Rewan moved closer, placing a hand on Kaian's shoulder and gently squeezing it. This small gesture and reassuring touch brought an end to the bloodlust.

'Verdante again? How did this one sneak inside? He wouldn't blend into the environment with that complexion.'

'I don't know, but I will find out. That means I have to investigate, but you should not be alone. The bodyguard we picked from my cadre, stop sending her away. I want you protected when I'm not here until this matter is sorted.'

The stern look of the white-haired man provoked a dramatic eye roll from the king, but Kaian didn't care. Instead, he bent down and started searching, rifling through the servant's outfit till he heard a strange rustling sound. He used his dagger to cut open the stitches, only to find a folded note. Rewan instantly reached for it and frowned, reading its contents.

Disable the king. The rebellion is in motion. Be ready to act when you receive the signal.

The letter was again marked with three wheat ears, and Rewan walked to the table, pouring himself a good measure of wine before leaning on the corner.

'What do you think?' Kaian asked.

'Many things. We need to dispose of the body without alerting the servants, so we can avoid war with Verdante, which will happen if the court learns about the attacks. The noble's pride will demand justice, even if I don't care about these provocations,' the king said slowly, sipping the wine.

'Do you want me to deploy my resources to Verdante? We can give that peacock Tobias a taste of his own medicine and see if this calms him down.'

The king smiled as Kaian tried to hide the glee from his voice, suggesting he would be more than happy to take on this task

113

himself. 'I love you,' Rewan said, laying his head on Kaian's shoulder, and those simple words made his lover sigh.

'So, that means no?'

'I told you I want to avoid going to war. We can't throw this country into more turmoil, and killing Verdante's ruler would mean just that. Why do you think I sent Ina there? If anything happens, I, as a king, would be as shocked as the others learning about her misdeeds, and I can deny Cornovii's involvement in any mishaps that might occur.'

'And I can see how happy you are with this decision.' Kaian stroked the king's cheek and looked at him with concern. 'You don't have to sacrifice her. There are other means to calm the South.'

Rewan's abrupt laugh surprised him as the king detangled himself from his embrace. 'Then who should I sacrifice, Kaian? Youngsters barely trained to be in an army, the southern peasants? Ina has the means to defend herself, and she has a dragon. Jorge said—'

'You listen too much to that old goat!' Kaian's outburst stopped the king's explanation, and his monarch's frown dropped into silence before he replied to his lover's words.

'She would understand.'

The slight tremble in his voice was like a bucket of ice water for Kaian's anger, and he approached Rewan, taking the wine out of his hand and embracing him. 'My love, Ina is like a horse that allows us to ride its back because it is unaware of its strength. One day, she will learn the full extent of it, and when this day comes, I want her to be a friend by your side, as there will be no means of forcing her to be a servant. No more political games with this one. If you wish to do something, tell her exactly why.'

Rewan nodded, relaxing under his lover's touch before his lips twitched slightly. 'I wonder why she took our nature mage with her? It's not like she wants to grow some roses at Castle Thorn, yet Jorge seemed thrilled when he heard.'

'I told you, that old goat has plenty of his own secrets. The problem we have now is that both the marshal and the captain of the palace guard are away from their posts. No matter how talented Sa'Ren Gerel is, he can't supervise the army and secure the palace, so we're back to where we started. You need a bodyguard with you at all times. Please, accept my recommendation or choose someone else from my staff.'

'Why can't it be you?' Rewan's voice carried a yearning that made Kaian smile.

'Because to keep you safe, I must do more than stop some random assassin. The mastermind behind the plot must be found and neutralised. For that to happen, I must find and kill them. We both know your tastes in the bedroom, but as long as I have your love, it matters not who shares your bed, especially if this helps you control the court. I may even join you occasionally.'

Kaian's remark released the tension in Rewan's posture and tore a laugh from the king's lips. 'You are one depraved son of a bitch, and I have a sneaking suspicion you just want more sex. Fine! Send me your bodyguard, but make sure she knows my boundaries. No simpering maidens of any sort.'

Kaian nodded and approached the king with a predatory grin. A few years older than the king, he still couldn't believe the stripling his family insisted he protect would so effortlessly capture his heart. From their first meeting, the master assassin had been impressed by Rewan's intelligence, cunning, and ruthlessness. Only after several years did he appreciate the gentleness and humour he kept hidden behind a mask of debauched excess. This insight encouraged Kaian to defy his family and their support of Princess Sophia, working to keep this amazing young man alive as his sister isolated and discredited him. The loneliness the two men shared created a bond that grew until, one day, Rewan surprised Kaian, kissing him one night on a stroll through the gardens.

He watched his lover retreat towards the bed, a taunting smile on his lips. Kaian's grin widened, even as he called for the guard to remove the body from the room. The assassin knew Rewan hoped for an end to the constant fighting, but both men knew, deep down, it never would. Kaian had long since been determined to live in Rewan's shadow, sharing his love with the future queen, but until that happened, his lover's nights belonged to him, and he intended to take full advantage.

Once the guard removed the corpse, Kaian's lips captured his royal prey, connecting them in a long, seductive kiss before he pushed Rewan roughly onto the bed.

'I want you so much,' he whispered, moving over Rewan's body, nails scoring the tense muscles under his touch. When the king's hand tangled in the silver strands of his hair, pulling him down for a more intimate kiss, Kaian happily yielded, moaning as he fulfilled his lover's request.

While they lost themselves in their passion, the guard who carried the dead assailant to the backyard gasped in terror when the corpse's eyes turned milky white, and purple flames burst into life on the dead body. Before he could call for help, nothing but ash remained, and even that disappeared as the spring winds gusted over the ground.

CHAPTER NINE

Ina woke up, confused and groggy, looking around at the strange surroundings until the previous night's memories flooded her mind, and she groaned, the fog lifting from her mind as she realised she'd fallen asleep instead of guarding her friend. The words to a bawdy folk song rang out as Velka belted out the popular tune, gleefully rattling dishes to the rhythm, almost distracting Ina from the pain of her poorly tended wounds.

In disbelief, the witch looked at her smiling friend, thinking this must be some weird fever dream, but the pain from her arm and leg focused her mind too well for it.

'Velka, what in Nawia are you doing?'

As soon as she asked, her friend turned, her bright smile widening as she looked at Ina, waving two eggs around as if that answered the question. 'Making breakfast? I couldn't find anything else, and our host is not here. Do you think she would mind? I left a few coins on the table, but I'm starving. So, it's not as though we're stealing, hmm?'

'No, we are not, and if the mamuna has any objections, I will have another talk with her.' Ina rose to her feet, hobbling outside to relieve herself and look at the horses, ignoring the wide-eyed stare of her friend. The mamuna was unlikely to harm their mounts, but the witch wanted to make sure. While standing next to her orein, she let the mountain spirit sniff her leg, shrugging slightly when Zjawa gave her a querying look.

'I know. I wasn't paying attention last night. I was tired and shouldn't have ignored you. I'm sorry.' Ina had always talked to her animal companions, often feeling more comfortable with them than humans, and Zjawa felt almost as aware as Boruta, though not quite as judgemental. 'Just don't tell anyone what a klutz I am. The amazing royal witch, tripping from calamity to calamity. Mar and Ren would never let me live it down.' Ina cuddled her cheek to the orein's soft coat when a sudden spasm almost brought her to her knees.

The orein lowered herself slowly to the ground, helping to ease her ailing rider to the ground. Ina gently unwrapped the makeshift bandages and sucked in a shocked breath at the sight of greenish tendrils spreading out from the wound. She placed her hand on the damaged tissue and called on her magic, but the mamuna's venom resisted her limited healing skills. Much to her consternation, she could see the source of the problem, but fixing it was entirely different.

'Well, I guess we need to find a healer.'

Ina hobbled to a broken-down old trough and, using the cold water, tried to remove as much green pus as possible without making the wound worse. She had just finished applying new bandages and took one of the remaining potions when Velka's blonde head poked through the door, and her friend shouted.

'What's taking so long? Breakfast is ready. Come back before it gets cold.'

After only a little grumbling about clueless valkyries, Ina joined her friend, sitting next to a wobbly table with a plate of scrambled eggs between them. Ina watched quietly as Velka munched through the yellow mush with the hunger of a marching army.

'Why aren't you eating?' asked Velka between the bites, and Ina smiled.

'I'm waiting.'

'For what?'

When Velka suddenly paled and rushed outside, Ina followed at a leisurely pace, grinning mischievously as she spotted the blond mage bent over a small fence, feeding the fish with the remains of her breakfast.

'For this,' she said. 'Serves you right for not telling me you are pregnant. What in Lada's name were you thinking? You should be lounging around the palace, not dragging your passenger around with me through swamps and fires. What if something happened to you or your child? How could I live with myself, Flower? I would happily die to keep you safe, but don't think I would hesitate to beat your sorry arse for risking your baby's life.'

'How did you find out?'

Velka's calm was getting on her last nerve. Pinching the bridge of her nose, Ina took a moment to study her friend's expression. Still pale and sweaty, she saw a stubborn challenge in her eyes, as if the discovery of her secret pregnancy was the essence of the problem.

'You really don't remember? Our lovely host turned out to be a mamuna, and she was trying to take your child. It took a little gentle persuasion to convince her she would not make a good parental figure.'

What little colour remained on Velka's face washed away, and she staggered, placing a hand on her tummy. 'I thought you were exaggerating. Did she…?' the nature mage stuttered. The realisation of what could have happened shocked her, and when her friend wobbled, Ina rushed over, locking Velka in a tight embrace before slowly lowering her to the ground.

'Breathe… Everything is fine. Your boy is well, I already checked. Now breathe, and don't you dare faint on me. I'm sorry for yelling at you, but my concern got the better of me. You are my sister in everything but blood. Take deep breaths… I will look after you, Velka… I will always look after you.'

Ina rubbed her friend's back, and her calm, compassionate voice seemed to ease the tension. When Velka looked up, the tears in her eyes were eclipsed by the most beautiful smile.

'It's a boy?' The dreamy expression lasted only for a moment before Velka, with inhuman strength, grabbed Ina's injured arm, forcing the witch to place her hand on her friend's stomach. 'Is he healthy? Will he be more like Daro or me? Can you feel his magic?'

Ina hissed at the pain from her wound and struggled in the nature mage's grip. 'For fuck's sake, woman, let me go. We are kneeling in the middle of a swamp, and you want me to do divinations?'

Velka released her hand with a frown at Ina's unusually sharp reaction and looked at her forearm. Bloody green pus seeped through the bandage and clothes, staining the mage's fingers. 'Ina? What exactly happened?'

'I told you it took a little work to get her off you, but she won't be a threat anymore. Now, please get yourself ready. I promise I will tell you more about your boy, just not now.'

Velka nodded solemnly and returned to the cottage, packing their small bags while Ina saddled the horses. When both steeds were ready, Ina approached the biggest tree and pressed her forehead to the rough bark.

'Leshy, if you can hear me, please help. I don't know where we are, but I must get us out of this forest,' Ina said, inhaling the stale smell of the swamp and the more vibrant scent of wood, leaves, and barely budded flowers. Despite all their troubles, she felt at peace, embracing the quiet dignity of the forest. The memory of those early days in exile rose to the forefront of her mind when, lost to despair, the witch had wandered off, finding herself in front of a majestic, ancient tree and had rested her head on its warm, welcoming bark. The feeling of something unfurling inside, opening to the world, took over, just as it had back then, and Ina whispered, 'Your autumn girl needs you, Leshy.'

Far away in the city of Osterad, a large, black cat woke from a comfortable nap in front of the fire and stretched, back arching down and claws piercing the soft cushion beneath. His outline shimmered, slowly fading into the background. Soon, only the cooling impression on the pillow testified to his presence.

At that exact moment, the doors of the mamuna's cottage crashed open as Velka, a shocked expression on her face, burst out into the open, looking at Ina as if she had seen a ghost.

'Ina, what have you done?' she asked, her gaze snapping back and forth between the verdant forest and her friend.

'What?'

Ina's dumbfounded face made Velka's frown deepen. She approached Ina, poised as if to battle a horde of monsters from the shadows. When nothing happened, she placed her hand on the witch's shoulder.

'Tell me what you did a moment ago, please.'

Ina looked at her friend, blinking rapidly, taken aback by these sudden, serious questions. 'I only asked the Leshy for help. I talk to the trees sometimes, and before you start, I'm not mad. I know he is not here, but it calms me down and helps me think. I fear the poor forest god has become my shoulder to lean on, and if he's ever listened, he must be tired of my rambling by now.'

Ina felt a gentle blush warm her cheeks when she admitted this strange habit, but Velka shook her head and looked at her friend with a half smile. 'I think he listens, Ina. Your plea woke up the forest. I know you can't feel green magic, but it was so... I can feel them. The trees will show us the way, and... there is love behind the magic. Ina, I think the Leshy cares for you a great deal.'

'Yup, I know. Gods love the heralds of chaos, mainly for the entertainment we bring.'

Velka loaded their bags on the horses, laughing giddily. 'I would give my right hand to be cherished by the Lord of the Forest, and here you are complaining. Oh, Ina, you are deliciously bizarre. Let's go. Your trees are shining like a beacon, showing us the way.'

Velka's mood was bright and free, her laugh full of vigour, unrestrained by worry as she delighted in the magic surrounding her. Ina followed, grumbling about gods and helping the wrong mage, as nothing in the forest looked any different to her. The nature mage guided them through foliage that looked impenetrable to the witch but became an impossibly wide path as they approached. Soon, Ina had to admit her friend was right, and despite the throbbing pain in her wounds, she focused on enjoying the smooth ride.

The picture of an unkempt, bearded man shimmered in her mind, flashing her with a mischievous grin, and Ina reached out, touching the branch of a low-hanging tree, gently trailing her fingers over brightly free oak leaves.

'Whatever your reasons are, thank you for everything,' she whispered, and the branch swayed gently, caressing her cheek.

It didn't take long to return to the main road, and Ina sighed with relief, seeing the hard-packed dirt stretching out before them. They set off at a brisk pace in order to reach the next settlement before dusk. After their adventures, the horses had rested and followed her command eagerly, so it didn't take more than a few hours to emerge from the forest to the fields and meadows surrounding the small town.

Men-al-Tol was an ancient settlement near the river, its buildings still showing the influence of the high elves that had once built their enclaves here in Cornovii. Despite falling into disrepair after the elves abandoned the area, the subsequent human population's rebuilding of the town retained the delicate symmetry of elven construction, and almost every house was covered in intricate nature-inspired carvings. Ina pulled up her hood, hiding her hair and face, and when Velka threw her a questioning look, she answered with a shrug.

'This way, I might get to sleep one night in peace, so let's try to look as casual as possible.'

The dubious look her friend gave her left Ina grumbling under her breath. She didn't want to worry Velka, but the throbbing in her wounded arm and leg was now a searing pain that forced a gasp every time there was an accidental jostle, and Ina wasn't sure how long she could hold herself upright in the saddle. Much to her relief, the town looked quiet and ordinary. Its citizens busied themselves with usual daytime activities. Although two lone women riding into town initially gained a few surprised stares, Velka's cheerful questioning soon earned them directions to the tavern. Ina, in her current state, decided it would be best to let her friend do the talking.

While waiting for the rooms to be cleaned, Ina learned it would take them less than a day to arrive at Castle Thorn and the town, despite its idyllic look, also struggled with food shortages. Of course, the innkeeper didn't mind telling her how much everyone blamed the king.

'But why the king? He bought the grain with gold, and I heard they even abolished taxes for this year.'

The innkeeper snorted a brief laugh and shook his head. 'Can you eat or drink gold? We are lucky here because most people held back their winter supplies in case of a late spring. Plenty of others got blinded by the sight of all that gold and now turn to Marzanna with hungry resentment in their eyes.'

'I saw your fields. The wheat and early vegetables are sprouting nicely. Even if you're short on supplies, it should be enough to survive till full spring and summer,' Velka said, curious about the conversation.

'Yes, our fields survived. The elven blessing still anoints this land, but further south, I heard the earth is foul. What little vegetation is rotting, and people are getting desperate.'

Ina listened quietly to this exchange. The scene was exactly as Hem had described. She felt the key to the southern problems lay in providing people with the means to live, as peasants were unlikely to revolt if they had a field to plough and livestock to feed. Before she could enquire further, the servant announced their rooms were ready, and both women gathered their belongings and followed the girl upstairs.

As requested, a small bowl of steaming hot water had been provided and, throwing her bag in the corner, Ina sat heavily on a chair. She listened to the bustling Velka, happily singing for a moment, taking comfort in the joyous sound. Since Ina learned of the pregnancy, a weight had disappeared from the blonde valkyrie's shoulders, which made the witch happy in a way she struggled to understand. Ina looked at the water and started undressing. The shivers and cold sweats that ran over her body in the last hour were a bad sign, and knowing Velka, she could burst in at any moment to ask Ina to check on her child.

With a heavy sigh, the witch began unwrapping the bandages, biting her lip when the stench of decay made her gag. Ina examined her leg for a moment, unsure what to do, then closed her eyes, trying to come to terms with her predicament. Whether it was magic, mamuna's venom, or swamp fever, it caused a problem her magic couldn't fix, and it kept spreading through her body, leaving her weak. Even the ointment she applied after the injury hadn't worked. It'd only slowed the progress. She had little choice but to trust the local healer or use the last of Nerissa's gifts, hoping it would be enough to get her to Thorn. After their less-than-welcoming reception at the previous village, and knowing that one look at her meridians would reveal the nature of her magic, jeopardising her mission tipped the scales.

Ina hobbled to her bags and shook the content onto the table. Scrolls, healing potions and clothes were mixed in a pile, and the witch kept throwing things aside till her hand locked on one of the healing gems. The last of Nerissa's gifts from her previous adventure shone in Ina's hand with a soft blue light as she whispered the activation formula.

The bliss that followed when the pain subsided and her skin lost its necrotic hue was immense.

'Bless your old bones, aunty.' Ina breathed in relief, pouring clean water on the wound. Even such a powerful spell wouldn't heal her completely, but at least she was almost sure she would arrive at Thorn alive and maybe even with two working legs, which was good enough for her.

Ina had barely finished changing her dressing when Velka barged in with a plate of steaming buns. She paused at the entrance when she noticed Ina's exposed thigh with its thick layers of bandages. With a soft sigh, she placed the tray on the side and approached Ina, reaching her hand towards the witch.

'For once, you could wait and let me help you. You don't have to carry all the world's burdens yourself. Especially since I already knew you were injured. Did you truly believe I wouldn't notice you wincing every time you moved?'

'We have enough problems as it is. Fussing over a few scratches won't make me feel better.' Ina attempted to unwrap her arm, jumping when Velka slammed her fist on the table and approached her, towering over Ina. The deep frown on her face reminded Ina of one of the university teachers, and she couldn't help but smile.

'Inanuan Zora Thornsen, don't you dare patronise me, or I'll wipe that smile off your face with the back of my hand. Show me your arm.'

Ina was openly laughing, but she extended her arm to her friend. Velka unwrapped the fabric scraps Ina had used to bandage her wound in the hut. 'I'm not Mar or Ren and won't lock you in a tower because you were injured. You can ask for my help without losing your martyr's crown.'

Ina hissed as Velka tore the fabric from the wound, but much to her relief, the healing gem had driven the poison from her arm entirely, and she didn't have to explain the rot and her worries to her friend. A warm, fuzzy feeling spread through her chest as Velka fussed over her wound. *There's no better time than now to ask her about her troubles*, Ina thought, and took a chance to use Velka's tirade against her.

'Oh yes, Lady Velka "*I share my problems*" Powoj. It's not like you mentioned being pregnant before or during our journey. I suspect I would still be living in blissful ignorance if not for the mamuna and her pathetic attempt to snatch your boy.'

Velka's hand stilled for a moment before, and with a deep sigh, she reached for a jar of ointment. 'I was going to tell you … but so many things happened, and I didn't want to worry you.'

'I know, but since my return from Liath, we met almost daily, and you didn't say a word. What if someone had hurt you? Or the baby? I felt bad enough bringing you with me, but now? How will I explain to that lumbering oaf you call a husband that his son has a flat head from all the running away we did?' Her words were teasing, but Ina frowned when Velka averted her eyes, avoiding her gaze.

'Flower, you did tell him, yes?'

'It's complicated.…'

'There is nothing complicated about this. Either you told him, or you didn't. Is this why you were so upset when we left? Didn't he want a child?'

Velka busied herself with packing their medical supplies, and her silence made the witch growl quietly. 'Velka, don't make me channel my inner aristocrat. What did that pig-headed husband of yours say?'

'He didn't really want children.' This muted response and Velka's hunched posture made Ina jump out of her chair and wrap her arms around the mage in a reassuring hug before pacing around the room.

'I will rip off his dick and shove it where the sun doesn't shine, and what's left, I will throw to the scavengers. What was this idiot thinking? I will sort him out. I promise he will be a good father or a dead one, and he will apologise to you for telling you to get rid of the child.' Chaos was swirling around, answering Ina's anger, damaging everything it touched.

'Ina, no, he didn't say that—'

'Don't defend him. He doesn't deserve it, and he does not deserve my sweet, loving flower—' Ina was building up to a crescendo of righteous indignation when Velka shouted.

'Ina, stop, please! He doesn't know. I only asked if he wanted to have children.' They stared at each other for a moment before Velka broke the silence. 'I asked him if he wanted to have children, and he said no, but he doesn't know he will have one, anyway.'

Ina approached her and, thrusting her chin out, stared at the nature mage for a moment. 'Tell me *exactly* what he said.'

'He said, "Give me a few years before we consider having children. I want to enjoy my wife's company before her attention is stolen by someone else or something stupid like this."'

Ina rubbed her temples, trying to set things straight in her head. 'So, he didn't say no, just not now, and he didn't know he was already a father when you asked. Velka, I don't know how you did it, but now I feel sympathetic to the snarky bastard. After your little speech about leaning on a friend, don't you think Daro deserves to have you lean on him?'

'Ina, I'm forty. Much too old to be a mother. It will be half-orc and half-human, and gods know how that will affect whatever magic he inherits. We took the same classes. Orc magic is all sex and mushrooms. People will gossip, my family will probably cast me out, and I'm scared. I know I've fucked up, and Daro might never forgive me, but I don't know what to do. I didn't plan this.' The last few words were uttered in a flood of tears, so Ina gathered up the much taller woman in her arms, stroking her back gently.

'You should have talked to me. I can't imagine what you were going through bottling this up inside for so long. Now listen to me, you frustrating, bone-headed mage. First, we live longer than ordinary humans, so you're still young enough to spawn an entire coven. Second, children are always more beautiful than their parents, and you two are already sickeningly pretty. If the boy has magic, it will be even better, and who cares what people think? As for family… it's not like they care about you, anyway. Besides, you have me, your sister by choice, Mar, Ren, and even that scaled harpy, Ayni. So you will tell Daro, and if you want, I will be there to ensure he shows the appropriate amount of happiness.'

Velka's sobs intensified, and Ina was at a loss for what else could console her. *If I could only project the serenity of the forest like the Leshy had for me*, she thought, and suddenly Ina had an idea. With one hand on Velka's belly, she said, 'Cast a linking spell with me. Try to read my mind.'

'Why? Aren't you sc—hate it? Don't you hate it?'

'I trust you, so trust me and do it. Don't use force, but skim over the surface.' Ina smiled when she felt the first touch of her friend's consciousness sliding over the surface of her mirror spell. Since Liath, it had become second nature to keep it in place, ready to repel any psychic attacks, as she couldn't allow herself to be anyone's puppet, not with the burden of chaos she carried.

Slowly, she reached for chaos, siphoning a small amount from the fire, placing her hand on Velka's barely round stomach. Her magic brushed against the tiny spark, and she projected the image on the mirror in her mind. The magical energy moved and wiggled, and Ina dutifully conveyed the impression, hearing her friend gasp in surprise.

'Ina, is it...?'

'Your boy. I'm sorry I don't know more, but I can feel it's male, who carries magic that differs from yours or mine, and he is fine, Velka. Everything will be fine, and you will be a wonderful mother.'

CHAPTER TEN

Ina glared at the ray of sunlight through half-closed eyes. 'Gods, I hate mornings.' Muttering curses under her breath, she crawled out of bed. The wound to her thigh reminded the witch that it wasn't healed with agonising jolts of pain every time she moved. She clenched her teeth, squeezed her eyes shut and told the room to stop spinning, or she'd hex the entire building.

Using magic last night cost more than Ina realised, and now she was paying the price. The memory of Velka's wonder at seeing the baby growing inside her was worth it, though. With a deep sigh, she decided her friend needed to return to Osterad because, sure as Veles's pit, the witch didn't intend to drag a pregnant woman into any more danger.

Ina's options were somewhat limited at the moment, with Nerissa at Castle Thorn needing her help, this damn wound, which required a skilled healer's help, and the rebellion she suspected her grandfather was most likely involved in, which all meant there was no way to avoid going to Thorn. Still, putting Velka and her unborn child anywhere near the influence of that conniving old lord felt wrong.

With a sudden burst of energy, Ina stood up, kicking the bedside table in her frustration, and then nearly passed out from the pain shooting up her leg.

'Damn it all to Nawia. I need to persuade Velka to go home. That way, the old bastard can't hurt her.'

Decision made, Ina gathered her belongings, stuffing everything into her bags without trying to organise it. She would need to push the orein hard today. Otherwise, she wouldn't have the energy to defy her grandfather when she reached the castle. The thought of Mar's anger at her for not staying out of trouble transformed the grimace of pain on her lips into a brief smile, as the thought of the dragon's caring wrath improved her mood, giving her the energy to face the world.

The world, it seemed, was ready for her. Velka was already in the dining chamber, eating an enormous breakfast. Ina shook her head in disbelief, especially when her friend, who usually avoided greasy food, finished a dribbling pork belly, and the empty bowls testified she had already demolished more than one serving of porridge.

'Have mercy on your horse, Flower.' Ina sat gently, paying attention not to hurt her injured leg, but Velka only shrugged and pushed away the empty dishes.

'I'm done unless they have some pickles. How are your wounds?'

'All good, like brand new, but we need to talk. I want you to go back home. Castle Thorn will be a viper's nest of conniving bastards, and with the baby....'

Velka stood up, stubbornness radiating from her every gesture. 'Inanuan Zoria Thornsen, if you think you can get rid of me now, you are sorely mistaken. I will be travelling to your family home

132

by your side or five feet behind, throwing pine cones at your head, your choice. Now sit down and eat. You look like a ghost.'

With Velka storming off to get ready, Ina looked at the bowl of porridge the innkeeper placed in front of her, her appetite driven away by the pain. But, considering the food shortages in the region, she felt compelled to try at least. While waiting for Velka, she waved at the innkeeper.

'Are there any troubles on the road to Thorn? Marauders? Magical beasts or spirits?' she asked, keeping a casual tone.

'No, Lady, just patrols on the roads. And the guards question anyone who enters the town. They don't like strangers, and the old duke is very suspicious.'

'What do you mean, patrols? Are they expecting trouble?' Ina bit her tongue before openly admitting she was a ducal house member, but the innkeeper didn't seem to notice.

'This I don't know. The old duke never explained why, but they are hostile to non-humans, and some fae folk even got attacked.'

'Well, it looks like we'll be safe on the roads then.'

What the fuck did my grandfather do this time? News of murders on the highways will reach the king. I need to sort it out before Rewan decides he doesn't like me enough to spare the Thorn family. Ina's thoughts drifted, and she barely registered the innkeeper's answer.

'I hope so, my lady. There are rumours. No one has seen the old duke for some time. They even say he sent for his sister to heal him, so it must be serious. Some say he lost himself to madness, others that he sold himself to Marzanna, but the Thorn doesn't protect us anymore.'

These rumours shed light on what was happening with her grandfather, and Ina nodded slightly, eating a few more spoonfuls of porridge when the innkeeper shared even more information.

'They say his granddaughter will arrive from the capital and help with him. I heard she is terrifying. You came from the capital, have you seen her? Is it true what they say that she wears crimson robes and rides a dragon?'

'Who does?' asked Velka, who came down with their bags.

'Lady Inanuan, the royal witch. They say she can even move mountains.'

As the innkeeper explained, Velka's azure eyes sparkled with unbridled amusement, making Ina desperately shake her head.

'Oh yes, my good man. She rides the dragon so hard it makes him roar, and she moves mountains with a wave of her hand. She is a terrifying woman who can strip the flesh off your bones in a blink of an eye.'

Velka was enjoying herself far too much, describing, in-depth, the terrifying qualities of the royal witch, when Ina grabbed her hand and dragged her out of the inn as fast as her pain allowed.

'Are you out of your mind? Why would you spread that kind of horseshit around?' Ina was royally pissed, but Velka didn't seem to care.

'You wanted to go unnoticed, so who will they search for now when the gossip spreads? A hobbling pale woman or dragon-riding crimson witch that can move mountains?'

Ina stopped abruptly upon hearing this and turned to her friend, inspecting her for a moment. 'Velka, you are a bloody genius. Well, you have free rein. Make that gossip of yours work for us.'

'I know I will. You should trust me more. I keep telling you that nature mages are as dangerous as any sword-wielding soldier, but no one seems to believe me.'

'You are the most dangerous woman I know. Now get on your horse. We have quite a distance to cover.'

Velka muttered something under her breath, but Ina barely heard it focusing on getting on her orein without letting the rest of the world know she could hardly walk. In the end, her unusual mount bent her long neck and pushed Ina's rear end with its massive head, throwing the witch onto the saddle. Velka looked at her with suspicion.

'Are you sure you're fine?'

'Yes, there is nothing we can do now anyway, so the sooner I get to Castle Thorn, the better. Nerissa can help, or if she's busy, my grandfather has some excellent healers there, and if he's obstructive, there's always Aunt Mirena.'

Ina's faint smile didn't convince her friend, but Velka didn't argue the point, turning her horse towards the gates.

'Let's go. I'd hate to see you end up as a plant fertiliser.'

'I can't be fertiliser. I'm rotten to the core. Only thorny and poisonous plants would grow on me,' Ina said, joining her friend on the road, and the two women set off, leaving the town behind.

After a few hours, Ina was close to tears. Although spring was beautiful in the South, the women weren't enjoying the scenery. Ina focused on keeping herself upright whilst keeping her magic under control, occasionally hissing through her clenched teeth when her injured thigh knocked the saddle. Even Zjawa's smooth gait couldn't prevent the occasional bump and jostle.

Velka wasn't faring much better, swaying as her stomach failed to settle, and their initial brisk pace soon turned into a slow trot with frequent breaks. The first was the location where a severe bout of morning sickness had deposited the excellent breakfast from the inn. Velka sent apologetic glances each time she had to dismount to visit some nearby bushes, with Ina waving her away as she tried to handle her pain and irritation with dignity.

'Remind me to check if you are pregnant next time we embark on a kingdom-saving mission,' she finally snapped, immediately regretting her harsh tone as she saw her friend hunched over next to the horse.

'I'm sorry. It was never this bad before, like something in this dammed forest worsened my symptoms,' Velka apologised weakly.

'I'm sorry, Velka, it's not your fault. I'm cranky and fed up, that's all. I'm happy you are here.' *Gods, I'm such an idiot,* the witch scolded herself. *I shouldn't have lashed out at her.*

The witch kicked the orein to a trot, getting a bite on her uninjured leg for the offence, and they covered a reasonable distance before Velka had to dismount again. As Ina awaited her return, the unmistakable screeching of wheels grabbed her attention. A decent-looking trade cart appeared with a small group of people travelling together for safety. Ina felt exposed, standing in the middle of the road, holding two horses, and as expected, the cart came to a halt, with a few men moving forward to surround her.

'Good day to you, Lady. Why are you standing alone out here on the road?'

'I'm waiting for my friend while she attends to her... needs.'

Ina pointed to the nearby bushes where, brushing the leaves off her skirt, Velka came out to greet them. The men looked at each other.

'And to where do you travel?'

'To Thorn, we have family there, and my friend, being with child, wants to see her mother.'

Velka raised her eyebrow and looked at Ina, but the witch shook her head slightly, asking her not to contradict her. Suddenly the canvas of the cart opened, and a mature, very round-looking matron came out and, resting her hands on her hips, gave Ina a stare that would impress Nerissa.

'How dare you drag your friend along these roads on horseback without a single man to escort you? What if a mamuna attacks her? Or the Leshy? For the gods' sake, what were you thinking?'

Ina stared with an open mouth at how this strange woman gently took Velka by the elbow and led her to the cart, despite the nature mage's protests and the worried looks she sent to Ina.

'What...? Why?' the witch said, floundering at the bizarre turn of events.

An older man, clearly the leader of this small group, waved the men off and turned towards Ina. 'My wife likes to help. Your friend will be safe, and we welcome travelling with a mage. You are a mage and a lady, yes?'

'How do you know I'm a mage?'

The man took a moment before his lips twitched slightly, and Ina felt as if she had asked the wrong question. 'Your magic is all around you. I was born with the sight, so I notice these things. That's why I lead these travellers.'

It was a reasonable explanation. The common folk were just as likely as the nobles to be born with the gift of magic, although they weren't given many opportunities to train or even recognise their talent. Those people often found themselves as leaders or oracles, some simply known for their green thumbs, unique gifts in rearing livestock or healing skills. Those with more dangerous forms of magic, especially if they struggled to control it, were killed or descended into madness. Ina couldn't resist and gently touched the man's consciousness. He flinched but didn't stop her attempt to examine his thoughts, and Ina sighed gently. He was a natural seer, and it was doubtful he'd encountered them by accident.

'As we are both travelling to Thorn, we will gladly join you, and if your wife can keep my friend from visiting the bushes, I will be eternally grateful.'

She tied Velka's horse to her saddle and watched as the man nodded and climbed back on the wagon, snapping the reins over his horse's head. Ina heard retching sounds, the smell of mint and cucumber telling her Velka was sick again, but after a moment, the awful noise subsided, likely medicated with some peasant remedy. Still, she was grateful there would be no further stops on their journey.

'Why are you going to Thorn? To get supplies?' the man asked. The journey would take a while, and she needed a distraction from her painful leg. Making conversation with the travellers was as good a distraction as any other.

'No, although I heard they have plenty. We are headed further south to visit a temple there. Not just any temple, but a true chram, dedicated to Marzanna. They say miracles are performed there.'

'Miracles from Winter's Death? I'm not sure I would want one of those.'

Ina chuckled, but her laugh died when she saw the man's serious face looking back at her through angry eyes. 'I'm sorry. What miracles happen there? I've never heard of a chram in the South, so please forgive my ignorance.'

'This chram is new. A dedicated volkhv started building it several years ago, and after the first miracle occurred, thanks to his devotion, the faithful began flocking there and helped to complete the building. Now, when you come before the statue of Marzanna bearing a sacrificial offering, she will release a loved one's soul so they may see all the beauty of Marzanna's realm.'

'What made the priest so dedicated? In my experience, people are not keen to burden themselves with such heavy tasks, no matter their reason.'

The man laughed and snapped his whip over the horse's head, forcing the tired animal into a trot.

'Initially, he was the same as every other volkhv, a money-grabbing lech, but when his dead wife rose from the grave and told him to build the temple, he changed his ways. Marzanna's glory cannot be denied.'

Ina nodded at the traveller and, lapsing into silence, nudged her orein to canter slightly ahead of the cart to give herself time to mull over this new information. Too many strange coincidences were appearing before her: the crops failing despite the weather, the fervour of the villager's belief in Marzanna, especially as the goddess had never performed a miracle before. Then there was the rumoured revolt of the nobles and her grandfather's complete withdrawal from his demesne.

The crops failing and an upsurge in religious fervour made sense, but why not pray to Lada, goddess of spring, fertility, and love? The revolt was unusual, too. There were rumblings of discontent, but the king had tried to help, even giving the nobles hope their daughters might soon be queen. And then there was the question of why Castle Thorn had become so withdrawn.

Something was missing, some elusive piece of information she couldn't grasp. Was it a foreign government or a group of malcontent mages? Who had the power to affect an entire province this way? Ina sighed in frustration, carefully rubbing her thigh as she thought about the problem.

The answers were not forthcoming, and the more she thought about it, the less she understood. Verdante wouldn't curse the fertile land they intended to use. A necromancer could raise a corpse, but not the spirit of people's loved ones, and no matter how much she tried, Ina could not recall a mage, or even a spell, powerful enough to curse a whole province.

'You there, halt!'

The shout startled Ina, making her jerk the orein's reigns. Zjawa reared in indignation, her talon barely missing the head of a shocked guard.

Several moments passed before Ina calmed her racing heart and her agitated mount. It wasn't until she'd regained control of her breathing that she finally turned towards the source of the voice. Then, the witch noticed the magical barrier manned by a few guards and a mage.

Cursing under her breath, Ina knew that had she not been so tired and distracted, not to mention in so much pain, she'd have seen the obvious blockade before almost crashing into it. Behind her, the strange seer studied her reaction intently, making her blush in embarrassment. She turned to the guards and sneered at them for their inaction; not one of them had moved an inch to help her bring the distressed orein under control.

Her voice, dripping with disdain, lashed at the soldiers. 'Step aside, good man. I am Lady Inanuan Zoria Thornsen, headed back home to Castle Thorn. My grandfather is expecting me. If this is the welcoming committee, I would appreciate it if you'd remove the barrier and let my companions pass.'

The leader looked at her, and a smirk ghosted over his face before he answered. 'If you are Lady Thorn, you can open this barrier yourself.'

Ina looked at him, then at the barrier, and slowly dismounted Zjawa. When her foot touched the ground, she realised her condition had deteriorated, and mustering her remaining strength, the angry witch approached the shimmering wall with what she hoped was a confident swagger, not a painful hobble. As soon as her fingers touched the barrier, Ina felt a jolt of power shoot through her body, but she was prepared for this and let it flow into the ground.

The magic revealed a surprise. Her wounded leg was a vortex of chaotic power. Smiling, Ina teased a few tendrils of that chaos and gently pushed them into the barrier, corrupting the shimmering lines that anchored it in place. She could create enough of a gap for a rider to pass, but that wouldn't satisfy her anger. Closing her eyes, she found the weakest link in the structure, and with the flick of her wrist, she destroyed the power that held the barrier in place, smirking when its magic imploded, launching its maker several feet backwards.

'Is that good enough, or do you need another demonstration of my skills? Because I would be thrilled to show you what I can do.'

Her voice was polite, but the unmistakable threat forced the squad's leader to bow his head as the rest of the guard stepped to the side, letting her small group pass, each murmuring quiet thanks for sparing them an unpleasant experience. Once they were further along the road, Velka emerged from the cart and joined Ina on her own horse.

'Well, that was an interesting encounter. Did you know they have elves and a shifter in the cart? It would have been difficult for them to pass if the guards carried out an inspection.'

The frown Ina directed towards the cart caught the caravan leader's attention, and the man ducked his head, avoiding her eyes. Ina sighed quietly, turning back to the road ahead. 'It's not the first time someone has used me, and likely won't be the last. I don't blame them for taking their best chance to bypass Thorn. What about you? Are you well enough to ride? We need to get to the castle today, and my dance on Zjawa didn't do me any favours.'

Velka smiled, gently tapping her stomach. 'Yes, the goodwife's mint and cucumber concoction performed a minor miracle on my sickness. I'm sorry to have delayed us so much.'

The caravan leader looked pleased when they announced their decision to go on ahead. He confirmed the road led straight to the city and Castle Thorn, so gathering the last of her strength, Ina set a brisk pace bringing them swiftly to an adorable panorama as they emerged from the forest. They stopped for a moment, looking at the picturesque city with its green walls and the ribbon of the river glistening in the afternoon sun. The elven architecture blended with southern ostentation was just as Ina remembered; a stark contrast to the sturdy, brooding feel of Castle Liath.

'I could live here.' Velka's dreamy smile lit her features, distracting Ina from her pain as she turned to her friend with a question in her eyes. 'Why green walls? It is an odd choice for a defensive barrier.'

'Velka, you out of us both should know the reason. Castle Thorn, remember? The walls are white, but the elven blessing on the land encouraged rose vines to grow at such an incredible rate that they covered the walls, giving the town its unique appearance. You should see it in the summer when the roses bloom. It looks like a pure bridal nightmare.'

After seeing the goal of her journey so close, Ina relaxed slightly and set a slower pace, letting her friend enjoy the scenery.

Velka's voice cut through the silence, the words leaving an unexpected pain behind. 'Ina, you are a part of all of this. For the first time, I envy you, my friend.'

'It's not mine. I'm just a minor and irrelevant granddaughter of the old duke.' Ina didn't understand why her friend suddenly became so diffident, as Velka had never expressed a sentiment like this.

'It's in your blood, Ina. Even the trees talk to you, whilst I'm just a glorified gardener.'

'Aha, a glorified gardener who fought off Sophia's monsters, saved her husband and keeps me grounded when I lose myself in chaos. You are a miracle, Velka. If I could give you all of this, I would.' Unsure of what else to say, Ina reached out and grabbed her friend's hand, hissing when her thigh rubbed over the saddle.

'I know. Now, let us get you into the loving embrace of your family before you grow fur like Boruta. You sound like a furious cat with this constant hissing.'

Ina nodded, taking this change of the subject with relief. It wasn't the right moment to talk about her friend's insecurities or her own family issues, but she promised herself they would have a good talk once she had a clear head and enough mead.

CHAPTER ELEVEN

Mar shifted in the saddle, trying to balance the weight of the unconscious troll. After wrapping Hem's body and loading him onto Woron's back without dropping him on the other side, the stallion had given Mar such a look of annoyance that he'd promised his mount an entire week's worth of honey sticks when they were done. The marshal wasn't confident that the innkeeper would even survive the journey. It took a lot to take down a troll, and transporting him this way wouldn't help. *At least Ina would be proud. Oh, and probably tell me to suck it up.* Mar smiled, thinking about his little spitfire and her need to help the injured. It was a relief when the forest opened up, and the green fields appeared in the gaps between the trees, the midday sun warming the fallow fields.

'Ugh, were you wearing a knuckle duster when you hit me?' Daro grunted with chagrin before looking over at the troll's body. 'What are you going to do with him?'

'Not much. We will find the nearest healer and leave the innkeeper with a heavy purse and our best wishes. I can't delay our journey for a man I don't even know.'

'Glad to see you haven't lost your common sense completely, Captain.'

'Daro, how many times must I remind you? You're the captain now.'

His friend didn't answer. Instead, he kicked his horse, forcing the tired animal to speed up, and, biting back a curse, Mar had to do the same. Even so, he only caught up with the orc at the town gates.

'What the fuck is wrong with you? You are as moody as a stripling asked to clean his room, and you forced not just the horses but this poor man to endure hardship for a few minutes gain.' Scolded like a young recruit, Daro sagged in the saddle but didn't reply.

The town guard eyed them suspiciously, clearly aware two bulky men with massive swords meant trouble. His attitude didn't change when Mar asked for the healer's house. Still, the man had seen enough problems in his life not to question them and hastily pointed them in the right direction.

Mar felt out of place as they wandered down the street between the heavily decorated buildings, especially with the attention their presence seemed to garner. It was a relief when they finally dismounted and carried their unconscious burden into the healer's home, where they were greeted by the wide-eyed stare of a young girl who quickly turned, disappearing into the backroom screaming.

'Master… Master, we have another one.'

Her high-pitched voice, full of fear, was promptly answered, and a balding elderly man came out, pausing at a safe distance.

'How can I help you?'

Mar looked around, trying to locate a bed or even a table where he could place the troll's body, but Daro quickly answered.

'We have a wounded man here, and we pay in gold. Where can we put him?'

The healer came closer and pulled the fabric off the troll's face. 'In the graveyard? He will soon be entering the afterlife in this state.'

'But he's not there yet, and you're supposed to be a healer.' Mar's tense voice and the coiled violence in his posture finally reached the healer's attention, and the old man pointed to the back room.

'Take him back here. I'll see what I can do, but this will be costly.'

Free of his burden, Mar rolled his shoulders, releasing the tension in the strained muscles while the healer examined his patient. The deep frown on the man's face didn't bode well for the unlucky troll, but Mar didn't want to wait for a prognosis. His good deed was completed, and it was time to continue their journey to Castle Thorn.

Suddenly, the healer's assistant started shouting in her shrill voice, catching the dragon's attention. Even through the closed door, it was clear the girl was arguing with someone, and when he heard her answer, he strode into the front room.

'No, I told you so before. We haven't seen anyone marked with three wheat sheaves. Stop coming here.'

Upon entering, he first noticed an old woman tightly wrapped in a shawl, trying to push some small coins into the helper's hands.

'Please, let me see him. I need to make sure. Please, I will pay.'

'Who do you want to see?' The faded blue eyes of the woman met Mar's question.

'My son. You bought an injured man here, and I need to see if it's my son.'

147

'She comes here every day wanting to see our patients, alive or dead. Since her son left, her mind has become confused.' The assistant tried to guide the old lady out of the house, explaining the situation, but Mar stopped her.

'It is not your son, goodwife, unless you gave birth to a troll, but if you tell me about your boy, I can look around. My companion and I will be wandering the province for a while.'

The woman rushed to Mar's side with a speed he didn't expect from a lady of her age and grasped his hand. 'Good lord, it is not true that he left. They took him, the men from the South who serve the young lord. They came to our house and talked to him, promised glory and riches if he followed them, and that was the last time I saw my boy.'

'But why are you looking for him in a healer's sanctum, asking about wheat sheaves?'

'He wrote to me, good lord, every week. He was so proud and sent me money. He said they trained him to be a soldier, that he'd already earned the golden wheat sheaves.' The woman started sobbing, so Mar gently sat her down on the nearest seat, ignoring Daro as he rolled his eyes. The old woman patted his cheek when he crouched next to her.

'You are a good, strong, kind boy, just like my son. His letters stopped coming three months ago. That was the last I heard. He said he was afraid because people kept disappearing and that he would run away and come home.'

Mar suspected where and how the young men disappeared, but he didn't have the heart to tell the grieving mother that her precious boy would never come home. Instead, he stroked her hand and answered with a reassuring smile.

'We will look for him, and once we find him, I will tell him his mother is waiting.' His words calmed her, and this time, without protest, she let the assistant lead her out of the healer's sanctum.

'You know he's dead, don't you?' Mar turned around, surprised by the assistant's question. When he remained silent, she added, 'I saw it in your eyes. Master has the same look when he knows the patient is gone but wants to give the family a few moments of hope.'

Mar approached the counter and reached for a quill and paper, scribing a brief note before passing it to the assistant with a few coins. 'Yes, I know. Now be so kind as to send this note to Gruff at the *Drunken Wizard* in Osterad. He will help if there are any issues with your new patient.'

Mar gestured for Daro to leave as he headed towards the door. Once outside, he greeted Woron with a friendly scratch, leading him to the nearest trough for a drink, only for his friend to step in front of him, frowning.

'Mar, there's nothing more you can do here. The faster we get to Thorn, the better. Then, we can alert the king that Verdante is recruiting here. They must have a communication crystal in the castle.' Daro's sombre voice left no doubt in Mar's mind that the orc understood the gravity of the situation.

'He already knows, my friend. This was Rewan's plan all along. The only reason Ina is here now is that her grandfather preempted our plans and forced her to head south early. Once that situation is resolved, we'll investigate the insurrection before they can start a war. The fact that Verdante's agent has free rein in this area tells me the nobles are supporting their efforts.'

'So what are you going to do?'

'I have a mission for you, my friend. Once we make sure your wife is safe and you apologise profusely for whatever shortcomings or misdeeds you're guilty of, I will ask you to travel around, knock on a few doors, talk about the weather, and check on who allowed Verdante to recruit on their lands.'

'Mar, I don't have any shortcomings and misdeeds.'

His protests released some tension, and Mar burst out laughing. 'You have so much to learn. It doesn't matter what you have or haven't done. You will apologise anyway or face Velka's wrath. Remember, Ina will be there. As for me, I will stand there looking smug when those two strigae go for a pound of your flesh.'

Understanding suddenly flashed on the orc's face when Daro finally joined Mar's merriment. 'All I ask from you is to distract your woman when I am dealing with my own,' he said, and Mar shook his head, climbing astride Woron.

'That will never work, my friend, but I will try it for your sake.'

Velka frowned when Ina swayed in the saddle, looking paler with each passing street. The hour it took them from the city gates to the castle felt like an eternity, and even Zjawa carefully chose her steps, snapping at anyone who got in her way.

'Will you manage? The meeting with your family, I mean?' The mage asked, and Ina forced a smile.

'Do I have a choice? I don't think they'll dare hurt Nerissa, but with my grandfather, you never know. Just be prepared. He is not the nicest person and has certain views on… well, non-humans. Even non-mages aren't liked.'

'What do you mean?'

'He was always peculiar, but Nerissa mentioned he got worse recently. Now he firmly believes mages should rule the world and everyone else should serve them, particularly the non-human races. He is a moron, but a moron with mind magic so powerful it makes Liander look like a petulant toddler.'

Velka's sudden laugh startled Ina, who blinked rapidly and looked at her friend. 'And here you are bedding a dragon, befriending trolls, and your best friend is pregnant with an orc's child. Someone would think you were trying to get under the old man's skin.'

If you put it like that, it sounds like I did. Ina's lips twitched, amused at her thoughts, pondering what the old man would say. 'Just promise me you won't take one senile man's views to heart, and if things turn ugly, you'll run back to Osterad and alert Mar. Still, the rest of the family isn't too bad, just not strong enough to stand up to him.'

Velka nodded, but they had to stop the conversation when the gate guardian approached them.

'State your business.'

The quick command, without a word of courtesy, got on Ina's nerves. Despite the pain and exhaustion, she straightened up in the saddle for the second time today, channelling her inner Nerissa. 'I'm Lady Inanuan Zoria Thornsen returning home at the request of the Grand Duke of Thorn, and you will treat a lady of this house with respect.' Ina saw the guard's pupils widen when tendrils of chaos wrapped themselves around her like a cloak.

'The crimson witch.'

The words came from the side, and an irritated Ina noticed she'd missed the arrival of a much younger guardian. Her expression filled with disdain when she looked at the man, pinning him under her stare.

'My Lady Thorn to you, or royal witch. Now go, alert the family of my arrival, and you….' Ina turned towards the first guard. 'Call the stable master. Our mounts are tired and in need of sustenance.'

She pushed past the guard without waiting for his response, enjoying the satisfaction of his fear as he scrambled backwards. She dismounted in the courtyard, trying to get as close to the main entrance as possible, unsure how far she could walk. Ina stroked Zjawa's long neck and whispered into the beast's ear. 'Be a good spirit. We don't need more trouble today.'

Ina set off at a stately pace, allowing the servants time to open the door for her. Everything was exactly as she remembered, maybe a little grubbier. Specks of dust swirled through the light from the stained glass windows. She heard Velka gasping in pleasure when the carved stone columns opened out into a room dominated by a cherry tree that proudly extended its branches to a gap in the ceiling.

'You never mentioned it was so beautiful.'

Although her friends' attention was on the beautiful blooms, Ina's mind and will were focused on the hunched figure sitting on a small dais. *Glad to see you look like an old mushroom,* she thought. As soon as this crossed her mind, the man on the wooden throne sneered.

'You know I can hear you, mongrel, and who's the wretch you're dragging along? Your servant?'

Ina took a deep breath, trying to calm her thoughts. The mirror spell she relied on so much gave her very little protection against her grandfather's intrusive thoughts when she was this agitated, and the witch cursed under her breath.

'This is Lady Velka Powoj, a talented nature mage in the king's service, as you well know, you nosy old goat. Now, care to tell me where you're keeping Nerissa?'

'Peasant upstart then, but at least one with magic.'

She could feel his magic brushing against the now steady mirror in her head, and a rasping laugh shook the halls.

'You think this will stop me, girl? A useless trick, but at least you've finally learnt something. Why did you take so long? Did you spend the time rolling in the filth with your dragon?' The old man spat on the floor, muttering. 'How could such a prestigious family come to this? All is falling. All is tainted.'

His disdain was palpable, and Ina was so focused on fighting his mental attacks that she nearly missed seeing a tall, dignified man standing behind the throne.

'Father, please, that's not how we welcome family home, especially when my niece looks so tired. Ina, Nerissa is no longer here.'

A strained half-smile was all Ina could manage for her uncle Cyrus, his intervention lessening the force of the old man's venom. Ina liked the quiet scholar, always smiling, especially when reading another esoteric tome in the library. His magic was potent, just like all descendants of House Thorn, but it manifested peculiarly.

With no talent for spellwork, he was dismissed as useless by her grandfather, even though Cyrus was a genius at recalling any information he'd seen. However, the awe-inspiring part of his talent was that he could recall information that anyone in the room with him had seen. If it wasn't for his father's iron will and hatred keeping him in Thorn as a family librarian, he could have been so much more, but what did he mean Nerissa wasn't here? Her musings were halted when the old duke raised his voice, looking at his son.

'Welcome? She is not here to feel welcome. She is here to do her duty, not waste her talent on that fatuous king. You all are useless wastes of Thorn blood, but all that will change. I will choose your path, and I will choose your husband. A human mage who will use your magic to fix the South. You will obey him, girl, or I will crush your mind and those you care about.'

Ina felt her world narrow to this madman's rage-filled words.

Where is Nerissa? What have you done to your sister?! If you hurt her… I'll crush your dreams. She pushed the thought through her mental wall. *I will not marry or obey any man of your choosing, and as for the beast you hate so much? I let him enter my body each night, and I loved… every… single… second… of… it.*

Ina pushed her remaining power into her words, summoning visions of the passion and possessiveness of her dragon. She saw the old man flinch, and his thoughts were overcome with raw fury. Chaotic magic erupted from her body, and shocked at her strength, he lowered his defences, and a long-buried memory of a younger Nerissa, crying, begging him not to force her to sterilise her grandniece, rose to the surface of his mind together with the sound of his cruel words.

This mongrel will not breed. It's enough she has the blood of the Leshy in her veins, but now she wields chaos? How tainted will you allow our bloodline to become, Nerissa? Do as you are told. Ina gasped as her grandfather, unrepentant of his actions, used the revelation to attack her.

See what she did to you? Your perfect great-aunt? She maimed you, and you came here to save her, you stupid child. His rasping laugh echoed through the silent chamber as he enjoyed the horror on Ina's face.

Even at her best, Ina would have struggled to contain the fury that followed his words. Now overwhelmed by the old lord's madness, she saw what this fanatic had done to her. He had maimed her, breaking his sister Nerissa's mind to do it, casting out his daughter because she dared to love a man he didn't accept. Her control snapped, and the swirling chaos around her burst outwards, filling the room with quivering red tendrils.

'Abomination!' the duke screamed, scrambling backwards on his throne. 'I should have chained your mind, destroyed your will, killed you even. But, like a fool, I listened to your mother's pleading, only restricting your emotions, and even with this, you cannot control yourself. Thankfully, now I have the chance to rectify my mistake.'

His mind assaulted her with the power of a thunderstorm. So far, no one had penetrated the witch's barrier when she was conscious, yet this feeble-looking old man crushed it with ease. That thought frightened her more than anything else, and chaos lashed out, destroying everything it touched in eerie silence. Ina felt the pressure on her mind disappear, and in relief, she desperately fought to control the raging magic, crying out as, with one last effort, she cut off the source of the power, her mind falling into a black void, moments before her body hit the floor.

Velka was the first to her feet when the maelstrom of chaos suddenly disappeared. After her friend's warning, she'd expected an unpleasant welcome, not a magical battle.

Fingers shaking as she covered her belly, the nature mage realised this was the first time she'd seen the full manifestation of the witch's power, and couldn't restrain a shiver of fear, even as she rushed to Ina's side to help her. Velka checked for signs of life, a lip caught between her teeth as she scanned the fevered body. Barely finding the lightest trace, she sobbed in relief as the faint breath repeated.

'Where is Nerissa? Call a damn healer, or I will bring the roof down on your heads.' Velka hated the panic in her voice and the empty threats she issued. The younger man from the dais rushed over, pausing when the desperate mage snarled at him, looking down with concern in his eyes.

'My name is Cyrus. I'm Inanuan's uncle and would never harm her. Not all of our family are bigots. Nerissa left weeks ago after fighting with my father, but now isn't the time. We should take Ina to the infirmary for my wife to examine her. She is nearly as good as aunty is at healing.'

The relief that flooded through Velka left her sobbing as she nodded her agreement. Lifting his niece with surprising ease for such a svelte man, Cyrus set off with a swift but steady pace. Ina's uncle issued curt orders as he walked along the corridors, commanding the servants to see to his father's needs. Velka suspected the mage battle had left the old lord unconscious or at least too debilitated to care for himself, but the gentle mage felt herself hoping he didn't survive the encounter after his unforgivable treatment of her friend.

'Why are you looking after Ina? Why not your father?' she asked.

'Because I loved my sister and still love my niece. As for my father… he was never a kind man, but over the last year, he's changed so much I barely recognise him. You heard the vitriol he spewed. I don't think the old fool's even sane anymore, but his magic is as strong as ever, if not stronger. Today he crossed the line, and once we get Ina some help, I will do what I can to remove him from power in Castle Thorn. It will take some work. My father had those who supported his visions, but I will handle this.'

His response and the determination in his eyes reassured Velka, but her relief didn't last long. As soon as they crossed the threshold of the infirmary, a buxom, approachable woman rushed in their direction.

'I heard Ina is back….'

She stopped in her tracks, taking in the lifeless witch. 'What did that bastard do to her this time?'

With a furious snarl, the woman turned, snapping out orders like a sergeant-at-arms, sending servants scurrying back and forth, preparing the room as she undressed Ina. When the healer cut away the bandages from the witch's leg, the stench of rotten flesh made the nature mage gag, and she was grateful when the healer sent her to the corner with a dismissive wave.

'I'm Mirena, this lumps wife,' she said, pointing a thumb towards Cyrus. 'You shouldn't be near someone with swamp fever, especially in your condition. When did this happen? I haven't seen anyone at such an advanced stage… and still alive. Gods, I wish Nerissa was here.'

'She fought a mamuna because of me. I didn't know. I promise I would never… Please tell me she will live.' Velka sobbed while Cyrus and Mirena exchanged a concerned glance.

'She will live. I may not be an arch-healer, but I will not lose my niece to this sickness, even if it leaves a nasty scar. Cyrus, send for your aunt. I don't care what quarrel she has with that senile old goblin, she is needed here. Now you, girl.' The look she turned on Velka was as hard as flint, but strangely comforting. 'Go and rest. You need it, and I don't want any distractions while I work.'

Velka felt Cyrus take her by the elbow and lead her back to the main corridor.

'I will take you to your room. Ina will need time to recover from her injury, but when she wakes up, she'll need a friend by her side after that battle. My wife is a talented healer, so please trust her and allow her to work.'

Velka let him lead her away, and the servants he called escorted her to a room, assisting with the laces as the mage disrobed for the night. Afterwards, she lay on the bed, crushing a pillow in her arms in a feeble attempt to comfort herself. *I'm not cut out to be a hero,* she thought as she cried herself to sleep.

CHAPTER TWELVE

*A*m *I dead? If the afterlife is this bright, I'll drag myself out of Nawia and kick that old bastard's arse for sending me here.* Ina nearly wept with relief as a shadow blocked out the light, then coughed as she caught a whiff of something awful. With stinging eyes, the witch pried her eyelids open, and a blurry form of a woman emerged from the shadow.

'Nerissa?'

As soon as her great aunt's name appeared in her thoughts, Ina sat up on the bed. Was she here, after all? Had Cyrus lied to her in the great hall? With her thoughts finally focused, Ina looked back at the woman, this time taking the time to concentrate, now finally recognising her. 'Aunt Mirena? What are you doing here? No, what am I doing here? Is…?'

The witch slowed her breathing and looked down at her leg. The pain was now a dull ache, and the limb was swaddled in what looked like the kitchen's entire herb collection.

'Inanuan, I'm glad you finally decided to join us. How is your head? Your grandfather didn't hurt you, did he?' She looked at Ina with a gamut of emotions running across her face too quickly to be identified. 'Here, drink this. It will help with whatever damage the old bastard caused, and it will speed the recovery of your leg wound.'

'Where is Nerissa? Did she heal me, or are you the miracle worker who saved my leg?'

'All I did was clean up the wound and keep you in the land of the living. Nerissa performed the miracle and is now in her room, exhausted. You were in a terrible state and decided to fight your grandfather? I'm sure the arch healer will have a few choice words to share with you over that.'

Her aunt looked at her, amused pity in her eyes, and Ina shifted uncomfortably under the compassionate gaze. 'And how is our esteemed patriarch? Will he start another fight, or has he given up on trying to control my life?'

Emotion drained from Mirena's face, her gaze dropping to the ground, and Ina exhaled slowly, hoping he hadn't ordered her locked in the dungeon till he found a suitable match for his whore of a granddaughter.

The witch readied herself for bad news as her aunt took a deep breath.

'He had a stroke, child. There will be no second round or… well, or anything, for that matter. The duke is in bed and unable to communicate with the rest of the world. Even Nerissa doesn't seem hopeful, though I doubt she's particularly motivated to help him after his latest crime. Cyrus tried to communicate using his mind magic, but we both know it's not his strong suit, so his failure could mean anything.'

'Is this my fault?'

Ina hated herself for the small voice and guilt that suddenly swept through her. Her grandfather was a terrible person, and

Ina hated him for his actions, but she hadn't wished him harm. However, it looked like losing control of her chaos had done something to his mind during their fight.

'Inanuan, don't you dare blame yourself for this. That old fool was a terror and controlled everything and everyone with his abilities. He barely slept or ate, sitting in his office like an evil spider at the centre of his web. That much strain would harm anyone. Your confrontation was the last straw, but I suspect this was bound to happen eventually.' Her aunt's voice was like honey, soothing Ina's worry, and the witch dared to smile.

'So, is Cyrus now the lord of the house? How did he take it? Did he have any trouble with Grandfather's cronies?' Ina asked, remembering the rude welcome and the soldier's disdain.

Mirena just shrugged and approached the bed, holding a plain grey dress. 'He will get used to it, and if you ask me, it's all for the best. Cyrus wasn't on speaking terms with your grandfather, opposing most of his ideas, but until you incapacitated the old fool, he couldn't do anything. No one could without the risk of him destroying their mind. As for the rest, a few demanded your head, but as my husband so eloquently put it, he was happy to dismiss them from Thorn to allow them to present their grievances before the king. Now dress and let me take you to the bathhouse. After you're clean, the servants will help you up to your room, hopefully before your friend kills all the plants in the castle with her worrying.'

'I'd like to see how Nerissa is, please.'

'Later, child, your great-aunt is resting. We almost drained our magic trying to cure your fever. I promise she is safe, but please, let her rest.' Ina's objections died on her tongue, and she meekly nodded, pulling the dress over her head before following her aunt outside. Mirena hadn't been exaggerating. The garden looked afflicted by months of drought, leaving the witch overcome by the display of friendly concern. She would have to talk to Velka about how her mood affected her magic.

Washed, dressed, and with freshly braided hair, Ina sat in her room looking out at the city beneath her window. So much had changed since she left here. Suddenly, the old man's thoughts, exposed by his anger, returned to her. Had he really bespelled her emotions? Ina thought about her past, how no matter how well they treated her, she never committed to anyone. Then Mar came into her life, and despite how devoted he was, she kept trying to push him away. *Was it the geas or my past that made me distrust him so much?* Biting her lip, Ina shook her head. The geas might play the role, but she bonded with Velka from the first day her friend invaded her dorm space like a flowery, unstoppable force of nature. After her family treated her, she simply distrusted men, and the geas only enhanced her feelings.

Suddenly, the door bounced off the wall, and Velka entered the room in a frenzy, locking her in a tight embrace. 'Never do that again. Don't you ever dare try dying on me, or I swear to the gods I will plant the most obnoxious weeds on your grave and tell the bards to sing the ballads there every night.'

Ina let herself enjoy the moment before detangling herself from Velka's embrace. 'You wouldn't dare. Your sweet nature wouldn't allow this torment. I can deal with flowers but not bards.'

Velka pinned her with a challenging stare, but before she said anything, they both heard the rumbling of Ina's stomach, and the witch grinned, embarrassed. 'How long was I with the healers? I'm starving.'

'Just over a day. Your uncle took you there after your fight and the mayhem you unleashed in the grand hall. They called for Nerissa because you were that bad…' Velka sniffled and paused for a moment. 'So you know that your grandfather…?'

'Yes, I already spoke with Mirena. She said I was just the trigger, not the cause. I wish he hadn't tried to break me with his magic. After Liath, I couldn't allow it. The things Tar'eth made me do, I couldn't allow anyone to control me ever again, and my grandfather… He is a horrible man, but I never wanted this.'

Ina looked at Velka, her memories of mind control and the bloody battle resurfacing. Her heart started racing, breath shuddered in her chest, threatening to choke her, and Ina felt, just this once, she had to share the darkness she carried. 'I'm afraid, Velka. My magic can be horrifying, and under the control of someone else? The last time it happened, I almost killed Mar and saw what chaos magic did to Tar'eth, to the battlefield…. Since I returned from the forest, I'm constantly fighting not to become the monster everyone thinks I am, but the truth is… The truth is, it's becoming harder. Whenever there's death and destruction, I feel this need, this desire to take it all, to keep fuelling the chaos and destroy everything around me. The magic that comes from inside feels natural, but when induced by violent death… it is so addictive and tastes so good. I am so afraid that if there's another war, it will be the end of me because I'd prefer to be dead than turn into a crazed monster or allow another madman to use me for my power.'

She choked on the last word, and Velka sprang to her, wrapping her arms around Ina's shoulders. 'Shhh… Striga, stop. What are you saying? What death? Ina, you are not a monster; I don't care what anyone says. As for the rest? You have me, Mar and Ren to keep you sane. Well, as sane as you've ever been.' Velka's cajoling

163

eased something inside Ina's chest, and she sniffled before looking at her friend.

'I'm sorry, the old fart's attack affected me more than I realised. Let's eat something. I'm sure everything will improve once I stuff my face with food and mead.' The crease between the eyebrows was the only sign Velka didn't believe her sudden change of mood, but the witch was grateful her friend didn't argue when Ina grabbed her hand and pulled her towards the doors. The ironclad wall she built around her feelings was back, and Ina already regretted letting her gentle friend see the ugly cost of her magic she tried to hide from the world.

Breakfast was a surprisingly pleasant affair, though the small group of people seemed to be dwarfed by the size of the dining room. Ina appreciated the lack of formality when she sat beside her uncle, observing her cousins bickering about their responsibilities. It differed so much from her memories that she couldn't help but ask. 'Since when are our family gatherings so lively? Or maybe my memories are clouded, but this feels different.'

'About a year ago, the duke stopped joining us at family meals, preferring to eat alone in his quarters. We took the opportunity to introduce fewer formalities at the dinner table,' Mirena said, and Ina's eyebrows shot up when she pointed out the heated debate on the superiority of ink against paint in drafting diagrams. Her cousins took this scientific research to a new level by drawing the mentioned diagram on the table with the sauce.

'You call it fewer formalities?' She chuckled and dabbed the table, sending tendrils of chaos that lit up the sauce artwork in red flame.

'Ina!'

Her cousin's shocked reactions were identical, and she burst into laughter when they attempted to douse the flames with drinking water, this gentle prank lightening her mood.

What made me tell Velka about chaos? I've only worried her more, she thought, cursing herself for a moment of weakness.

'We need to talk. My father… wasn't always like this. Please meet me in the library after breakfast.'

Her uncle's quiet voice spoiled the moment of entertainment, and Ina turned in his direction, nodding lightly. 'I'm full, anyway. We can go there as soon as you are ready, and can we ask Nerissa to come as well? I thought I would see her at breakfast.'

'I already asked her to join us,' he said as they headed upstairs.

The library was as she remembered, and the musky smell of books was so comforting that, for a moment, she observed specks of dust dancing in the morning sun rays that fell through the sparse windows, lighting the otherwise dark environment.

'You wanted to talk, what about?' she asked when they finally settled in the comfy chairs.

'About my father and our future,' he said.

The sight of Nerissa gesturing to everyone to stay seated as she entered brought a smile to Ina's face. She stood up and, approaching her great-aunt, placed a soft peck on her wrinkled cheeks. 'I… I'm glad you are all right,' she stuttered when her aunt reciprocated the awkward greeting.

'I am too. Now, why did you come here? I thought you knew better than to believe my brother could imprison me. Come, sit down and listen to what Cyrus has to say.' The harsh words were laced with tenderness, but following the command, Ina dropped to her seat like a chastened pupil.

'Mirena thinks my father will never recover, which makes me in charge of our house. There are some family secrets that need to see the light of day, or we'll never become the family I wish us to be.' Ina nodded, frowning but otherwise remained quiet, observing how her lack of response made her uncle twist restlessly in his seat.

Finally, he blurted out in distress. 'I'm sorry, Ina, for what my father did to you. There is no excuse, but whatever you hear next, please remember we are still family and... Gods, this is so difficult. Ina, no one was strong enough to resist his coercion. We all fell victim to his mind magic, twisted words and belief he wanted what was best for the House of Thorn. Now I can only beg for your forgiveness.' He turned to Nerissa, his eyes pleading for help but receiving only an empty stare. Ina sighed, observing her great-aunt's face lose all colour.

'That doesn't bode well.'

'No, it doesn't. But I want you to know my father wasn't always like this. Although he was always a peculiar man, his hatred towards everyone who was not human started after you were born.'

'You're trying to tell me it is my fault?'

'No, Ina. I'm sorry, I'm not good at this. Nerissa, can you please help me? He is your brother, after all.' He pleaded again, but the old healer lowered her eyes to the floor when Ina sent her a questioning look.

'Your magic terrified him. Where we saw a toddler's temper, he saw a chaos mage decimating all life, and he changed. He blamed your father's old blood or the rumours that his family was not entirely human, and he focused this hatred on anyone non-human.' Cyrus stood up, pacing in the small space, clenching his fists.

He must know I don't blame him for his father's actions? Ina wondered, observing how distressed her uncle had become. 'You never mistreated me, Cyrus. I don't blame you,' she said, trying to calm him, but much to her shock, he turned and bowed in front of her chair, clasping her hands and locking them in a tight embrace.

'You should blame me—all of us. We were all to blame. The day you returned with your mother, when your chaos manifested so violently, he forced Nerissa to make you barren. I never saw him so afraid, so unhinged. He violated his sister's mind to get what he wanted, and she can't even look at you now, so ashamed of what he has done.'

'Oh…'

'There is more. I know you were always troubled, exchanging lovers, rarely making friends.' Cyrus stopped, and deep sadness flashed through his face when he shook his head. 'You were such a lively child, so trusting and open, but he put a geas on you, making sure you let no one stay long enough to love them. And we, the rest of the family, saw what he did, and we let him convince us it was all for the greater good.'

Cyrus searched Ina's face for condemnation or forgiveness, but she felt strangely calm and gently pushed him aside, approaching her great aunt, who flinched when Ina's shadow fell over her. After a moment's silence, Ina kneeled and placed her head on the old woman's lap.

'I'm so sorry for what happened to you. It must have been hard to live with this burden. All I care about is that you tried to look after me the best you could, which was no easy task. I'd never blame you, aunty.' She felt a trembling hand stroking her hair gently, and a quiet sob escaped the old woman's throat when she tried to speak.

'I could not protect you and your mother or stand up to my brother, so yes, I failed you. I have no excuse, but I want you to know there was not a day I didn't regret what happened. If I could fix it….'

'Please don't be sad. I'm not made for family life, so in a way, it is better.' Ina cut her short, standing up. She rubbed her neck while looking at her family, all three of them harmed by the man who was now lying impotent in bed while his victims had to carry on. 'Everything is as it should be. Whatever happened in the past made me who I am. I'd like a moment alone, but I want to talk to you both later,' she said, walking towards the doors. She'd come here to ensure Nerissa was safe and free to leave. Seeing her solved one problem, but plenty of things still needed to be dealt with, just not right now. First, she needed to calm the raging anger that threatened her control over chaos. For that, Ina granted herself a moment of solitude.

Ina wandered into the garden, stroking the fresh green leaves and budding flowers. No matter how hard she tried, she couldn't get rid of the burning desire to run upstairs to smother the old man with his pillow. *Would it make me feel better if I did it?* she thought as she replayed the conversation in her mind.

Years of conditioning prepared her to expect the old man's hatred and her family's inability to stand up to him, but that wasn't the reason for her anger. To see her great-aunt so broken, so despondent, and all because of something she had no control over? No, Nerissa deserved more for the years spent caring for the hellion that was Ina, cut off from family and the home where she grew up. Without thinking, Ina wandered to her favourite childhood spot and sat on the boulder next to an ancient oak tree. Gently stroking the harsh bark, she sighed.

'You survived so many storms, and so will I,' she mumbled. The texture of the bark under her fingers changed as a familiar presence wrapped her in its warm embrace. Ina closed her eyes and opened herself to the experience while the tree bark changed into flesh and the crude masculine arms wrapped around her. She inhaled the primordial forest's deep, rich scent that finally calmed the blizzard of her anger.

'Leshy… thank you.'

'I will always come to you, my little witch.'

'My father, did he come from the forest?' Ina already knew the answer, but she needed to hear it.

'Yes, and no. He was the last of the long line of my descendants, but he was human, just like you and your mother.'

'Your descendants? I thought he was the child of a forest spirit, but you…?' Ina frowned as the answer was not exactly what she expected and she shivered hearing his raspy laugh.

'Where do you think your auburn hair came from, my autumn girl? My Lady Willow was just like you, and I promised her I'd look after our offspring.'

Ina sighed deeply, thinking about all those years in the Black Forest when his company kept her sane, holding back the despair in the darkest time of her life.

'I will be the last one,' she said, thinking of her family deeds, and Leshy nodded, stroking her hair.

'Yes, you will be. Everything eventually ends, but you, my harbinger of chaos, will burn the brightest in a long line of exceptional people.'

'I don't want to. All I ever wanted was a carefree life with the few people who are close to me.' As soon as she said it, she felt his smirk against her cheek.

'That is not who you are, but you won't be alone, my fierce, loving Ina. The forest will always guard your dreams. Now go, your friend will worry, and I would prefer to keep this tree alive.' She felt the comforting presence fade, soft flesh hardened under her touch, and opening her eyes, Ina found herself pressed against the rough tree trunk.

'Sure, Grandad. I have an existential crisis, and you're worried about your precious foliage.'

As if responding to her words, the oak crown shook in silent laughter, and the witch sighed, standing up and heading back to the castle. *I will have to tell Mar.* Even the thought of losing him when he learnt the full extent of the mess she landed in this time felt unbearable, and the witch pounded her chest, trying to draw in a breath to ease the pain.

'Oh, for fuck's sake, since when has he become the sole reason for your existence?' Ina hissed through her clenched teeth, fighting with unwanted tears, but she knew this couldn't be kept secret, and deep down, she knew Mar needed to know.

It didn't take long to find her uncle and great-aunt as they still sat in his office, worrying his lip raw. 'You are not guilty of your father's misdeeds, Cyrus. We can't fix the past, so stop fretting. I'm no teenager to lash out whenever I'm unhappy. Nerissa, I've known I was barren for years and came to terms with this. That my family did this to me was… difficult to digest…' Ina stopped looking at Cyrus's pained expression, forcing a tight smile. 'It doesn't matter anymore. We have other problems, and I hope you will help solve them. It is time for Castle Thorn to take responsibility for the province they're supposed to govern, and what is it with this damn blight?'

Stupefied, her uncle couldn't stop staring until her words brought the light of hope to his eyes. 'You exceed my expectations, niece, and I gratefully place the family resources, including my humble abilities, at your disposal. I am happy to see how you've matured. When I heard the bard's tales, I admit, I expected....' The shrug he gave her left Ina even more exasperated.

'What? That I'd call you a limp dick? Turn you into a dragon, or order the entire Castle, including the cows and chickens, to kneel before me? Never trust the bloody blustering poets, but don't misunderstand; despite my anger, I know to direct it at those who deserve my ire. Now, let's get back to the issue at hand. What's happened to Thorn? I barely recognise the province! Crops not growing on fertile southern soil? Starving peasants who barely remember they're part of Cornovii? Not to mention the cult of Marzanna, which almost killed us on our way here!'

Her speech was interrupted by Velka, who, tired of waiting, joined them in the library. When Ina smiled and welcomed her friend, Cyrus gestured to the table and removed a large map from the shelf. The intricately detailed patterns showed the province of Thorn in all its glory, and Ina gasped, enchanted by the sheer beauty of the craftsmanship. Cyrus pointed to a small city near the southern border.

'If you are looking for the heart of the problem, you must seek it here. So far, all information points to Alsia as the centre of rebellious activity. We never had trouble with the old master of those lands, but it is an entirely different story since he died and his son took the reins.' The mage started pacing back and forth, shaking his head. 'I told my father we needed to go there. Nothing suspicious, just a routine visit, but I was always told no, with no explanation. Then the visits started, and the old fool removed me from all my family duties.'

'The visits?'

'Yes, a few times a year, and it was always the same mage; tall with raven hair. Father smuggled him into his private office in the middle of the night, but when those visits stopped, his behaviour grew more erratic.'

Nerissa looked at Cyrus, and Ina noticed her aunt's thoughtful expression, but before she could speak, Velka interrupted. 'Don't tell me he got worse than spouting nonsense about tainted blood?' she said, laying her hand protectively on her round belly. Ina realised her friend had stopped wearing large, loose clothes. Now in a light house dress, no one could miss her pregnancy. Cyrus looked at her gesture with a gentle smile.

'Yes, his newest obsession was to make "*magic triumph*," and to set magic users up as the ruling class of Cornovii. He gathered supporters around, mainly mages unhappy with their positions. Those idiots and soldiers they managed to convince or coerce fled after learning my father's reign had ended. Not that any of them posed a significant threat or will be missed. As for my father, despite his hatred, he even called for Nerissa to return home. He told me he wanted to unite all the mages of our family because the time was coming for change.'

Nerissa snorted contemptuously. 'And I left as soon as he told me. If not for an ailing noble and his wife, I'd have been back in Osterad already. She seemed to contract one illness to another, making me suspicious of their intentions.' Nerissa was visibly angry, and Ina made a mental note of this tidbit, adding it to what she already knew. The witch looked at the map silently, trying to connect all the dots, and one thing stood clear. Her grandfather was involved in the southern rebellion and was collaborating with someone, probably a magical user.

The young nobleman and the city that was the centre of discord needed to be investigated. Then there was also strange sickness to the soil and Marzanna's cult spreading like wildfire among the peasants. Ina felt it was all connected, but she couldn't find the sense or reason and was becoming overwhelmed by the situation.

'Cyrus, I have to warn you. I will use a communication crystal to message Rewan—I mean, His Majesty. The old duke is neck-deep in all of this, which will weigh heavily on our family, but it will be even worse if he finds out from someone else.'

'I understand. Do you need my help? Our family crystal is tuned to the university and the palace's general communication rooms. Those channels won't provide the necessary discretion.' The tightening of his lips that followed this simple answer clarified Cyrus understood the gravity of their predicament, making her grateful he didn't try to stop her.

'No, Jorge provided a spell to contact him directly, and unfortunately, I need to be alone for that conversation, but he will safely inform the king for me. There is also one other thing. Whatever is affecting the land is the primary cause of peasants' distress. We must sort that out first. Providing food and reversing the rot will calm the mood, and without distressed commoners, it will be much harder for the nobles to recruit foot soldiers. I will ask the university to send mages skilled to deal with such a problem to see what they can do about it.'

'Why? I can do it.' Velka's offended tone surprised Ina, and she looked at her friend with interest and concern.

'Are you sure? I don't want to expose you to any danger. Not in your condition.'

'Ina, I'm the best nature mage this bloody country has, and you're pushing me out because I'm pregnant? I said I could do it, and I will. All I need is a workshop, a library, and a few smart servants to help.' The outrage in Velka's voice made Ina smile. Her friend had a sweet nature, but was proud of her skills and didn't like anyone encroaching on her domain.

Cyrus cut in to prevent an argument. 'How about Nerissa and I help you? That way, we can keep Ina happy, and I can at least try to be the leader this province deserves to have.'

Her uncle's words smoothed down everyone's ruffled feathers, and Ina nodded before continuing. 'I will leave you to it. I don't know much about plants and soil, and I'm grateful you took this burden off my shoulders. I will head to the tower now to send the message. And uncle, it will be fine, I promise. Rewan owes me a favour or two. This family will survive, but if he asks for grandfather's head, I won't object.' Ina stood up, bracing herself for the upcoming confrontation with the judicial mage.

Ina headed for the tower, leaving the excited chatter behind as Velka and Cyrus dived deep into planning the magical research. Each step that took her towards the crystal felt heavy, as the witch didn't know how she could possibly explain her family's involvement and if she would be able to keep the promise given to her uncle.

CHAPTER THIRTEEN

Communication crystals had always been a mystery to Ina. The principle seemed simple, but like all high order spells, creating a device that connected across the world to any another device of its kind took countless diagrams and calculations that only certain order mages could efficiently handle. The rest of the magical world had to rely on pre-tuned crystals with sigils that provided the necessary connection. The sigils were so complicated to recreate that the witch still remembered the headaches they'd caused all those years ago at university. The crumpled parchment she removed from her satchel held the diagram Jorge insisted she carry in case of emergencies, and Ina attempted to recreate the complicated and precise pen strokes on the crystal's surface. Her efforts were childlike in comparison, leaving her hoping her amateurish scrawl would still work.

As Ina poured her magic into the completed spell, she watched it light up, calling out loudly, just in case.

'Jorge? Can you hear me?'

As her voice echoed around the stone room, Ina winced, then crossed her fingers, begging the matching gem in Jorge's house to connect. Moments later, the distorted but distinctive voice of the order mage filled the small space.

'Ina?'

The witch sighed with relief and moved closer to the gem. 'Oh, thank the gods. I made it to Thorn, but a few mishaps slowed us down. How is Mar?'

'Already on the way to you, with a furious orc desperate to find his wife, but this is no time to talk of trivialities. There was another assassination attempt, and I'm unsure how long we can keep it quiet. Did you find anything?'

'Rewan's unharmed?' Her heart skipped a beat when she asked the question. The king was an annoying pain in the arse, but he was her pain, and somehow she'd grown to like the manipulative bastard. Jorge reassured her that Rewan was uninjured, with Kaian now bullying him into accepting a permanent bodyguard.

'Now tell me what you learned. Contrary to you, I don't have a bottomless pit of primal power.'

Ina rolled her eyes, but he was right, and it was time for a few confessions. She detailed her journey; the twisted and fastly spreading cult of Marzanna and the strange blight ravaging the province that left the vegetation stuck in endless winter, creating a food shortage for everyone that counted on the spring produce. The most serious revelation she left for the end.

'There's more, I'm afraid. It looks like Duke Thorn was involved in some idiotic mage conspiracy. Cyrus noticed a strange visitor and changes in his father's behaviour. My welcome here ended in a mage battle that left the old fool in a coma, so we can't gain any information from that quarter. All we know is his increased usage of mage supremacy rhetoric. How is this happening? Don't these idiots remember what caused the mage wars?'

'Ina, some people at the university believe in this view. I didn't know it had spread outside, but some mages think the world would be better if ruled by magic users. Arun is trying to keep a lid on it, as we don't need the common folk chasing us with pitchforks when they find out mages think they should rule the world.'

Ina sat down and pinched the bridge of her nose. 'When did you intend to inform me of this? And Rewan, does he know? The situation here is so convoluted, with so many issues, that I don't know if I have the skills to unravel it. Can you come here or use your magic to tell me what in Veles's pit is going on?'

'Ina, we both know it doesn't work like that. I'm needed in the capital to find the ringleader. Besides, I can't see future events in the South. That usually means you or another chaos mage is disrupting my spell.'

'Jorge, so you're dumping this crap in my lap... again?'

'You are a judicial mage. We gather information and divine the patterns. Now, before you tell me patterns are your weak suit, I'll tell you what I told the king when he asked for my recommendation. Trouble gravitates to the chaos inside you, and plans fall apart at the slightest touch when you exert your influence. So trust your instincts and, for once, utilise the talents that surround you.'

The connection began sputtering as Jorge finished, the communication crystal flickering. Ina knew she was running out of time, but the mention of talent awoke the hint of an idea. 'Tell Sa'Ren Gerel to listen to his dreams.'

'What?'

'Just tell him. That's all I ask.' Ina finished right before the crystal dimmed, breaking the connection. Ina pulled her knees up, squeezing her legs as she thought through her options. Cyrus needed to prove the family's loyalty to the Crown. With his talent, he would be the best person to search through Lord Thorn's correspondence and accounts. Velka had already staked her claim on the problem with the blight, and Ina admitted it removed a considerable part of the growing burden off her shoulders. *That leaves me with a necromancer in league with bandits, Marzanna's cult, and a potential war with Verdante, probably involving the rebellious nobles. If Mar and Daro are on their way here, they can help with the nobles, or at least the leadership. Marzanna's cult will be my job, and I'll let the local guard captain know about the necromancer. I can try using my bond with Ren to brief Rewan, as Jorge will protect the university more than the king. It serves me right for not learning the palace communication pattern.*

Ina jumped off the chair, heading to Cyrus's office. He would know the schemata for a dream-walking spell. In a much more optimistic mood, she smiled to herself. The conversation with Jorge went better than she expected, with the judicial mage refraining from asking about her family's involvement, and her uncle deserved a bit of good news before she asked him to dig into his father's private affairs.

Ina found Cyrus pacing a groove in his carpet. As soon as she told him what she needed, he silently turned towards the window, considering his options. Just as she was about to play her trump card, her judicial mage privileges, her uncle turned back, frowning.

'It's not that I don't trust you, but if father were involved with the magic supremacy movement, it would be considered treason.

Do you trust His Majesty enough to gamble our lives? Mine, Mirena's, our children's… even Nerissa's would be at stake.'

Ina placed a reassuring hand on her uncle's shoulder, shaking her head. 'I refuse to acknowledge guilt by association, and I doubt Rewan would be so shortsighted to execute such a rich resource as our family, unless he didn't have a choice. I don't need your permission to dig up the old man's dirt, but I would prefer your cooperation. There's more at stake than just our family. If you help dismantle this conspiracy, it would be another reason to accept Grandfather as the sole culprit.'

Cyrus nodded and gestured for her to follow. She was taken to a small room at the back of the old duke's bedroom. It looked tidy, with no unnecessary papers cluttering the polished surfaces. As Ina studied the room, she realised it was as soulless and empty as her grandfather felt.

'I realise this looks rather sterile, but it's a reasonable place to start, so I'll leave you to it while I look through the estate records.'

The words barely registered as Ina stared, unseeing, thinking about the situation in which she'd placed Cyrus. She felt sorry for him. Trapped in an uncaring family, forced into a loveless marriage, and while they seemed to have reached an accord, the beginning of their relationship had been complicated and marred with scandal. Now, once again, his father's actions had created an untenable situation that the innocent had to suffer through unhappily, and all she could do was find out what he'd done.

Over an hour later, Ina was ready to incinerate every inch of the room in frustration. Despite pulling out every drawer, reading each piece of parchment, and even pulling apart the seams of the chair's padding, she hadn't found a hint of wrongdoing, not even that damn wheatsheaf motif. Finally, she sat heavily on the chair, sneezing as wadding exploded into the air. Did he hide the evidence somewhere else? But why bother? No one would dare trespass in his private chambers, knowing the duke could destroy their mind in a fit of pique.

Ina's thoughts raced as she rocked on the chair, breathing slowly to calm her racing mind when she decided it was time to enter the old duke's bedroom. With a snort at how ridiculous she felt, the witch stood up and headed in, pausing to look at the shrivelled body lying motionless on the bed. Two servants were tending to the duke whilst casting nervous glances in her direction.

From this angle, the old bastard didn't look intimidating, but Ina still felt tingles of fear tugging at her chest. *I'm still afraid of him. Even after all these years, I'm afraid.* This realisation was not pleasant. Ina noticed tendrils of chaos beginning to curl over the pale skin of her hands. It took a conscious effort to dissipate the magic and send the petrified servants away. Alone in the spacious bedroom, Ina slowly approached the bed, pulling up a chair. Green-grey eyes, faded but similar to hers, looked back with frustrated hatred. The old man tried to speak, but all he managed was the slow flow of drool onto his pillow.

'Well, will wonders never cease? It seems Nerissa was wrong; you are in there. I… I just wanted you to know… I forgive you.' Ina watched as her words seemed to ease the fury contorting the old man's face, and she smiled bitterly. Now it was her time to talk, and maybe, this time, he would listen to what she had to say.

'I forgive you because your cruelty made me the woman I am today, not the meek, simpering lady you hoped I would be.

The geas you forced onto me as a child? I broke it, choosing love over mistrust, even if it may hurt me later. No longer can your spell take my happiness away. I want you to know I will never reject the man who is part of my soul. I may not give him a child to continue the Liath line because of you, but I will stand by him for as long as I live because, despite your schemes, I love that oafish, beautiful dragon.' Ina blinked rapidly, and the truth in her words solidified into a determination to live her life and never look back in fear.

'You could have taught me so much and helped me wield my magic, but you cast me aside, stripping me of choice and forcing those around me to suffer. You were wrong all this time. Chaos didn't make me a monster, nor did your abuse. I am proud of the woman I have become, and nothing that you, or the power of chaos, can do to me will ever change that fact.'

Ina paused, blinking back unwanted tears, then blew out an exasperated breath, scolding herself. *Oh, for fuck's sake, stop acting like a toddler craving acceptance. He doesn't care what you say, and you shouldn't care about his opinion.* She massaged the bridge of her nose to stop the tears before looking back at the duke with a smirk. 'As for your intrigues, I will find and unravel them for no reason other than to spite you.'

Her last remark was petty, but Ina could not resist this little revenge. The old duke and his magic would haunt her nightmares no longer.

The smirk on her lips disappeared as the duke gagged, and Ina cursed, unable to watch him die. Leaning over and turning the helpless man onto his side, she gently patted his back. The anger inside drained away at the pitiful sight, but being closer meant she could finally make out words amidst the choking.

'It was her... king... n... my fault.'

The words were so garbled that Ina could hardly understand, but they reminded her of why she was here originally. When the duke's breath evened again, Ina inspected her surroundings. The room, almost as austere as the office, yielded little to the witch's searching gaze. The rose crest of Thorn above the duke's bed, and a detailed picture of Lada in a sea of wheat under the midday sun, were the only decorations on otherwise bare plaster.

Listen to your intuition. Jorge's words echoed in her mind as she studied the picture, her feet moving forward of their own accord. The longer Ina looked at the picture, the more real it seemed, the goddess of love and harvest drawing her closer, inviting the witch into the beautiful setting. It looked so alive, so enchanting, that Ina leaned in, on the verge of stepping forward and joining the goddess, when a sudden commotion from the castle yard snapped her mind back into focus. She frowned, walking to the window, curious about the noise, when a deep voice, amplified by the castle's stone walls, shouted.

'Where the hell is my wife?!'

Ina burst out laughing. *Jorge, you manipulative bastard, you knew they were close.* It seemed her asset had arrived with Daro, the irate husband, wreaking havoc in this seat of high-born mages. With a mischievous grin, she turned to the bed. 'I will see you later, Grandpa. I must greet my dragon and his orc friend, and while there will be no offspring from this reunion, it won't be for the lack of trying. Especially not tonight.'

The door to the bedroom slammed closed behind her as Ina rushed downstairs, arriving just in time to watch the drama unfold. Velka stood, calm and collected, on the castle steps, her hands resting on her rounded belly as Daro paced, yelling some colourful curses in the orcish language. "Ivuldad bosharkand" sounded very poetic. However, she remembered those particular words from many a bar fight, and they weren't complimentary. Ina sighed and looked over, meeting Mar's eyes. The warmth that flooded her gave a spring to her step as she approached the Lord Marshal.

Mar slid off Woron's back with practised ease, gathering her up in his muscular arms, squeezing until she squeaked, fending him off and slowly relaxing as he breathed in her scent, savouring the moment. Ina pressed her head to his chest, disregarding the arguing lovers, basking in his warm embrace. Mar leaned down, and she felt his chin resting on her head when he finally spoke. The words were whispered with a delicious growling rumble.

'I don't know if I should spank you or kiss you for leaving like that.'

'Well, let me know what you decide, my mighty warrior.' His words elicited a response neither one expected, and Ina raised her chin, a challenging look blazing in her eyes.

'You left the king's council chamber like a savage goddess without a word on what prompted your sudden departure, and do I need to mention your injuries? And don't try to deny it, as I felt each moment of your pain.'

Ina reached up and grabbed Mar's beard, pulling him down for a tentative kiss, nipping at his lips as uncertainty turned to desire. When her dragon picked her up into his arms, she leaned back, smiling.

'Have mercy, woman, not here... Where is your room?' He walked forward, leaving Woron to the care of an eager groom, only to stop as Daro blocked their way.

'Oh no, my lady, you are going nowhere until I hear why you dragged my wife on this dangerous adventure.' Ina's eyebrows rose, and she untangled herself from Mar's embrace. When she turned to face Daro, her face was the icy mask of the royal witch.

'So I'm lady now to you, Captain? As for your wife, I will let her tell you why she went on an adventure with me rather than warm your bed. Castle Thorn has an excellent healer, and I'm happy to show you the way when she finishes her explanation.'

Velka, who had listened to Daro's ramblings with polite gentleness, coughed, trying to hide her laughter, then grabbed her husband's shoulder. 'We are going to the garden now. I will sort this out, Ina, and I'm sorry he's being difficult.'

'You don't have to apologise for anything, my love…' started Daro, but Velka cut him short.

'We are going, so not another word.'

Ina saw Mar hiding a smirk behind her hair, trying to spare his friend's blushes as Daro was led away by the blonde valkyrie like an unruly child. As soon as the bickering couple disappeared behind the building, the dragon turned to Ina and threw her over his shoulder like a barbaric raider.

'Where were we? Ah, yes, your room. Point me in the right direction, my love, or should we sneak into the stables? Unless you want me to go to the old duke to ask for your hand in marriage?' His remark brought harsh reality back with a thump. Ina shook her head and gestured for Mar to put her down.

'There are things we need to discuss first. The situation here has become a little complicated. Let's talk to Cyrus first.'

'Cyrus?'

'My uncle, the old duke, is … well, indisposed, but I promise I'll explain soon.'

A kaleidoscope of emotion flashed across Mar's face as he reluctantly put her down. 'What aren't you telling me? We will go to Cyrus, but first, we'll discuss it privately. I know you were injured. I felt it, so please don't try to hide behind protocol or family. Daro almost killed the horses to keep up with my need to see you. Even now, I am barely holding the dragon at bay. I must know you are safe and well in this den of vipers.'

Ina gestured to her body before tilting her head wryly, but one look at Mar's expression and she shook her head, chuckling softly. 'Fine! We can talk in private. Just keep your hands to yourself, dragon. You can be very distracting.'

Before she could take a step, Mar picked her up and looked around. 'Directions, please, my damsel. I'm awfully lost in this floral maze.'

She burst out laughing, pointing to a small entrance to the side and, from there, straight to her room. The ease with which her dragon carried her up the stairs sent a shiver down Ina's spine, and she placed her head on his shoulder, playing with the wild hair peeking out of his loosened collar. A deep rumbling growl triggered another shiver, causing her to look up into his liquid-gold eyes, and the connection between them flared to life, showing her precisely what Mar was thinking. The witch bit her lip and pointed to the door of her private quarters. 'I've changed my mind. My uncle can wait a moment. I wouldn't be able to focus now, anyway.'

Mar's throaty laugh reverberated with joy and desire. 'Thank the gods. I thought I'd be on my knees and begging.'

As soon as the doors closed behind them, Mar pressed her back against the solid timber, but when her hands tangled in his unkempt hair, he grabbed her wrists, trapping them above her head, leaning down to whisper into her ear. 'No, my love, your dragon missed you and will remind you what he's capable of.' The roughness in his voice felt like velvet, and Ina nodded as he released his hold, fingers trailing downwards, sparks of excitement igniting over every inch of their delicious trail.

As his knees touched the cold floor, Mar gripped the hem of Ina's skirts, lifting them slowly, the warm caress of his breath following the path of his hands, stopping as they reached the jagged scar on her thigh. Ina opened her mouth to explain, but stopped as he spoke.

'Ah, so that's what I felt.' His calm reaction surprised the witch into remembering to speak.

'Aren't you mad?'

'Mad enough to burn the city down, but it was your battle, and you won. That doesn't mean you will escape my wrath, Striga. You will endure every moment of your punishment,' Mar said, his kisses trailing upwards with elaborate slowness, driving her crazy.

'Mar, stop teasing, please.' Ina moaned when his breath caressed her folds, biting her lip. Suddenly, something changed, and they both stilled before Mar resumed his exploration. The gentle kisses were replaced by the slide of a tongue, a tongue that split and lengthened, touching her more intimately than she'd ever known, and if not for the grip of his hands on her thighs, she would have collapsed from the pleasure.

'Oh gods, that… What the….' She was breathless. Her heart was racing, desire surging with each delicious swirling touch, threatening to explode at any moment. Tendrils of magic curled and eddied, flowing down over his body like a playful kitten, nips of pain tickling his skin as the threads of control slipped from her fingers. Mar's grip on her hips intensified, and she heard a growling voice distorted by partial transformation.

'Let go, my love. You are safe with me.'

Her world exploded when pleasure erupted from within, crashing through her like a magical wave as she lost herself in pure bliss.

Mar cradled Ina on his lap, eyes full of love as he gazed down at her, gently brushing away unbound strands of hair from her face. The desire to taste his spitfire had felt so visceral, so instinctive, that he hadn't been able to resist. They'd both been surprised when his tongue had transformed, but his lady seemed to enjoy it. Ina's acceptance of his dragon never ceased to amaze him. *You are my miracle. My beautiful, fiery miracle.*

'You have no idea how much I needed that,' he said, smiling when she opened her eyes.

'I'm always happy to help, but what about you?' she asked suggestively, looking down at where his hard cock pressed into her rear.

'I can wait. We have the entire night for you to shackle me to the floor with your magic and practice your dragon riding.' He playfully kissed the tip of her nose, reminiscing on their first night together when she'd angrily pinned him down, fighting for dominance. She enjoyed their little power plays, and he loved how she expressed her passion. He was glad to see her smiling. Her beautiful face, glowing with contentment, satisfied something deep inside him.

'I love you.' His simple declaration seemed to sober her, and Ina looked at him with strange tenderness and vulnerability while reaching up and gently stroking his cheek.

'I know.'

Mar sighed and pressed her to his chest. It was always *I know*. He knew she loved him, and while Ina could say this to the trees, her cat, or through their link, she could never manage it straight to his face. Still, he was a patient dragon who hoped that one day she could say it, and when she did, her heart would fully belong to him.

'Why are you frowning?' The witch sounded unusually insecure, her voice filled with caution, and he cursed himself for worrying her.

'I'm thinking about the wound on your leg. Is it fully healed?' Mar sighed at the sceptical look on her face and added, 'And I should tell you what we learned on our travels.' She still didn't look convinced, but ignoring her expression, the marshal settled Ina more comfortably on his lap and recounted the events of his journey, then listened to the witch's adventures. When they finished, Ina stood up, holding a hand to help him.

'Time to talk to my uncle. I have a rudimentary plan, but there are so many issues to tackle that if they are connected, I'll never understand how they are woven together. It feels like the South is suffering a death of a thousand cuts, and I only have one bandage.'

Just as the witch was about to continue, they both staggered, falling to the floor as a wave of magic rolled through the castle, carrying the psychic scream of a dying man. Mar pressed his hands to his ears, but they couldn't stop the mental assault. Ina, however, jumped to her feet and started running.

'Quickly, something's happened to the duke!'

CHAPTER FOURTEEN

Ina raced down the corridor, Mar one step behind. It had been less than an hour since she left the old duke's bedroom, but the mental torment in that scream had been unmistakable. Cyrus appeared before her, crashing through his father's door, broadcasting his anguish to the world even as he commanded the servants to bring Nerissa. Right before entering the room, Ina stopped, turning to Mar.

'Please wait here. Whatever's happened in the bedroom, Cyrus and I will handle it. I… don't want him to meet you like this. My grandfather has peculiar ideas regarding racial purity and is already unstable. He's still the most powerful mind-mage I know, and if he's… Well, I don't want him lashing out at you.'

'What if he attacks you?'

'If he does, he will assault my mind, not my body, and that is something you, even as a dragon, can't fight. Though I doubt he can do anything if my uncle called for the healers. Still better to be safe than sorry, and whilst I can shield myself, your mind is wide open.'

Nerissa pushed past. Her petite frame, crowned with silver hair, seemed to dominate the room, her usual brusque manner slightly ruffled, and Ina followed, leaving Mar, frustrated, trying to restrain his desire to keep her safe.

The witch almost smiled, grateful he trusted her judgement, but the sight she was confronted with chased that thought away. Her grandfather lay on the bed, blood trickling from his lips, unnaturally pale, his chest no longer moving. Pale wisps of chaos told Ina that whatever magic Nerissa was preparing to use on her brother would be fruitless. His soul had already departed on its journey to Nawia.

'There's no point, Nerissa; he's already gone. Only a necromancer can revive his body now.' There was a lack of emotion in her voice, and Cyrus turned, studying her face, openly grief-stricken. The sadness she understood, but his anger was a surprise.

'Ina, you were the last person in the room with him. What happened?'

'Are you asking what I saw or whether I killed him?' Although Cyrus didn't accuse her directly, his question's undertone was clear, and the sooner they clarified this situation, the better for all involved. 'No, I did not kill him, and although I didn't wish him well, I wouldn't go as far as murder.'

'But the scream....'

'We all heard the call, and I can assure you, your niece was otherwise engaged and very focused on her task when it came.' She hadn't noticed Mar entering the room, but assumed he'd overheard the conversation and decided to step in.

'What do you mean, engaged? Who are you?' Cyrus's expression betrayed his doubt. Although Ina couldn't blame her uncle's lack of trust, his accusation stung more than she cared to admit. Still, she needed his cooperation, and despite her embarrassment, it was best to disclose their activities.

'He's trying to spare my blushes. We were fucking each other senseless when we felt the duke's mind scream. So, if you could kindly stop accusing me of murder, I'll introduce you. Your Grace, this is Lord Marcach, scion of Liath, Lord Marshal of Cornovii. Lord Marcach, this is His Grace, Cyrus, Duke of Thorn. He is also my lover, uncle, so be polite.'

Mar rolled his eyes at her speech, but bowed respectfully to Cyrus before moving to Ina's side protectively.

'I'm the man your father was so displeased to see by his granddaughter's side. As Ina eloquently explained, she was busy welcoming me to Castle Thorn. Therefore, she couldn't be responsible for whatever happened in this room.'

You are so sweet trying to defend me, Ina thought as she looked up at Mar. He focused on her uncle, expecting the older man to challenge him further. From the corner of her eye, she saw Nerissa stepping away from the body. Her great aunt's face looked indifferent, but Ina knew her well enough to recognise the sadness she tried to hide and something she didn't expect to find—a hint of fear. Apart from his children, the old duke's death would upset no one, but whatever caused his death needed an explanation, and Ina suspected his passing had closed many doors to her investigation.

'Do you know what happened? He looked quite alive when I left him.'

'I'm not sure, but I can't sense magic, and this bleeding suggests poison. I can check later in the infirmary, but I must cut him open to find any answers.'

All eyes were on her, awaiting a decision, an uncomfortable reminder she was a judicial mage, but before Ina could speak, purple flames erupted from within the body, engulfing it. Nerissa fell backwards, but Ina rushed forward, warding the fire with chaos to contain the destruction. She couldn't sense any magic or magical artefact, but the unusual colour of the flames, and the speed they consumed the body, couldn't be explained otherwise. *It has to be magic, or alchemy,* Ina thought as she edged as close as she could, sniffing the burning remains, then gestured to Mar.

'I need your senses. I can smell sulphur and some metal, but there is something else I can't identify.'

Mar sniffed the air, an unreadable expression on his face. 'It is sugar. The sulphur stench is overwhelming, but there is a hint of caramel under it. What the hell is it?'

Ina closed her eyes, recognition niggling at the back of her mind. She knew she had learned about it. Her alchemy teachers ensured their students knew not only transmutation and alchemic magic but also poisons, toxins, and unusual compounds used by the various races, all as part of their training. Now, she just had to recall where she'd seen purple flames. *Purple fire… purple death… purple flames of death,* she thought, muttering curses under her breath until the long-forgotten knowledge snapped into place. Ina opened her eyes and looked at the expectant gathering.

'It is a necromancer trick from the north. Purple flames of death. I'm not sure how they did it here, but if you mix sulphur with sugar and….'

'Metallic salt. It will explode, burning brightly and consuming everything that contains water, like dead bodies, leaving only the ashes to be gathered by the family.' Her uncle must have seen her memory, finishing the explanation for her, and looked at the ash mound on the bed—the last remnants of the greatest mind mage in the history of Cornovii.

'But how? Did someone feed him with it? Also, it needs a catalyst, a surge of power, to start the process. The fire came from within, and he was fine when I left.' As her uncle looked around, Ina ruminated aloud as Cyrus's magic catalogued everything in his sight.

'Death itself can be a catalyst, and you should already know this. You don't need a spell when violent death can be the catalyst for a reaction.' Nerissa pointed out the obvious with a few words, sending Ina back to her school days. The witch felt her cheeks burn under her aunt's disapproving look, but to her relief, Cyrus broke the protracted silence.

'There is a spoon under the bed,' he said after a moment, and the members of the Thorn family looked at each other.

'Interrogate the servants and the mages in the castle while I check the spoon. Could any of the renegades that fled the castle have returned? Would they be able to access the duke's bedroom? I think I should check to see if any residual poison remains. Do you have a workshop I can use?' Ina's mind whirred into a higher gear while she tried to recall as many of her alchemic classes as possible.

'I can talk to the servants, but interrogation? I wouldn't know where to start. All I know are facts and figures. If they recall a situation, I could tell you what they remember, but little else.' Her uncle looked so lost, thrust into a position of such responsibility.

'That's more than enough,' Mar said, looking at the floundering noble. 'I will take on the responsibility of questioning your people, and if you allow it, Captain Daro shall assist. He is a very intimidating figure, which can be useful in such situations.'

'You intend to hurt them? I cannot condone the torture of our staff. I guarantee their loyalty.' Cyrus spluttered, visibly distraught. Mar flashed a predatory smile, and Ina was unsure if it was meant to reassure or frighten her uncle.

'Oh no, all he'll do is puff out his barbarian chest, growl a little and show his fangs, and if this doesn't loosen tongues, I will show them my dragon.'

Despite herself, Ina couldn't help smiling as the image of Mar's tongue flashed in her mind. *But I love your dragon,* she thought, smiling to herself.

Not only was he versatile, but Mar's dragon was magnificent, with steel blue scales streaked with golden lightning, and Ina loved it. She would still adore his dragon half, even if she hadn't fallen in love with the man. Since he learned from Ayni how to merge their minds during flight, calming her fears, Ina had dared to fly with him, learning to trust his instincts the same way he trusted her magic. His fangs and scales were not frightening to her, but were instead an alluring prospect.

Ina was startled from her thoughts as her great aunt's words caught her attention. 'What do you mean, you're leaving? When?'

Nerissa responded to Ina's question with an exasperated sigh. 'I just told you, child. I'm leaving for Osterad as soon as possible, even if it means using a portal. Whoever came up with this plan studied at the university, and I'm going to shake that noble institution till some names fall out. First, my brother's nonsense about magical rulers, now this? It's past time to knock some heads together.'

Ina listened to this pronouncement with shocked, wide-opened eyes. Portals came with such an expense of magic that some less powerful mages were bedridden for days. She barely realised Mar and Cyrus were about to leave until her dragon leaned over, giving her a soft peck on the cheek and whispering into her ear.

'I will see you at dinner, as your aunt said, hopefully with some answers. Don't worry, my love, we'll get to the bottom of this. But I must admit, seeing you take charge gave me some idea of how I want to spend the evening.'

Lustful beast, she thought, her eyes lingering on his body as he disappeared down the stairs. Alone in the room, Ina turned back to the bed to collect the spoon and ashes, pausing when her eyes fell on the painting of Lada. The Lady of the Spring looked at her again, and Ina remembered where her search had ended before Mar's arrival disturbed her investigation.

The witch deposited the ashes onto a silver platter, placing it carefully alongside the spoon on the Duke's dressing table before approaching the painting of Lada. This time, Ina was prepared. She closed her eyes and trailed her fingers over the golden frame, exploring each nook and cranny, finding nothing. There had to be something, and Ina's intuition pointed her at the painting itself. With her eyes closed, she concentrated on its magic, letting it fill her body, and there it was, the unmistakable touch of the duke's mind, a prickly harmful piece of nastiness designed to enthral its victim, all the while hiding something.

Since that fateful night in Liander's clutches, Ina suspected the only way her enemies could control her was by controlling her psyche, and Tar'eth proved her theory right, almost forcing her to kill Mar. *Why had you left me unprotected despite knowing the danger?* She thought about her grandfather when his spell brought unwelcomed memories. In a sudden burst of anger, Ina hit the wall below the picture, ready for the cleansing pain, but it didn't come. She looked at the hole in the facade, and a sly smile tickled the edges of her mouth as she tore away the remaining veneer, uncovering a small door.

With a jaunty flick of her fingers, Ina sent a small pulsar through the door as she opened it, ready to combat any nasty surprises, but all that was illuminated was a meticulously ordered archive of letters, maps, and books. Too tight for the witch to relax comfortably, the room offered a wealth of information, so Ina began gathering documents and bringing them into the bedroom. The shudder that travelled down her spine at the thought of reading through this many letters left her cursing, but they needed to be catalogued at the very least. Ina glanced over the ones that responded vaguely to the old duke's complaints about the monarchy and the world in general, but the more recent letters carried dark undertones.

Ina's heart stuttered as she read a report on her romantic adventures, not only with Mar, but also Ren and, much to her surprise, a list of suitors she had never even met, let alone bedded. She could understand the account of Mar and Ren if the informant was too lazy to check their facts, but these other men? The letter stated she was hopping beds with an orc, half of the guards, and even Gruff. As if the troll, easily old enough to be her father, had ever looked at her romantically.

'Oh well, I hope you paid well for this piece of fiction, Grandfather,' she said, looking at the empty bed before opening another. This one came from an elder of Kaian's clan, reassuring the duke that the unrest in the South was part of the plan and to not worry about the peasants or the sudden popularity of Marzanna's cult. Ina frowned as she looked at the piece of paper. Her grandfather seemed involved, but not in the way she suspected. He wrote subversive letters about replacing non-magical nobles with mages, but instead of actively participating in a coup, he isolated himself from the world, even abandoning his own demesne.

Ina opened the last letter, this one more of a note, commending the old duke on luring her out of Osterad and telling him to keep her in Thorn, no matter the cost. Although this letter was signed only with the mysterious wheatsheaf symbol, the handwriting was too similar to the last to be anyone other than the elder of the Water Horse clan.

Ina closed her eyes, rubbing her temples, unsure of what to do with this new information. This letter could destroy both Kaian and his relationship with the king. Whilst ruthless and more than capable of using sex in his schemes, the silver hair advisor seemed genuinely in love with Rewan. It would pain her to destroy a man she respected, whose dry humour and darker-than-grey morality had wormed their way into her heart. No, there must be an explanation. So, for once, she would give the assassin the benefit of the doubt.

'My love, it's time for dinner… Ina, is everything all right?'

She heard Mar's voice and opened her eyes to look at him. Whatever he saw in her face had him rushing across the room to sit beside her, pulling her into his tight embrace.

'It's all right, my spitfire. Whatever you've found, we will face it together.'

She looked up, listening to the steady beat of his heart as he stroked her back, trying to ease the burden she carried. *I could listen to this sound for the rest of my life. My oafish overbearing dragon, somehow life is easier simply having you around*, she thought, the tight knot in her chest relaxing. Ina trailed a finger over his jawline before straightening her back.

'You can dim those golden lanterns of yours. I'm fine, but I've encountered a problem that bears some thought.'

Lips twitching at her remark about his ever-changing eye colour, he turned her around to face him. 'Should I hear the long or the short version? If it's the short version, we can sit here and talk it over right now, but if this is a big issue, we can disappear after dinner and discuss the problem in depth. Mirena was most insistent on your attendance, so maybe we should avoid upsetting another healer today.'

Ina looked through the window at the pale moon slowly rising in the sky. 'I lost track of time. I'll be lucky if my aunt hasn't given my plate to the hounds. Let me secure his archive, and we can go. There is more to talk about than my current findings.'

With a smile at Mar when he offered her his hand, she stood up, bumping against his hip before straightening her skirt and smoothing her hair. It only took a moment to weave a simple illusion over the letters and the archive, something to keep the servants from prying before the witch shared her findings with the family. As soon as it was done, she took the dragon's hand to head down for dinner.

'Let's go. I'm starving and curious to see if Velka tamed her raging orc after sharing her little secret.'

'What secret?'

'Oh, you will see. Just be ready to defend your damsel in distress.'

'Ina!' Mar was half roaring, half laughing when she pulled him down the stairs towards the noisy dining hall.

It felt wrong, but other than Cyrus, no one showed the slightest ounce of grief. There was a small amount of anxiety from the looming threat, but mostly, there was a sense of relief at finally being free from the contemptible mind mage. Mirena and Cyrus sat on opposite sides of the large table next to Velka and Daro, with her cousins sitting a little further down. Ina relinquished Mar's hold, gesturing towards the empty chairs as she approached her uncle and placed a hand on his shoulder.

'Are you alright?' She saw his forced smile when he turned to look at her and awkwardly patted her hand.

'Yes, there was no love between my father and me, but the circumstances surrounding his death have left our House in a difficult position. I hope we can discuss it later, or better yet, in the morning. Let's eat and enjoy each other's company as a normal family would.'

There was so much bitterness in his words that Ina bit her lip as it suddenly occurred to her that this quiet bookworm, who'd spent most of his life in the family library, was now the Duke of Thorn and had to shoulder its various responsibilities. She sat at the table and raised the nearest glass of wine. 'A toast. To Cyrus, the new Duke of Thorn. May your troubles vanish with the first blush of spring, and discontentment burn away in chaos fire.'

Her salutation, with its veiled threat, was met with surprised stares, as if it had only just occurred to everyone that there was a reason to celebrate during this dark time. The gathered company raised their glasses, and the conversation around the table became more relaxed while the family helped themselves to the food before them. Ina nibbled on the fish her aunt had thoughtfully prepared, studying the troubled couple across the table. Velka was eating enough for two and refused to look at her husband, while Daro continually glared at her and Mar, tearing apart his meat like it was an enemy's flesh.

Something wasn't right. When Velka told her Daro didn't want to have children just yet, Ina thought it was just a misunderstanding. Still, looking at his frosty, hostile expression

201

and how those two ignored each other, her fist involuntarily clenched, and she felt the urge to punch him.

'What an asshole,' she muttered, making Mar look at her.

'What have I done this time?' His curious yet amused expression told her it was more of a rhetorical question, but Mar still catalogued any possible transgressions.

'Not you, Daro. He should be happy about Velka's pregnancy. Instead, he's behaving as if she tricked him, forgetting how many people it takes to make a baby,' she whispered, confident that Mar's hearing would catch the near-silent words beneath the general conversation. However, Ina forgot her man hadn't heard the news, or that it was a secret.

'Velka's pregnant?!' Mar exclaimed, silencing every conversation in the room.

'What?' Daro jumped out of his chair and turned towards his wife.

'Ina!' Velka looked at her friend with alarm.

'Oh shit, you haven't told him? What were you doing in the garden?' The colour drained from Ina's face, and she covered her mouth, looking at the angry orc. An angry vein pulsated on his forehead, and Velka appeared close to tears.

'He didn't let me say a word, lecturing me on the dangers of the South, how I should be at home tending to my plants instead of traipsing through the countryside with you. How could I interrupt that when my loving husband berated me for not seeking his permission to make my own decision?'

'Because I fucking love and care about you, and I was worried you'd get dragged into another one of Ina's catastrophes. What is wrong with wanting you to be safe?'

Ina looked at her friends and sighed in resignation. 'He has a point, Velka.' She shrugged at the accusation in her friend's eyes. 'But he is also an asshole who should carefully consider his words. If you say anything now, Daro, you'd better say how happy you are at this wonderful news, or gods forgive me, I will turn you into a wet splat on the floor.'

Daro looked at her like he didn't understand what Ina was saying. 'Of course, I'm happy. Scared shitless, worried whether I'll be a good father, but I am happy. It doesn't mean she was right to run off like this, especially in her condition. What if something had happened to her or the baby?'

Mar moved to stand up, fists clenched, but Ina placed a hand on his shoulder, keeping him in place. The budding smile on Velka's face and the small leaves sprouting from the wooden table were enough of a sign that the conversation was heading in the right direction, and Ina pointed to the doors.

'I think it is time for round two of your conversation, and this time try to talk to each other like adults. We have enough trouble here without a silly misunderstanding causing more. Daro, so that you know, Velka was safe with me. I would sooner die than let something happen to her or the baby,' Ina said, feeling the scar on her thigh ache, reminding her how close she was to doing just that.

Velka grabbed the orc's hand and nodded to Ina. 'He knows, and you are right, but it doesn't mean I forgive you for revealing my secret.' Despite her words, the nature mage appeared happy, and Ina noticed how the massive orc sheltered his wife when they walked out of the dining room. *Thank the gods, now they can finally talk properly,* she thought, sitting down and briefly apologising to the rest of the family.

'It's no one's fault, but I don't think any of us has the capacity to discuss the recent events right now. Let's meet tomorrow after a decent breakfast.' Cyrus smiled at her, and Ina felt grateful he didn't force the issue. They were all tired, and whilst delaying the discussion wasn't ideal, mistakes from exhaustion could be fatal.

They finished the meal, and despite Mirena's objections, Ina invited Mar to her bedroom. The night was bright and crisp, making the stroll to her room relaxing and pleasant. It felt good to have his arm around her while caressing her shoulders in slow, lazy strokes.

'Ina? Today, talking to Daro, you were very… reasonable.'

'I know,'

'And how did it feel? To be a reasonable woman?' he asked, making her look up to see a mischievous smile on his lips.

Bloody tease, she thought, chuckling slightly before answering. 'It hurt, Mar. It hurt so much that I don't think I can sleep tonight.' When he burst into laughter, she playfully swatted his butt, and the dragon bent, kissing the tip of her nose.

'Well, I can take care of that, but promise me one thing. If you ever decide to carry my child, please let me be the first to know about it.'

His words silenced her, and her happiness instantly drained away. Ina saw his frown as she distanced herself from him and avoided his hands. The witch needed space before she lost the courage to tell him the truth. It hadn't mattered before, but Ina always knew she'd have to tell him, eventually. Not that tonight would have been the right time, but his words and Daro's reaction made her acutely aware she couldn't delay it any longer, even if it meant facing living her life without him.

'About that… We need to talk.'

CHAPTER FIFTEEN

A feeling of dread washed over Mar when he heard the words every man feared. He'd barely arrived, and everything was going wrong. With his thoughts racing, the Marshal followed Ina to her room, his gaze darting over her tense shoulders and downcast eyes. What could have triggered this reaction? Despite the dire circumstances, his spitfire had been warm and inviting until he mentioned Velka's pregnancy. Mar stumbled, grabbing the doorframe, fighting his transformation as a sudden flash of heat and possessiveness surged through his body at the thought of Ina being pregnant.

The thought of his little witch carrying his child was simultaneously exciting and worrying. Not once had Ina mentioned motherhood, and he suspected she didn't want children. The more he thought about it, the more idiotic his assumption felt.

'Mar? Is everything all right? Close the door, please.'

He realised he was still standing in the open doorway, staring at her like a rabbit would a fox, while Ina was already seated, gazing at him in confusion. 'Sorry, I just stumbled over my thoughts.'

Ina burrowed into the pillows, a wry smile ghosting across her lips before her expression sobered, and her whole body stiffened with worry.

Mar fell to his knees, placing his hands on his lady's lap, and blurted out as the tension grew too thick. 'If you are with child, we…' he stuttered. She sharply raised her head, making him stop, unsure what to say, trapped in his lack of experience. 'I want to say I will support you, whatever choice you make. I love you.'

'What? No. Is that what you were thinking?'

For a moment, he felt disappointment at her vehement denial, but one look at her, so fragile and determined, and all he wanted was to gather her in his arms.

However, Mar knew that would be a mistake. That was the first lesson he'd learned about Ina; never smother her with affection when she had something to say. So, bracing himself for the worst, the dragon waited, giving her the time she needed. The torturous silence made Mar's imagination run wild as Ina played with a strand of her hair, looking at the flickering fire. He was so focused on remaining calm that he nearly missed her whispered words.

'I'm barren.'

'What?'

'I'm barren. I can't give you an heir for Liath or be the lady your domain deserves. I should have told you earlier, but… initially, I didn't think it would matter, and then later, I couldn't let you go. I'm sorry for being so selfish. I know the realities of life, and I won't hold you or your family hostage to my feelings.'

'Is that why you keep pushing me away, my love?' It felt like a massive weight had been removed from his heart, and he would have laughed in relief if not for the worry etched onto her face.

'Ina, although it is not yet official, I'm no longer the scion of Liath. We may have helped the elder races emerge from the shadows, but there's no way a dragon can be the Duke of Liath. I discussed it with my father, who agreed to groom one of my many cousins for the job. The only reason it is not yet known is the slight chance he doesn't find anyone suitable, and I will have to step in.'

'Why?'

'Politics and common sense. I know, not your favourite subjects. I spoke with Ayni about being a dragon, but she was... unsure. As I wasn't born a pure-blood dragon, she doesn't know if I will inherit all of their characteristics. In short, I could live as long as a human, centuries like a dragon, or something in between, like a mage.'

The sob that escaped her lips hit his chest like a warhammer, and he gathered her into his arms, holding on tight as Ina squirmed to escape. 'I'm sorry I didn't tell you. I should have mentioned my plans, but you never seemed interested in titles or politics, and with how busy we've been lately, I simply forgot.' He stroked his lover's head, unsure what caused her tears as she curled against his chest, hitting him continuously over the heart. 'Is it because you wanted to be a mother? If this bothers you, we will ask Nerissa or travel the world to find a better healer. All I want is you, and I will do whatever it takes to make you happy.'

His words seemed to worsen the situation, and a slight panic edged into his eyes as Ina was now sobbing with her head buried in the material of his shirt. He remembered his father's words from their parting in the winter. *'Son, you have won yourself a passionate woman there, so I'll offer you one piece of advice. Shut up and listen. If a man keeps talking and his woman isn't, he'll fuck it up. So remember that and keep your hobnailed boot out of your mouth.'* As his lips quirked upward at the memory, he took the advice and sat there, stroking Ina's back till her crying subsided, and his complicated woman turned her red face towards him.

'You are such an ass, Mar. I thought I would lose you when I told you. I've been a coward and delayed telling you, knowing you'd one day leave me for a proper lady to carry on the Liath line while refusing to accept it. Then there's the situation with Ren and how difficult I can be to live with. I... I was worried this would be the last straw and that you'd resent me for stringing you along. Now you tell me it was never an issue? You're lucky the door is behind me, you arse.' The final insult came with another punch to the chest, much harder than before, but Mar just laughed, grabbing her fist and kissing it till she squirmed.

'Communication is not our forte, is it my spitfire? Now, I promise you that was my last secret, so please, my proud, beautiful woman, tell me anything you think is an obstacle to our love because I swear to you now, nothing you say will tear us apart.'

He saw her tilting her head and braced himself for the storm, only to hear, 'I want both you and Ren in my bed.'

Mar coughed and spluttered in disbelief, clasping Ina's face in his hands as he searched her expression, catching the twitch of her lips that hid an impudent smile, her eyes looking everywhere except for his searching gaze. 'Is that so? It appears something will hurt tonight, my pride or your rear, when I spank some sense into you. I would allow this trifle if I loved you less, but you are mine and mine alone. As long as you decide to stay by my side, no other man will share your touch, not even Ren.' The coy smile that blossomed on her lips relieved the tension in his shoulders, and while resting his forehead against hers, he closed his eyes and asked, 'Tell me, my love, what is so bad that you'd rather risk my anger than face your pain?'

Ina's touch was the only thing that kept him seated as he listened, shocked to the core at how the old duke used his magic to force Nerissa to do his bidding, about the geas that influenced her emotions, and about the rest of the family, who were too weak or too scared to stop it. Mar controlled himself by sheer force of will, the trembling of his fingers the only sign as he lovingly stroked Ina's hair, but he couldn't keep the admiration from the words that slipped through their bond. *I am the luckiest man alive. It's a miracle you could trust anyone after this.*

'I forgave him, Mar. I'm glad I did it when he could hear me. He took his hatred to the grave, but I'm finally free of it. There is one last thing, though I'm unsure how accurate it is. I learned about it by looking through the university's old manuscripts about chaos magic.'

'Go on, let me hear it.'

'In one of them, an overblown bombastic saga about the mage wars, it is mentioned that the sacrifice spell was used to stabilise unhinged mages.'

'Stabilise?'

'I think Cyrus may know more, or at least know where to find it, but I understood the link formed from the sacrifice spell helps keep the madness from using chaos at bay, and it's permanent. There is an issue, though. I didn't perform the sacrifice spell. I tried, but when I was on the brink of death, the magic in my soul tangled with the spell, and there's no telling what difference that made.'

'And what if this link fades or gets broken?'

'I don't know, and forgive me for saying this, but I hope I never find out. I know we haven't talked about this, but when I'm at my worst, I feel you and Ren, and it's like two lights holding back the overwhelming darkness. If the bonds ever break, I hope someone merciful will kill me like a rabid dog before I become my worst nightmare.'

Mar didn't like this discussion's direction, her words echoing his father's, especially when he knew she meant every word. With a deep sigh, he kissed her forehead. 'Well, tell me when the connection fades, and we will sleep with Ren.' Mar covered his concern with a jest, but Ina instantly sat upright.

'No, he is my friend, not a tool to be used. I don't need to sleep with him, just be close. Wait… did you just say *we?*' Mar felt tears fill his eyes when he tried to restrain his laughter, looking at her bewildered expression. It took Ina a moment to realise he was teasing her, and she grabbed his beard, pulling him down. She was trying to act angry, but the amusement in her eyes contradicted her harsh words.

'Marcach of Liath, I will hold you to your word, and you will regret it one day. Since you exposed all my secrets, are you sure you don't hide any?'

'It is not a secret, my love, rather something I've learned while talking to Ayni, something I may do for you, for us.' He saw her eyes sparkle, curiosity brightening her face.

'Well… what are you waiting for?' she asked, visibly impatient.

'Dragons can make other races live as long as they live by sharing their dragon's spark, but it is for life.'

'Like the sacrifice spell?'

'More like a *"you die, I die,"* spell. In the same way that we move our bodies in and out of the Other, dragons can connect other races to that realm using their own vital force or spark, as Ayni called it, but there is a catch, if one of us dies, the other person's life bleeds into the Other, and they die as well....'

'No!'

He hadn't stopped talking, but she had already pushed him away and jumped to her feet. 'You are a bloody idiot to even think about it. I'm a walking disaster, and neither of us expects me to live long and prosper. There's a good chance you'll live forever. Why would anyone do such a thing? And here I thought I was supposed to be the insane one in this relationship!'

The smile that curled Mar's lips was predatory. He'd expected his spitfire to react like this, and the sight of her pacing, magic swirling, dancing in a fiery aurora teased his senses. No, unless she rejected his love, he would not allow her fear to push him away this time.

Despite Ina's protests, Mar wrapped his hands around her waist and pulled her against his body, pressing a long, hungry kiss to her lips. He felt her melt under his touch, and warmth spread through his chest. The gods must have made this incredible soul for him, so passionate, so receptive, challenging him to become the best version of himself. The woman who healed the rift between his human and dragon halves, making him whole.

'It is too late, my spitfire. I cannot live without you. I choose not to live without you, and if you leave me, I will go to Nawia and tear your soul from Veles's hands myself,' he whispered, leaning down and gently biting her neck.

'You are an idiot.' Ina purred, arching under his touch.

'Maybe, but I am your idiot.' He felt the visceral need to mark her again and leaned towards her neck, grazing his teeth harder against her flesh. 'Say it, Ina... please.' He desperately needed to claim her, but would never do this against her will. His body shivered, translucent scales forming on his skin, and Ina opened her eyes, surprised by his reaction, before tilting her head to expose the soft, vulnerable flesh. He felt her magic wrapping its tendrils around him in a gentle caress as she answered his plea.

'Yes, Mar, I'm yours.'

The droplet of blood teased from her skin by his teeth tasted of magic and apple pie, lingering on his tongue like the finest of wines. Mar closed his eyes, holding onto the sensation until the soft brush of Ina's hand brought him back to reality.

'I'm sorry, I didn't mean to bite so hard,' he said, but she stopped him with one finger firmly pressed to his lips.

'Oh yes, you did, or at least your dragon instinct did. I wanted it, too. Your eyes were like molten gold, declaring your need with all your heart, and if you are ready to accept me as I am, then I don't mind the dragon in you marking me as his trophy.'

'Never as a trophy, Ina. My dragon has claimed you as his mate. You are a powerful, passionate woman, and my heart has been yours since the palace ball. The sash and daggers don't lie, my spitfire. Our bond is more than magic and grows stronger every day, so I hope your stubborn mind will accept my soul's spark one day soon.'

'You are a contrary, possessive dragon, Mar,' she said, but he was pleased to notice the shy smile on her face as she played with his beard.

'I am, but I am your dragon.'

'Yes, my love, you are definitely mine. Let's not forget I marked you first with my magic.'

He closed his eyes, inhaling this incredible woman's scent, basking in the feeling that they belonged together, as Ina ran her fingers over the hair on his chest as if petting a cat, a reminder of their first encounter, when he'd awoken from the healing with her still asleep, stroking his chest and almost purring herself. He whispered, leaning close to her ear, teeth grazing over the delicate shell. 'I will never let you go. You are mine, my beautiful chaos. Your magic chose me when your heart couldn't, and I bear your mark with pride.'

His ever-present possessiveness grew stronger, but Mar didn't try to limit it this time. Ina had accepted his mark, affirming her commitment. She might be the strongest and the most unpredictable mage on the continent, but for him, she was a wild rose, a delicate soul wrapped in deadly thorns that only bared its beauty to those she trusted, and he intended to protect her till the end of time.

The quiet voice that slipped from Ina's lips nearly broke his heart. 'I don't want to face this alone, Mar. I fear there will be no happy ending at the end of this adventure.'

Mar sighed, pressing her a little harder against his chest. 'Then we'll discuss it now. If we can organise a plan of action, it will feel a little less daunting, and whilst our friends and family are all dedicated and good at what they do, your grandfather's death means they might not have the luxury of complete clarity of thought.'

'Don't underestimate Cyrus. His skills are comparable to Jorge's, just focused on the past. He is the greatest source of knowledge in Cornovii. If Grandfather hadn't kept him close to home, I'm sure Cyrus would be running the Magical University. The man is a walking archive.'

Mar nodded before adding, 'I'm not questioning his abilities, my love, just his emotional state. If we take charge of this mess, it will allow Cyrus to focus without feeling guilty. With Verdante aggressively recruiting dissatisfied peasants and using them as spies, we need his help. I'm unsure if we can prevent another war, but we must try. Otherwise, Cornovii will be like an injured stag in the forest, its blood attracting predators from every direction.'

Ina bit her lip, thinking over his words before she raised her head, and he could see the sorrow in her eyes. 'I don't know how, Mar, especially now with the possibility of Kaian's involvement. Who can we trust with our findings, or where can we turn for help? Then there's the blight and the twisted cult of Marzanna. I asked Jorge for help, but he only offered his usual cryptic nonsense.'

'Why do you mention Kaian? We both saw how he looks at Rewan. I don't think he would betray…' Mar began, but something in Ina's face stopped him. 'You wouldn't say it if you didn't have proof. What have you found, my spitfire?'

Mar was shocked into silence as Ina shared her findings with him; the archive, its letters, and the damning wheatsheaf motif. Whoever the court spy was, he was well-placed, untouched by Kaian's purge, and had known Rewan was sending Ina from the moment the decision was made. More worrying was that the spy who disclosed their secrets could be the man sharing the king's bed, the perfect place for any assassin to be.

'I hope there is some other explanation. I like him and don't want to believe I misjudged his character so badly.' Ina looked so disturbed he felt the need to defend the king's assassin.

'There must be a reasonable explanation for this. Kaian isn't close to his family. Don't forget, he may be a renowned assassin, but that doesn't mean he'd be any good at finding spies, so please, don't convict the man on his family's actions just yet.' As hope slowly bloomed on Ina's face, Mar stroked her cheek, gently smiling.

'We still need to inform Rewan. We can't endanger his life over sentiment. I think I have a way to do it. It's best not to include Jorge, as it will probably ruin his magical predictions if I'm involved. With our bond still strong....' The guilty look Ina cast at Mar did not go unnoticed. 'I can try dream-walking and project a message to Ren. I've never done it before, but I can still try. Just not tonight, as it's a spell that needs some preparation.'

Mar welcomed the delay, picking up the subtle shudder running through the witch at the mention of dream-walking. When his hand slid over the fabric covering Ina's thigh, his fingers gripped her leg firmly, and they both winced at the pain he caused. The kisses he rained down on her neck almost drowned out the muttered apology that followed as he lifted the witch's skirts to expose the still-healing scar.

'Tell me about the necromancer, the blight, and how you ended up being hurt like this.' He forced his voice to be calm, but the sight of her injured skin awakened a wave of anger that threatened his control. His breath quickened, eyes flashing gold before Ina reached up to cup his face.

'It's all right. It doesn't hurt me anymore... much.' She gave him a reassuring smile, and the laughter in her voice eased his mind.

'Just tell me, please, and don't skip the details because you think it'll make me angry,' he said, closing his eyes, taking refuge in her touch. Ina sighed and recounted the story of her journey, from getting lost, the bandits and meeting the necromancer's puppet, then to the village, where the townsfolk tried to burn them in the tavern, before finishing with the encounter in the mamuna's hut and her fight.

Mar felt her magic coating him, easing the searing rage roiling through his body. Ina had been attacked three times, and he hadn't been there to defend her. It didn't matter if she handled each situation. They were supposed to face these dangers together.

'That's it. I will be back in a moment.' Mar wasn't sure what he planned to do, but the thought of flying over the hostile village and burning it to the ground had a distinct appeal. He attempted to leave, his anger feeding his desire to transform, only to notice Ina's magic no longer easing his anger but pinning him to the chair, and his mischievous woman slid off his lap, looking at him with an unreadable expression.

'I'm sorry, but I knew you'd overreact, so I took preventative measures.'

She may have said sorry, but her soft, alluring tone conveyed a very different message. Mar strained against the restraints, eyes blazing with a fierce golden light, the chair creaking ominously, threatening to break. Just as the dragon glanced at his hands, considering a partial transformation, Ina stepped between his legs and slowly removed her kirtle.

'I shouldn't feel this way, but your willingness to fight for me is so enticing.'

He watched her slowly undress before growling a command. 'Release me, or I swear to the gods I will rip this room apart and bend you over my knee.' The regret on her face made him smirk, but Ina withdrew her magic, and as soon as he could move, he grabbed her and placed her across his lap.

'You will never again pin me to the floor or any other object to contain my anger. I will manage it myself,' he said, lightly smacking her bottom, and when she turned and looked at him wide-eyed, he scooped her up and carried her to the bed. The sound of her chemise ripping startled them both, and Ina gasped when he cupped her breast.

'You can do whatever you want with me, my lady. If tying me down to have your pleasure entices you, I can grant you this boon, but never try to hold me back when I'm worried about your safety. You are all that matters to me, and I will incinerate anyone who tries to hurt you.'

Ina's pupils widened when she moaned softly, and Mar's breath caught when he saw it. Taking her wrists in his hand, the dragon trapped them over her head, and his anger evaporated, replaced by curiosity. His other hand drifted down to find a pool of wetness between her legs. Curious of her reaction, he lightly nipped her nipple and growled when she arched under his touch.

'I still have much to learn about you,' he whispered, before claiming her lips in a deep, possessive kiss whilst keeping his lover restrained, toying with her body.

His lips moved over her skin with light grazing kisses while his fingers teased her opening. Ina's magic roiled, surging, trying to break his hold, but Mar swatted it away. He leaned down, his breath warm as his lips caught her delicate earlobe.

'No, whatever you think you want, your body needs to yield to your dragon tonight,' he whispered in her ear when her impassioned cries heralded her climax. Mar, hard as a rock, flipped her onto her stomach, grabbed her hips and pressed his hardness to her tight, slippery entrance.

'Look at me, Ina,' he said, and when she didn't listen, he grasped a handful of her hair, forcing her to look up at him. 'I want to see the pleasure in your eyes when I take you.'

He slid inside her, savouring the ecstasy that radiated through their bond. Ina cried at the invasion of her body, arching her body to take him fully. Whatever need drove him tonight felt primal and predatory, but the soft caress of chaos on his skin told him she felt safe with it. Mar took pleasure from the look on her face while he slowly and deliberately moved inside her, forcing her to yield.

His love radiated through the bond as he savoured her moans. As if answering his thoughts, Ina closed her eyes, letting the waves of pleasure take her away, her willing submission driving him to the edge. When her second orgasm overwhelmed her, Mar lost control, his passion peaking as he exploded deep within her.

As they collapsed on the bed, his cock still nestled inside, Mar curled around her, his arms wrapped around his lover protectively. As he struggled to stay awake, satiated by their encounter, Ina spoke, her quiet voice full of wonder and surprise.

'That was strangely liberating. I never thought I would like things that way, but with you, I do.'

He inhaled her scent and wrapped the duvet around their bodies. 'Because, in your heart, you know I would never hurt you. Now sleep, my spitfire. It will be a tough day tomorrow.'

CHAPTER SIXTEEN

The clashing of swords and exuberant cheers woke Ina from a deep slumber. The shiver that ran down the witch's spine as she remembered the previous night left her smiling, even when she noticed the empty place beside her. She no longer felt a dark cloud hovering over her relationship with Mar, as if their mutual acceptance of each other had broken whatever curse had been trying to keep them apart. Ina's smile grew into a satisfied smirk. Last night, for the first time in her long, passionate sex life, she'd allowed a man to take control entirely and had enjoyed every last second.

Her throaty laugh brightened the room when her fingers touched the tender mark on her skin, left behind by the amorous dragon. Mar, or rather the beast inside him, took his piece of flesh. It thrilled her to see how happy it made him, and it surprised her how happy it made her. *Well, he earned the privilege,* she thought, trying to justify her contentment, standing on the cold stone floor with a mischievous glint in her eye. *It felt so good to trust him completely, and it was long overdue.* She couldn't help but smile, thinking about last night and how it changed her life.

Ina pulled a simple grey dress out of her wardrobe, her mind turning to the rest of the day. She almost had a plan formulated, but with her luck, something would sidetrack her efforts, and she would end up doing the complete opposite, just like yesterday. The blush that reddened her cheeks clearly showed how easily she became distracted.

When she stepped in front of the mirror, Ina used the image to concentrate on the barrier in her mind, probing and strengthening it. Hidden safely inside, the witch could feel the blazing energy of her link to Mar, brighter than ever before, and after trailing a light caress over its surface, she sought the silvery connection to Ren.

Her moonlight guardian, her family. Ina couldn't remember when she'd called him this name for the first time, but the title perfectly fitted the quiet warrior and his energy. His presence was always there, guarding her during the darkest night and soothing her soul like fresh, cool water, and Ina wished she could tell him how happy she felt. She could feel his happiness and surprise when he noticed her presence through the bond. Ina knew she shouldn't disturb him, but today would be difficult, and she needed to feel he was still there, grounding her as she readied herself for the next calamity.

A wave of steadfast affection flooded her, bringing tears to her eyes, and Ina withdrew from the connection. 'I miss you so much, my friend.'

Her whisper was drowned by the thud of the door bouncing off its hinges as Mar barged inside. 'What happened, my love? I felt a call… Why are you crying?'

'It's nothing. I just missed Ren and touched the bond. Now I miss him even more.' She chuckled, shaking her head when he rolled his eyes. 'Why did you wake up so early?'

'Too long living as a soldier, so I went to practise for a while. Then Daro came down, all grumpy and worried, wanting to share his fatherly fears, then telling me how stupid he was for not noticing things, so it took more than a few hits to the head to clear his mind. Please be patient with him when you see him. The news hit him hard, and now he's feeling paranoid after Velka told him about the mamuna's attack.'

'You mean like you are when I get a little sad missing a friend…?'

'Ina, I'm so going to spank you properly one day, and not the way you like it.'

His grizzly tone and exaggerated eye-rolling made her laugh. 'Well, we will see about that, dragon. Just remember, you can only do certain things *because* I like them.' When his facial expression changed from concerned to predatory, she realised his dragon took her words as a challenge. Ina approached him and placed her head on his chest.

Standing there, she was the perfect height to listen to his quickening heart, and she almost started purring when he began stroking her hair. 'We will have the time for this later. Now, I need you all in the library after breakfast. Could you please tell Daro to bring Velka whilst I talk to Cyrus? Yesterday left us at a disadvantage, and I'm afraid we have little time to plan the next steps.'

Mar looked down, amused by her chastising tone, before gently kissing her forehead. 'Yes, my liege, I will do it now. Please, no more brooding because you know I can feel it, and trust me when I say I don't look good crying.'

After finding a servant to ask her uncle to meet in the library, Ina slipped into the kitchen and stole a plate of pastries. When she arrived for the meeting, Cyrus took one look at her, mouth full of pie, carrying the rest like a drunk servant and sighed, far too familiar with her antics to argue over bringing food into his sacred temple of knowledge. Ina shrugged apologetically. When everyone else arrived, the food soon disappeared into hungry bellies. Once she was sure those gathered had finished eating, Ina launched into her speech.

'I have a few ideas I'd like to discuss with you. You may not like them, but please, if you could refrain from interrupting till the end, I'd appreciate your patience.' With Mar already frowning, Ina continued, her eyes asking for his understanding. 'Mar, you mentioned hearing about dissatisfied peasants being recruited for an army, and I think our rebellious nobles are likely involved in that. Cyrus and I discussed this previously, and Alsia seems the most likely location for this, so I would like you and Daro to investigate the noble in charge, especially as it's your area of expertise. If he is just a rebellious youngster, find out who is pulling his strings, but I think you're more likely to find the centre of the southern rebellion there.'

'How can you be so sure?' Daro looked at her, frowning, and she noticed he'd instinctively moved closer to Velka as soon as she mentioned the journey.

'As I said, the information I received from Cyrus points to Alsia as the source of the problem. Mar mentioned Verdante might be poaching young men to be soldiers, and I doubt that could happen without some southern lord's blessing. This also raises the question of why Verdante would incorporate them into their army. Sending them to fight their countrymen is asking for trouble.'

Understanding blossomed on Mar's face, and he nodded in agreement. 'I wouldn't. For a soldier, there is a big difference between fighting for a cause, no matter how irrational, and fighting in the ranks of a foreign army against your own country. My gut feeling says, whilst Verdante might be bankrolling this, those enlisted are in some southern lord's private army.'

Ina leaned over the table, flashing a mischievous grin. 'That brings me to the real reason for your visit there. I want you to convince whoever is in charge there to meet with the king on the fields of Alsia in two weeks. It should be enough time for the army of Cornovii to arrive.'

Cyrus, who had listened calmly to her plans, pushed his chair back and started pacing the room. 'Ina! I thought you wanted to avoid a war? People are already starving, and those farmers are fodder for the killing fields. If there's fighting, an entire generation may be lost, and the South may never recover from its food shortages if no one's left to plough. Please think about it, child. There must be another way.'

'There will be no war, uncle. Well, hopefully not. I thought about it a lot last night....' A blush tinted Ina's cheeks as she glanced at Mar before continuing. 'Whilst the southern nobles might take the gold of Verdante to finance their rebellion, they know if there were an invasion, they'd be forced to submit, even if they welcomed it. All we need to do is nip this idiocy in the bud before they are ready to fight a war that will weaken the country, allowing that invasion to happen.' Her cheeks burning, Ina desperately avoided looking at Mar, whose eyes blazed with a golden light, his lips curled in a satisfied smirk.

'And how are you going to convince them?' Cyrus looked calmer, as if he acknowledged the logic in her explanation.

'The first part should be easy enough; finding the rebel's army. I don't think they're ready to fight, or we'd already be at war. If Rewan can bring his shiny new army, with its shifters and mages, a dragon or two'—she shot Mar a querying glance, inviting him to object, but the dragon simply smiled—'breathing fire and acting like the king's loyal pets. I think that would be an awe-inspiring sight. Add in the "*crimson witch*," and that should prevent any bloodshed.'

Velka shook her head in disbelief. 'You really think that would work? Won't they fight, anyway? If the king is there, wouldn't it be their best opportunity to replace him? Or are you planning to make everyone kneel as you did at Liath?'

'I don't have that kind of power, Velka. Maybe I could with the full chaos regalia, but with the gems I have now, it would take too much death and destruction to subdue both armies. Even with the deaths of hundreds of men, I barely held them long enough last time, and we are trying to avoid a conflict, so, as much as I hate it, we'll give Rewan a chance to wave his dick around and hope for the best.' When Ina's voice faltered, Mar took over, giving his lover a sympathetic smile.

'We'll want to show them fighting the king is suicide. It's a bold plan, love. The army will need to be seen to do that, but if they are seen, it will allow the rebels to change tactics and attack differently. How are you planning on persuading Rewan? Before we left, Kaian's plan was a discrete cull of the rebel leaders. This is much bigger, unless you plan on forcing him as you did my father in Liath?'

'Killing the rebel lords was the plan to stop the assassinations. We now know they've built an army, and that changes things. I'm going to dream-walk and contact Ren. The king's dreams are warded, and Jorge has his own agenda, so Ren is the only one

I trust to inform Rewan of what's going on, especially after we found those letters. Once the king knows the situation, I know he'll agree to my plan and bring the army.'

Cyrus nearly leapt out of his seat again at the mention of dream-walking. 'It is too dangerous, Ina. How can you consider connecting your mind with his in the dream realm, knowing your mind is vulnerable to magical attacks while the spell lasts? What if he traps you in his dream? You're a talented witch, but when it comes to mind magic, even a novice could best you.'

'Uncle, it's Ren. If he wants to dig through all my dirty secrets, he can do it with my blessing. I trust him with my life.'

'Really?' Mar's grumpy statement made it clear he was not happy with the idea, but Ina was confident of her decision.

'Yes, really, Lord Marshal, and once we intimidate the southern lords, they can choose between a gruesome death and loyal servitude, then the army can return to Osterad, leaving provisions for the starving farmers.'

Daro slowly clapped till Velka elbowed his side. 'That hopefully will sort out the rebellion, but how do you intend to deal with the blight? Army provisions won't last long,' he said but stopped, hearing a knock on the door, and a moment after, Mirena came in carrying a tray of drinks.

'Do you mind if I join you?' she asked, already taking a free chair.

'Yes, please. Perfect timing, in fact. We were just about to discuss the blight. Velka has already started looking into any likely causes, and if you could offer her your expertise on medicinal plants, aunty, I'm sure she'll find the solution. In the meantime, I will look into Marzanna's cult. Something there doesn't add up, and my instincts tell me they're involved somehow. Even if they aren't, those idiots are making a difficult situation worse.'

'You want to harness my pregnant wife to work on the blight, without knowing if it can harm the baby? Have you no shame, woman?'

Daro's outburst snapped Ina's back straight, and while she looked at him blinking rapidly, she heard Mar mutter, 'Told you he was having issues.' However, before she could respond, Velka leaned over, fixing him with a furious glare.

'Daro Vakmu Yargrat, you did not just say that! I am a nature mage of the highest order, not some invalid or delicate flower. Ina needs my help, and I finally have the opportunity to prove I am more than just a glorified gardener. So sit there, do as you're told, and stop being such an arse.'

The anger in Velka's words had more to it than her reaction to the Orc's thoughtless insult, and Ina felt pity for Daro as he lowered his head, utterly dejected. When he muttered an apology, the witch reached over, laying a supportive hand on his shoulder, just as Mar asked.

'How exactly do you plan on dealing with Marzanna's cult?'

'I will travel to the temple and see what I find. Maybe she is just like the Leshy or Skarbnik and only needs a bit of friendly persuasion....'

'Alone?'

'Well, yes, you all have your tasks. This will be mine. Unless you know a better person to deal with it?'

With a mulish expression, the dragon answered. 'No.'

'Mar, I'm not asking for permission. Please, if we want to tackle all the issues, we all need to play our part. I wish I could wait for you, but we don't have the time or anyone to help.'

'No, Ina, you misunderstand. I'm not being overprotective. It is too dangerous for anyone to go alone. They already tried to kill you in Hem's tavern, and you aren't expecting me to fight the rebels alone, so how is this any different? I agree you are the only one able to face Winter's Death, but how do you expect to hold off her followers as well? Please let us think of another solution before you go into danger alone.'

'I can go with her. I know these lands, I have some useful defensive magic, and I'm a healer. Cyrus can help Velka. His knowledge of healing plants is just as good, if not better, than mine.' Mirena, quiet so far, suddenly joined the conversation, and despite her confusion, Ina jumped at her aunt's offer.

'Thank you, Mirena. Now, is there anything else I'm forgetting?' Mar still didn't look happy, and Ina began losing her temper. 'Lord Marshal, I know I'm trying to avoid using death to fuel my magic, but I'm not so naïve as to refuse to defend myself on principle. We will be fine.'

'Ina, why can't you just humour me for once?' Mar pleaded, exasperation colouring his voice. Ina glared at him, ready to argue her point, when Daro broke the tense silence.

'Well, now you know how it feels.' His crossed arms and tight lips radiated frustrated anger, and she couldn't blame him after Velka scolded him like a child in front of everyone. The words he'd thrown in Mar's face were so hilarious she couldn't help but laugh, and soon everyone joined in as the tension dissipated.

'I think that's all we need to discuss for now. Mar, Daro, if you could organise yourselves for the journey. If you need help, the chamberlain will happily lend his assistance. Velka, if you want to find a space to set up your workshop, Cyrus can advise you. I'll have one last look for any evidence left behind from grandfather's immolation, then get ready to leave.' Realising there was one more thing, Ina suddenly exclaimed. 'Oh! Uncle Cyrus, I nearly forgot. Can you show me the spell matrix for dream-walking before tonight? And Mirena, I know it's a lot to ask, but could you be ready to go by morning?' When her aunt nodded, Ina pushed her chair back and bowed lightly before playfully ruffling Mar's hair.

'I will go to Grandfather's room. Mar, please don't look so angry. It is a good plan, and you know it,' she said as the rest of their group left the library. As the room emptied of everyone except her and the disgruntled dragon, Ina turned with a heavy sigh, heading to the door. If he was going to be unreasonable and not listen to her argument, so be it. Before she could take two steps, Mar caught her, the cage of his arms preventing any thought of escape.

'Why can't you wait till I come back from Alsia? This stubbornness will get you killed one day, woman. You are like a stray cat balancing on the roof's edge who thinks she has nine lives, forgetting that there is a dragon who refuses to live without you. There are too many things we don't know, my love.' His voice sent a shiver down her spine, the promise in his words frightening her, but Mar hadn't finished yet. 'No, I can see in your eyes you aren't going to listen. At least promise me you will be careful and won't charge into danger. Just see what is going on there and come back to me. Use our bond, fuck it, use Ren's if you must, just… promise me you'll be careful.' He bent down, and even as she tried to push him away, Ina felt the familiar touch of dragon scales forming over his body.

'You crazy, overgrown lizard. I'm not a bloody cat, and I've already promised to be careful. Anyone would think I want to get into trouble. Now calm down before you transform and destroy my uncle's library. He'd never forgive you for such blasphemy. Please trust me. I am a capable woman, a powerful mage, and I have no intention of meeting Veles anytime soon. Now, will you let me work? We still need to capture whoever killed Grandfather, not to mention I have a diagram to draw, and we both know I'm no good at order magic.'

Mar stepped away, turning his head to the side, but she knew he was trying to rein in his frustration. 'Can't you see why I'm worried? You've been attacked three times already, and that was before they knew why you were here. Even your luck has its limits, Striga.'

The sigh that escaped Ina's lips sounded so dejected Mar's lips curled to snarl. 'I'm sorry, Mar. I know you don't like it, but my decision has been made. I don't want to argue with you.'

'Then don't,' he snapped, stalking out of the library, leaving the witch biting back curses at his oafish statement.

After taking samples from her grandfather's room, Ina went to her uncle's workshop, but focusing on the tests she needed to carry out proved impossible. That bloody possessive, infuriating dragon kept intruding into her thoughts. Mar was intelligent and should have understood that she was just as worried about his mission to Alsia, but would never stop him from heading into danger. Shouldn't that go both ways? Hadn't he learned she could look after herself?

'Well, he'll have to learn to live with it,' she said, turning back to the iridescent residue on the spoon. Her uncle's alchemic workshop was well-equipped and allowed her to perform analyses she wouldn't usually be able to. Yet no matter how hard she tried, she couldn't find any trace of magic or poisonous plants. All she learned when extracting the components was that one of them turned purple while mixed with water, while another burned with a green flame similar to basilisk venom, which should be impossible as they'd been wiped out in Cornovii decades ago. Were there any other creatures with such deadly venom?

Ina asked Cyrus for any books on poisonous creatures and animals, then spent a frustrating hour unable to find any helpful information. *If only I could ask Kaian. He was far too good an assassin not to know about such things.* As soon as the thought crossed her mind, Ina exhaled and hid her face in her hands.

'If any of you interfering gods are watching, please don't make him my enemy. I have few friends, and I really like this one.' She uttered the silent plea with little hope, then opened the book on the section on northern creatures. There was a picture of a lizard with the title *Basiliscus Parvulus*. The description left Ina cold. This reptile, a denizen of the northern marshes, was a mutation of the basilisk, unable to turn victims to stone, but whose bite caused its victims to bleed from all their orifices. This matched the sudden and rather gruesome death of her grandfather. Moreover, the boiled venom served in food would create paranoia and speed the ageing process before finally stopping the heart or causing bleeding in the brain.

Cyrus had mentioned his father changing in recent years, and Ina believed his sudden involvement in the rebellion, bizarre behaviour, and magical theories were the response of slow, deliberate poisoning and woe to her; all traces pointed north, the same place the scion of Water Horse House controlled.

'Kaian, what the hell is going on up there? Did your family send the assassin alchemist here?'

There was nothing more to find, and now she'd have to talk to Ren and somehow deliver this devastating news to Rewan. But how could she tell the king that the man he loved could be the very reason for his troubles?

CHAPTER SEVENTEEN

Ever since Jorge had given him the cryptic message about trusting his dreams, Ren hadn't managed a single good night's sleep, and those he could remember were full of blood and roses. Were they supposed to mean something? This was why he avoided mages. Why give you a simple explanation when a complicated one could keep you under their control?

It didn't help when, during sparring, there had been a sharp tug, deep inside, the bond with Ina flaring into life with longing and sadness. It was so strong he'd dropped to one knee, nearly getting skewered by a pupil for his trouble, and had to fight the urge to gallop to the South to find his friend. Instead, he settled for heading home and packing a bag, ready for the call to arms.

Her silence made it clear Ayni wasn't happy with his preparations, but Ren couldn't explain the feelings churning inside.

'You are worried about Ina.' It was more a statement than a question, but all he could offer was an apologetic smile. Her words did, however, help settle his mind.

'Yes, I don't know what's wrong, but the bond between us filled with such sadness, it… left me unsettled, and this message from Jorge… something has changed and I… I'm sorry. I don't want to upset you.'

Ren watched Ayni sigh, not revealing her emotions. The dragoness moved close and, reaching up, slowly stroked her fingers over his tense shoulders.

'Rest. We can't do anything about it now, but if you still feel like this tomorrow, I will fly to Thorn and drag your little witch back here, even if I have to fight Mar to do it. I might even refrain from biting her.'

Her statement brought a smile to his face, and Ren took her hand, kissing the inside of her palm. 'I don't deserve you, my lady, but I'm grateful for every moment you spend with me. I love you, Ayni.' The depth of his feelings for Ayni still surprised him in their intensity, and he would be eternally grateful for the happiness he never thought would be his in this lifetime.

'I know,' she said with a smile, pushing him towards the bedroom, 'but you have to rest now, or I will start worrying.'

After taking Ayni's advice, Ren spent several hours fruitlessly trying to sleep. The moon had risen and was well on its way to meeting the horizon when the quiet warrior felt his bond with Ina come to life, pulsing in his chest. The urge to sleep was overwhelming, reminding Ren of Jorge's cryptic command.

Was this connected? Determined to find out, he slowed his breathing, attempting to use a relaxation technique he'd learnt as a child. Initially, nothing happened, and Ren spent considerable time staring at the inside of his eyelids, but when his body relaxed, he heard the one voice he would recognise anywhere, even the darkest pits of Nawia.

'Ren, thank the gods, that was too much like my university days. Ugh, I hate order spells. Can you hear me clearly?'

'My lady, what is going on?' he replied, amusement at Ina's exasperation in his tone.

'We need to talk about the war. Gods, I missed you so much. Do you know Velka is pregnant?'

Chaotic as usual, Ina emerged from the mist, and he felt her ghostly arms wrapping around his torso, almost tackling him into a hug.

'No, I didn't know and missed you, too. What is it? Was that the reason you felt so sad this morning? Did you learn how to talk using the bond?'

'No, it is a dream-walking spell, and I have little time. It took most of my strength to help you sleep, so I must be brief. I need you to talk to Rewan and prepare the army.'

'So the war is certain.'

'No, but I need Rewan to bring the troops to the fields of Alsia in two weeks, all in their finest armour, with mages and shifters. I need it all, Ren, with full fanfare. I also have a favour to ask. Please convince Ayni to come as a dragon. I know it sounds strange, but I want to intimidate the rebels into submission and to do this, they have to see Rewan, not as a king barely holding onto power, but as a leader who commands dragons, as well as a chaos mage. Please convince the king and Ayni that this is a good idea. Oh, and bring as many supplies as the soldiers can carry. People are starving here, which is the main reason for the unrest.'

Ren looked around at the images appearing before him. Ina's thoughts, whilst disorganised, still showed the problems she faced. 'I will persuade the king to lead his army; he'll probably jump at the chance. Don't worry about Ayni. If I go, she'll join me and likely enjoy the opportunity to stretch her wings. The mages will be more challenging. Since Nerissa turned up, the university has been locked down, with not even rumours escaping its walls. Why do I have the feeling you're involved?'

'I have no idea why you'd think that… however, I might have a few thoughts on the matter. Unfortunately, I don't have time to explain. Right now, there is one more thing to deal with. Gods, this is difficult.'

Ren looked at her projection, pacing pensively, and although more translucent than earlier, he saw the worry on her face. 'I will do what needs to be done. Just tell me, my lady.'

Ina stopped and looked at him, and he saw her eyes darken in sadness. 'Kaian, he may be involved. I found letters from his elders implicating his household in the palace coup and the southern rebellion. The old duke was poisoned using venom from a creature indigenous to the northern swamps. Then his body was incinerated using a trick northern necromancers used to extort money from distressed citizens to calm the risen in their graves.'

She looked at him, biting her lip to stem the worry. 'So many connections to the north, and the Water Horse House rules there. Although I have nothing directly pointing to Kaian, I can't ignore those findings, especially with someone feeding the rebels Rewan's secrets.'

Now he understood her distress and hesitation. 'Ina, if Kaian wanted to assassinate the king, he's had plenty of opportunities. He shares the king's bed and has always protected Rewan. I will talk to Rewan, but it's difficult to believe Kaian is the spy at court.'

'Ren, I like him too, and I like him a lot, but who knows what hold his elders have over him? Maybe Rewan is still alive because Kaian complies with their requests. I don't know, but you must prove his guilt or innocence because we can't have a spy in Rewan's bed, even if it breaks his heart. Use truth-seekers if you must. Jorge or Nerissa can help, although I would prefer you didn't inform Jorge just yet.'

'I will speak with the king and see what he says. I will sort it out, my lady, and I'm glad I will see you in two weeks.' He saw the deep crease between her eyebrows soften, and her ghostly fingers brushed his cheek. He couldn't feel the touch, as Ina's figure was almost entirely translucent, and her voice faded as she spoke.

'Ren, once this ends, I will find a way to release you from our bond. You deserve to be free without being affected by my moods and problems.'

There was so much sadness in her voice, but Ren barely paid attention. The thought of losing her presence left him feeling an incredible sense of loss. 'Ina, don't you dare! Don't you bloody dare. You promised I would be your guardian. Have I failed so badly that you'd push me away?' Her figure faded away before she could answer, leaving him wide awake, clutching his chest to reassure himself the woman who'd helped change his life so much was still there.

With Mar and Daro away on official business, Ren was often called to brief the council on state security. The meetings were dry affairs, with indolent, prejudiced aristocrats questioning his every decision. Today was no different, and the Acting-Marshal couldn't wait for the meeting to be over so he could request a private audience with the king.

'Sir, if I might ask for a moment of your time?' he asked when Rewan finally adjourned the meeting.

'Yes, of course. Wait for me in my office, Sa'Ren.' Rewan waved Ren off as he continued his conversation with the chancellor, shrugging off a look of exhaustion as he did, not noticing the respectful bow offered by the quiet warrior.

Ren could barely contain himself by the time Rewan walked into his office, heading straight for a carafe of wine.

'Tell me you have good news. Is my army ready? Kaian and Gruff's spies mentioned suspicious activity at the Verdante border. We can't wait much longer to confront that threat.'

'The army is as ready as it can be given how long we've had. As for the rest, that's what I'm here to discuss. I've spoken with Ina....'

'Is she back? Has she finished her investigation already? Why isn't she here?' The desperate hope in the king's voice left Ren feeling increasingly uncomfortable.

'Your Majesty, in answer to your first question, no, the Lady Ina has not returned. She has, however, contacted me via arcane means and asked me to convey a solution to the rebellion, as well as some rather unsettling news.'

After taking a deep draft of his wine, Rewan took a moment to control himself before turning back to his visitor. 'Yes, sorry, the lack of sleep recently has left me a little frazzled. Please go on with the royal witch's message.'

As Ren revealed Ina's plans, the king's eyebrows rose sharply, his mind working through the implications and problems until, at last, he nodded. 'That could work. Yes, that could actually work, but....' Turning his sharp, assessing gaze on the warrior, the king asked, 'Will you be ready? Travelling to the southern border with the pageantry she wants will take at least a week. The mages may be able to assist with the provisions, which could save some time, but it's still a difficult task. Hmm, yes, talk to Jorge about it, or better yet, Arun, and tell them I would consider it a personal favour. Otherwise, he'll dismiss you and tell you his alumni are not pack mules.'

'Yes, Your Majesty. There is one other thing I need to talk about.' Ren hesitated, but Rewan waved him off with a slight huff.

'Then talk. With all these preparations, we have no time to dally.'

'Ina thinks she's discovered a link to the court spy, or at least a definite connection to the southern rebellion, and it involves Lord Kaian's household.' The colour drained from Rewan's face at Ren's words, and the warrior quietly admired the determination that kept the king upright at the possibility of a loved one's betrayal.

'Continue, but be mindful of your accusations.'

'After confronting the Duke of Thorn, Ina searched his correspondence and discovered letters from the elders, or I should say, the current head of the Water Horse House supporting the palace coup and the southern rebellion. The poison used to murder the duke originated in the north, as well as the method used to destroy the body. We know information is leaking from the court, and I have to agree with Ina as much as it pains me. The assassin master has access to everything Your Majesty does or thinks.'

'Do you have substantive evidence of Kaian's involvement? Please, Ren, I need to know.' The anguish in the king's voice revealed the depth of the monarch's pain at the potential betrayal.

'No, nothing substantive. That's why I'm here instead of talking directly to Jorge. Ina also wants to believe Kaian is innocent, just a pawn in his clan's machinations, and not the person betraying you, but she needed you to be aware of the possibility.'

'I will ask Gruff to look into it, Sa'Ren. Thank you for the warning. It took courage to breach this subject to the man who could order your death. Prepare the army and not a word about Ina's scheme. Let all believe we are heading for war while I attend to my love life and the kingdom's future.'

Ren's bow, performed in the style of Imperial Yanwo, showed his deep respect for the king that put duty before his feelings. 'I see why Ina considers you a friend. If it helps, I don't believe Lord Kaian is involved, and he deserves the benefit of the doubt, just as you deserve love. I will take my leave, Your Majesty. I will inform the dwarven artisans that you require your armour fitting as soon as possible.'

'Thank you, and if you speak with Ina, tell her I appreciate her giving Kaian a chance to explain.'

Rurik looked at the dying flames in the small fireplace, reminiscent of Ina's wild hair. Despite his best efforts, the witch had yet to take the last piece of chaos regalia, the circlet that would turn her from an extraordinary mage into a force of nature. He could almost see luck twisting around her even as he piled problem after problem into her lap; the nobles, Verdante, and even a province-wide blight, but instead of reaching for the easy option, she harnessed the dragon, Velka and her family to find a solution.

He should have foreseen it, especially after Liath, when she showed such inventive thinking to solve the conflict. Instead, he focused on inciting the southern nobles, losing his foothold in both the Magical University and Osterad. A soft knock at the door diverted his attention from his plans, and as soon as he answered, a tall young man in dark robes walked into the room.

'Master Rurik, I've just returned from Osterad. I have news you may find interesting.'

Rurik instantly smoothed his features into a mask of polite interest. He'd learned long ago that mages must flaunt their self-importance to be useful. 'Ah, Master Raleigh, long time no see. How are things in our noble school? Any news on recruitment of our compatriots?'

'No, I'm afraid there's been a setback at the university. The arch-healer returned to the halls, and since that moment, truth-seekers have been interrogating anyone they can get their hands on. Several of our members managed to flee, but far too many were taken away. Arun even excised the magic of those deemed guilty of crimes against the ancient laws.'

I should have killed her when the duke failed to recruit her to our cause, but destroying such talent is unforgivable. Shame she turned against us, he thought, rubbing his neck when tension tightened his muscles into a knot. 'Does the king know?'

'No, Master Arun is trying to avoid a scandal, and so far, both he and the judicial mage have kept this a secret from the Court.'

'Well, at least those fools have enough sense not to expose our plans to the sheep. Did they suspect you, Raleigh?'

'No, Master. I had been sent on a mission by the dean before the purge.'

'Good, go back to Osterad, but don't announce your return and report any developments at the Magical Council. Do you know how to communicate via cadavers?'

'Yes, Master, but I don't have enough magic....'

'I will give you a communication crystal that should solve the issue. Our vision will come true as long as the chaos mage dons the regalia.' Rurik kept his frustration at Arun from his voice, even as he cursed the man's lack of foresight. Once confronted with such a widespread movement, he'd been sure the old battle mage would understand his vision. A world where no one would ever be enslaved again, where all monarchs answered to a power that protected the innocent and destroyed the guilty; one that could challenge the gods themselves.

'But why her, Master? I met the woman. She is just a witch, not worthy of ruling us. She keeps rejecting her magic, and even if you force her to wear the regalia, what guarantee do we have that she won't turn against us?' The young necromancer's outburst brought a benevolent smile to Rurik's lips.

'Then you didn't encounter her sense of justice? Once we reach our goal, I will gratefully stand before her as she judges my crimes and likely step into the halls of Nawia with a smile on my face.' The shock on Raleigh's face was evident, but it felt good to talk about his plans, even the part his mother didn't know, and Rurik allowed himself a minor indiscretion.

'When I was your age, Master Raleigh, I wasn't a mage, but a slave on the docks of Dancik. I didn't know about my talent or my parents, knowing only the stroke of the whip, but one day, everything changed. I lost my only friend in this world and brought him back from Nawia, only to realise I'd just animated his corpse. Do you know what the citizens of the free cities do to mages who commit such crimes? They are drowned in the bay to appease the sea and to prevent interference from any judicial mage.'

'What does that have to do with Ina and the chaos regalia? I thought you wanted mages to rule the world. Is this just for revenge, Master Rurik?'

'No, Raleigh. Revenge is useless and accomplishes nothing, though I... I do admit to those feelings once. I wanted to kill them all, to kill the king who defiled my mother, to see the life drain from the eyes of the woman who sold an innocent child to avoid the shame and guilt, but then I met Ina. A mage who bowed to no one, able to manipulate life itself. It was a profound moment.' Rurik smiled, remembering their first meeting in the tavern when Velka brought him to show off their love, and what he learned that day changed his life forever.

'I still don't understand. How does that help us? She listens to no one. Even if you put her on the throne, she won't listen.' The younger man was visibly anxious, pacing around the room, making Rurik sigh.

'Maybe you are too young to understand, but it is not about power. Ina will never be swayed from what is right, protecting everyone with unlimited magic. She will be above kings, above laws. Do you know how she ended up in exile? To protect the sacred boar, for that innocent animal, Ina stood before the king and defied him, and from that day forth, he was known as Limp Dick Roda. Even now, she is a force to be reckoned with, forging her path despite my manipulations. I'm in awe of what this woman can do. With her leading the way, there will be no child slaves, no senseless executions of mages, and no chained shifters tortured for the entertainment of the drow nobility. Whatever she touches is transformed. She is a true chaos archmage, and for this, I'm ready to sacrifice myself, to sacrifice all of us for her ascension.' Voice raised in a fanatical zeal, Rurik slammed his fist onto the table, the young necromancer in front of him looking on in horror.

'You are insane. I thought you did this for us, not for her. How will this make magic rule the world if you put all the power in the hands of that insane bitch?'

'Be mindful of your words, Raleigh. Do you want to be the one to rule the world? You all wanted that, and that's why you were so easy to manipulate, but no matter. Whether or not you want to, you will serve me. You are too deeply involved to step away from this path.' Rurik's hand shot forward, grasping his companion's neck, his dark gaze sinking into the young man's mind, forging a geas that not even death could break. His victim writhed in agony, the grey strands of the spell entwining with his soul, before finally hanging limply in the necromancer's grasp as the magic dissipated.

'Go now. You have a task to fulfil. Use the communication crystal if you hear anything important, and if you want to find me in person, I will be in Alsia.' His victim sagged to the floor, then slowly crawled away, sobbing in despair.

CHAPTER EIGHTEEN

I t seemed Mar decided Ina's desire not to argue could be accomplished by not talking altogether. That, coupled with Daro's resentful glances, drove the witch to distraction. After performing the dream-walking spell, Ina was exhausted. Cyrus patiently talked her through the complex pattern, but that didn't stop the mistakes, the misfiring spellwork, nor the tremendous drain on her energy once she finally made contact. If not for their bond, Ina doubted she could have talked to Ren at all, which didn't help her mood. With Mar silently standing guard, watching each mistake and leaving when the spell ended, her frustration and anger grew.

Her mood didn't improve when, too tired to undress, Ina collapsed alone in her bed. The witch couldn't help but feel betrayed by Mar's lack of understanding when the sound of dragon wings propelling her lover into the night sky chased her mind into slumber. As conscious thought fled, dreams of desolation, dying forests, swirling desert sands, and bleached bones tormented her sleep, until finally, Ina woke drenched in a cold sweat, with chaos magic swirling and sparking over her arms. Still not fully awake, she barely registered an almost scorching heat that surrounded her with a feeling of safety, calming her racing heart, and the red vortex slowly disappeared. As she slipped slowly back to sleep, the heat beneath her hand became a familiar, muscular, hairy chest.

'Sleep, my love; it is just a bad dream. I am here for you. I will always be there for you.'

It was barely a whisper, but the dragon's reassuring scent and slow, steady heartbeat chased away the terrors. Ina embraced him tightly, lulled back to sleep by the loving embrace. However, as the dawn sun woke the witch, she was alone, leaving her unsure if it had all been a dream.

The longer she reflected on the evening's events, the more uncertain she became until, lost in thought, Ina found herself in the stables with her orein. When laughter rang out from the men as they prepared for their journey in the armoury, Ina's anger returned in full force. *Fine! If you want to throw a tantrum, so be it*, she thought, tightening her mount's girth with such force that Zjawa turned to nip her shoulder.

'How can one man be so annoying? You give him your heart, your body. I even submitted to the sexy damn beast, and then he does this? Giving me the silent treatment because I didn't listen to his illustrious advice? What an ass.' Ina continued to ready her mount, banging and crashing around the stable as she ranted.

With everyone busy elsewhere, Ina relaxed, venting her resentment to the strange mount while packing for the journey. 'He knows I don't have the time to sit on my arse and wait for the mighty Marcach to help his little damsel. I am a bloody chaos mage. What can they do to me now when I have my magic to protect my body and a shield to protect my mind? Pray that I trip and stab myself or spray goat's blood in my face?'

'Ina, why are you shouting at the horse?'

The voice behind her startled her, and both Ina and Zjawa turned to look at her aunt with equally baffled expressions. 'I was not shouting at her. We were talking,' Ina said, attempting to explain the situation.

'It doesn't make it any less strange whether you were talking or shouting at the animal. Anyway, are you ready? You mentioned you wanted to depart early.'

'Yes, I am.' Ina pointed to her outfit and packed bags. Her aunt gave her a quick, assessing once over and chuckled.

'Are you sure you won't try to rob someone on the journey, carrying a sword like a brigand?'

The witch looked down at herself and smiled. The sturdy brown leather trousers and vest she had chosen for the journey, together with a linen shirt and thick wool cloak, didn't announce her occupation or status. The sword Ina attached to the saddle and daggers on her belt were more suited to adventurers or free company fighters than a royal mage. The only thing she couldn't hide was her flaming copper hair, but Ina tied it in a warrior braid, hoping it would be enough to mislead the casual observer. 'I look perfect for the job I'm going to do. Let's go before Mar decides he wants to be an even bigger arsehole and tries to stop me from going anywhere.'

'Don't be too harsh on him, my dear. He is a man who is worried and helpless to protect you.'

'I know, but how he expresses his worry is simply infuriating.'

Her aunt's laugh filled the stables before she jumped onto her horse. 'Come, Ina. We have quite the distance to cover, and I want to spend tonight in an inn before we have to face the volkhv or his followers.'

The sigh Ina gave in reply was deep and sad as she mounted her orein to follow her aunt to the gates. *He didn't even come to say goodbye,* she thought, as they left the protection of the city walls, heading, for the moment, towards Alsia. The reminder of Mar's destination further soured the witch's mood, and she wished the crossroads would appear before she grew too maudlin.

A thundering noise startled Ina from her thoughts, the sound crystallising into the heavy beat of galloping warhorses, and Ina turned her head to see two riders approaching them at breakneck speed, the massive black warhorse of Liath leading the charge. A brief moment of joy seized the witch's heart, then quickly soured as Mar caught up, grabbing Zjawa's bridle as Woron wheeled to face the two women.

'You will not stop me, you lizard-brained idiot. It is my job….' Ready to blister his ears with righteous indignation, Ina's words were silenced when Mar reached out and plucked her from the saddle, crushing her lips in a deep, possessive kiss. Longing, love and respect flashed through their bond, overwhelming her senses as she returned it passionately.

As the kiss ended, Mar rested his head against Ina's, growling out the only words he could manage. 'Promise me you will be careful, that you won't hesitate to eliminate anyone who poses even a hint of a threat, and won't willingly walk into danger alone.'

Ina stroked his bearded face and kissed him once more in gentle parting before climbing back onto Zjawa's saddle. 'I will be fine, trust me a little.' She tried to reassure him with a smile, but Mar squeezed her hand, giving her a determined scowl.

'I trust you, but also know you. The real you, not the brazen witch you want people to see. You would rescue the downtrodden and helpless, even if you put yourself in danger. So promise me you will prioritise your safety because you, my lady, hold this dragon's heart in your hands.'

Ina shook her head, trying to pull away, but he didn't let go until she gave him her word, his reluctance clear as her hand slowly slipped from his grasp. With a deep bow and a blown kiss, Mar turned his horse and waited beside Daro as Ina slowly rode away.

'Remember, Ina, you promised. And with the gods standing as witnesses, if you get yourself killed, I will go to Nawia and wrestle Veles for your soul.'

Mirena frowned at such blasphemy, but Mar's brazen words brought a smile to Ina's face. It might not be the perfect goodbye, but it was one that any woman would want when embarking on a dangerous mission.

'Be safe, Mar. And remember, if anything happens to you, I will tear Nawia apart to bring you back, just to beat you senseless for upsetting me,' she said with a laugh, pushing Zjawa into a trot, leaving the men behind, coughing and laughing at her words.

The snort that came from Daro was full of mockery. 'Dragon's heart? More like your bollocks, you sap. If you're so worried, why did you let her go? You should have disciplined your woman.'

'And that's from the orc who was just brow-beaten into packing spare undergarments by a pregnant nature mage.' Mar's voice was sarcastic, but his burning gaze never once left Ina as she disappeared into the distance.

Despite her cheeks announcing to the world what had just happened, the journey to their first stop was uneventful, leaving Ina plenty of time to ponder the next steps of their expedition. As her aunt predicted, they arrived at a small village just before sunset and easily procured two rooms for the night. As the tired witch was getting ready for bed, Mirena came to her room with two steaming mugs of herbal tea and sat down to talk.

'Ina, I didn't ask before, but I feel I should now that we're alone. What is going on between you and the scion of House Liath? I know you have shared a bed and bonded after performing the sacrifice spell. After hearing about it, your grandfather banned the bards from the city for months. However, there is something different, something deeper than a spell-binding here. It's not every day someone offers to fight Veles for your soul.'

Ina sipped her tea, wincing at the overwhelming taste of honey. Mirena's habit of over-sweetening her drinks till you couldn't identify the flavour was a running joke in the Thorn family. 'It is difficult to describe, but Mar and Ren's presence tempers the desire to stop controlling my magic. I was always told to never let go and never give in, that the strange desires inside me were wrong and would cause nothing but pain to my loved ones. All because chaos mages, forced to fight wars, were overwhelmed by the tide of death and destruction, then went mad, wiping out friends and foes—a scourge of the battlefield. The rush of power that comes from destruction is so alluring and addictive. I felt that captivating call at Liath, but Mar and Ren were there, and countless lives were saved as their love held back the insatiable hunger for more power.' Ina gave Mirena a shy smile, unsure why her aunt watched her so avidly.

'I cast the sacrifice spell....' Ina winced, feeling guilty for not being entirely truthful about the spell she'd cast. 'Simply because I had no choice. Mar, my safe passage back to Osterad, was dying, so I did what needed to be done. It was the same with Ren, though I was given less choice then. Somehow, from this, affection grew between us, especially with Mar. There was something, a golden spark, that called to me more than Ren's quiet care. I can't take all the credit from Mar, though. That stubborn dragon fought for our love so fiercely that I'm sure he's the reason that old goat's geas failed.' When Ina looked over at Mirena this time, it was impossible to decipher her expression. 'You shouldn't worry about him fighting Veles. I doubt the god of the underworld is less able than the Leshy or Skarbnik at handling himself.'

'Ina, don't joke about this so casually. Your attitude to the gods will one day bring you bad luck, and I hope you never have to face Veles for your impertinence. They may favour you now, but there will be a price for such disrespect.' Mirena paused, sipping her tea. 'Now, do you have any plans to deal with the cult of Marzanna?'

The witch smiled with a mischievous glint in her eyes. 'How do you think I got this peculiar mount of mine? She was a gift from Skarbnik for helping a crippled grandfather, making the Lord of Liath carry his brushwood to a nonexistent cottage. As for the Leshy, he taught me more about potion-making than anyone at the University. The old gods treat me like a plaything for their entertainment, and as I can't do anything about it, I give as good as I get. That is what I am counting on now. I have no plans to deal with Marzanna, but I believe I can reason with her if she's only killing the crops to entertain herself at the peasant's expense. Or I will appease her if there is something she needs to calm her wrath. If not, at least we will know what we are dealing with.'

'That is insanity, child. I wish your dragon had stopped you before we came on this trip. Even if you can find her, she will freeze you with one breath for your insolence. How do you plan on talking with Winter's Death?'

'The same way I'm talking to you. Aunty, I don't know why, but the gods are seeking me out. Maybe they're bored or simply using me, but being frightened helps no one.' Mirena's words echoed Ina's worries too closely, but now wasn't the time or place to voice them. 'Please don't upset yourself over this. I'm more worried about those exploiting the situation and the peasants they've tricked than the goddess. We will fix what we can, and hopefully, Velka will find how to bring spring back to the South.'

Ina wondered why Mirena supported her plan if she had so many doubts about it, but it was late, and the witch was too tired to argue. At this point, it was more important to get some sleep, so she'd worry about it tomorrow. Exhaustion must have been catching up with the witch as a sudden wave of dizziness forced her to drop her mug on the table, and Ina turned to her aunt in embarrassment.

'Can we discuss this tomorrow? I am tired and likely not making much sense, but I promise I will make my plan work. Besides, this syrupy goodness made me drowsy. I should get some sleep.'

'It is just a few sleeping herbs. Marcach mentioned you had a nightmare and asked me to help you sleep tonight,' her aunt said, and Ina couldn't help but roll her eyes. That explained why she could barely keep her eyes open.

'Never do that again. What if someone attacks us at night?' she said, shaking her head and letting her aunt lead her to bed and tuck her in like a toddler.

'I bought enough beer for the locals to ensure no one will be sober enough to attack. Sleep, child, you need it,' she said, closing the door behind her.

No, they will come for more money. You flaunt your wealth, and now they will come for more because there is no easier job than robbing two defenceless women. Ina tried to get out of bed, but her limbs and thoughts were sluggish, and soon, despite her desperate attempts, the witch drifted into a dark, dreamless sleep.

It was well past midnight when Rurik noticed that two rough-looking men had quietly broken into the room. They must have noticed the women's arrival at the inn, and greed overtook all sensible thought when they saw a large green pulsating gem on the younger female's finger.

'Is she sleeping?'

'Yes, the tavern wench told me the other woman brewed two sleeping draughts before providing beer for the entire village.'

'Let's grab the ring and go. Only mages are brave enough to flaunt magical stones, so we need to be quick, or we'll miss our chance. That black robe in Alsia pays well for magical stones.' The younger of the two men nodded, moving forward silently and reaching for Ina's ring, only to gasp in pain as his fingers touched the green gem. Magic erupted from the peridot, wrapping itself around the terrified thief's hand, and the sleeping woman's eyes snapped open, glowing with the same light that pulsated in her ring. As the magic holding him captive moved up his arms, the thief screamed in anguish as the life was drawn from his body. Suddenly, a powerful grip seized the scruff of his neck and dragged him from the deadly magic.

'Imbecile, do not touch what you cannot comprehend,' said a cold, dry voice, and the thief stared at the tall hooded figure that saved his life. Scrambling backwards, the brigand rushed out of the room, barely noticing the caved-in head of his lifeless companion. With a nonchalant flick of the wrist, the robed figure animated the body, which ripped off its shirt and cleaned up the evidence of its own demise as the hooded man walked over to Ina's glowing form.

'You should be more careful. If I wasn't on my way to Alsia, those sleeping herbs could have been your end. What was that woman thinking?' He flinched when a ribbon of chaos touched his bare skin and held his hand over the glowing stone on her hand, muttering a spell in an old dead language. As the glow slowly faded and the swirling chaos receded, Ina's eyes closed, and a sigh escaped her lips.

'The regalia defended you, my beautiful chaos,' he said, covering her with a blanket. The woman in front of him looked so fragile. The tiny wrinkle between her eyebrows showed a person who cared too deeply, yet she was filled with a power that could decimate a kingdom.

However, to reverse the curse he'd cast on the land, she would need more, and he hoped the clues he left in Marzanna's temple would encourage her to complete the regalia. If this wasn't enough, the southern nobles were ready to take action, and as soon as Cornovii's army arrived, it would trigger Verdante's response. *You will need a lot of power to subdue them all. Once that happens, they will learn who the true ruler of Warenga is, and I will be there, pointing out the injustices your new power can redress,* he thought, absentmindedly stroking Ina's cheek.

His mother was wrong, advising him to kill the dragon. Ina was emotionally bound to this fierce male, and his suddenly awakened heritage gave Rurik another advantage if he played it wisely. Marcach already loved her, and if Rurik pushed him in the right direction, he could gift her eternal life, or at least a greatly enhanced lifetime.

The thought of an eternal sorceress and her consort filled the necromancer with a renewed sense of purpose. To see that vision fulfilled would make the sacrifices, the deaths—even his own—worthwhile. Rurik brushed the stray hair from Ina's forehead, looking at the key to his plans. So far, her wilfulness had frustrated his schemes, but not once had she disappointed his expectations, growing in power with each trial she overcame, striving to protect people even at the cost of her own life. His thoughts drifted to the moment he almost lost her to the chasm in Liath, and Rurik ground his teeth, standing slowly.

'I will need to keep a closer eye on you, Ina,' Rurik said, placing a simple tracking spell on her ring. He had already spent too much time here. His face was well known at Marzanna's temple, so that meant taking a step back, but he had to ensure he knew where the witch was in case he needed to reach her quickly. With a last look around, the necromancer cast an illusion spell on the remains of the blood his newly risen corpse hadn't removed, then left the room.

On the way to his horse, he watched as the reanimated corpse bashed in the head of his former associate. With a smile and another casual wave of his hand, the corpse collapsed, and he scattered a few gold coins between the two bodies. In the morning, the good folk of the village would find two thugs who died fighting over gold neither would ever spend, the perfect ending to their benighted existence.

Saddling his horse, he thought of talking to his mother, but as she was already busy, he decided against it. The dragon was already on the way, and he had to ensure everything was under control. He had to evaluate Marcach and learn his triggers in order to goad him into offering Ina his longevity, and for that, he needed to meet the dragon face to face.

He whispered a quick cantrip, checking if he could detect Ina, and a fiery red dot flashed in his mind's eye. His beautiful chaos was safe, for now. He leapt onto his horse, riding off in search of the dragon, looking forward to the challenge of getting to know the man with whom she shared her bed.

CHAPTER NINETEEN

Zjawa daintily picked her way through the mud and early morning frost. Ina had been concerned when Mirena led them northwards, leaving the main road, almost trespassing on the fields. As her aunt seemed to be sure of their direction, she let go of her worry and focused on thinking about their plans.

'I met a peasant on the way to Thorn who mentioned they performed miracles at the temple, something about talking to a dead relative. I think it would be the perfect excuse to explain our visit. A pilgrimage to beseech Marzanna for one last conversation with a dead relative, maybe a husband or brother?' Ina said, startling her companion.

'What? Why? How will that help?'

'First, we would be one of many pilgrims. Second, if they claim Marzanna lets you talk to the dead, they must take us to her. I've brought enough money to convince anyone we'd be willing to pay for the privilege.' Mirena's frown effectively communicated her distaste at the idea, but as far as Ina was concerned, it was the only way to gain access to the temple without raising suspicion.

'When do you think we will arrive?' she asked, making Mirena look over.

'At this pace, probably right before evening service. There should still be enough daylight to look around and maybe find a place for the night before you start your antics.'

Why does she seem so unsettled? Does she believe this cult is more than a group of charlatans and can actually raise the dead? It's not like we will call Grandfather from Veles's cauldron. That bastard is better off where he is. Cyrus will make a much better Duke. The thought of her uncle brought a warm smile to Ina's face. He was dealing with the situation surprisingly well, supporting her despite their history. Mirena also looked after her, clucking over her like a mother hen. Ina had to admit last night's potion helped tremendously, and the dreamless, peaceful night gave her the rest she needed. Ina absent-mindedly stroked a finger over her ring, feeling its steady and powerful pulse synchronising with her body and magic.

'You checking on the chaos regalia?' Mirena's question took her out of her thoughts, and Ina nodded.

'Yes, it feels almost like they are a part of me. Just like Skarbnik said, they are connected with my magic now. Hopefully, I will look as good as Sowenna when they bury me with them.' Ina's words and bitter laugh caught Mirena's attention.

'You saw Sowenna? And… the rest of the regalia? Why didn't you take it?'

Her aunt's sharp voice gave Ina pause, but she shook it off. The legendary limitless power of the chaos regalia appealed to many magic users, so her aunt's question shouldn't have surprised her. She would bet that her relative considered her insane for leaving such a treasure behind, and after all her help, she owed her aunt an explanation.

'There is a darkness in me. I told you about the hunger that rejoices in death… no, not death—renewal. Violent, constant renewal. I felt it in Liath, and it frightened me so much that I let myself fall into the chasm I opened, choosing death over becoming the cause of some insane cataclysm. Mar saved me because he clearly doesn't have enough trouble in his life. Since then, I have tried to separate myself from chaos caused by violent death. Still, even before I knew how deeply death affected my magic, I left the circlet behind because I felt its power and feared I would lose all sense of myself once I placed it on my head.'

'You can't know that. Imagine how much good you could do with such immense power. Kings would bow to you….'

'Or I would become a second Sowenna. I read about her in the university library. She didn't start out as a monster. Why do you think my story would be any different? I'd be just another hero striving to do good that drowns the world in despair. I need no kings bowing to me, and I will help where I can, solving problems as they occur in my own chaotic way.' Ina thought this answer would be sufficient, but when Mirena tried to convince her further, Ina tightened her hands on the reins, urging Zjawa into a canter.

'Let's speed up a bit. I want to have more daylight to view the temple grounds,' she shouted over her shoulder, hoping Mirena would take the hint.

The temple appeared on the horizon sooner than Ina expected, and she pulled Zjawa to a halt, ignoring the accusation in her unruly mount's stare. While waiting for her aunt to catch up, Ina pulled her hood up, hiding her hair in the fur-lined fabric.

'Try to look sad, not angry, and remember, we are here to talk to our dearest relative, a brother who died without telling us about his hidden assets,' she said while Mirena huffed quietly, tightening her lips before they led both horses to the temple grounds.

It looked more like a small village with a few cottages than the centre of a new religion. There was even a makeshift tavern doing brisk business in the centre. One thing was clear, everyone still had the same helpless expression and starving faces as the rest of the province, but there was something else here. Ina felt it as they crossed the village edge, a feeling that tugged and twisted the soul; a perversion of nature. It took the witch several moments to repel the foul magic and create a shield. She noticed Mirena struggling from the corner of her eye, hastily casting the same spell.

'Now we know where they get the power to perform their miracles. Do you need help?'

'No, it simply caught me off-guard. I didn't expect someone would try to steal my energy,' her aunt said, leaning heavily on the saddle.

Ina directed the orein to the chram, or small temple really, that loomed over the small settlement, disproportionally large for the pilgrim's needs. Large oak timbers held up a sweeping shingle roof crowned with a carving of three wheat sheaves, but what surprised Ina the most was how little attention their arrival garnered, as if the people were indifferent to the presence of armed strangers.

'Let's go inside and see what's causing this,' she said, dismounting and tying Zjawa loosely to a wooden beam. The magic of this place unsettled her orein, raising Ina's suspicion that the spell affected the magical creature as well. She pressed her face to its long neck, stroking it to calm the restless spirit while whispering in the orein's ear. 'I need to check this out. I'm sorry. I will try to be as quick as possible.'

They entered the building without issue. The guards cast them an inspecting glance but didn't try to stop them. They walked into the dark interior, a few scattered torches the only relief from total gloom, until a massive man with a fearsome face stood in their way. Ina pulled her hood up further and bowed to hide her face. 'Please, good sir, we came from afar to pray at the Lady's shrine. We need to see our brother, and I heard only Winter's Death has the power to help us.'

Her words were met with a silence that lasted much longer than was comfortable, but in the end, the man blinked and uttered a few words, pointing to the darkness ahead. 'Volkhv will help. Go there.'

Ina mumbled her thanks, heading off and ducking under the enormous man's arm, Mirena following hesitantly. Just as the darkness seemed impenetrable, a door appeared, its outline wreathed in a sickly yellow glow. The witch stilled for a moment before grasping the handle and pushing it open, stepping through confidently, ignoring the warning in the back of her mind. The light from hundreds of candles blinded her, and Ina cursed several gods before grabbing the hilt of her sword when someone suddenly spoke.

'Come closer. I've been expecting you. The prophet told us you would come to kneel at our Lady's feet and awaken Winter's Death from her slumber.'

Ina faltered momentarily at the mention of a prophet, unsure how to deflect their certainty at her identity, then shrugged her shoulders and tried to brazen her way through with the deception.

'You must be mistaken. I'm just a simple pilgrim, hoping to see my brother one last time. Can you help us?'

The wizened male stepped closer, looking over Ina's shoulder before slowly nodding. 'Yes, yes, please forgive me, young lady. If you would follow me to the shrine? Once you begin your prayers, I will speak to your companion about your journey.'

His sudden change of attitude and eagerness to lead her to the most sacred place in the temple was suspicious, but she couldn't back down now. The look she gave Mirena was uncertain, especially when she saw her aunt staring at the volkhv, hand pressed firmly to her chest, but before the witch could say anything, Mirena turned and nodded. 'Go, it's alright. I'll be fine.'

Ina followed the volkhv to a small door, stepping inside as the priest waved her through into another darkened room, only to stop at the stench of death and rotten flesh.

'For fuck's sake, what is that stench?! And darkness again? Can't you decide what you want?' Ina wasn't addressing anyone in particular, masking her fear with the brazen statement, hoping to cause some reaction, even if this meant annoying the goddess of death and rebirth. She waited for a moment, quickly glancing back at the closed door. When no one came to criticise her lack of respect, Ina cast a light spell and sent the pulsar into the rafters.

'Well, that explains the smell,' she mumbled, looking at the corpses arranged around the room like some macabre prayer circle. It was an extraordinary presentation. Each body knelt towards Mariana's statue, arms outstretched to hold their neighbour's hands. A sharpened stake had been thrust through their ribcage from behind, presumably through their hearts. Ina's curiosity overcame her disgust, and she leaned in to study the nearest body, gasping when her breath blew the hair to the side, revealing the long point of an elven ear. *What the hell happened here?* she thought, grabbing hold of the stake to remove it, only to hiss in pain when a curse so vile she could taste the evil blistered her unprotected skin. The eyes of the elven cadaver opened, and she saw the light of the underworld focus on her face.

'That's enough. What the hell were you thinking torturing those spirits?' Ina stepped backwards, fighting to suppress nausea while fending off the offensive magic. She looked at the indifferent statue with disbelief and anger, unsure of what to do next. Marzanna stood, unresponsive and uncaring, despite the insults Ina threw at her feet. *Should I pray or what?* she thought, disgusted at the very idea. As she felt her grip on chaos fray, a soft golden light flickered to life in the corner, instantly grabbing her attention.

'Oh, look who's finally turned up. It's gone time we had a friendly talk.' Ina stopped trying to hold back her magic, allowing it to surround and coat her body like a shield. As she readied herself to fight, the figure that emerged from the light was anything but Winter's Death. Petite, with a flowery wreath crowning her golden hair and dimples on a youthful face, the goddess who appeared looked like a peasant maiden waiting to dance with her May lover. Ina blinked rapidly as the vision crouched next to the elven bodies, holding her hand above the baleful green chains running from the circle to the inert statue.

'So, you finally came to free her? It took you long enough, autumn's child.' The woman's voice held the wisdom of ages, in complete contrast to her youthful radiance.

Ina shook her head in denial and confusion. 'I didn't come here to free anyone. What is going on here? Why is Marzanna chained to this place by this sacrilege, draining the life from the land and its people?'

'Did my brother not send you? And really, who knows why humans do anything? Perhaps your friend, the volkhv, knows.'

The complete lack of understanding on Ina's face was apparent as the goddess huffed in annoyance and tried again. 'The Leshy, your… guardian. Did he not send you to free our sister?'

Suddenly, things fell into place, and it was Ina's turn to huff her frustration. 'No, I imagine he forgot to tell me about such an important detail, not that he's talked to me recently, but why would he make my life easier by offering any information? What could be more entertaining than sending the clueless witch to a temple and letting her burn her hand on a curse?' Ina was in the middle of her rant when a hearty laugh shocked her into silence.

'Skarbnik told me you were amusing, but he didn't tell me how much. Free my sister, autumn's child, and I will bring forth a spring so beautiful they will sing about it in ballads. I cannot stay much longer. The curse only gains strength from my presence, so give me your hand.'

When Ina threw her a dubious look, the goddess shook her head. 'Don't be an obstructive child. If you can't trust Lada, who can you trust?'

The witch hesitantly reached out and, moments later, nearly collapsed as the pure power of life swept her away in a sea of joy. The spring goddess laughed again as Ina wept, feeling a love she had only felt for the dragon who stole her heart. She barely sensed the heat flowing into her body till it grew to the strength of the blazing sun, burning every nerve under her skin, forcing a tortured scream from her lips even as the witch ripped her hand from Lada's grasp.

'There, all done. You have an unusual way of thinking, child. You should never be afraid to love those you hold dear and never turn away a shield on the battlefield. Call on me when you find a way to free my sister; I may even decide to help.' Lada's voice faded, and Ina stared in disbelief at her arm, golden scales now coiling up around her wrist and forearm. The goddess Lada had branded her with a tattoo of Zmij, which seemed to move, twisting and stretching beneath her skin as she stared.

'Oh, for fuck's sake, couldn't you give me a cat or a horse?' she shouted at the empty corner, trying to remove the winged, golden serpent from her arm before having to explain another god-given gift to Mar. *What is it supposed to be, a god's mark, a protective spell? Would it be too much to ask that just once, these gods could give me a straightforward clue?* Ina shook her head, focusing on her surroundings. She had to break the vile chains and stop the curse before it destroyed the land, but she didn't know how.

Ina looked at the sacrificial victims, took a deep breath, and grabbed a stake—only to turn the air blue, cursing the fickle gods as she fought the unbearable pain. With gritted teeth, the witch pulled, only falling back when her strength gave out. Even though it frustrated her, Ina couldn't help her curiosity at such a puzzle. *The blackened wood must be the spell's anchor, piercing the heart to hold the soul in place, using that to draw... something— energy?—into the chains and then to the statue. But how does it rot the crops? Maybe if I use chaos to destroy the anchor?* The desire to do just that swept through the witch, leaving her gasping, shocked at its power. When Ina saw her peridot glowing, she realised she'd almost given in to the craving.

'You will need more than your gem to free her. Winter's Death was chained to this land by a curse older than antiquity. I am now the bearer of its power and the only one who can release her. I can free the lands from the grasp of Winter... if you give me your regalia.' The volkhv's voice behind her made her twist around, hands raised, ready to cast a spell.

'How could you cast such a sick curse? No one deserves to suffer like this.' Ina looked at the priest, his arrogant sneer sending a shiver down her spine. 'And why do you want Sowenna's gems? Only a chaos mage can use them. To anyone else, they are just cursed stones.'

The smile that stretched the old man's lips was so hideous the witch took a step back, almost tripping over the bound corpses, but more terrifying was the faint crimson light that shone above his outstretched hand.

'He thought I was a foolish old man who believed in gods who abandoned humanity centuries ago. He thought I would be easily fooled, but I knew what you were, knew the gem's real power. Did you think you were the only one that could command chaos? I also hold its power in the palm of my hand. You may have money and privilege, but I have Winter's Death bound to my service, and you cannot defeat the power of the old gods.'

'So you've already gone insane… but your magic, I can hardly feel it at all. There is the stench of death magic, but hardly any chaos.'

'No, little witch. I am a chaos mage and smarter than you. Your precious aunt is in my custody, so give me your gemstones, or she dies, painfully. If you bring me the circlet, I will release her and even dissipate the curse as a reward.'

'You wish me to trade one life for many?' she asked, looking at her enemy. Was he the one who taunted her in the forest? It made a sick kind of sense. The power in the spell behind her could easily control the revenant they'd encountered. Ina's thoughts raced as she tried to fit the priest's demands into the puzzle of the South. His words reeked of insanity, but the volkhv was calm and controlled with a brutality that allowed him to sacrifice the souls of the elves to further his plans. One thing, however, didn't feel right, giving the witch an idea. 'Who is the mysterious man you mentioned? Won't he fight you for the regalia?'

'Is that what concerns you, child? It doesn't matter. Once I have them, you will all bow your heads to me. Even gods will respect my power. Stop delaying the inevitable and give me your gems.'

'No.'

'Then you and your aunt will die, and I will take them from your cold, dead body. Kill the old mage!' he shouted, and two shadows rushed into the corridor, disappearing in the light. *Bloody hell, I didn't even notice them. I need to save Mirena before they hurt her,* Ina thought, moving forward until a bolt of energy hit her shoulder, sending her to the ground. It felt like boiling tar was burning her flesh, and Ina screamed.

The old man laughed as she collapsed, reaching for her necklace whilst she was helpless, but Ina's determination to live and protect her aunt was stronger than her pain, and she rolled away from his grasping hands. Her eyes filled with a swirling red when the maelstrom of chaos threatened to escape her control, pure rage sweeping away all rational thought.

She threw her hands forward, pushing him back with a blast of raw magic, but doing no damage as he protected himself, destroying the surrounding area instead. The volkhv attacked again, narrowly missing her head as Ina dived to the side, feeling the curse's power bolstering his strength. *This bastard is raping the land of its life force whilst I try to hold back, trying to control the chaos.* Ina knew she would lose this duel if she didn't fight with all she had. Calling her fire vipers to life, she leapt forward to attack.

'You were not born to chaos, necromancer, and I was trained to fight by the best.' Ina's words were brave, but as she lashed out with her fire vipers, he withstood the onslaught, laughing, before stepping back. With an agility that belied his advanced years, the volkhv reached down, grabbed the chains of the curse, and lashed out, just as Ina had, using its vile magic to cause as much damage as possible. The witch fell back, eyes widened in shock, deflecting the chain away with her vipers. *He is copying my moves. Fuck, if those chains hit me, I'm dead!*

Ina ducked to the side as the chains snapped at her face, but again and again, the volkhv attacked, and her desperate defence began to fail. The voice in her mind returned gleeful and demanding. *Attack him with chaos. You can feed on his magic, just as he is. Magic moves in both directions, so use that knowledge and steal his power.* The darkness in her soul spread, virulent and all-consuming. Distracted, Ina failed to protect herself, and the cursed magic struck her shoulder again.

Gods help me. If I lose control, I will burn this place to the ground. How can you ask me to sacrifice Mirena and the innocent villagers to survive? Her prayer must have fallen upon deaf ears as the priest broke through her defences again, wrapping the chain around her wrist, and, as she screamed out in terrified agony, Ina lost control, chaos blossoming around her like unfurling fiery wings.

Suddenly, the magic attack stopped. The man's eyes widened in dismay as a red stain spread across his chest, and he fell forward with a loud thud, revealing the instrument of his demise—a dagger thrust to the hilt in his back. With his death, the magic he had controlled erupted, burning its way into Ina's body, overloading the already weakened witch with the force of a thunderstorm. She heard her saviour gasp, but Ina could only scream out one command. 'Get out… Everyone get out or die!'

Nothing could stop the raging storm, and chaos leapt outward, obliterating everything it touched.

As the sound of screaming reached her ears, the witch recognised Mirena's voice and wept as she fell to her knees, trying to regain control of the maelstrom burning through her soul. She needed to slow the destruction and allow her aunt to escape to warn the villagers, but even forcing the power into her peridots failed to help. Worst, her thoughts became a muddled, blissful oblivion, beckoning her mind into madness until something caught her tattered mind's attention. Something was writhing beneath her skin, and as she looked down, the eyes of a golden viper stared back, capturing her mind in its gaze.

'I am Inanuan Zoria Thornsen, and no god or power will control me,' she choked out, reaching for the bonds anchored to her very essence. Focusing on the gold and silver strands that were part of her spirit helped Ina regain control and concentrate on the raging storm. *If you had the circlet, you could claim all this power.* The intrusive thought awakened a cold fury that the witch used, thrusting her mind into the vortex, ignoring the pain and turning the magic towards the chain on her wrist.

'Take your circlet to Veles, whoever you are, you bloodthirsty arsehole!' she shouted, forcing the energy into the chains as magical fire engulfed the room, incinerating everything around her, lighting up the night sky as the walls and roof disintegrated. Despite that, the statue stood untouched and indifferent, mocking her efforts.

The goddess of spring was right. The curse fed on life and magic and was now trying to steal hers.

'Oh, I don't think so,' she murmured. Tears streamed from her reddened eyes, almost blinding her. Even as she fought, Ina felt her fury washing away as the bonds within her soul shone with love and affection, allowing her to control the curse's magic. Even then, she couldn't break the spell and releasing this much power into the world would devastate the landscape for miles around. As a last resort, she returned the magic to its purpose, allowing it to bolster the chains imprisoning the goddess, falling to her knees in defeat. Marzanna's corrupted statue and the sacrificial victims remained intact, surrounded by a circle of scorched earth, evidence of both the strength of her magic and that of the obscene spell.

Ina exhaled slowly and dared to open her eyes. Her quick response had prevented the death of innocents, and although the curse was still in place, the temple was destroyed, with the cult's leader no longer able to deceive any unsuspecting peasants.

Mirena approached her cautiously, and Ina winced at the wariness in her expression before forcing herself to relax and attempt a smile.

'Well, that didn't go as planned. I hope Velka and Cyrus can find a better way to deal with it because I have no idea how to break this curse.'

'This man, he was a chaos mage as well?' Her aunt took a long, measured look around the magical battlefield and swallowed hard when Ina shook her head.

'He had a small amount of chaos, just as any necromancer does, but he couldn't use it. While he had a connection to death magic, I don't think he could have cast this curse. I think someone else helped him set it up, then bound him to it as added protection. When we fought, if not for the power of the spell, he would have been an easy target, but it was like fighting a dark volcano. All the life this curse drained from the land stood against me, and if not for you, I would have lost. Unless it wasn't you who sank the dagger into his rotten heart?'

'I knew they were up to no good, so I used my magic to steal the dagger and, after dealing with their thugs, rushed back to help.'

Ina leaned on her hand to stand up, collapsing back and cursing the pain in her shoulder before glancing up at Mirena with a hopeful look in her eyes.

'I would appreciate a little more help, aunty. And if you could heal me, I'll love you forever.' Ina smiled her most charming smile before turning her attention to the cowering villagers. The witch sighed. 'We need to head back to Thorn and ask Cyrus if he's heard of this spell.'

After a bit of grumbling, Mirena and Ina headed back to their mounts, only to be surrounded by the previously morose peasants, each now reaching out and touching the witch's clothing. Attempting to speed up, the women hurried to the horses, leapt on their backs, and rode away to escape the strange phenomenon.

'What is going on?' Ina asked, panicked.

'You survived the fire intact, more like a goddess than a living being, especially with crimson fire burning in your eyes. What do you expect, pitchforks and torches?' Her aunt's pragmatic answer didn't relieve Ina's panic, nor did the sudden commotion behind them. While the awed peasants saw her as some kind of deity, the surviving temple servants and cultists didn't share their opinion. They quickly grabbed whatever makeshift weapons were close to hand and were now rushing towards them.

'Great, you had to mention pitchforks and torches. Time to go, aunty. The quicker we resolve this curse, the quicker the farmers will plough the fields and not try to kill us.'

CHAPTER TWENTY

The road felt like an endless tunnel, surrounded by grey, muddy snow and a misty haze that isolated them from the rest of the world. After the bittersweet farewell with Ina, the two warriors had finished their preparations, setting off soon after. Mar reminded himself, yet again, to relax his hold on the reins whilst Woron danced in reaction to his rider's tension. It was difficult to accept Ina heading into danger with, in his opinion, inadequate support, but the strong-willed witch had decided, leaving him no option other than to follow through with his part of her unconventional plan. At least she opened up to him about her worries, and he took comfort from the warmth transmitted through their bond, proof that Ina accepted and returned his love.

'Oh, for f… Just stop it.' The orc seemed irritated, unhappy at leaving his wife to deal with some unknown plague that killed off all vegetation.

'Stop what?'

'You look like a court jester, smiling like a fool, then frowning like an old hag. It's obvious who you're thinking about, but as we're heading towards the rebel camp, it might be helpful if you could find a moment to consider the danger and devise a plan that doesn't involve us being hung, drawn and quartered.'

'You heard the plan. We present ourselves as envoys to the rebellion leaders, so subtlety would be counterintuitive. We politely ask if there's any possibility of a peaceful outcome. If not, we announce the imminent arrival of the king and his new army, then invite the rebels to meet them on the battlefield.'

'Mar, that is insane. We will end up with our heads on spikes over the town gates, and for what, a dream? Did you even get confirmation from Ren that the king agreed to this, or are we tugging the lion's tail for nothing?'

'Ren will handle the king, and if you could stop blaming Ina for your problems with Velka, you'd see her plan has merit. Do you want to go into battle facing terrified farm boys? It would be a pointless slaughter and exacerbate the crop shortage. No, if we can avoid that, I will do whatever Ina asks of me, even if it means pretending to be the king's pet and begging for a tummy rub.'

Daro sighed, lowering his gaze to the road. 'That's not what warriors do. Is there even a role for me in this grand plan?'

'We are not just warriors anymore. We are leaders. This is not about our egos, but about protecting those who rely on us, including the soldiers who trust our judgement. All I ask is, don't let them goad you into a fight. I'm sure some of the southern lords won't be happy to accept a peaceful solution and will aim to start a fight with a volatile orc, unworthy of his position,' Mar said with a smirk before pushing Woron into a trot, and the massive orc's gelding neighed unhappily, trying to keep up with the larger warhorse.

'I am not volatile, and I'll have you know I earned that position with my blood and sweat.'

Mar laughed, hearing the angry tone in Daro's voice, then took a deep breath to concentrate. He had to focus on the task ahead. In order to succeed, he must be the personification of the Lord Marshal of Cornovii, there to negotiate for peace. However, keeping up appearances would be nearly impossible, with no inn or guest houses on the way to Alsia.

Just as he was considering making camp in the damp, cold conditions, a small hamlet appeared through the mist, and the marshal smiled in relief.

'Let's ask for shelter here. It will allow us to wash up and dress for the upcoming confrontation. Otherwise, the gate guards will assume we're mercenaries or spies.' Daro nodded and waited patiently while Mar negotiated with a peasant for lodging, even as the man cast worried looks at the intimidating orc. In the end, the man offered them space in the barn and a full meal, which was a generous offer, considering the blight.

After cleaning and feeding the horses, the warriors washed up, then settled down for the night, relaxing with the meagre food they'd received from their host. The barn was warm, with enough hay to make a proper bed, even for a dragon. After washing in freezing cold water, he contemplated transforming to warm himself until Daro's voice snapped him back to reality.

'Mar, before we go to Alsia, promise me if anything happens to me, you and Ina will take care of Velka and my boy.'

'What's gotten into you lately? What happened to the carefree orc I know and respect?' Mar leaned over and punched Daro in the shoulder.

'I just... I've never really cared about much in my life, just lived for the day and never thought about the future, but since I met Velka... then finding out she's pregnant... I can't stop thinking about it. I'm a soldier, as you said. I can die anytime, but you… dragons live forever, and Ina can subdue armies. Velka and Ina are like sisters, so I know she'll help. For as long as I've known you, once you've given your word, you've never broken it. Please, for me.'

Mar nearly laughed at the earnest tone in Daro's voice, but when he looked into his friend's eyes, his expression sobered, and he nodded. If someone told him a year ago that the flamboyant Daro, who hadn't seen a skirt he wouldn't chase, would become a dedicated family man, he'd have called them fools and laughed in their face, but now with that truth staring back at him, Mar reached over and clasped his friend's arm.

'I will look after him if the situation demands it, and although I can't speak for Ina, I know she would put herself between Velka and the god's wrath if they threatened her friend. Now, go to sleep. We need to be rested to face tomorrow and avoid getting ourselves killed. If you act particularly stupid, I may withdraw my promise, so be on your best behaviour,' Mar said, smiling to offset his harsh words.

Daro turned to the side with an annoyed grunt and an obscene gesture while Mar settled back to sleep. Talking about Ina made him want to feel her close, so, eyes closed, he searched for the connection between them. It was hard to suppress his worry; the gods seemed to delight in using his spitfire to entertain themselves. All he could do was hope their games wouldn't end in her death. As the quiet noises of the night slowly lulled him to sleep, Mar lost himself in the warmth of the bond, basking in Ina's love.

Next thing Mar knew, it was morning, and an evil cockerel was crowing loud enough to wake the dead. The young orc was snuggled up to his back, snoring in his ear like a faithful wife. *Gods, I'm glad Ren isn't here, or I'd never hear the end of it,* Mar thought as he extracted himself from Daro's embrace, seeking some fresh morning air.

When he returned, Daro was already up, finishing the last of his warrior braids. He looked at every inch the peacock Mar remembered, and the marshal chuckled slightly.

'I see you took my words to heart. Let's see what I can do to match your pretty hair,' Mar said, stripping naked, ready to transform his skin into the dragon-scaled armour of Liath.

'Fucking hell, Captain, I thought you were a dragon, not a werewolf!' The orc stared at his naked body. Mar looked down at his hairy chest before smirking when he noticed Daro couldn't take his eyes off it, although he wasn't prepared for the orc to reach over and stroke him like a pet. 'So soft, like a kitten.'

Mar pushed him away with an annoyed growl before transforming with practised ease. The soft pink tinting his cheeks was the only sign he felt embarrassed. He hadn't expected anyone to notice the subtle changes he'd made to his body, knowing how much his witch liked them. 'Keep those orcish shovels to yourself, or I will rip them off. Ina likes it that way, and if my woman's satisfied, I am happy to oblige.'

'Oh, I wish I had that ability. I would do so many things with my cock. Make it longer or wider, even give it a curve to get those extra special places. Would it be possible to make two, do you think?' Daro was roaring, his laughter so infectious that Mar couldn't help but join in.

'Did you not hear when I said my woman was satisfied? I meant that in every way possible. It's safe to say your ego wouldn't survive such an ability.' Lifting his hand and waving his pinkie, Mar snorted. 'Should we ask Velka which is larger, your cock, or your ego?' Laughing at his joke, the Marshal threw a cloak over his armour, striding to the horses. Now every inch the noble commander, with Daro following behind, hand raised in his own obscene gesture. Once mounted, they headed off towards Alsia, the banter continuing until they saw the first armed patrol.

The two warriors grew silent when they noticed the size of the patrol, the overt display of force worrying. Mar took a moment to lean over and mention their earlier conversation to Daro. 'Remember, do not allow them to provoke you. With this many soldiers, the leaders must be confident of their position.' Mar straightened up when they were noticed and met the soldiers with an amiable smile.

'Who are you, and what brings you to Alsia?' The soldier who asked was too pale to be local, most likely a recruit from the north, his up-tilted ears displaying a shared ancestry with the drow.

'I am Lord Marcach of Liath, Marshal of Cornovii, and this is Captain Daro of the King's Guards. As to our purpose, I shall divulge that information to your liege lord. You may escort us to his residence.' The authoritative tone made an impression on the patrol leader, and the man stepped back, reaching for his sword while his companions surrounded the two warriors.

'It's the king's dragon! Surrender your weapons and prepare to be taken prisoner!' the guard all but squeaked, lacking the authoritative tone of Mar, and his voice was filled with nothing but terror.

'Now, whilst I appreciate the fear in your voice, you do not have the authority, or the men, to enforce that request.' Mar raised his right hand slowly, willing it to transform as it moved, smirking as the stink of fear increased. 'Not to mention, I am a living weapon and could kill you all without a moment's regret. Take me to your leader, or get out of my way. Make your choice.'

His demonstration had the desired effect, and after a quick muttered exchange, the soldiers backed away as their officer turned his horse, gesturing towards the town. 'Come, I'm not fighting a fucking dragon. I'll take you to the commander.'

As they followed the soldier through a gate to a rough palisade, Mar studied his surroundings, paying particular attention to the trainees attempting to learn basic swordcraft. From their general appearance and lack of skill, it was clear these men had come straight from the fields, hands more used to the plough than the deadly steel they now carried.

He could see the flags of several free companies, noting the slovenly mercenaries lounging around and drinking instead of training, including a handful of liveried warriors from a few southern noble houses.

The army didn't seem adept or disciplined, but their ranks stretched as far as the eye could see. Mar's lips thinned with concern; an overwhelming force could defeat a smaller, better-trained army. It was becoming more imperative to avoid an armed conflict. The resulting bloodbath would cripple Cornovii for generations if it survived as a nation at all.

The town itself was unimpressive, a typical gathering of ramshackle buildings that sprang up wherever an aristocrat set up home, with its principal street leading to a market square and continuing to a large mansion. The only difference was the extensive military activity. The soldiers here appeared better trained than those outside the town, and as he watched, Mar noticed the subtle feline movement of those who were used to killing in the shadows. One of the assassins approached Mar's guide, leaning in to talk with the nervous soldier before bowing politely to Mar and gesturing to the building.

'Dismount, please, my lord. I understand you do not wish to part with your weapons, but you can't ride inside.' His words, heavy with sarcasm, contradicted his polite bearing, and Mar exhaled slowly, feeling the hostile stares at his back.

'Of course, I would never presume to be so rude. I would, however, appreciate knowing the name of the noble I am about to meet.'

'That would be up to His Lordship, if he so chooses,' the man said, stalling for time as a servant ran into the house, likely to warn their master of Mar's arrival.

Mar waited patiently, and when Daro moved forward, he placed a hand on the orc's shoulder. 'No, we wait. This is the game of aristocrats, just simple posturing to put us in our place. Especially as we are the king's envoys.' The look he gave to their escort made the man step back in fear, only relaxing when the servant appeared at the door and beckoned the visitors to enter.

Mar didn't rush. His long, slow steps made the guards nervous and brought a knowing smile to Daro's lips, but the orc didn't comment on his friend's haughty manner, especially when they were led to what one could only be described as a throne room, if not for the fact it was in a country manor. The young man sitting on an ornate chair surrounded by several severe-looking men observed his visitors with disdainful arrogance, and Mar couldn't help comparing him to King Rewan.

Maybe it was because they were of similar age, but where Rewan radiated a calm confidence and, for those who knew him personally, a sense of humour and informality that let his advisors speak without fear of retribution, the man in front of Mar was the complete opposite; arrogance and disdain pouring from him in waves. He glared at Mar and Daro before finally beckoning them closer.

'What brings the king's pet and rabid dog to my house? Did Rewan finally come to his senses and give up his claim to the South?'

Mar clenched his fist, the only sign of his irritation. *This man is an idiot. How could he organise the rebellion if he can't even greet an envoy?* he thought, suddenly hearing Daro's voice.

'And who might you be? I haven't heard of any accomplished military leaders from the South. Maybe you should call your father so we can talk to the person in charge?'

Mar couldn't decide whether he wanted to rip out his friend's tongue or burst out laughing. Daro's barb flew true, and the face of the young noble turned a disturbing shade of purple. The covert sniggering of his older companions told the marshal it wasn't the first time they had heard such an insult. Still, plenty of young nobles leapt up, shouting their outrage, and Mar stepped forward to control the situation. 'What is your name, sir? I have a message from the king for the man who leads this… gathering.'

The young man stood up from his makeshift throne and approached Mar. 'My name is Prince Wawrzyniec. I am the Lord of Alsia and its provincial holdings. I can't wait to hear what my good cousin wants so desperately that he sent his overgrown lapdog.'

Mar was close to grabbing the annoying brat by his throat and shaking some reason into his empty head when an older gentleman stepped forward, offering him a welcome nod.

'Welcome, Marshal. As my liege so eloquently inquired, may we ask what business brings you here, with only one companion accompanying you? Although we all would hope His Majesty acknowledges the sovereignty of the South, I doubt this is the reason for your visit.'

Mar moved his attention to the older man, recognising the actual leader, despite Wawrzyniec standing before him, quietly fuming after the older man's interjection. 'I understand Verdante has already acknowledged the *sovereignty* of the southern province. However, Cornovii is very fond of this part of the country, and, if needed, we are ready to show how much we appreciate them.' Mar took a wild guess, but the man's accent, manner of dressing, and tanned skin, combined with his curly blond hair, told the marshal his origins lay further south than the edge of Cornovii's border.

Wawrzyniec didn't even attempt to hide his fear, turning to the older gentleman, his eyes begging for help, but the southerner looked Mar in the eye with a smirk, acknowledging the marshal's assessment of the situation. 'After the palace coup and the war in Liath, we look forward to this display of appreciation, however lacklustre it may be. I'm surprised the Crown forbore recruiting soldiers from the South, but I suppose finding loyal soldiers in a province only remembered when it's time to steal their food may be a difficult task.'

Mar returned the smirk with one of his own, sinking all his anger into the expression as he remembered the crying woman searching for her son at the healer's compound. 'At least we don't coerce naïve farmers to fight a war under false pretences. Tell your liege that angry dogs can easily tear off a thieving hand reaching for another man's goods, and as your puppet so eloquently acknowledged, the king has plenty of those.'

The man laughed, and for a moment, his image seemed to flicker, a hint of black hair and pale skin overlapping that of the Verdante noble, but the effect disappeared too quickly to fully register. Before Mar could question him, the prince interrupted, poking him in the chest.

'I am in command here, and you will answer to me, not my advisor. What do you want? And remember, one disrespectful word and my knights will kill you on the spot.' Each word was accented with another poke to Mar's chest, and seeing Daro move forward, his hand drifting to his axe, the dragon grabbed the young noble's hand and squeezed.

'You command nothing, boy. Verdante has used you to weaken Cornovii, and if by some miracle you succeed, they will take it away from you. Being foolish and gullible is no excuse for the trouble you have caused your people. I should drag you to Osterad and give you to Sa'Ren Gerel. If he agrees to train you, you may, if you're lucky, turn out to be a reasonable human being.' This time, it was Mar who made his point with force, squeezing a little tighter with every sentence until the young prince buckled, falling to his knees and whimpering. With the helpless prince at his feet, the marshal looked over to the shocked faces of the surrounding nobles.

'His Majesty King Rewan challenges you to meet him on the field of battle during the spring equinox in the fields of Alsia. You will be accorded the honour of dying for the freedom you think you are fighting to gain. Unless you choose the honourable path and bend your knee to your benevolent monarch to beg for the lives of your soldiers.' Mar released Wawrzyniec's hand, and the young prince scrambled backwards, avoiding the golden fire in the dragon's eyes. Instead, it was the southern noble who stepped forward to answer.

'We will be there, Lord Marshal, and time will tell who the winner will be in this dispute.'

Mar turned to leave, satisfied his message had been delivered. He smiled at the memory of his father recounting his favourite saying, *'Mar, every war is won before the battle starts. If your opponent believes you are unbeatable, you will be unbeatable.'* Unfortunately, this prince and his supporters were puppets for the strange advisor. The marshal shook his head to clear his thoughts. The next move would rely on Ren and the king arriving with the army. Hopefully, Mar's assessment was correct, and Verdante would wait to fight whichever army won the coming battle, taking advantage of their weakened state to conquer the country.

'What are you thinking about?' Daro asked quietly as they rode towards the town gates. The guards who tried to prevent them from departing quickly stepped aside after one look at Mar's blazing eyes. Now, away from the camp, Mar could turn to the orc and share his thoughts.

'This rebellion is weak, unprepared. The young man posing as the leader has no experience, charisma, or any actual power, but I'm worried about this southern noble. He is controlling and far too confident. I can't help thinking something about him isn't right.'

'You mean except talking for the actual leader and highlighting he is from Verdante? He couldn't be more obvious if he tried.' The orc's pragmatic viewpoint brought a smile to Mar's lips.

'Exactly. Why did he want us to know who was pulling the strings behind the scenes? It would be easier to let the young fool get himself killed so he could take over. You saw how the nobles deferred to his command. This man has the respect of the more sensible men, which means there's a back-room deal we don't know about.'

'This I don't know. I leave the politics to you and Ina. Hopefully, her trick will work, as there will be no glory in killing those farm boys.' He gestured back towards the noisy camp and rolled his eyes.

Mar sighed and pushed Woron into a light trot. 'They may be untrained, but even our army will suffer significant casualties against those numbers.'

'Then tell Ina to make them kneel. It worked last time.'

'That power came from hundreds of deaths, and we don't want anyone dying if we can help it. Not to mention she's only human and can't save your lazy arse every time we get in a little scrap. We have ten days to prepare, so let's use this time wisely instead of counting on another miracle.' Mar slapped Daro on the back of his head, and Woron leapt forward into a gallop, his rider laughing even as he thought about Ina and her mission.

CHAPTER TWENTY-ONE

Ina stood on the balcony overlooking the city of Thorn and studied the sedately flowing river and the flourishing greenery far below. The blight affecting the province struggled to gain a foothold in this area, possibly repelled by her family's magic, but Ina couldn't stop thinking about the fields and forests she'd travelled through on her recent journey. That the lifeless feeling of the flora touched her heart surprised the witch, especially when confronted with such lush growth.

Her visit to Marzanna's temple had left the sour taste of defeat in her mouth but had revealed some answers, even as it left Ina with even more questions. The volkhv had claimed to be the mage controlling the curse, but the strength of his chaos magic was minimal. That spell withstood every ounce of power the witch had thrown at it. How could such a weak mage manipulate a curse that could steal enough power to imprison a goddess?

As Ina rubbed her tired eyes, she hissed in pain as her shoulder ached in remembrance of her recent battle. Mirena had treated the injury with her usual calm efficiency, but the wound caused by the curse's chains was still aching and discoloured. Thankfully, her aunt reassured Ina that the ugly marks should fade quickly, and the witch trusted the healer's judgement.

Sleep beckoned as the latest energy potion wore off. While it had been essential to use the dangerous concoctions in order to escape their persistent pursuers, Ina was now regretting their use as every muscle in her body twitched incessantly whilst she desperately craved oblivion.

She'd already told Velka and Cyrus about the curse, her findings leaving her uncle with a pensive frown before he rushed to his library. Velka simply came to Ina and embraced her in a suspiciously motherly hug, sending her friend to bed to rest with a decisiveness that made the witch smile.

A sudden commotion at the castle gates caught her attention, and Ina squinted, trying to see what was happening there. Mar burst through the gates, pushing the guards to the sides before jumping off Woron and grabbing one of them by the neck, shouting into the man's face. Ina sighed slightly and turned away, heading down. *He must have felt my injury through the bond*, she thought, readying herself for the lecture that would likely come from the raging dragon.

When the great hall doors exploded inwards, nearly crashing off their hinges, a furious, muddy dragon striding through the gap with a sour-faced Daro in tow, she knew it would be more than just a lecture.

'Ina! What in Veles's name did you do this time?'

'Why do you always assume I did something? And stop throwing people around; they don't deserve to be manhandled.' Mar's dishevelled appearance finally registered, and it occurred to her that sending him to Alsia might have been more challenging than she appreciated. 'Why are you so dirty? Did you get into a fight? Are you hurt?'

'Don't even try changing the fucking subject. You were fighting, injured, and lost control of your magic. I thought I'd lost you.' Mar strode forward, his arms surrounding her so quickly that Ina gasped, which then turned into a moan as he lifted her off the ground, kissing her with desperate relief. 'Never do that to me again. Do you hear me? Never. I nearly lost my mind thinking you'd died.'

Ina could feel his heart racing, squashed against his chest as she was. The witch could also feel something else. Unfortunately, it wasn't what she hoped to feel, but a strange frisson against her skin, and she realised Mar was struggling not to transform. 'Ina, when you reached out for help, and I wasn't there, it nearly killed me,' he said, pressing his forehead to hers before she gently stroked his bearded cheek.

'Hush now, you big oaf. I'm not so easy to kill. I survived whilst my opponent is ash, floating away on the breeze. You have been fighting too, and you look much worse.' She said, picking a flake of dry mud from his beard, trying to lighten the mood, but she heard Daro snort.

'Oh, we weren't fighting. We were all noble and diplomatic. It wasn't until we were halfway home that the idiot fell off his horse like a ham actor swooning on stage. If that wasn't bad enough, he turned into a dragon, causing the horses to bolt and me to land in the mud next to him. Even Woron couldn't withstand his roar. Whatever you did to him left him flightless, so he spent the night groaning with his scaly ass firmly stuck in the mud. It would have been amusing if muggins here didn't have to catch the horses. Now, if you'll excuse me, I have a wife to kiss.'

Ina gasped, blinking rapidly as she threw her arms around Mar's neck and pressed his head to her chest. 'I'm so sorry. I didn't know. If there is a way to remove the bond, I will find it. I can't let you be shackled to me if you get hurt whenever I do something dangerous.' The low growl that rumbled in his chest made her stop and look into the golden irises of the dragon.

'You will not remove our bond, even if you find out how. You are mine, and I am yours. We share each other's pain along with the joys. I would, however, appreciate you finding a way of warning me when you go into battle, as this is the second time you've left me flat on my back.' He seemed much calmer, but still held her painfully tight. 'If you want to repent for your sins, tell the servants to prepare a bath and food, and while I get clean, I'll answer your questions about Alsia.' He lowered her to the floor, his hand lingering on her wounded shoulder as if reassuring himself she was all right. Only then did he let a wicked smile grace his lips, reminding Ina of the time she'd questioned him back in Osterad.

Ina mirrored his smile and gave him an exaggerated curtsy. 'Yes, my lord, I think this will be the best way to retrieve every piece of information. I will do my best to ensure your cooperation and promise you will be unable to hide anything from me.'

'You are such a minx, Ina. Love, you scared me, and I am finding it difficult to deal with that fear. So much so that I almost wish Ren were here to help you protect yourself better. Maybe you would listen to his quiet scorn better than my blustering roars.'

Mar's sad chuckle chased the witch down the corridor as she pretended to look for a servant, but as soon as she disappeared around the corner, Ina gasped, supporting herself on the wall and biting her knuckles to suppress a pained sob. *Oh gods, how could I have hurt him so badly? And what about Ren? Did the bond cause him pain, too? I'm so sorry. If I could take it back, I would*, she thought, feeling guilty for the price they paid for her recklessness.

Spring was not the best time to march an army anywhere, let alone the pastoral South, and despite Ren's best efforts, their column moved at a snail's pace. The last few days slogging through the mud had worsened an already tense situation. After passing on Ina's revelations, Ren heard the king had called in the truth-seekers. The advisor had been found innocent, but judging by the distance between Kaian and Rewan, along with the subsequent mood, such an intensive interrogation had broken the trust between them and might never be repaired.

Ren decided discretion was the better part of valour and busied himself checking on the supply wagons. It was, coincidentally, where Ayni was, travelling with the healers who chose not to ride on horseback, and the quiet warrior spent a few moments enjoying the sight of her keeping busy, repairing soldier's clothing.

'Don't strain your eyes, mi'khaira; the soldiers don't mind wearing torn clothing.'

The dragoness looked up, meeting his gaze, a beautiful smile gracing her lips. 'It is no strain for a dragon's eyes, but I wouldn't mind stopping for a rest. I could fly us to Thorn if you'd like?'

'We could, but the rest of the army would become jealous of my beautiful dragon soaring overhead when they are stuck in the mud,' he said, but the prospect of seeing his friends was very appealing. 'We will stop in Madron soon. Now, if you would excuse me, I need to speak with Kaian.'

Ren rode away at a slow trot and approached the king's advisor, feelings of guilt and pity uppermost in his mind. Kaian's cheerfulness was gone, and now he looked like the incarnation of death, every inch the king's assassin.

'Come on, Kaian, stop pouting. He had to do it, but we both know he loves you. It was the only way he could protect you from the spectre of suspicion. This way, no one can question your loyalty, which is more important than ever right now,' Ren said quietly alongside the man who had become a close friend.

'If he truly did, he could have just questioned me under oath instead of interrogating me with magic.'

'Put yourself in his shoes. This wasn't about him not trusting you. Do you think he would sleep with someone he didn't trust? He might have sex with you, but actually sleep? Once we found out your family was involved in sedition, Rewan did the one thing that would protect your reputation; he used the mages to verify your innocence. As painful as it was, that interrogation saved your life and allowed him to justify keeping you by his side. We are headed to war; he could not leave Osterad with the court thinking the king cares more about his intimate relationships than the safety of his kingdom. So if you must be angry, be angry with Ina or me. Better yet, be angry at your bastard relatives for putting you in danger in the first place.'

'I was angry at you and Ina, but once those mages started rooting around in my mind, I knew where I went wrong. I remembered my father being so pleased when I got close to Rewan, how he encouraged our friendship whilst supporting the old king's every excess and refrained from restraining Sophia's harsh reforms. With

Rewan facing so many attempts on his life, it felt natural to ask my father's advice, and I placed one of my most trusted assassins in Rewan's bed, never realising her loyalty was to my family, not me. I was the one who placed the spy in the palace. Unwittingly yes, but you were right, and I almost got Rewan killed.'

The bitterness in Kaian's voice didn't escape Ren's attention. After riding for a moment in silence, he asked, 'We all make mistakes, but the question is, what are you going to do now? This kingdom and the man who leads it need you, so don't let your guilt and resentment stop you from making the right decision. Visit him tonight, Kaian.'

The assassin met Ren's gaze, and amusement flashed in his eyes. 'Who are you, and what have you done with the quiet Ghost? I'm sure that man wouldn't push me into the king's bed.'

'Someone has to.' This answer made Kaian laugh long after Ren left to lead the column on the last stretch to Madron.

When the army finally made camp and settled for the night, Ren found a secluded space on the outskirts of the encampment, leaving Kaian in charge of Rewan's security as he dined with some local aristocrats. The citizens of Madron took the sudden arrival of the king and his army with great trepidation, mainly concerned about their food supply. However, a generous donation of grain and dried meat made the locals much more amenable to the army's presence. With the atmosphere much soothed, Ren could finally relax.

He lost himself in the slow, deliberate practice of his Jian kata when searing pain ripped through his shoulder, throwing him off balance, and invisible fingers reached into his chest, tugging at the bond he shared with Ina. The sensation was so overwhelming that the tired warrior had to support himself on his sword to not fall to his knees.

'What is going on, my lady?' he said, closing his eyes and focusing on the desperation behind the connection. At that moment, the bond felt so tangible that he could almost see the silver strands binding him to the woman he had sworn to protect.

Ren sat back on the frozen ground, crossing his legs and laying his sword across his knees, focused on his breathing, offering whatever strength Ina needed to the connection.

'What are you doing? Ren, what is wrong?' Ayni's voice, full of concern, interrupted his meditation, leaving him dizzy when Ina reached for the bond again.

'Ina is injured,' he said, cold sweat pooling under his collar.

'I see…' Ayni's concern was now tinged with anger, but she sat beside him without further comment, offering Ren comfort just by being there. It felt like an eternity as Ren concentrated, feeling Ina's emotions as she battled, frustrated at being too distant to help. Eventually, despite the pain he still felt through their connection, the witch stopped drawing strength from the bond. Heaving a sigh of relief, the warrior turned to Ayni, smiling as she offered a hand to help him stand.

'Does it hurt like that often?' Ayni's quiet question turned his smile wistful, her concern filling his heart with a warmth that drew his hand to stroke her cheek gently.

'No, this was… intense, and worrying, but thankfully it is fading now. Ina is usually reluctant to call upon the bond, so something dire must have happened. I'm sorry, mi'khaira, we can no longer afford to travel so slowly. I will have to push the army to increase their pace.'

He stroked his companion's cheek again, beckoning for her to follow him to their quarters, but Ayni shook her head. 'I will be there in a moment. I need to stretch my wings, now more than ever, if I'm going to spend the whole day in a rickety wagon.' Ren tilted his head, scrutinising her expression before forcing himself to nod.

'Don't stay out too long. We both need to rest before tomorrow.'

By the time the dragoness joined him in their room, Ren was fast asleep, yet it must have been late, the dark circles under her eyes noticeable when he lightly kissed her in the morning. Her warm, inviting smile nearly distracted him from his duties, but with a teasing nip of her bottom lip, he made his escape and was soon dressed and shouting orders at the sluggish soldiers in the encampment. Ren had hoped Ina would visit him in a dream to explain the previous day, but instead of her, he dreamed of the forest and took this bizarre dream as a sign she was well. Still, his concern about her wouldn't recede, and despite feeling guilty, the warrior drove the army at a blistering pace until a red-faced mage approached him, proposing they use magic to ease the soldier's burdens.

Ren was unsure if he wanted to hug the bejewelled mage or punch him for offering help at such a late stage. Once cast, the relief in the soldier's posture made the slight delay worth the time as the army moved forward with a spring in their step, reaching the outskirts of Thorn earlier than expected. At the first sighting of the castle, Ren rode over to King Rewan's side.

'Your Majesty, I will ride ahead and announce your arrival.'

Rewan and Kaian gave him an amused look before the king nodded in agreement. 'We noticed you were eager to arrive early. Go check on my royal witch and send her my regards. Kaian, tell the column to take a rest and clean up. We should give our hosts a spectacle to enjoy, don't you think?'

Ren glanced at Kaian, realising the two men had repaired a few bridges, then bowed in gratitude before replying. 'Thank you, Your Majesty, for your understanding.'

With that, the warrior gave his horse a firm command and leapt forward into a gallop, barely noticing Kaian stopping and taking control of the army.

The wind flowing past, the speed of the horse, and the freedom of the moment brought a grin to Ren's face. When he heard another horse, followed by the sight of Ayni chasing after him, he let out a war cry from his homeland, the sheer joy of the moment eclipsing the uncertainty of the situation.

'You didn't think you could leave me behind?' she asked, breathless from the ride.

'Never, my love. I'm just happy to be free of responsibility for so many lives, even for a short while,' he said, surprised by his little white lie.

'Ren, I know you are worried about Ina and don't want to hurt my feelings. I can see how much you missed her. You don't need to hide it from me, my love.'

He smiled bashfully and lowered his eyes to avoid Ayni's gaze. 'You are an exceptional woman,' he said when he leaned over to kiss her hand.

'I know. Now let's ensure our third wheel is fit and well so we can return to our extraordinary normality,' she said, galloping off, a carefree laugh trailing behind, daring him to chase her.

Ina slowly walked up the stairs, lost in thought, her discussion with Cyrus and Velka weighing on her mind. The spell causing the curse draining life from the land had ancient origins. Even with his talent, Cyrus had to search the library vault to find any reference to the devastating spell.

During the mage wars, in a desperate attempt to starve an invading army, an unknown mage slaughtered his compatriots, tied their souls together and cursed the soil, leaving nothing but desolated land. However, there was no mention of a counter-spell, and the curse had eventually burnt itself out. Ina suspected that was the genesis of the eastern desert, a thriving nation in legend.

After that revelation, the three mages looked at each other, horrified, until Cyrus began muttering, his eyes glowing. Velka fell backwards, but Ina looked relaxed as she glanced at her friend. 'It's my uncle's talent asserting itself. He'll be fine in a moment.'

With a groan and a curse, Cyrus looked at the two ladies. 'It appears one of you read something recently, mentioning an attempt to send an envoy to the drow empress, Sowenna, and the death of spring, but it never happened thanks to her untimely death from the chaos madness.'

Ina echoed her uncle's groan, realising she had read the story. 'That was me. It was a cautionary tale on the perils of chaos magic. During an attempted coup, the prince consort sacrificed himself to save their daughter, but in doing so, the empress lost control, spiralling into madness which only ended once she'd broken the world by raising the Grey Mountains and died. Unfortunately, they didn't say why they thought she could help.'

Despite finding a reference to chaos magic, it hadn't provided any answers on how to deal with the current situation. Still, Ina knew she couldn't let the southern lands fall prey to the ancient curse. She considered asking Skarbnik for the last piece of regalia. "*Come to me whenever you are ready to take it,*" were his words, but she didn't feel ready, doubting her ability to remain sane if even the mightiest chaos archmage lost the battle with temptation.

At the mention of an unaffected area within the circle of cursed corpses, Velka suggested that must be where the spell linked to the earth. Perhaps there would be a way for her to commune with the primaeval earth spirit to disrupt the link enough for Ina's chaos to cut off access to its power source, effectively destroying the spell.

Although Velka's proposal couldn't solve all their current problems, it was the best they had for the moment. The witch agreed to proceed as soon as the theatrics with the southern rebels were over. Ina had still neglected to tell her companions of her meeting with Lada and the promise she'd brokered with the spring goddess.

Her thoughts drifted to the day of Mar's return. The bath with him had quickly transformed from getting the hairy warrior clean to them both getting very dirty, ending with them apologising to the servants for flooding the floor.

Ina hadn't needed to question the thoroughly filthy male. Instead, he offered insight into the rebellion and reassured her he thought her plan would work. The only concern was the strange southern noble. After reviewing his revelations, she felt overwhelmed by how many threats there seemed to be in the province. *One thing at a time, Striga. Whose sinister mind could construct such a convoluted and layered plot?*

Deep in her thoughts, Ina tripped over an uneven step, heading face-first for the ground, until a strong, calloused hand snapped out and pulled her back against a solid, familiar chest. Her gasp of surprise slipped into a sultry moan, which devolved into a disgusted grimace.

'Mar, you smell like a fox's arsehole. What have you been rolling in?'

'I was waiting for my sparring partner to come down for her daily sword lesson, but I found out she was busy with gods and curses. Instead, I had to pummel an angry orc who wouldn't stop muttering about bloody witches and poor pregnant mages. I also feel a little lonely and useless when you confer with Cyrus and Velka all day while I wait for Ren to bring my army here.'

'They should be here soon,' Ina said, avoiding Mar's eyes, gasping when he scooped her into his arms and, jumping two steps at a time, carried her to their room.

'Rest, my love, you look tired. In the evening, I will fly and check their position. I know you are worried about how your little adventure affected Ren, but he is a resilient warrior, and I suspect I took most of the impact. If not, I will be one very embarrassed dragon.' Mar sat next to the fireplace, pulling Ina onto his lap, and stroked her back, slowly kneading her tense muscles.

A forceful knocking interrupted their discussion, and the door opened after Ina shouted her permission. Seeing the two people wo entered, Ina gasped joyfully and leapt up to greet them.

'Ren! Ayni! Oh gods, did I hurt you?' Ina ran towards the hastily approaching warrior, who caught her mid-run, laughing as he hugged her close.

'Don't be silly, my lady. It is just pain. You were the one injured, so please explain what happened,' he asked, exhaling slowly to relax his tense posture.

Behind them, Mar and Ayni exchanged greetings before Mar nodded at the pair, eyes rolling.

'Ayni, would you care to join me? I haven't flown in a while and could do with stretching my wings.' Ina blushed in embarrassment as Mar greeted the dragoness, realising she'd completely ignored her in the excitement of seeing her guardian. Removing herself from Ren's arms, Ina offered an apologetic smile to the other woman.

'I'm sorry, Ayni. Welcome to Castle Thorn. I'm glad you came.' Her formal greeting earned her a smirk before Ayni nodded to Mar.

'I think that is an excellent idea. I need some fresh air, and Ina needs to brief Ren on recent events. Should we see if you can still catch me?'

Her remark, a blatant reminder of her mating dance with Mar, made Ina frown and step forward, but Ayni had already left the room, chuckling. As he followed the dragoness, Mar leaned down, stole a kiss and whispered in the witch's ear.

'I won't even try,' he said, following Ayni, who had already disappeared up the stairs.

CHAPTER TWENTY-TWO

Mar closed the door behind him, leaving the two friends looking at each other with unaccustomed wariness. Ren broke the awkward silence first, a wry look on his face as he gave Ina another hug and asked, 'My lady, you worried me. Can you explain what happened?'

With an embarrassed wince, Ina squeezed Ren's hand, allowing herself a moment to enjoy the strength of their bond. It felt so comfortable having him near, and the witch sighed with contentment. 'I missed you so much, my friend. It wasn't a comfortable journey, and I often needed your advice. I'm sorry I had to reach for our connection. I know how much it hurt Mar, so I hope you weren't left prostrate in the mud.'

Her last remark caused the taciturn warrior to laugh. 'No, I didn't end up in the mud, but I could feel your emotions as you fought, and your injury didn't feel like an ordinary wound. Feeling your pain and fear, unable to help, was far worse than any physical pain I might have felt.'

'I will find a way to release you from the spell. That will be better for everyone, and Mar alone should be enough to ward off the madness.'

'No, you won't, Ina. How often must I tell you I'm content with this arrangement?'

'Ren, but Ayni… that's not fair to either of you.'

'I know your words came from concern, but I could not love a woman who would ask me to abandon my family just because they sometimes ask for help. Ayni understands, and her love is unchanged by the connection that saved my life. Even if you found a way to dissolve the bond, it wouldn't change our friendship or my respect for you. I am humbled when I see how you care and change things for the better, despite struggling with your own demons. You helped me change from the ghost of my former self to a man who is happy, feeling complete, and living a life as exciting as any in the court of Yanwo. So please, accept my decision to be bonded and never mention dissolving what is so precious to me again.' Ren's eyes narrowed when she sighed with relief. 'What do you mean by warding off the madness?'

Ren looked confused when Ina revealed the origins of the sacrifice spell and that its healing properties were a by-product of the bond, not the purpose. The witch explained its function was to prevent a chaos mage from losing touch with reality and destroying everything around them.

At this point, Ren lost control of his legendary restraint, leaping from his seat to pace back and forth as he snapped out, 'And you want to remove it? You're saying that the only reason you can hold back when chaos takes over is the bond you formed with us? How many times… No! The times we've spoken of your fear that you'll become another Sowenna and break the world, yet you want to remove the one thing preventing it? Because I deserve a love unencumbered by this so-called shackle? No! We will never speak of breaking the bond ever again. You will never free Mar or me and draw whatever you need from us to keep yourself safe. No hesitation or second thoughts because the alternative would break us all.'

With tears in her eyes, Ina stood up, stepped in front of the agitated Ren and placed a hand over his heart, looking into his eyes as she smiled. 'I am blessed with men with no instinct for self-preservation. It doesn't sit well with me to see you suffer because I fought some bastard with stolen power, but have it your way. I promise I won't search for a way to release the spell,' she said softly before turning and walking onto the balcony. She sighed as she watched the two dragons weaving and diving in the sky.

'It feels awkward, but I'm happy. I know we are living through interesting times, and everything keeps falling to pieces, but I have Mar, Velka, and you; that's more than anyone deserves. I even like the current king, mostly. Speaking of our dear monarch, did… Was Kaian involved with the rebellion?'

Ren, finally relaxed enough to smile, joined Ina in watching the dragons whirl around each other joyfully in the sky. 'Kaian has been proven innocent, and while it was a messy affair, both he and the king will be joining us soon. The Water Horse House, it seems, were supporters of Sophia, and when that scheme failed, they must have expected to be purged, so they looked for a way to distract the king's attention. Rewan appointed Kaian as the new duke, but cannot deal with them yet.' Laying his hand on Ina's shoulder, Ren lightly squeezed the tense muscles. 'My lady, you still haven't explained how you were injured. For my peace of mind, please tell me what happened.'

Ina detailed her adventure, observing how Ren's face lit up when she described fighting with her sword, frowning when she got to the more gritty details.

'I should have come with you,' he said, but before he could add anything more, a blast of wind buffeted their clothes, and a dragon's roar almost deafened them.

'The king is within the city walls. Sa'Ren Gerel, get your hands off my woman, or I'll dance with your dragoness.' Mar's voice was laced with laughter. Still, Ina sent a weak whip of chaos at his swinging tail.

'No, you will not. I'm a jealous woman, and since both of you rejected my offer to release you from the sacrifice spell, your fate is sealed. Also, Ayni is a lady who wouldn't take used goods, and you are definitely a well-used lizard.'

The roar of laughter from the dragoness made everyone look up in fear, but Ina waved her hand in dismissal. 'Shoo, both of you. Land and change, and I'll send a servant to warn Cyrus and Mirena to be ready for the king. If we want to keep up appearances, we must provide a suitable welcome for the mighty king. Mar, can you help settle the army? There's a field next to the river where they can set up a temporary camp. Ren, you must be tired. I will find you and Ayni a comfortable room so you can get ready for the evening. I want to discuss our plans with you all at dinner. We have much to do and not much time for it.'

Her words spewed out of her mouth at the speed of a racing horse, but instead of carrying out her orders, her friends looked at her with growing amusement until Ina rushed out, running to Cyrus's office just as a servant shouted, 'The king! The king is coming to the castle!'

Ina stood in the great hall right next to the chair of the High Lord occupied by Cyrus. Mar, despite his amusement, flew to welcome the arriving army, leading them to the allocated area, and now they waited on the king. Rewan was kind enough to give Cyrus and his court a moment of preparation, slowly marching through the city and graciously accepting greetings and well wishes from the surprised citizens.

When the sound of trumpets cut through the quiet buzz of conversation, Ina braced for the pomp and circumstance of a royal visit, knowing there'd be a meeting afterwards for the actual discussions. After all, she was the one who'd accused his lover of treason, and no matter how good her intentions were, it was better to clear the air before they headed into conflict.

Rewan entered the great hall with typical nonchalance, frowning when he noticed Ina standing stiff and proper behind her uncle's high chair. He raised an eyebrow, tilting his head towards her uncle, and the witch answered with a half smile and shrug that provoked a sigh. Rewan straightened his back, striking a very regal pose as he approached Cyrus, who had already moved to the bottom of his small platform, bowing low when the king stopped.

'It is a pleasure to meet you, Duke Thorn. I hope my royal witch hasn't caused any inconvenience during her stay,' he said, reaching his hand towards Cyrus, who kissed the royal seal before straightening.

'No, Your Majesty, my niece has been very useful, especially after my father's premature death, making significant progress with the issues concerning the southern province. As the new head of House Thorn, I would like to reaffirm our loyalty to the throne of Cornovii and put our every resource at your disposal.'

Cyrus and the king exchanged more pleasantries, but Ina's gaze was fixed on Kaian, who stood quietly in the group of court members. Ina noticed a few mages around him she didn't recognise and men in military outfits she'd met once or twice. Suddenly, the doors opened again to reveal Mar and Ren marching forward. Ina reluctantly smiled at their attempt to impress the southern court's spy. Mar had once again used his dragon magic, dressing in blue steel armour with the crest of Liath proudly displayed on his chest. His massive body projected an aura of leashed menace, while Ren sported Yanwo court robes, ash grey silk contrasting dangerously with polished black leather.

Daro was right behind them, his captain's livery somehow modified to incorporate the finery of the Steppe orc chieftain, but Ina only noticed when Velka nearly swooned, muttering, 'He is so handsome.'

'They all are very pretty, but the best part is that they are a force to reckon with, and whoever is watching the king's arrival will see that now.'

'Your Majesty, the army encampment is established, with patrols and sentries in place and under orders to detain anyone spying on their deportment,' Mar barked out, snapping a sharp military salute, making Rewan smile. Ina could see the pride in the king's eyes when he looked at his military commanders.

'Thank you, Lord Marshal. Your efficiency is, as ever, a great source of comfort in these trying times. I look forward to seeing that talent in action on the battlefield. However, for tonight, it would please me greatly to relax in the company of House Thorn and take a moment to consult with our royal witch.'

Every inch the regal monarch, Rewan commanded the room whilst still able to put everyone at ease, impressing Ina and even Mirena, if her deep curtsey was any indication.

'Your chambers are ready, Your Majesty. My daughter would be honoured to serve in your chambers to help you relax after such a long journey.'

It was not uncommon for noble houses to offer daughters to serve travelling kings to curry favour, but this, coming from her aunt, surprised Ina, and she looked at her aunt sharply. Thankfully, Kaian saved the day.

'My lady, whilst we appreciate House Thorn's offer, the king is a very private man and prefers the company of those he knows intimately. The one request we would make is the presence of Lady Inanuan so that we may consult on her latest exploits.'

Ina could barely restrain her laughter when she noticed her cousin's jealous glare aimed at the master assassin and the king, as well as Mar's hand hovering over the hilt of his sword. The dragon's golden eyes looked at her, prompting her to refuse, but Ina suspected there was more to the offer than an intimate conversation.

'I shall prepare myself,' she said with a long-suffering sigh. She risked a glance at her dragon, silently urging him to restrain himself. Ren's deep frown told her he didn't like the idea either.

Only Daro seemed oblivious to the situation, because even Velka whispered, 'Are you sure? That's... Rewan has a history.'

'Yes, mostly fabricated to avoid being slaughtered by his sister. Besides, he is too intelligent to demand things he knows he will never get,' she said, watching Mirena lead the king and his entourage out of the room.

'Ina?' Mar's voice was almost a growl. They were still in the grand hall, and although it cost him a lot, Mar did his best to maintain his composure. Still, his possessiveness tickled the mischievous streak in her soul. *I'm a wicked woman, but I like him like that*, she thought, sensing the dragon's presence through the bond. The beast in him was ready to stake its claim right there in front of everyone, and Ina felt the heat crawl over her cheeks under his intense gaze.

'Mar? Forgive me, Lord Marshal, I need to prepare.' She turned on her heel, hastily retreating when he moved forward to catch her hand. Judging by the heat in Mar's molten eyes, she feared that if he caught her, more than just her cheeks would blush.

It took more than a few moments and several curses to remove the heavy court dress before braiding her hair and slipping into a light house dress, covering the thin fabric with a heavy cloak. Once she felt comfortable, Ina set off for the king's temporary accommodation. Rewan was already in his bathroom bathing chamber, soaking in a large, heated tub with steam rising from the hot stones. Although Ina considered this a perk of magical homes, whether great or small, as the greatest invention of civilisation, she hadn't expected him to actually take a bath. After grabbing a towel and throwing it over the king's hips, Ina found a seat far enough away to avoid being splashed and sat down, blatantly staring at Rewan's body.

'What was so important that you called me here, risking the dragon's wrath? We both know Mar won't take kindly to you ogling my breasts.'

Before Rewan could answer, the doors opened again, and two men walked through the thickening steam. 'Your Majesty, we are here to add an extra layer of security.' Mar's voice was dripping with sarcasm, but as she caught sight of them, Ina couldn't prevent the inelegant snort that escaped. It wasn't that each one wore what she could only describe as a personal arsenal upon their bodies, but the fact that those weapons were almost all they wore, except maybe for a loincloth and pride. When the two warriors posed on either side of the door, Ina choked on laughter and grabbed the bench to stop herself falling to the floor as she tried to wipe the tears streaming from her eyes.

'Mar, we were trying to make any spies think it was a meaningless dalliance, not a briefing on the situation in the South. I'm not here to stroke his ego, or anything else, for that matter. Please find something and cover yourselves up. Do you know how distracting it is to have three naked men before me? Ren, I'm surprised you agreed to join him in this escapade. Aren't you supposed to be the sensible one?'

'My lady, as you can see, we dressed appropriately for men guarding the king when he is otherwise engaged, and we wouldn't want our liege to come to any... lasting harm.' The warrior's reply, unphased by her accusation, was directly aimed at the king, and when Rewan fell back, laughing uproariously, it was clear he understood completely.

'All I wanted was to thank you for finding the threat in the palace and to ask if there was any information that couldn't be shared in front of a war council. However, as most of us are already here, please explain why I am leading my army around like a flamboyant mummers troop. We can return to the subject of meaningless dalliances afterwards....'

Mar's interruption was firm as he stepped between the king and Ina. 'I would suggest you drop that subject, Your Majesty, and I would appreciate you averting your gaze from my future wife's body.' The witch, about to snap at him, glanced down and clamped her lips shut when she noticed the effect of the steam on her dress, her cheeks flaming red at how transparent the material had become.

Kaian chose that moment to walk into the room, smirking at the sight that greeted him. 'Well, this is an unexpected pleasure. Aren't we supposed to be discussing why we brought the army?'

Ina's sigh was as long-suffering as it was heartfelt. 'I have a plan to avoid bloodshed. If we arrive at Alsia with the most intimidating, well-organised army and generously offer food, aid and a full amnesty of all soldiers for the rebel lord's unconditional surrender, then they might go home without any fuss. Mar told me most of the rebel army are simple farmers, the majority press-ganged into service and easy to impress, so he would be the best person to discuss the details. Our only concern is an unknown southern noble who seems to be the puppet master behind your cousin.'

Mar spoke then, his thoughtful expression sober despite the strange outfit. 'We believe he may be a Verdante noble. There was a moment when his appearance flickered strangely, so most likely a magical disguise, but he controlled Prince Wawrzyniec with an iron will.'

The fierce look Kaian gave Mar lowered the temperature of the room. 'Give me a full description of him later. I think removing anyone who can strengthen that coward prince's spine would be best.'

'It is an appealing idea, but I think it would be counter-productive. We can use him as our messenger to Verdante, a trusted witness to the unassailable strength of Cornovii's army.' Ina stood up and started pacing as she talked, her dress clinging to the curves of her body. The surprise on her face when she was suddenly enveloped in a thick towel left the king and Kaian laughing whilst Ren pulled the witch back to the chair, forcing her to sit back against Mar.

'I'm sorry, my lady, but this is too distracting.' He nodded, pointing to her wet clothing. 'So we go to Alsia with a well-trained army, mages casting breathtaking spells, and two dragons above them all, breathing fire and causing havoc?'

The men looked at Ina as if she'd grown a second head, and the witch sighed in frustration, fighting to free herself from the towel. 'Look, when it comes to waving swords around, I know men lose what little sense they were born with, but it will work, especially as there's an eclipse that day. I talked it over with Cyrus, and, with the judicious use of chaos and my two anchors to keep me grounded, I can create a spectacle to overawe even the most jaded of soldiers. That's all it will be, though, a spectacle. No one will get hurt, so it would help, Your Majesty, if you could step forward at that point and make your offer. I'm sure that will be enough to make them surrender. If not... well, we all know what happens then.'

Rewan sat up straighter in the tub, appreciation and hope in his smile, before he turned to look at Mar.

'Lord Marcach, I will leave this to your capable hands. I am sure you and Sa'Ren can coordinate the army to be prepared for every eventuality.' When both men nodded in agreement, Rewan turned back to the witch. 'Ina, if this works, I will shower you with gold.'

'I don't want gold, but if you're in a giving mood, give Ren the recognition he deserves. A title and some land should cover it; you know he deserves it. I also want you to restore the House of Willow and give the title to Velka and Daro. They may be commoners, but they have served you faithfully, and as my father was the last male of the line, I may cede it to whomever I choose.'

'I don't need it, my lady.' Ren's voice was barely audible, and his face, pale even in the heat of the bathhouse, told her all she needed to know.

'Yes, you do. You've served Cornovii with honour and decorum and keep me sane. That role alone deserves a handsome reward. You live here, not as a sword for hire, but as the Dragonlord of Yanwo.' Ina approached him and placed a hand on his cheek. 'I can't give you much, but I will give you all I can,' she whispered as he turned his face and kissed her palm.

'Dragonlord?' Rewan's surprised voice broke the moment, and Ina turned around with a mischievous grin.

'Your Majesty, may I introduce you to Sa'Ren Gerel, Prince of Yanwo and bonded partner of the sea-green dragoness, Ayni? We are fortunate to have such a noble warrior call Cornovii home.'

'You are always full of surprises, Lady Inanuan, but a request for Sa'Ren to be granted a title has already been accepted. As to the House of Willow, if the Leshy gives his blessing, I will offer no objection, so it seems you will have to take a reward.'

'Good luck with that, unless you can guarantee a future where I'll not kill everyone I love in a vortex of madness? Just be a king worthy of those who serve you. Now, if you'll excuse me, I need to help with the preparations for dinner. Velka also mentioned a viable way of breaking Marzanna's curse, and as Mar decided I can't take part in any orgies, I shall leave.'

'Ina, I'm so going to spank your arse for this.' Mar growled when she bent to kiss him, and the towel slid down, leaving little to the imagination as the witch's linen dress plastered itself to her body.

'Promises, promises. This is the only place in the castle that's safe from eavesdropping, so I will take my bosom out of sight to let you focus on your plans. See you at dinner.'

Ina walked out, leaving the men to their discussion. The spring chill left her shivering in the damp dress as she headed back to change, a smile teasing her lips as she thought about the meeting. Rewan was not attracted to her, that much was clear, so using his quarters to meet had felt like a wonderful idea. After seeing the wild look in Mar's eyes after she agreed to attend the king, the witch knew he would be joining them, which prompted her choice of garment, hoping to tease that wildness into action later. When her dragon arrived, half naked, that hope had grown... until Ren appeared, just as unclad, changing the moment from the sublime to the ridiculous.

While rushing to her cosy, warm room, she bumped into Velka in the corridor, and her friend grasped her cloak to steady herself.

'Why are you wet? Oh, we need to talk,' she said, rubbing her moist palms over her dress, and Ina chuckled lightly.

'That's what happens when you're in the bathroom with four men. Come to my room so we can talk privately.' Ina waved to a servant and requested a snack and some tea before clasping Velka's hand and dragging her along. When the door closed behind them, Ina dropped her cloak to the floor, and Velka gasped.

'Four men? And you showed up in... this?'

'Oh, we both know Rewan and Kaian only like skinny women, and Mar knows my feelings. I didn't expect Ren to come as well. It was only slightly embarrassing, but his feelings have changed, and Mar seems more relaxed. I feel like fate has smiled, giving me a man to love and a friend to cherish.'

'Ina, you managed to dream-walk with Ren, which shouldn't be possible for a mage with your talent. Then Mar felt your pain in such a physical way it forced his transformation. Do you think it's because of the spell? Have you thought about reversing it?'

'Yes, and yes, but they both refused to break the bond. It might be selfish, but I'm happy they did, Flower. I know I shouldn't, but I do. Let's stop talking about my crazy life. Did you find a way of countering the blight?'

'Yes, and no. You can't destroy the statue or the sacrifices you mentioned. They are protected by the power they drain from the land, but you can cut them off from the magic that fuels them. If you can isolate the spell long enough, the curse will burn itself out, just like it did in the wastelands.' Velka looked at Ina's face, brightened by hope, and shook her head. 'Don't get your hopes up just yet. I can create the barrier, and the soil will hold my spell, but I can't sustain it. Redirecting the magic being drawn into the curse won't help. The sheer magnitude of power needed to hold the shield would burn out anyone stupid enough to try. Even linking a full assembly of twelve mages wouldn't be enough.'

'Can you channel the magic through me?'

'I can, but it is raw chaos siphoned from the whole province, and the curse will fight hard to reach it. Even with your gemstones, you may be ripped apart. Maybe if you had that circlet you mentioned? Cyrus said a chaos archmage, fully linked to the regalia, could control it. He said that kind of power could create new life or destroy the continent. Only the user's willpower limits its use. Ina, maybe it is time for you to take it?'

'No, I can't trust myself to control it. I'm not the sort of person who should wield such power. People annoy me, so if one too many idiots insult me, I may well erase a continent. Let's do it my way, Velka. Trust me, I can handle it.'

Her friend wanted to argue, but Ina pulled a few dresses from the wardrobe and waved them in front of the mage. 'It's all set. You will cast the nullifying barrier and redirect the land's magic to me, and I will use it to sustain the barrier until the curse burns itself out. We will take care of this after the theatrics with the rebels.'

She put a dress to her chest before reaching for another. 'For now, I need your help with something much more important. Which one should I wear to look irresistible but intimidating for dinner?' When Velka raised an eyebrow, baffled by the subject change, Ina added, 'Spies and men, you have only one chance of making a good impression. Besides, it is fun to dress up for the occasion every now and then.'

CHAPTER TWENTY-THREE

Ina almost regretted asking her friend's opinion about her outfit, but now, finally dressed and prepared, she had to admit Velka had a good eye for fashion. As she looked down at the dress, the witch glimpsed a flash of gold and, remembering the encounter with Lada, pulled back her sleeve to study the strange tattoo. The legendary Zmij, a winged serpent, fangs dripping with deadly venom, coiled around her forearm, looking so alive, its eyes seeming to follow her as Ina moved her arm, but apart from this strange phenomenon, it was just an inconvenient reminder of her promise to the spring goddess. However, Ina doubted that was the case, as every time she'd thought to mention her latest encounter with divinity, she was distracted by something else.

Lost in thought, Ina gasped when a muscular arm wrapped around her waist, pressing her to a firm chest, and a familiar metallic scent washed over her.

'Tut, tut. What if I was an enemy soldier attempting to take advantage of a pretty lady?' Mar said, and the playfulness in his voice brought a smile to her lips. His beard brushed at the base of her neck, giving her a delicious rush of goosebumps, and as revenge, Ina stretched, pressing her backside to his breeches.

'An enemy soldier would be dragging his sorry arse from the trees below, but I have a soft spot for bearded dragons, so you can take advantage of me for a little longer, especially since you are so warm,' she said, leaning on him and letting his hand trail along her arm in a soft caress.

'What is this, my spitfire?' Mar asked when his hand stroked her forearm, and Ina realised she had forgotten to lower her sleeve.

'Nothing, just ... I wanted to bear the mark of a dragon.'

'Ina, you have many talents, but lying isn't one of them, and if you ever want to have a visible sign, wear my wedding ring. So, what is it really?'

The witch rolled her eyes when he grabbed her wrist, stretching out her arm to study the golden image more closely while she detailed her encounter with Lada and the promise she gave to the goddess of spring.

'It is incredibly lifelike and compliments your skin. Want to bet that's the Zmij's actual appearance? Do you think it's supposed to do something?' Mar raised his voice when the music her uncle arranged became louder, followed by Ayni singing.

'Nothing so far, not even during my fight with the volkhv, and I had my arse handed to me back there. If not for Mirena, I would've struggled to survive, so I think it's just a pretty reminder, though this is the gods we're talking about.' Ina paused, listening to the enchanting song before continuing with a smile. 'Ayni has a beautiful voice, don't you think?'

'So we must wait and see what Lada has planned,' Mar said, teasing her with her favourite phrase. 'And yes, she has a beautiful voice. She also loves Ren, so try being a little nicer to her. Now, fancy telling me why you wore such a thin dress to see Rewan?'

'Don't be obtuse. You're the military genius. It is difficult to eavesdrop there, and men always overlook weak women desperate to fuck the king, so it was the perfect misdirection. Besides, I was the most dressed out of all the people there. I should be asking why you and Ren paraded around, barely clothed, flaunting your masculinity in front of the two men you knew would appreciate it.'

'Ohh...' Mar's eyes widened as if the thought of being enticing to another man hadn't occurred to him.

'Yes, *ohh*, you bloody oaf, displaying yourself like this. All that furriness is mine, and don't you forget it,' she said, grinning as she gestured towards his body.

Mar fought his laughter but failed, shaking them both as he expressed his happiness. 'I love you, woman. You've turned my life upside down, driven me insane more than I care to admit, and you are absolutely wonderful. My only regret is that I didn't follow you into exile when Roda cast you out.'

'So trust me, dragon, when I say there is no one else for me. I could stand naked in front of an entire army, but only you could touch me.'

'I do trust you. However, I'd appreciate you not testing that statement, or we might find out how thoroughly I touch you.'

Mar turned her around, looking down to capture her gaze, and she felt his mood shift. As his frown deepened, Ina braced herself for unpleasant news, but as the silence stretched out, she began losing her patience until the dam burst, and he spoke. 'I've been thinking about Ren, how close you are and, well... I know it is important to you both.' Mar stroked her cheek as he searched for the right words to express himself.

'You know how Ayni shares a mind connection with Ren? When we were flying, she told me Ren had nightmares of losing the bond and being unable to protect you without that connection. What you told me about the sacrifice spell made me think maybe I was wrong in asking you only to choose me. I know his presence calms you down in a way mine never could. You need him, and he needs you. Ayni knew it too, so she asked me to allow….'

'Stop right there. Whatever crazy idea you have in that thick dragon's skull, the answer is no. If you're suggesting what I think you are, then whilst it might help control my magic, it would make everyone miserable. Before I knew you both well, the thought of sharing your affection had its appeal. I was lonely, and you were an infuriating oaf who I fell for against my better judgement. We are different now, and I will not share my love for you. If that means I must work harder at controlling my chaos, so be it.'

Mar's proposal felt so ridiculous that Ina had to resist the temptation to break the tension with a joke. Instead, she wanted to allow her dragon to express his feelings. Whatever Ayni had told him left Mar willing to deny his very nature, but he seemed to struggle to put it into words. Ina realised that to help him, she had to make an admission of her own.

'Mar, I let you live in my house, sleep in my bed, and make love to me every night, not because of the bond, but because I love you. Yes, the spell is strengthened by that intimacy, to the point my sanity is as safe as possible, but that's not why I do it. I want you happy, both of you. Ren was right when he said we are family, and we'll always care for each other as a family should.'

She searched his face for understanding. A soft smile blossomed on her lips when the stunned dragon lifted her hand, kissing her palm. Mar leaned forward, pressing his forehead to hers, locking her in a tight embrace and through their bond, she felt he struggled to contain his emotions.

His reply, when it came, was barely a whisper, laced with a pain Ina didn't realise Mar had held inside. 'I so wanted to hear you love me, but shame on me, it was my insensitive words that forced you to say it. I can endure anything as long as you are safe. You said before that the bond keeps you stable when you use your magic, so how can I deny you that protection? When Ayni mentioned Ren's nightmares, I thought you were in danger, and I would rather see you bed my best friend than get hurt. I'm sorry, Ina, I feel like a fool. I thought I was doing the right thing.' The anger Mar directed inward shocked the witch, and she grasped his chin, forcing his gaze on her face, looking at him in frustration.

'I know Ayni thinks I'm one step from a killing spree, so she'd best not be having this same conversation with Ren, or I swear I'll maim the pair of you. You are a wonderful man, Marcach of Liath. I love you. You didn't force anything, I'm sorry I made you wait to hear it, but I do love you, and don't you dare to doubt it, you foolish dragon. I'm truly grateful that you're trying to put my safety before your pride and happiness, but casual touch will be more than enough to stop the bond from fading. I'm not sure how chaos mages did it during the mage wars, but I doubt they fucked everyone they met to stay sane. Besides, I'm getting better at controlling my magic, so accept that you are my one and only dragon.'

The music faded, making Ina aware of how long they'd spent alone, engrossed in this bizarre conversation. 'We need to go down. Did you set a date to march for Alsia? We need to go soon if we plan on arriving on time.'

'We will go in two days. It will be easier now, as Cyrus offered soldiers to help distribute supplies to the local populace. Without that to delay us, arriving at the battlefield shouldn't take long.'

'Good, I don't want to exhaust the mages, or the show won't be as spectacular as we need. I hope this works, Mar. It doesn't feel right, slaughtering farmers and boys to appease some bastard's ego.'

'It will work, my love. Let's join the party before the court wonders what we're doing for so long alone on the balcony.'

Mar took her hand, leading them inside, and Ina was acutely aware of all the accompanying stares as they walked through the room. Not that she minded, but Mirena's disapproving look was the one that jarred. Ina always thought her aunt was on her side, fighting the old duke the same way the witch did. Still, there'd been a distance since they returned from the temple. After her bathroom conversation with the king, Ina felt her aunt's disapproval whenever she looked at her.

When she reached the king's table, Ina sat next to Velka and Daro, leaning over to rest her head on the nature mage's shoulder. 'Thank you for your help, Flower. Now I almost look as ladylike as you. Can I ask you another favour? Mar said the army will be travelling to Alsia in two days, and I was hoping you'd stay here to prepare the spell for Marzanna's curse. If Daro stays to keep you safe, it will ease my mind, knowing you are in charge of the preparations.'

The orc saluted her, but Velka's frown told her she didn't like the idea. 'Ina, I'm not baggage to be left behind when you no longer need it.'

'No, but your role is different. You will be the hero who will free this land from the shackles of the blight. My role is to escort His Loftiness as he deals with his unruly subjects.'

'Is that so?' Rewan's voice interrupted their exchange. 'In that case, I should offer a reward for such heroic work. The House of Willow has too long been inactive in our realm, so if Mage Velka can rid the land of its cursed winter, I will grant her the title of Lady Willow with all the privileges and land that comes with the position.'

A shocked gasp travelled around the room, with only four people grinning at Velka's and Daro's expressions. Ina was impressed at Rewan's manoeuvring, preventing discord within the court by offering to reward the nature mage for an arduous task and not bestowing the position to a favoured supporter.

Raising a glass to the suddenly pale Velka, Ina winked and toasted her friend. 'To Lady Velka, soon to be Contessa Willow, Saviour of the South. I can't wait for the bad limericks at the *Drunken Wizard*.'

The banquet lasted a few more hours before people began slipping away to bed, leaving the servants to clean up after the feast. In a rush to finish their work, no one paid attention to the woman who stalked past the kitchen door towards the castle gardens.

Rurik sat in the shadows beneath the willow's canopy, watching the bright lights in the castle as a haunting voice wove a spell of beauty through the chill night air. He knew the wait till the end of the banquet would be long and pulled his cloak tighter around his body, hoping the spell woven into its fabric wouldn't drain too much of his energy. When Ina and her dragon appeared on the balcony, he smiled, observing their exchange. Although he couldn't hear much, the man's gentleness spoke louder than words, and he was happy she had someone to love. His experience taught him that people with something to lose were less likely to be self-destructive.

He must have dosed off as the next thing he knew was the sound of quiet footsteps and an urgent, hissed question.

'Rurik, are you here?'

'Yes, Mother. How was the feast?'

'Raucous and annoying. The army leaves in two days, but it is all theatrics designed to frighten the rebels into giving up without a fight. Make sure your little puppets aren't frightened into surrendering. Even with two dragons, Ina doesn't have the strength or guts to stop a determined enemy. This is our chance to bring the king to his knees and make them pay for what they did to us. That witch will never be your chosen one; she refused to claim the circlet and will never be confident enough to wield its power. Focus on escalating this battle into all-out war, so you can make your perfect kingdom once Cornovii and Verdante have bled each other dry.'

'No, too many will suffer if the war gets out of hand. We just need Cornovii weakened to the point they'd accept the rule of a benevolent council of mages. Only commoners suffer in a war, and that was never my intention. I am not a monster, mother, but I will do what is required of me.' Rurik shook his head, looking at his mother with determination. 'The rebellion was never meant to succeed, so let nature take its course. The Verdante army is close enough to the battlefield to witness who the real power behind the throne is, so let Ina have her moment.

There's still a good chance she'll claim the regalia to destroy the curse, so make sure to encourage her.'

The woman gave Rurik an irritated glance and shrugged. 'I said I would support you, but I see no other way for you to succeed if you don't crush Roda's vile seed before it takes root. He doesn't even have the grace to take a queen, flaunting his white-haired lover just as his father did. You shouldn't pin all your hope on the curse to force Ina's hand. Instead of retrieving the circlet, she and the nature mage plan to perform some ridiculous ritual they think will work.'

'I know you hate the late king, but please be patient. If we persuade Velka that Ina needs the regalia, I know she'll convince her friend. I will wait for the army to depart, visit the castle as a mage council messenger, and use our former relationship to gain her trust. Once she understands the situation, I'm sure Velka will talk Ina into using the circlet.'

Rurik's mother pulled her shawl tighter and shrugged. 'I have to go before my absence is noticed,' she said, turning to leave, but the necromancer was already lost in planning his next steps.

Rurik wandered the streets of Thorn, enjoying the crisp night air and pondering the next steps of his plan. First, he would have to earn Velka's trust again. Their last conversation at university in Osterad left her in tears. When she asked him why he was so obsessed with Ina, in his arrogance, he said that silly and naïve girls shouldn't try to understand what they couldn't comprehend. He had to make amends.

Maybe she would be more open to talking if he arrived injured, asking for help. He would need to open up about his past; the enslavement and pain that motivated his desire for a better world. *That should be enough. It wouldn't be for Ina, but*

Velka is gentler, and once she cries over my scars, I will help her with the spell. After all, we both want the blight to end. All I need is to convince her to tell Ina we need the regalia to fight a curse no one from the past could break.

The thought of meeting with Velka gave a spring to his step. He understood his mother's objections and hatred, but didn't share them. After all, the southern rebellion had been years in the planning, but the closer to the goal he was, the more doubts rose in his mind. All he'd ever wanted was to see the continent united to end the suffering caused by poverty and slavery, ensuring no one of noble birth or wealth could escape justice. He knew bringing together all the races and countries with such a goal would be nearly impossible unless they were confronted by an unstoppable magic willing to make a stand.

After escaping slavery and finding magic, Rurik had thought that was the end of his suffering, but at university, the noble-born mages had added their mark to his scars for being a filthy death master. He'd been reminded those in power did as they chose when his tormentors were freed, their bribery of the officials blatant and obscene.

When he met Velka and Ina, he'd cynically seen just two more dissolute nobles, but he should have known better. They never mistreated him, offered encouragement, and were genuinely interested in learning about his magic, despite having no talent with the dead.

The moment Ina refused to kill a helpless frog changed Rurik forever. As he watched this tiny female stand up for a creature of no significance, empowering it to defend itself, he saw his path and how to change the world for the better.

At the sight of his lodgings, Rurik ducked inside and paused, savouring the heat, even as it assaulted his senses with the smell of sweat and a hint of stale beer. With a goal in mind, his younger self had made many mistakes, assuming justice prevailed for those willing to fight for it. With one failure after another, he learned people will do the right thing only when all other options are removed. So, slowly but surely, he'd schemed, manipulated, persuaded, and threatened. He committed one shameful act after another to unite those with magic into a cause worthy of following until, finally, he was on the cusp of success.

His mother asked him to abandon his quest, but how could he? All those deaths in the war and those caused by the blight stained his soul, but Rurik wasn't looking for salvation. Would his misbegotten life not be wasted if he gave up now? *I am the monster lurking in your dreams. I became the darkness so that you can see the light.* His crimes could not be forgiven, but he took comfort in the fact that the world would be a better place once it was finished.

CHAPTER TWENTY-FOUR

The following two days passed in a whirlwind of meetings and packing, preventing Ina from spending any time with Mar or Ren, as both men made last-minute changes and plans in the army camp. She pursed her lips, looking in the mirror as she absent-mindedly brushed her hair. The people she had seen, Cyrus and Mirena, spent their time expressing their concerns that without the circlet, Ina would struggle to have enough power for her plan, but it still didn't feel right, not even with such significant problems to face.

'What will be, will be,' she said to the mirror, turning at a knock on the door and walking over to open it. The witch stood in the doorway, blocking the entrance in her surprise at seeing Ayni with a large box in her arms.

The dragoness tutted and rolled her eyes before speaking. 'Are you going to invite me in or stand there like a gaping fish?'

'Choices, choices… Oh, come in, Ayni. I'm not in the mood to fight with you tonight.' Ina tried to be civil, especially since she hadn't seen Ayni much except at the banquet.

After the ladies sat down, Ayni handed Ina the large package with a tentative smile. With her curiosity piqued, the witch took the remarkably heavy box from the dragoness and opened it, gasping when a shimmering wave of red scales poured into her hands.

'It is beautiful, but what is it?' Ina looked up at Ayni with genuine interest, glancing back down as the touch of the supple metallic material reminded the witch of flying on Mar's back, and the realisation struck her. 'Ayni, this is dragon skin. How the hell did you get hold of dragon skin?'

The dragoness raised her eyebrow and looked at Ina with amusement. 'I have plenty of it on my back. This is my peace offering, my apology for the trouble I caused when we first met. I crafted a flying suit and harness to protect you on Mar's back. It will keep you warm and deflect most weapons whilst still allowing freedom of movement.'

'I don't know how to thank you. It is beautiful.' The witch removed her jacket and put on the crimson coat, feeling it slide onto her arms in a cold, strangely sensual way. She was reaching for the trousers when Ayni's words stopped her.

'It's not just for you. Your last injury hurt Ren terribly. He has nightmares each time you need the bond or get injured, so I hope this will keep you both safe.'

The beautiful gift took on new meaning for the witch and gave an insight into how much the dragoness cared for her friend. Ina studied Ayni closely until she reached over and gathered the woman into a hug. 'I'm sorry you've been dragged into this, Ayni. It was meant to be a healing spell, not lifelong bondage. Thank you for the gift and the thought behind it as well. I hope you both find lasting happiness together.'

The dragoness awkwardly patted Ina's back and pulled away, looking uncomfortable. 'Yes, well. Keep yourself safe, and everyone will be happy.'

The smile on the witch's face disappeared as she concentrated on dressing in the supple outfit, jumping slightly as Ayni reached over to help adjust some of the more problematic straps, tutting until Ina could move easily in the unusual garments. In the mirror, Ina saw the person most of Cornovii feared, the crimson witch who had forced an entire army to kneel at her command.

'It is beautiful, but why crimson?' she asked, sighing heavily, dreading the answer.

'It… Well, when we arrived at the capital, there was a song popular in the taverns, the "Ode to the Lady of the Crimson Veil and the Dragon of Liath." I remembered your embarrassment and couldn't resist using it. Whilst it may cause you to blush, everyone knows that tale, which makes it perfect for the spectacle you intend at Alsia, no?'

'The gods must be enjoying this.' The face in the mirror seemed to be surrounded by several ghostly, familiar figures, pale compared to the vibrant crimson figure, sending a shiver down Ina's spine.

'Why do you think I'm willing to sacrifice a piece of my hide to protect you? Mortals and gods don't mix well, so I will do everything I can to protect what's mine from their games.'

'I promise to keep him out of the gods' way if I'm able, Ayni. He is my friend and will always hold a place in my heart, but he loves you, and I will fight to keep that safe.' Ina heard the panic in her voice and realised Ayni must have heard it too as the dragoness placed a hand on her shoulder.

'Ren is a complicated man, and as you're not trying to steal him away, I can live with your unusual friendship. You must have some value if my rider cares so much.' Ayni's amusement at her own joke made Ina smile until the dragoness grabbed her hair, pulling it tight. 'Now sit down. It is time to braid your hair, and if I'm going to roar at the king's command, you will be his goddess of war.'

Ina groaned, helpless under the stronger woman's hands, as Ayni expertly sectioned the long strands and plaited them into a thick dragon-scale braid.

Before she could admire the intricate hairstyle, trumpets announced the king's appearance. Ina stood up and clasped Ayni's hand in hers. 'I know I'm not a friend yet, and our only connection is the man who loves us both, but I'm grateful for the generosity of your heart. You are a much better person than I am, and I'm glad you found each other.'

She released the stunned dragon and walked out of the room, but it wasn't long before Ayni followed, and soon, both women arrived in the courtyard. She saw Rewan and Kaian exchange amused looks when she mounted Zjawa, so she made a surreptitious, rude gesture in their direction. With a laugh that surprised everyone, King Rewan set off, leading the small procession to meet the army outside the city gates.

As they greeted the saluting soldiers, Kaian dropped back to talk to the witch. 'Ina, you upstaged the king today,' he said with a grin, and when she turned to him to protest, he raised his hand slightly. 'No, it's good. We are here to make an impression, and with that outfit, you'll make a much better target than the king ever could.'

'Oh, gods, give me strength,' she muttered, provoking his laughter before he left to rejoin the king.

The journey continued once the army, with a smoothness that surprised Ina, joined their ranks. The witch almost wished it hadn't been so seamless, as Mar felt confident to leave the ranks to join her. He promptly tested the strength of her new armour, striking her with various weapons, then checking for any damage before nodding in satisfaction at Ayni's spectacular gift.

The curse played havoc with the weather, and the soldiers had to slog through mud and submerged roadways, causing delays and frustration, making Ina worried they wouldn't make it to the battlefield in time to take advantage of her secret weapon, forcing her to use more magic than she could afford. Thankfully, Mar continued the march until late in the night, and at sunset the next day, they arrived, tired but satisfied, at the fields of Alsia.

The army's efficiency as they made camp increased Ina's admiration for Ren and Mar as, with a few terse commands, a small town sprang to life in less than an hour, with protective earthworks following soon afterwards. Ina caught Mar's attention at a break in the fevered activity, pointing to the castle. 'Why is nothing happening? I'm sure I heard them blowing trumpets earlier.'

'They are safe behind their walls,' he replied, shrugging. 'Hopefully, tomorrow they will sally forth to do battle. They seemed eager enough when I confronted them, but in the cold light of day? When do you expect your special event?'

At the slight change of subject, Ina pulled out the scroll with Cyrus's calculations and looked it over again. 'Late tomorrow morning. I was worried we'd arrive too late, but now I'm worried the rebels will attack tonight instead.'

'No. Despite seeing our professionalism, I don't think they take us seriously and will want to humiliate the king with as many witnesses as possible. The only question is, will they confront us on the battlefield or force us to lay siege to their fortifications?'

Ina looked at the town, biting her lower lip. 'I'll need to use more magic if they stay in the town, and innocent people will probably get hurt. If they won't come, could you fly above and burn a few flags? Encourage them to move?'

'A few flags? I can burn whatever you want for your beautiful smile. You have been far too serious today, and I long to see you happy again.' Mar reached out, smoothing a few stray strands of hair behind her ear.

'I'm just worried. I was certain this plan was perfect when we talked, but I'm not sure I made the right decision. What if they don't surrender, or if Verdante joins the rebels? I don't even know if we can time it right to synchronise my magic with the eclipse. It requires precision, and I'm not the most organised person.'

'Focus on your magic, and I will handle the rest. You are not alone, Ina, not anymore. And despite the impression our chaotic life gives you, I am good at organising.' The softness in his voice strongly contrasted with the bearing of this tall, muscular warrior, dressed for death and mayhem. Her handsome dragon, always ready to provide the support she needed. Ina felt the tightness in her chest ease as his words melted away the tension, but much to her embarrassment, this relief brought tears to her eyes.

'Ina? Did I say something wrong?'

'Nothing. You are an oaf, too charming for your own good. Remind me of your plans.'

'Woman, you are so confusing sometimes,' Mar said, shaking his head. 'I won't do much. We will send a messenger, giving them the time to be on the field with the threat of two dragons burning the city down if they don't. Then I will fly around and, as you said, burn a few flags to emphasise our commitment. Then we have a good rest and food.'

'And this will work?' There was brilliance in the simplicity of Mar's plan, but she couldn't help doubting herself on the eve of battle.

'We will see, and if not, well, we'll improvise, but I will leave this part to you, my beautiful chaos. Come, your tent should be ready, so unless you want to see me puffing out my dragon's chest, you can get some rest.' Ina nodded and turned Zjawa over to a waiting groom, following Mar to a tent next to the king's, her mind picturing the image of a magnificent dragon dominating the skies.

The king's pavilion was set up on a small hill overlooking the site chosen for the battle, surrounded by his guards and military leaders. Ina watched Mar exchange a few words with Ren and a very flamboyant soldier before the stranger grinned and leapt onto an equally bedecked mare, heading off towards town. Moments later, Mar was replaced by a roaring dragon who slowly stretched his wings and leapt into the sky.

As soon as the young soldier entered the town, Mar circled above it, and Ina walked into her tent. She knew he would be flying until the messenger returned safely. He might train his troops mercilessly, with a good dose of menace, but he cared for every one of them. She was sure it would earn him the monicker *Mother Hen* if he weren't so scary.

She borrowed a shield from a very confused soldier outside and polished it with her magic to resemble a good mirror. After changing into a warm nightdress, she brushed her hair, noticing Mar's entrance in the reflection when he eventually returned.

'How did it go?' she asked without turning, and Mar sauntered over, taking the brush from her reluctant hand, his smirk frightening in the warped reflection.

'You are a very resourceful woman,' he whispered, kissing the top of one ear and trailing the brush through her tresses. Ina congratulated herself on already untangling them, enjoying the smooth glide of the bristles.

'Don't change the subject. How did it go? Will they meet us on the field of battle?'

'I'm sure of it after that little display. Wawrzyniec received the messenger with his usual arrogance, taunting the poor boy with torture and death, but after I accidentally demolished part of the roof, they released the messenger with only a few bruises. If you walk outside, you'll be able to see the damage; it is quite impressive.' He bent and kissed Ina's exposed neck. 'Will this satisfy my lady's order, or should I also burn their flags?'

He didn't stop there, sliding lower to her collarbone. The heat crawling over her cheeks prompted her to swat him away. 'Have some manners, dragon. We're in a tent.'

The sultry chuckle that roughened her voice only enticed him further. He lifted his lips to her ear, nibbling her earlobe. 'I have no manners. Dragons devour, and you smell so delicious.'

'Better than a dusty old roof, I bet.' Ina didn't know what made her say this, but as soon as the words left her lips, Mar's shoulders shook in laughter, and he raised his hands in surrender.

'Your mind works in mysterious ways. Yes, you smell much better than Wawrzyniec's roof, and I deserve a cuddle before we go for dinner.'

'We're not eating in here? Where are we going?'

'We have a tradition before battle in Cornovii. The commander and his officers tour the soldier's campfires, offering meat and drink to toast the gods for luck. This way, the commander learns the faces of those who fight for him, and the soldiers know their leader respects their loyalty.'

'After you chewed on the prince's roof, they already know you respect them,' she said with a smile, stroking his cheek. 'I don't have anything pretty except the armour Ayni made for me, but I will add some glamour to it, and if my plan works, the only casualty will be their hangover.'

Ina stopped a moment before taking a deep breath and looking straight into Mar's eyes. 'I want you to promise me something. If we fail and it ends in battle, the amount of chaos magic will be overwhelming.' The hitch in the witch's voice stretched out into a long pause, making Mar nervous as he waited. 'My love, I will need your help to control myself, and if everything goes wrong, you'll have to be the one who stops me.'

'What exactly do you want me to do, my spitfire?' Mar's voice was quiet. He didn't try to argue, already knowing her fears and worries.

'Knock me out, fly me away from the battlefield, even rip away my gemstones, but if all else fails, you have to kill me.' She placed her fingers over his lips when he protested. 'I don't have a death wish, but I think it was a mistake to avoid taking the circlet. If the chronicles are right, Sowenna made the necklace to store, the ring to manipulate, and the circlet to control chaos. How accurate that is, considering she broke the world... Well anyway, it's too late to worry about it now. I will do my best to stay in control and use the bond with you and Ren without hesitation; that is my promise to you. But if that fails, promise me you'll do everything necessary to stop the monster I might become.'

Mar took her hand away and shook his head. 'You mistake me for a hero, my love. A hero would sacrifice you to save the world, but the world can burn if it means I lose you.'

Ina smiled bitterly when she pressed her head to his chest. 'Then we'd best hope everything works out. You never know, maybe the gods will be helpful for once,' she muttered, feeling the Zmij moving beneath the skin of her arm.

When Ina walked out of the tent in the morning, slightly bleary-eyed from the night's revelry, she was confronted by an energetic and organised army already arrayed for battle. When Mar mentioned toasting the gods, he failed to mention only the divine could drink, yet somehow, the soldiers still threw a raucous party, despite being more sober than Svarog's virgins.

As a soldier gave her a nod and a wink, Ina remembered the brazen youngster who danced up to the king, bowed respectfully, then asked His Majesty to grant permission for him to kiss the royal witch.

'If I'm going to face death tomorrow, I would ask to be blessed by the Lady of the Crimson Veil's lips.' His grin had widened as he finished his request, though, from the looks on Mar and Ren's faces, death was much closer than he suspected.

'At least he didn't ask to taste the king!' she had exclaimed, standing up and approaching the young man, ignoring Mar's angry stare.

When he'd touched her mouth with his trembling lips, placing the kiss lighter than a feather, she heard him whisper, 'Will you keep us safe, my lady?' The realisation that this boy, barely old enough to be called a man, full of bluster and bravado, was genuinely hoping she would save them, humbled her.

'I will do everything in my power to keep you safe,' she had whispered.

She looked around. He hadn't been alone. Many of the recruits looked at her with a mixture of fear and hope, believing she would repeat the miracle of Liath. The burden of responsibility felt so heavy that suddenly she heard herself shouting, 'So, who else wants to kiss the royal witch for luck?'

The crowd of men had burst out laughing, but suddenly, a one-eyed veteran with a face so covered with scars only a mother could love it stepped from the crowd. 'Aye, Lady, give me enough luck to keep my beauty. If you ain't afraid to fall for such a handsome hero, that is.' The cheering this caused had Ina laughing and stepping forward to confront him. She grabbed his face and, despite his surprised struggles, gave him a fierce kiss.

'You are much too pretty not to get a kiss, though I must say, I only fall in love with heroes who transform into dragons.' She tilted her head, pointing at Mar, who stood there clenching his fists. With this last joke, the pedestal they'd placed her on disappeared, and the men surrounding her began chanting her moniker, each one dancing around and singing about the crimson witch.

'Enough, you bunch of ruffians. Kissing the royal witch is only allowed if you defeat me at arm wrestling.' Mar approached, wrapping his arm around her waist, and the moan of disappointment almost drowned out the singing, but even as they dispersed, the soldiers started another tune.

'Spoilsport,' Ina had said when he led her back to her seat, but Mar only smiled.

'The man you kissed saved many lives in the palace battle. That's how he lost the eye and earned his scars. The soldiers kept joking that even the king didn't have enough money to buy him time with a woman. I should spank your arse for offering yourself up like that, but I can't. The way you see the world…. Tonight, you gave him something more valuable than a kiss; you honoured his sacrifice, giving him the hope someone else will see past his scars.'

Ina sighed and let the memory slip away. *I promised to keep you all safe, and I will, whatever it takes.* She jumped on the orein and cast her prepared spell, the dragon skin armour shimmering with a crimson light. With a quiet plea, the witch allowed a sliver of chaos from her tight control and watched as it swirled around her like soft translucent wings. *I wish Velka could see me now. She would be so proud*, Ina thought, riding the orein over to the king and his entourage with the two dragons flanking them in all their glory.

On the other side of the valley, shining in the morning sun, was the rebel army of the southern nobles, their shiny armour in strong contrast to the muddy brown of the commoners in front of them. The look she gave the king was determined, even as the butterflies in her stomach seemed to grow blades on their wings.

'Your Majesty, we need to go closer so they can hear me.' At her statement, the king nodded to Ren, who commanded the army to move forward. The soldiers moved with such smooth coordination, it looked like a wave of steel flowing down the hillside. Before she pushed her mount to follow, Rewan reached over and touched her hand.

'Whatever happens today, I want you to know I'm grateful, Ina, not just for being the royal witch, but for being my friend. Now, go and put the fear of chaos into them, My Lady of the Crimson Veil.'

CHAPTER TWENTY-FIVE

Nervous energy coursed through Ina as she rode forward, and she allowed herself a moment, taking a deep breath and sinking into the persona of the royal witch. A glance at the stone in her hand indicated the time of the eclipse. It was very much her uncle's idea. From the very first time she mentioned intimidation as a weapon, Cyrus brought information about the eclipse. Later, with the head of the king's mages, he worked through the night to create a spell to predict the time of it accurately. Their surprise at the hug she'd given them in thanks still made her smile, but now the guesswork was removed from today's proceedings, giving her a distinct advantage.

Kaian rode beside her. His title of *King's Voice* a smokescreen for his actual job as bodyguard, which she did not entirely agree to, but the men insisted she needed protection and it was easier to accept his company than argue with the overbearing men. They approached warily, and Ina had to improvise a shield with an impromptu spell when a volley of arrows was sent to welcome them. After stopping close enough for their purposes, a second volley darkened the sky, only to disintegrate in dragon fire high in the sky, followed by a stream of insults, with *"royal whore"* being the most popular.

'Should I be insulted that they hate you more than me?' Ina's teasing made Kaian shake his head.

'I'm sorry to disappoint you, but I think they mean you,' he said, his mischievous grin reminding Ina how he seduced so many courtiers. Sobering slightly, he turned to the waiting army, took a deep breath, pressed a finger against a small tattoo on his neck and, using its spell to enhance his voice, announced the king's proclamation.

'His Benevolent Majesty, King Rewan, First of his Name, offers greetings to the people of the southern provinces. In so doing, he would like to remind the nobles of Cornovii that bearing arms against the monarchy is a dereliction of their sworn duty and a violation of their oaths of fealty. In his generosity and compassion, His Majesty will extend a full amnesty for those who lay down their weapons and surrender to his mercy.'

'You surely know how to wax lyrically,' she whispered, wishing they could enhance the enemy's voices, avoiding being this close to the army, but the roar of laughter that followed Kaian's words made it apparent surrender wasn't a consideration. Two armoured knights slowly rode out from the front lines when the laughter died down.

'Surrender to his mercy? What mercy? Paying us a pittance for our produce and stripping us of the means to feed our people for his war in the West? It has been years since Osterad cared for the South, taxing us into poverty and ignoring us when we faced disease and famine. Well, now we stand before you to claim our rights by strength of arms. Our army is three times the size of your pitiful forces, and we will not surrender to your tyranny.'

The impassioned words were shouted out by a man with fox-like features in plain armour, and despite the anger, his speech offered the witch an opportunity to negotiate. Unfortunately, his companion, a sallow youth in garish robes and sporting a jewelled crown, ordered him to be quiet and rode closer to Ina and Kaian.

'Tell that piece-of-shit usurper I won't be talking to him. He may send his dragon, but we've killed dragons in the past, and magic? We have the support of Castle Thorn and its legacy of mages. Tell him I will stick his head on my spear and display it over the town gates,' he said, and Ina had to close her eyes to compose herself before she laughed in his face. This idiot called the few stubborn mages who left her uncle's castle, unhappy with the shift of power, support? Still, his confidence gave her pause. *Is he expecting more people from Thorn to support him?* The thought was unsettling, but it was not the time or place to dwell on it.

Kaian looked at the man, then at Ina, who shook her head, letting him know she wasn't ready, muttering, 'Talk to the stupid one. Keep him busy.'

'The king heard of your difficulties, Prince Wawrzyniec, and came with supplies of grain and emergency provisions. We have the finest minds from the Magical University to study and remove Marzanna's curse from the land, and this is how you choose to thank him, with steel and insults that solve nothing?' Kaian continued to use the spell on his voice, and even Ina was impressed by how he weaved soothing promises and subtle threats in one breath. A murmur of discontent swept through the commoner's ranks, but the disdain on the noble's faces remained the same.

'Once we dedicate your blood to Winter's Death, the goddess Marzanna will lift the curse as our reward. Return to your incompetent king and tell him to die with honour, or as a coward; it makes no difference to me. This beautiful day shall go down in history as the day justice was served.' Wawrzyniec seemed to be very pleased with his clever answer, associating the weather with divine retribution, but the glowing stone in her hand told Ina things were about to change, and it was her turn to speak.

The witch exhaled, loosening her hold on chaos a little more and sought the bonds with Mar and Ren, stroking them with her mind as the crimson mist surrounding her grew, drawing everyone's eyes to her. 'Go to the king, Master Kaian, and tell him I tried to be patient as you negotiated with this idiot, but there is a limit, and this is mine.' Ina emphasised her statement by tossing the stone in her hand at the feet of the prince's horse, its bright light startling the animal into rearing, and she nearly missed Kaian's smirk as he wheeled around and cantered back to the king's side.

After finally regaining control of his mount, Wawrzyniec pushed forward, standing in his stirrups with a deranged look drawing his sword.

'Do you think we are afraid of you, woman? You stand alone in front of an army. Our mages will wipe you from existence before you draw another breath, witch.' His boasting tone took on a desperate note as the crimson hue of her magic grew, and with a little effort, Ina shaped it into wings that moved in an unseen wind. Her voice became an otherworldly whisper, saturated with power that reached the core of life's magic, making her presence palpable to every living being on the battlefield.

'Oh, you poor, foolish child, do you really think those renegades who fled Castle Thorn when I dealt with the old duke can stand against me? I am the harbinger of chaos and daughter of the gods. Men kneel for my pleasure, and the sun darkens at my command. The touch of my power will drain the life from your bodies and feed my magic till nothing remains but dust.' The glance she gave Zjawa reassured Ina as the orein whickered and looked back, unperturbed, but as the witch smiled, several men broke down in terror. With a dramatic yell, Ina thrust her hand towards the sky, exclaiming, 'The sun you called upon to witness this day of justice shall remove her gaze from your blasphemy, and you will know despair at my hand.'

With an outpouring of magic, the chaos mage called upon the crimson fire that expanded around her in an explosion of golden light, reaching the insurgent prince. Wawrzyniec screamed, charging her, weapon raised before his body was ripped from his saddle and thrown to the ground. Some soldiers moved forward to support their leader, their swords flashing red, reflecting her power, but they halted to hear her words.

'I am Inanuan of Thorn, Lady of the Crimson Veil. Today you shall see my power and beg for mercy.' Her voice, thunderous with command, echoed over the battlefield, and right on cue, the sun's glow darkened as the moon's pale disk slowly slid across it. The anguished pleas that followed told her the tactic had hit its mark. The rest were in the hands of the army and its mages.

She didn't have to wait long. On the first sign of the eclipse, Rewan's battle mages released their spells, deafening thunder booming, terrorising the rebel army. When the first bolt of lightning struck the ground, even Ina winced, her eyes closing at the terrifying spectacle. The ground shuddered as the army marched in step under Ren's command, their swords crashing against shields in perfect time, and Ina crossed her fingers that no bards made a song of her latest misadventure.

Ina watched as Wawrzyniec stirred on the ground, attempting to stand. As she looked around, ready to fight the soldiers who came for their leader, Ina realised she was alone with her captive. The undisciplined rebel militia and the conscripted peasants ran to escape the demonic witch and her magic, but much to her disappointment, the regular soldiers and mercenaries only stepped back, knuckles white on the hilts of her sword and hesitation in their eyes, waiting to see what came next. The man who was supposed to lead them squirmed, held down by her power, cursing and swearing, urging them to step forward, but there, in the darkness, the red glow surrounding her was the only source of light in the valley. To the terrified warriors, Ina was the vengeful goddess coated in crimson flame, and they flinched when she flicked her wrist, releasing a flare of light.

At her signal, another group of mages cast their spells. Black smoke spread overhead as a wave of magic rolled over her towards the fleeing peasants, shaking the earth and tripping them as they ran. Then as they tried to regain their feet, the roar of two dragons turned the rebels, herding them like cattle, leaving them cowering on the ground, unable to escape as the king's army marched forward, splitting to surround the prostrate people, their sword hilts still crashing against shields, as they chanted 'For Rewan and Cornovii' until no avenue of escape was left to the broken enemy.

The southern army was in disarray, but the core, nobles, and regular soldiers remained, but seeing their main force surrounded and overwhelmed, a few brave souls took command and tried to resist. Contradictory orders shouted in the air as they drew their swords. Even to her untrained eye, it was clear the desperate southerners could not resist the well-trained Cornovii army without a military genius or a miracle.

As the southern soldiers rallied for one last charge, the ranks of Rewan's forces stepped aside, leaving robed men and women standing alone, hands raised and chanting. Seeing this opportunity, the braver soldiers charged into the gap, weapons raised, only to scream as horrifying creatures burst into life before them or hammers of air smashed into their bodies. No matter how they tried to escape, they faced monsters or a wall of steel. A keening sound began growing within the surrounded army as more and more men fell to the ground, praying to the gods, King Rewan, and even the witch who terrorised their souls.

Still, some tried to fight, throwing themselves at Ren's warriors. Ina knew not all bloodshed could be avoided, but even with battle-hardened warriors showing mercy to the rebels, attempting to subdue rather than kill, she began shaking, shocked as the fear and injuries from the fight created a surge of chaos.

The power seeped into her body, caressing her soul like a demanding lover, insisting on being let in, offering the promise of unlimited power. The darkness in her soul blossomed into sweet euphoria, its seductive voice fanning her desires; to take just a little more, draining their strength, their vitality, to use the soldier's lives to destroy the curse and revive the land.

As the fighting raged around her, the witch remained still and silent, waging a battle within her mind, wordlessly repeating one man's name as she attempted to drown the desire for uncontrolled chaos, but just as Ina's gems glowed with a blinding light, there was a touch, a feeling of love and respect that eased the call of her magic, then two arms holding her close.

Enough of this. You are not a monster. Ina scolded herself as she turned to the side, looking into Ren's calm, trusting eyes as he leaned back and slowly let her go. In a panic, the witch looked at

347

his body for any damage from the raw chaos, but there were no wounds, and her friend smiled, gently squeezing her trembling hand.

'I felt your struggle, my lady. I will always protect you, even from your magic,' he said, before moving away to support the fighting soldiers. Cursing under her breath at stupid selfless idiots and with her bond to Ren burning brightly, she took an iron grip on her power, cutting it off entirely before another noise caught her attention.

The noise was her orein, growling at the frightened figure of the rebel prince as he tried to escape, but even as she realised this, Zjawa stepped forward and pressed her clawed fist to his chest, holding him down.

The horror in the captive prince's eyes made Ina flinch and look away, taking in the pandemonium before her. Whilst her plan hadn't guaranteed no one dying, it had been their best chance to avoid outright slaughter, but even the aftermath of a much smaller skirmish felt terrible, the mass of broken men adding to the weight of responsibility already on her shoulders. Still, it looked like Cornovii's soldiers, led by Ren, had gained control over the situation, and the last of the resisting rebels were subdued, wounded or dead on the field. Mar and Ayni dominated the sky, helping to keep the terrified militia cowed whilst still managing to look beautiful, making the edge of Ina's lips twitch into a subdued smile.

How can something so magnificent look so deadly? she thought, fumbling at the pouch on her belt, trembling fingers struggling to grip as they probed inside its depths until they found the object she needed. Her lips, nearly tripping over the words, released the messenger spell.

At her signal, two small groups of mages stopped chanting. Once the spells ended, the black smoke over the battlefield slowly dispersed, and the thunder faded into silence, revealing a bright, beautiful blue sky. The blood on the grass and scattered bodies were the only evidence of a battle, but most of the soldiers survived, and now the sun Wawrzyniec called upon as witness shone on the cowering rebel army, their captors surrounding them.

In the confusion and terror, no one noticed that the only casualties were those from the rebel army who stood and fought and a few unfortunate enough to be trampled in the panicked rout, but Ina still offered whispered prayers for their souls even as she turned and signalled for the king's party on the hill to join her.

As the healers descended to aid the injured, Ina wished she could turn her orein and leave the battle far behind, but she had to play her role till the end, as any sign of weakness could bring more death and anguish.

As they waited on the royal entourage, Ina turned to the two armies and stood up in the stirrups. 'I, Inanuan of Thorn, stand before you and offer you a choice. His Majesty King Rewan is a benevolent monarch and requested that I stay my hand from those willing to offer fealty and service to the Crown. So once again, I ask you to lay down your arms and serve this country and its people. For those who refuse, your life will be mine to take.'

Ina's voice was met with silence from the stunned soldiers, but rather than wait, the witch dismounted her orein, approaching the ranks and driving her point home. 'Look at those who fought against Cornovii and the blood of your brethren pooling at my feet. Look at me, chaos incarnate, the dragons in the sky, the mages, and the different races who oppose you today. Only a true king could gather such might, and his strength of character brought us together. So ask yourselves, do you want the king's protection or his wrath?'

The shouting of some braver soldiers focused the witch's gaze on their faces, only to realise they were looking above her head. As she turned, Ina glimpsed the king before a gust of wind nearly knocked her over, and Mar landed to her right, roaring and announcing the king's arrival.

'All hail King Rewan, Monarch of Cornovii and the Free Cities.'

His voice still echoing through the valley, the dragon reared up, spreading his wings, even scaring his own soldiers.

Suddenly, a whooshing sound and a broken cry caught Ina's attention. Mar's actions had proved enough distraction to embolden a soldier's hand, and he'd used the opportunity to fire an arrow aimed at her heart. As the witch looked in the direction of the sound, her eyes met those of the young soldier she had kissed for luck the day before as they clouded over in approaching death, an arrow piercing his chest.

Ina looked in disbelief as the young man fell to his knees, then collapsed, his hand reaching out and a contented smile on his lips. *They killed him, even though I promised to protect him.* Ina dropped to her knees, placing his head on her lap and stroking his boyish face. Somehow, his death hurt more than any other. She promised him life, but the touch of her lips brought him death, and when the magic of his life joined with her own, Ina felt the tears fall from her eyes. The healers rushed to his side, but she could feel his life slipping through her hands as the veil of Nawia came for his soul.

'I'm so sorry. I'm sorry I have failed you,' she whispered. Her tears fell on his face, and the man's eyes fluttered briefly, focusing on her.

'My lady... I'm glad you are s....' he whispered, red foam frothing on his lips. And just like that, he was gone; the chaos of his death dissipating in the air as she let it slip away.

Sorrow and the sense of failure awakened a fury the witch couldn't have imagined. Her piercing scream knocked back the surrounding people, shocking everyone into silence. Red fire burst from her skin, coiling about her before, shooting forward, scorching the ground as she searched for the culprit.

'Who did it?' Ina was seething, her voice death incarnate. As her hands moved up, a space opened up around a single soldier, a bow dangling uselessly from his hand.

Even as he turned to flee, her magic wrapped around his neck and dragged him back. Ina lost herself in her anger, no longer wanting to hold back. *He killed that boy as if his life didn't matter,* she thought, but even listening to the rattle of the man's laboured breathing as she lifted him into the air didn't soothe her fury.

'My lady, please, don't do this.' An unfamiliar voice cut through the focus of her rage, and she turned to see the old, scarred veteran from the feast. 'Mirek was a soldier, willing to give his life for someone he believed in, and he died knowing his actions saved your life. That is everything we hope for, to make a difference and not die in vain. So please, don't sully your hands with this man's death.' The veteran looked Ina straight in the eyes, his expression stopping her completely. He looked at her like she was a creature of pure goodness, worthy of such sacrifice, and the witch dropped her hand, releasing the gasping soldier.

Suddenly, the shock of moist roughness slavered over her neck, shocking a small scream from her lips as she turned to face her worried dragon.

'Mar.... Eughh, you disgusting lizard.' She wiped away the drool, abandoning the limp, barely breathing form on the floor as the dragon shimmered and changed into an armour-clad warrior before gathering her into his arms.

'Enough, my love. The soldier is telling you the truth. You would regret his death, especially if you react in anger.' Mar's soothing voice and gentle touch in the middle of her murderous haze were so surreal it took a moment to remember why she'd lost her temper. Still, he was right. She would regret it later, and this lowlife was not worth her guilt. Ina looked down at the gasping man, and as she opened her mouth to speak, the king interrupted.

'My Lady of the Crimson Veil, I thank you for your forbearance and for ending the battle so efficiently. We will bury your young soldier with honour, his family will receive a state pension, and his name shall be remembered. All Cornovii, not just my Royal Witch, will mourn my warriors.'

The interruption left Ina gaping, reminding her of her task. She recovered quickly despite the still burning anger and bowed to hide her embarrassment. 'You offer me great honour, my liege.' Waving her hand to the man still beneath her orein's foot, she continued. 'I lay before you, the rebellion's leader, ready to face your judgement.'

Rewan's expression was the picture of regal disdain as he studied his cousin, then turned to Mar. 'I would appreciate your assistance transporting this fool to my pavilion, Lord Marshal.' With that statement, he dismissed Wawrzyniec from his thoughts as he faced the remaining nobles. 'Find two among you who will speak for the South and your rebellion, and once you do, they will be escorted to my presence to plead your case. The rest of you bury your dead and tend to your wounds. Lord Kaian, see that the prisoners are given bread and water, and our troops are fed as they deserve.' With that, the king wheeled his horse away and rode back to the army's camp as Mar transformed and picked up the captured prince, flying off in the same direction.

Left alone with only the quiet presence of Ren behind her, Ina looked at her friend and reached for his soothing presence. 'Shall we go back to camp? Zjawa deserves a brace of chickens for carrying me during that circus. And I need a moment to come to terms with… everything.' With an affectionate pat on the orein's shoulder, the witch climbed into the saddle and turned towards the hill.

Ren's smile was soft as he answered. 'No, my lady, you go on ahead. I still have work, but I will make sure the man who protected you will be honoured for his sacrifice.' With that, he gave her leg a reassuring squeeze and headed towards the rebel army.

For the first time, she wished Mar and Ren could leave their duties and cluck over her like mother hens, soothing away her pain. Instead, Ina rode up the hill, lost in her thoughts, gasping in surprise when several mages stepped out to greet her.

'My lady, that was an impressive display. Would you care to join us for a meal? My colleagues and I have plenty of questions….' Leader of battle mages stopped momentarily, observing her baffled expression before flashing a disarming smile. 'Forgive us. Everyone wants to meet with you, a chaos mage fully in control of her magic; it is unprecedented. We had to follow the king's and Master Arun's orders, but many braced themselves for the possibility we would have to subdue a rogue, insane mage. Yet here you are, sane, winning the battle without a soul lost to fighting.'

Ina felt a blush crawl up her cheeks. *If they knew how close I was to giving in during the battle, how that man's actions… If not for Mar and that scarred soldier…* Her thoughts were jumbled, but the man before her didn't have to know about the darkness that tempted her soul to destruction. All it took to rear its ugly head was the thought of someone hurting those she promised to protect. Ina nodded slightly. 'I will come if the king allows. His Majesty may have other plans for me.' She smiled at the group as they stepped aside, then headed to the king's tent.

Several servants rushed around as Ina entered the pavilion, setting the scene for the upcoming meeting, creating a regal throne room in the small space. With a single wave, Rewan dismissed everyone, rushing over and enveloping the witch in a fierce hug as soon as they were alone.

'Ina, are you all right? Your idea, all of this… That was… I have no words other than thank you. For a moment, I thought I was going deaf. You are my miracle, Ina. I know it was hard for you, especially after that boy died, and I'm so sorry you had to go through this, but you saved so many lives.' His enthusiasm was infectious, and she reciprocated the hug, finding a strange comfort in their private interaction. For the rest of the world, she was the royal witch, serving the court of Cornovii. In private, she was helping a friend who was doing all he could to keep this country safe. Now, this friend was helping her, telling her precisely what she needed to hear.

'I'm glad I could help. Now that we've used the stick, I think it's time to win them over with the carrot.' Before she could elaborate, Mar, Ren, and Kaian walked in, each looking at the pair with differing expressions, and Ina promptly stepped away from the king.

Behind the three men trailed two muddy gentlemen, nobles by the quality of their bedraggled clothing, followed by Prince Wawrzyniec, his wrists and ankles in heavy iron shackles, cursing and fighting the soldier who held him upright. The two nobles flinched when they caught sight of Ina, eyes wildly seeking a means of escape, while the young prince sneered and jerked forward, fingers crooked as he tried to claw at her body, only to fall back as his gaoler pulled back on his chains.

Ina's response was a deep sigh and a roll of her eyes, but rather than react, she moved backwards, positioning herself behind the king to sit on a convenient chest. When the unrestrained nobles meekly knelt before him, Rewan smiled, allowing himself a moment of good humour before gesturing for them to stand up.

'You have spent enough time on the ground today, gentlemen. Especially you, cousin.' Ignoring his relative momentarily, the king addressed the other nobles in a condescending tone. 'I hope you don't mind that I came here to discipline an unruly family member.'

Wawrzyniec attempted to spit on the king, but the thick saliva fell from his lips to slide down his chin to his clothes, and despite her best efforts, Ina snorted, earning her a disapproving glare from the king before he addressed the rebels.

'Did you come to a decision on where you and your men's loyalty belongs, or should I ask my royal witch to repeat her... persuasion?'

Falling to their knees again, the older of the men spoke. 'The southern houses pledge their loyalty to the Royal House of Cornovii, Your Majesty.' Despite being on his knees, the silent man looked down, expression thunderous, with teeth and fists clenched. Rewan must have noticed this too, as he sighed in disappointment.

'Traitors! Cowards!' Wawrzyniec screamed and thrashed, kicking the silent man in the back until the abused noble turned round and punched him in the face, knocking him down, to which the king responded with a shake of his head.

'And that was the man you hoped would lead your province?' he asked, his voice tired and disappointed. With a new look of purpose shining in his eyes, the king turned to Ren. 'Master Sa'Ren, please tell our quartermasters to gather our spare stores and prepare a meal for the rebel—no, for our countrymen. Once they have relinquished their weapons, begin feeding them and organising provisions for them to return home.' When Ren nodded and left the tent, Rewan turned his attention back to the nobles. 'One of you will be free to return to your men to share the good news, whilst the other shall remain with my council to discuss the situation in the South and advise us on how the Crown may assist you in recovering from your troubles.'

'Your Majesty, the prince... I mean, Lord Wawrzyniec?' The nominal spokesman for the nobles looked at the king, a fearful hope in his eyes, whilst his silent partner moved forward aggressively, prompting Kaian to draw his blade, but Rewan raised his hand to stop him.

'Everyone makes mistakes. Yours was standing against Cornovii when it needed your help and not standing against the whispers of those who meant us harm. My offer of amnesty was not just empty words, but be warned. It was my will that withheld the hand of death today, so change your ways or pay the price. As for my cousin, he will travel with us to Osterad, where time and the tender care of his family will ensure he mends his ways and never threatens the safety of Cornovii again.'

The king looked at the contrite nobles for several moments before nodding. 'You may leave, decide between you who wants to contribute to rebuilding the South. That is all.' Almost as an afterthought, the king looked down at his moaning cousin in disgust and gestured to the soldier holding him. 'Get him out of my sight, clean him up, and find a secure wagon to take him to the capital. He's caused enough trouble.'

The soldier snapped a sharp salute and, following the other men, left the tent, dragging the unfortunate prince behind him.

A sudden commotion outside had Kaian looking through the entrance. 'Your Majesty, a Verdante emissary requests an audience,' Ren said, returning to the tent, the unexpected news bringing a deep frown to the king's face.

'Another of Jorge's predictions comes to pass, despite the chaotic disruption. Send them in, please,' he said before turning towards Kaian. 'Please be ready. After so many assassination attempts, I don't trust this one a bit.'

The man who entered was the southern noble from Mar's meeting in Alsia. Now wearing the Verdante king's insignia, the man stood with the bearing of a high-ranking lord, and Mar cursed at the confirmation of his suspicions.

Kaian's hands drifted to his sheathed yatagans, ready to strike, but the man bowed respectfully to the king, though his eyes never once left Ina's until Rewan's polite cough reminded him of his manners.

'Your gracious Majesty, thank you for allowing me to proffer congratulations on your decisive victory. It is my great honour to pass on the invitation of my liege lord, King Tobias of Verdante, leader of the Southern Marches, to join him at the border of our two great countries to discuss the recent disturbances that have caused great concern for His Majesty these last few months, and clear up any misunderstandings that may have arisen.'

Rewan stepped out from behind his protective lover, placing a grateful hand on his arm as the assassin drew breath to object.

'You may convey our acceptance of His Majesty's invitation. In three days, we shall meet at the border town of Elkan. Due to, as you say, recent disturbances, I shall bring my trusted advisors and a small force for protection. We wouldn't want any accidents during the meeting.' With Rewan's statement, the messenger's eye snapped back to Ina, and the noble visibly shuddered.

'Your advisors are welcome, all except the crimson witch. The demonstration of her power here today means her presence is too big a threat to my king's safety.'

'What about my royal dragon? Will Tobias object to this, too? Maybe I should arrive barefoot, dressed in sackcloth, to show my friendly intentions?' Ina snorted as Rewan's sarcasm left no doubt of his thoughts on such a proposal.

'The royal dragon is welcome. The Lord Marshal's honour is well known and trusted throughout Warenga.'

'What about my honour? You spew this nonsense in my presence, yet I still haven't ripped the flesh off your bones.' Ina smirked and stepped closer, seeing the emissary's breathing quicken. He stepped back, tripping over a chest and would have fallen if Ina hadn't grabbed his waving arm, pulling him closer.

'My lady, that's enough. Please leave him alone.' The amusement in the king's voice contradicted his words, and looking to the side, she noticed Rewan lightly shake his head. Ina released the man's hand and bowed to the king.

'Forgive me, Your Majesty. I simply wanted to see why my presence is so threatening, but, as always, I'm yours to command.'

'You are insane,' whispered the emissary, colour slowly returning to his face. 'I bid you farewell, Your Grace, and will present your answer to my king.'

Rewan waved him off, and the man rushed to the exit as if chased by a hive of angry bees.

'That was a welcome, if unexpected, outcome from your plan, Ina, but did you have to scare him so much? The poor man almost filled his trousers when you grabbed his hand.' Rewan seemed happy with the invitation, but the witch had another problem to address.

'He deserves it for offending my honour. I'm a threat to his king. What, he took me for an insane man-eating spider? Still, that settles the question of who you will take with you, especially as I have to return to Thorn. Velka is waiting for my help to reverse the curse, and with so many starving, I dare not waste any more time. Besides, you don't need me here anymore.'

'I will take the Lord Marshal and Kaian as advisors. The head of the mages and those nobles experienced in battle shall provide an escort. Sa'Ren, once again, I ask you to lead the army. Bring them close enough to the meeting place for a rescue if needed.'

Mar couldn't remain silent as Ina seemed determined to leave without him again. 'Your Majesty, I ask to be released from this duty to assist Ina with her endeavour. Her last confrontation in the temple was… challenging.'

'I will be fine, and I have your burly orc to protect the helpless maidens. He would confront the goddess of winter if his wife's safety were at risk. The king needs you for your military mind and as a means to evacuate if Verdante is setting a trap.' Ina noticed Kaian's thoughtful nod and rolled her eyes.

Ren joined the chorus of dissent. 'My lady, Mar is right. You should stay with me in the camp, and once he returns, we can all go to Marzanna's temple.'

Ina shook her head.

'No, if I sort it out, it will further strengthen Cornovii's position. If there's no crisis, then we won't argue over aid. I am grateful for your concern and promise to listen to Daro whenever he offers me sensible advice.'

Moving to her side, Mar leaned down and stole a kiss, smiling despite his worry and looking deep into her eyes. 'The fury you felt because someone shot the young soldier, that anger will be nothing compared to the wrath I unleash upon the world if you are hurt,' he whispered, sending a shiver down her spine as she looked back at the dragon, whose only concern was his mate. Yet he let her go. With a last tender kiss, he bowed and stepped aside.

The curtsey she proffered the king was slightly unsteady after that kiss, but Rewan waved her off before she could embarrass herself further. Not seeing Ren, Ina turned and left the pavilion, only to almost collide with the quiet warrior outside.

'Oomph. What the…' Ren's arms gathered her into his chest, and he squeezed her tight for a long, uncomfortable moment. 'Ren, please, let me go. It will be alright. You trained me well, and I am learning more about my magic every day.'

'I am your guardian and your friend, so I will always worry if you're in danger.'

Ina chuckled as she buried her head in his shirt, squeezing him back before letting go. 'I am lucky to have so many overbearing, loving men in my life. Now let go and help Rewan with the rebels while I prepare to leave.' Ren's arms slowly relaxed, letting the witch wriggle free, and with a wink and a wave, she slipped away towards her tent.

CHAPTER TWENTY-SIX

I na felt every mile of the journey in her aching thighs. She'd never been more grateful for a gift as she was now, Zjawa's smooth gait making a hard ride almost bearable. The thought of resting on an actual bed with a quilted throw to keep her warm nearly brought the witch to tears.

Once she arrived at Castle Thorn, Ina slid off the orein with a relieved sigh, promptly followed by a stream of muttered curses when her knees buckled, and the witch had to grab the saddle to avoid collapsing into the courtyard mud.

Turning to the stableboy, she handed over the reins, taking an unsteady step towards the castle. 'Take my mount to the stables, clean her and give her some chickens,' she said before asking a passing servant. 'Do you know where Velka, the nature mage, is?'

'Yes, my lady, she is in the library with a necromancer and asked not to be disturbed.'

Ina looked up at the castle walls, where a light glowed in the library window. *What necromancer? What the fuck's been going on here over the last five days?* The prospect of climbing the stairs to the library was daunting, but she couldn't leave these questions unanswered, even with aching muscles.

'Well, it had better be a friendly necromancer, as I'm not in the mood for polite conflict resolution right now,' she muttered irritably and began climbing, feeling her mood sour with each passing step, until an enormous shadow blocked her path.

On the top of the staircase, next to the library door, sat the orc sharpening his battleaxe with a grim expression.

'Daro? What are you doing here? Is Velka inside?' Ina asked when he raised his eyes to her.

'Of course you're here. I assume that means the plan was successful, or are you on the run? No, I wouldn't be lucky enough to get to fight for once. As for my wife, she locked herself in with some skeleton fucker and refused to let me in, saying I was disturbing their research. I have a bad feeling about him. Would it be a big loss if he had a little accident?'

The hope in the orc's voice made her smile, especially since it looked like she had lost the position of his least favourite person. 'Let me see what's going on. Velka doesn't usually like death magic. There was an incident a few years ago, so if she's cooperating with a necromancer, she'll have a good reason,' she said, stepping over his enormous axe and knocking on the door.

'Velka? Your lucky sprite is here. Can you open the door before I accidentally, on purpose, break it down?' she asked, almost politely. 'I'm tired, and there's an orc out here with an axe and a bad temper.' Turning the handle, Ina felt the spell holding it closed dissipate and nearly fell through the gap when the door was torn from her grip, and two pale arms grabbed her and squeezed the breath from her body.

'You are here and in one piece. No strange wounds this time, no?' When the witch shook her head, Velka released her from the crushing hug and pulled her into the room, waving at the tall, handsome man slowly walking towards them, his face familiar despite his bruises.

'Lady Inanuan, it is a pleasure to meet you again.' His low, pleasant baritone teased her memory, but unable to pinpoint it, the witch looked at her friend in confusion. With a dramatic eye roll and a surreptitious peek towards the stairs, Velka answered the unasked question.

'It's Rurik. Remember our uni time? He was my... that time you had your "little accident" with the frog?' Mild panic appeared in her eyes when Daro stood in the doorway, and the mage snapped her mouth closed and hid behind Ina's smaller stature.

Ina nodded slowly, looking at the man's face, suspicious of a necromancer appearing when they were trying to reverse Marzanna's curse, but smiled instead of voicing her misgivings. 'It is a pleasure to see you, Rurik. It's been so long, so please forgive me for not recognising you. If I may ask, what brings you to Castle Thorn?'

The twitch at the corner of his eye told Ina she hadn't kept the suspicion from her voice, but it disappeared quickly, replaced by a look of bitterness.

'I was looking for you, as you are the only one who can help me. I was asked to investigate Marzanna's temple by the local mage's circle, but when I arrived, I was accosted by the volkhv and two rather large acolytes. The next thing I knew, the building was burning, and it was all I could do to escape with my life. Well, my life and this.' Rurik pointed to the table, and a worn, slightly burnt scroll. 'I learned how to reverse the sacrifice, and once I learned it was you who destroyed the temple, I came here as fast as possible, knowing you would need the information.'

Ina sat down on the nearest chair and looked at the man who said he'd been sent to investigate the cult of Marzanna, knowing the council hadn't been aware of the cult when she was sent to the South. She poured herself some wine. 'Why should I trust you? This is a very convenient story, but I also know the Mage's Council was ignorant of the threat Marzanna's cult posed when I came south. Not to mention, we were attacked by a revenant on our way here. Is that a coincidence?'

'I was sent by the local mage's circle, not the council. There was some concern, but only that. We were unaware of the threat until I was captured. I still haven't contacted my compatriots to make a report, choosing to tackle the danger first. If you look at the scroll, you'll see I'm telling you the truth. I can't speak for whatever attacks you may have suffered, only that I had no involvement.'

'Ina, he got injured when the temple was destroyed, saving the scroll from the fire. I don't know about the rest of his story, but I've read it, Striga, it's real. Every horrifying detail of the curse is on that scroll; there's even mention of Sowenna and the regalia.' Velka's plea made Ina sigh, but she was too tired to argue.

With thoughts drifting to her grandfather's death and subsequent immolation, Ina couldn't help her distrust, but Velka seemed so sure, and she gave in against her better judgement. 'I don't trust you, Rurik. I might not have recognised you earlier, but that doesn't mean I forgot what you did to Velka. I don't know how you persuaded her to trust you now, but for her sake, I will give you a chance to prove me wrong.'

'Ina, thank you. I promise I didn't just believe his story, but once I read the scroll….' Daro was throttling the handle of his axe and not just holding it, unable to take his eyes from the necromancer. It was clear Velka had mentioned their past, but the witch was happy to use the orc's anger to control Rurik.

'I hope you're right, because the land isn't all that's suffering. This spell is torturing those elves, the moment of their deaths prolonged by the magic siphoned from the earth, trapping Marzanna and further powering the spell. I can't allow whoever did this to go unpunished, and I won't hesitate to kill them if needed.' Ina looked at Rurik as she said those words, her face a mask of icy fury.

'If you truly think I am responsible, I will surrender myself to the king's justice once we defeat the curse. Velka told me she wanted to isolate the bodies, preventing the energy of the southern lands from fuelling the curse, but it won't be enough. You must end the elves' lives, sending their souls to the afterlife. Only then will Marzanna's chains be broken. I can help with the death magic, but I can't kill them all without the power of the chaos regalia.'

'Ina, Rurik and I spent days deciphering the scroll. The spell is preventing the Death of Winter. We need to complete the feast of Maslenitsa, the symbolic death of Marzanna and the rebirth of the land by allowing those poor victims to die, then filling the earth with the magic of nature.'

Ina rubbed her forehead and looked up at Daro, who now stood behind Velka's chair, staring at the necromancer with a hostile expression. It was good to have someone she could trust with Velka's safety because her soft-hearted friend was staring at Rurik as if he was her saviour.

Taking a deep breath, Ina looked at her friend before speaking. 'So, to summarise, Velka. You want to create, then sustain a barrier between the sacrifices and the land, diverting the green magic back to the earth, while Rurik intends to use his skills to finally end the victims' lives? However, neither of you has the power to manage it, so you need me to fuel both spells simultaneously while Veles knows how many cultists are trying to stop us?' The witch sighed, closing her eyes, trying to imagine how to perform such a miracle. 'You realise the amount of magic needed exceeds the combined power of the Magical University?' Ina was trying to remain positive, but if anything, she was understating the amount needed.

It wasn't an awful plan. With enough preparation, mages and soldiers protecting them, they could probably manage it, but with three mages, an orc, and the last six soldiers from Castle Thorn, they'd be lucky even to make it to the temple.

'You need the circlet, Ina. The combined power of the regalia, bonded to a chaos archmage, is enough power to reshape the world. Used in this manner, we'll easily succeed.' Rurik's quiet voice made her look at him sharply. *Is that why he's here?* she thought when her gaze forced him to lower his eyes. It was the second time he mentioned the chaos regalia, and even if he was right, his knowledge about her affiliation with the gemstones was unsettling.

'The circlet is too far away, and we must act now. I will think about it once I've had a good night's sleep. Daro, please ensure we have everything ready for tomorrow morning. I want to go at dawn, and please see if we can take whatever soldiers are available. I doubt the cultists are all gone unless Lada finally decided to help.' Ina winced when Velka reacted to the mention of the goddess of fertility, and the witch changed the subject quickly, pointing at the two mages. 'I want you to find a way to work in close proximity. If I have to fuel your spells, I can't afford to split my attention too much.'

She wasn't convinced this plan would work, but with no alternative method and people starving, the witch wouldn't forgive herself if she didn't at least try this. Besides, Velka was positive she could do it and was the best nature mage in the kingdom. Her friend was in tune with the very spirit of the earth, so if anyone could heal it, that person was Velka. Then maybe she would finally stop belittling herself with this *glorified gardener* phrase that irritated the witch so much.

With a yawn, Ina finished her instructions, stood up, then paused. 'I have to talk to Cyrus and get some rest. Rurik, if you betray us, even Veles won't recognise you after I'm finished,' she said, and the tired witch left the library without waiting for a reply, unaware of the soft, proud smile that blossomed on Rurik's lips.

When they met in the morning, Ina was surprised to see Mirena dressed and ready to ride, but after the healer scolded the witch for not including her, especially considering the last time, Ina apologised and welcomed her to the group.

Cyrus bid them farewell with a worried expression, his gaze following Rurik's every move. Last night Ina had spent several hours bringing her uncle up to date with the rebellion, Verdante's intentions and the current situation, as well as her thoughts on the necromancer's coincidental arrival. The new Duke of Thorn had an animated, if whispered, discussion with his wife, but whatever had been said, Mirena kept her counsel and joined them at the gate. With the determination of a mother hen, her aunt fussed over Velka and even brought Ina a new, much warmer cloak. So with a last wave for Cyrus, they set off.

The journey itself was uneventful and surprisingly easy, especially with Mirena forcing strengthening draughts on everyone every few miles, but when the temple settlement appeared, Ina felt overwhelmed by doubt and worry.

As she'd talked to her uncle the previous night, he remarked on her father's connection to the earth, which gave the witch an idea. When she told him her thoughts, Cyrus had grown silent and, without elaborating, had agreed that it might work.

The gentle pressure she applied to the reins directed Zjawa next to Velka's horse, but it took Ina a moment to tell her friend the plan.

'My battle with volkhv gave me an idea. Once you set up the barrier, redirect the flow of green magic to me,' she said, and when Velka gave her a sharp look, Ina shrugged. 'Before you say anything, I know it's dangerous, but I intend to use my connection to the forest to siphon off some of the power as it returns to the earth. I know it could cause a magical overload or disrupt our spell entirely, but it's the only way I'll have enough magic for you both. I'll just need to concentrate on where to send the magic and maybe pray to the Leshy.'

'You know this is a bad idea, yes? The curse's anchor taps into the vitality of the land itself. Do you hear me, Ina, the land? It has enough magic to chain a god, and you want to take this all on yourself? Even siphoning a small amount could kill you.' The observant orc didn't miss their quiet conversation, and Daro moved closer, listening to the two women.

'I know it's not the best idea, but it's the only one I have, so let me take the burden of the spell, and if something goes sideways, your handsome and eavesdropping husband can snatch you away to safety,' she said, nodding towards the orc, who answered with a smirk.

'Hah, I bloody will too, but how about, just this once, you don't end up nearly dying? That way, I won't have to explain to the big scary dragon why I let you do something stupid, again.'

'What Mar doesn't know can't hurt him, or you, so let's keep it that way. Now brace yourselves because the remaining worshippers may not be friendly, and I would prefer to save our magic for the ritual,' she said as they passed the palisade, the orc pushing past, following her advice.

The place was just as Ina remembered, only the people were more lethargic, repeating tasks performed every day with such indifference that none of the work was completed. Velka moved closer to her friend, nearly crushing their legs.

'There is no green magic here. I swear I've never seen the earth so bereft of life, and this dragging weight in my chest is... You were right. I can feel the land dying, screaming in agony. There's no way this could've waited.'

'You haven't seen the sacrificial circle yet, and I'm sorry for exposing you to such an abomination.' Ina's pale face showed the strain she was under from the curse, despite strengthening her shields in readiness. She couldn't imagine how it would feel for a nature mage connected to living beings as deeply as Velka.

Even Rurik, who should be used to death magic, seemed strangely moved by the situation, whispering quiet prayers to Veles as they went. It made Ina reevaluate her judgement of him. How many had she killed in the last few months? Perhaps it was guilt she was feeling and blaming Rurik as a convenient scapegoat.

Unbothered by the inhabitants, the small group arrived at the centre of the settlement, where dark, barren ground marked a perfect circle around the statue. The elven victims were still there. Their rotten bodies, exposed to the elements, looked even worse, yet now it looked like they screamed their suffering to the heavens.

Ina signalled for everyone to dismount and turned towards Velka and Rurik. 'Tell me what you need me to do.'

Velka turned haunted eyes to Ina and shook her head. 'Nothing until I've drawn the sigils around this circle. I thought I would have trouble tracing the anchor, but the wound is crying out to my magic.' Reaching into her saddlebags, the nature mage removed a bag of salt and headed for the statue.

Rurik didn't look much better than Velka, unable to look away from the horrifying scene. 'I will need to go inside their minds and connect with what is left of the victims. Once Velka is ready, we cast. You will need to stand between us, close enough to touch if needed. Frankly speaking, this is new to all of us, so we'll have to hope for the best.' He gave her an apologetic smile, and Ina pulled Zjawa's saddle down and sat on it, watching as both mages drew their sigils.

'Very well. Let me know when you are ready to begin. Daro, please make sure our people are at a safe distance in case Marzanna thinks we're the ones who locked her in the statue and exacts her revenge.' The orc looked at her grimly, grinding his teeth, so Ina gave him a tired smile. 'I won't let anything happen to her, but I'll be too busy to do anything else. Please help me keep everyone safe.'

Daro wasn't happy leaving Velka's side, even for a moment, but he gathered his men and started moving the lethargic townsfolk beyond the palisade. Everyone let themselves be herded like obedient cattle, and this lack of resistance worried Ina the most. It was almost like the inhabitants of this place had given up on living. *Maybe that's why no one lives on the barren lands beyond the Black Forest,* she thought, not noticing her aunt sitting beside her. The cup in her hand made her shudder, but Mirena looked at her with motherly concern when she raised her head.

'Don't look at me like that. It will boost your energy and help you focus, so drink. The potion will last a few hours, but that's it. I'll help the villagers, see if we can break their lethargy or at least make them comfortable. There's nothing more I can do here unless things go wrong, so try to avoid that, yes?' she said, stroking Ina's cheek, and the witch exhaled slowly. With Velka and Rurik busy drawing sigils, Mirena was the only person with whom she could share her worries.

'Can I admit I'm scared? I've never worked with chaos on such a scale, and it's not just one spell. I'll be working three magical streams in just as many directions. In battle, it's all instinct and reaction, but here, I have to be in full control to avoid killing everyone, but each time I immerse so deeply into raw chaos, I feel one step closer to madness.' Ina wanted to say more, but the dreamy smile on Mirena's lips stopped her, so instead, she finished drinking her aunt's concoction.

'Ina, my lovely child, you don't know how special you are. Now be yourself. Let the chaos reign. That's all I need.'

It was an odd choice of words, especially after she'd mentioned her worries, but before she could dwell on it, Velka called her over.

'We are ready. Please stand here.' She pointed to the place in the diagram where the salt circle changed, drawn into a strange half-moon shape. When Ina raised her head, she noticed Velka watching her inspection with pleasure. 'That is an idea I had to incorporate your magic into the ancient drawing. This shape will gather any stray energy so that you can utilise it. How are you going to transfer it to us?'

'I need to channel chaos through my ring. It's hard to explain, but chaos becomes less volatile when I work through it. Once I do that, it's a matter of connecting with you. That's where things get tricky. In the past, the people I've touched with chaos have either been hurt, or fled in a blind panic, but hopefully, using the ring will help, so you'll have to relax and allow it to merge with your magic. In short, I'm not sure how you will feel, so let's hope for the best.' Ina sent a silent prayer out into the aether, crossing her fingers.

Leshy, please help me. I am here to free a goddess, but please don't let me hurt my family to do it. Channelling chaos, Ina opened herself up to the magic of her blood, that link to nature that had always been there, and reached out to her companions, merging with their energies and momentarily feeling their shock and pain.

Rurik winced. Her touch was enough to crack his impassive facade, but he quickly walled off his emotions, cutting off Ina from his psyche whilst keeping the link open enough to fuel his spell. Velka's reaction surprised Ina, as the nature witch opened up completely, embracing both the raw magic and the emotional burden, creating a connection she felt only with Mar and Ren.

My beautiful Flower, each time I think I know you, you surprise me again, she thought, feeling selfless love and complete trust through the connection.

Velka smiled back. 'Let's begin,' she said, and together with Rurik, poured their power into their sigils, weaving magic and making the lines glow.

Initially, Ina felt nothing. The two melodic voices chanted in beautiful harmony, but the pressure from the death chant slowly intensified. Rurik was drawing power through the bond, and Ina reached for her necklace to tap into its reserves, waiting for Velka to complete her spell. So far, everything had gone as planned. She caught Velka's look, warning her that the nature mage was ready to close the barrier, and Ina braced herself for a sudden influx of magic.

She thought she was prepared, but nothing could compare to this, not even the pain of healing Mar. Ina felt like a magical tidal wave was trying to force its way through her midriff, scouring the flesh from her bones as it passed. Ina's heart shuddered in its cage while her body jolted, muscles rigid with shock. The untamed magic lit up her veins, creating glowing red patterns on the witch's skin. *Breathe, you idiot, breathe. This was your idea, now deal with it!* Ina focused her mind, fighting for control over the wild torrent of power. Whether it was the sheer power of the witch's will or her prayer to the Leshy, Ina finally managed to drag a painful breath into her lungs, and her heart stopped trying to leap from her body.

Piercing, ragged screams burst from the sacrificial offerings, a sickly green glow burning in their eyes, when, as one, they slowly looked towards Rurik, their clawed fingers reaching for his flesh. His black aura fluctuated when the necromancer fell backwards, shocked as his spell nearly collapsed. Ina grabbed his arm, forcing more power through the open link, and with a muttered cantrip, Rurik strengthened his enchantment, freezing the remnants in place.

Worried and struggling to focus, Ina looked at Velka, whose quiet chanting created a beautiful coruscating glow, her barrier cutting off the curse's energy. The overwhelming amount of power diverted by that barrier was slipping from the witch's control. Ina fed more magic into Velka's connection to stop it, closing her eyes in relief as the pressure lessened.

Ina could do nothing else and focused on her surroundings, finding the strange tableau fascinating. On one side were five terrifying monsters, frozen with hate-filled eyes; on the other, a glowing rainbow over lush green grass slowly spreading outwards from their position. *I'm like a bloody power gem. Now we just need a giant to dangle me on a golden chain*, she thought, and the idea of her new function made her giggle.

Suddenly, the witch felt another change in Rurik's magic. A burst of fury and relief filled the link as the necromancer broke a single chain; the victim tied to its sick magic, crumbling to the ground, lifeless and free from torment. Despite the sweat beading on his brow, Rurik smiled as he focused on the next body, guiding its soul to the afterlife with a shaking hand.

As the second body fell to pieces, Marzanna's statue began cracking, the sound startling in its suddenness, and a new type of magic encroached on Ina's consciousness.

Velka's song turned shrill as more cracks appeared in the statue, and it became clear where the new magic came from as grey ropes of energy escaped their confinement and struck at the nature mage's barrier. Ina nearly panicked at the shrill scream almost deafening her, thinking Velka was hurt. Even as the thought came, the witch still heard her friend's chant in the background and turned to the effigy of the goddess, going pale when Marzanna turned hate-filled eyes towards her.

Ina cursed when a malevolent consciousness disrupted what little control she still had, and the darkness in her soul expanded, feeding on the wild energy burning through her body. Crimson, destructive chaos shimmered over her, sending a sensual shiver along her spine. *My loves, I need your help*, she thought, searching for the light of her bonds, finding nothing. The gold and silver threads that helped her resist the seduction of power were gone. She was alone, facing that all-consuming darkness with no help to fight it.

Her fear exploded in a maelstrom of chaos that shook the ground. Rurik stumbled, using the last of his magic to release the final soul, then cried out as his body was flung to the side by the whirlwind of Ina's power.

Velka huddled on the ground, her barrier still, miraculously, in place, seeming to glow brighter as Marzanna's statue exploded and Winter's Death emerged, her wrath focused on the one person still standing. With the power of chaos and the land's rebirth consuming her, unanchored and unprotected, Ina, Lady of the Crimson Veil, answered the goddess's fury with a chilling, serene smile.

Ina heard Velka shouting, but it didn't matter. Nothing mattered anymore but hunger and the power that was hers to take. A piece of the statue hit her cheek, searing the skin, and the witch looked up at the towering presence of the Winter Goddess. The Lady of the Crimson Veil held out her hand, and the magic within the circle stalled, leaving behind silence, freezing Ina's breath in the still air.

The land's life force built inside her, but it was not enough. Ina wanted more and reached for the pure essence of the goddess. The promise of peace and freedom unrestrained by mortality's shackles was alluring. Ina raised her gaze to the woman before her, looking into Marzanna's eyes without fear. With skin the white of glaciers and her body shrouded in mist and snow, Marzanna looked like a marble sculpture, her beauty hard and unyielding. Chaos reached out for the goddess, who looked at the crimson tendrils with condescension and grasped them firmly, pulling and trying to claim their magic, sneering when the witch resisted.

'It is mine,' Ina said, tearing the magic from the goddess' hands. Indignation flashed across Marzanna's features as she responded, her power crashing into Ina's chest, instilling a sense of wrongness and blame for forcing the divine into a chained existence. The divine magic of winter was tainted by the grey, hungry power of the curse, leaving it weak and ineffective, and Ina realised if she was to take the goddess' power, she had to get rid of that parasite. When fire exploded from her hands, igniting the curse, Marzanna's face twisted with fury, even as the grey sludge was burned away in the raw chaos, and Ina reached for the untainted essence of a goddess.

'You think to chain me again, human? Won't you have wasted all of your efforts? Your life, your friends, your family. They surround you with love, holding back the darkness you fear so much. Yet I can feel your desire to give in. You want to take everything and bring a true Winter's Death to the world.'

The smile that twisted the witch's lips was a parody of humanity, matching that of the goddess as she siphoned the power from the land, losing herself in the madness of chaos, fighting Marzanna and laughing when the goddess' eyes widened in disbelief. This was it, and all that magic would be hers now. Ina closed her eyes, feeling the touch of winter caressing her soul.

'Ina, no! Wake up! This is not you!'

The voice and a sudden flash of gold caught her fleeting attention. The Zmij slithered under her skin, answering the call of the green magic bursting through Velka's connection. Golden light erupted from Ina's arm, covering the nature mage like a shield, and Velka pushed forward, the atmosphere thick with immense power. The witch could see tears freezing on her cheeks while battling the magic, but it didn't stop her.

'Striga, wake the fuck up, call for Mar!' she shouted, screaming in shock when tendrils of chaos rammed into her body, barely repelled by Zmij's golden coils.

'No, not her.' Images from the past flew through her mind. The last shard of humanity still within her recognised her friend's love, breaking through the hunger, and Ina sobbed, tearing her power away while frost crawled over her skin.

'Lada, I need your help!' she cried, fighting to stay upright as the raging winter reached for her core. 'I won't die on my knees, and I won't die as a monster,' she said, looking at the winter goddess with sorrow.

'You're right. I am filled with darkness and crave to tear every piece of magic from your cold, dead heart. As for the rest, you are wrong. I'm more than the darkness and hunger. I carry the love of those who trusted I could stop the curse. So go ahead, take my magic, take my life if you must, then go back to whatever hellhole you call home. You are free.'

Ina could hear Velka's muffled cry. With one last effort, she strengthened the barrier spell protecting her friend and let go. The magic that caused so much hurt was now at peace as the witch gave it all up and closed her eyes, the smile on her lips echoing her thoughts. The Lady of the Crimson Veil dying at the hands of a goddess shrouded in frost. That would be one epic ballad, giving the bards the last laugh, after all.

A melodic voice broke through Ina's musings, forcing her to open her eyes. 'Leave her be, Sister. She is our herald and serves us well. It is time for the land's rebirth, Marzanna. Return to the underworld and release life back to this world.' Ina blinked in surprise, feeling Lada's hand on her shoulder, directing her power. Her chaos and the light of spring sprang forth, and, with a sardonic smile, Marzanna burst into flames and disappeared, waves of magic spreading out from her former position, almost bringing the witch to her knees.

The winter goddess was gone, and as the icy ground melted, the magical sigils were washed away, quickly replaced by thousands of sprouting shoots growing with miraculous speed, shocking Ina speechless. Suddenly, the witch was tackled from the side, and Velka's arms gathered her into her generous bosom, sheltering her from Lada's gaze.

'Why do you keep hurting her? Why?' Ina looked up from the smothering embrace, too weak from channelling so much magic to fight, and tried to reason with her friend before Lada took offence.

'Velka, it's fine. I'm fine,' she said, and her friend stomped her foot.

'No, you are not fine. You have too much of a bloody death wish to be fine! I could feel you fighting, but you were lost, so lost that I couldn't feel your soul. The magical overload broke you, but why did you lock yourself with Marzanna behind the barrier? The ground was shaking, drained of magic. I couldn't get to you until this thing helped me. Even when I felt how bad it was through our link, I could only watch because all I've got is my useless magic.' The last words were filled with tears, and Ina's face paled at hearing the woman who saved them all demeaning herself.

'If not for you, I would have lost myself to the darkness. You saved me, and I haven't even asked how you feel or how the baby is,' she said, more concerned about her friend than the spring goddess, observing this exchange with a genuine smile.

'Is that all you can think about now? You almost died there, and you're asking me how *I* feel?'

Velka gasped when Lada approached her, placing a hand on her round stomach without warning. 'Your friend will be fine. The Leshy's blood is stronger than expected for her to survive this encounter. And you, my child… the love you share with the world puts even the gods to shame.' Lada nodded to Zmij, who'd been hovering over the small gathering, and the beast wrapped itself around Velka's arm, making both women scream in unison.

'Blessed be the child and mother, blessed be the heralds of spring.' Lada's voice echoed throughout the settlement, and despite her exhaustion, Ina reached out, trying to push the goddess away.

'You are not fucking with their lives… I will do what you want me to do, but leave them alone,' Ina snapped, cursing Lada's bright laugh as the goddess vanished in a flash of golden light before she could finish. Ina turned to Velka, who looked at her belly with eyes full of wonder. 'I'm so sorry. I shouldn't have dragged you here. I will make them change their mind, I promise.'

Velka slowly shook her head. 'No, Striga, it… it is good. It feels right. I can sense my boy's magic now, and it is as powerful and green as life itself. Besides, being a herald of a goddess of love can't be too bad. Oh, Ina, it's over. We did it. We broke the curse!'

Ina looked at the happiness that blossomed on Velka's face when her friend looked around, seeing the ground covered with a green carpet of plants already spreading far beyond sight. *Oh, Flower, should I tell you that being the gods' herald can make your life difficult beyond reason? I hope the boy at least finds someone like you to rely on before the gods make him their plaything,* she thought.

Hesitantly reaching for her bonds, Ina hoped, with Marzanna and the blight's curse gone, whatever blocked her connection would disappear as well, but all she felt was darkness.

Velka gasped when the witch, pale with shock, fell to her knees, gripping her chest. Ina tried to control herself, but panic choked her. She couldn't deny it anymore. Whatever happened had nothing to do with Marzanna. The bond was gone, and no matter how hard she tried, she could no longer feel Mar or Ren.

'Velka, stay away from me,' she said, seeing the nature mage bending down to help her.

'What happened? Are you injured?'

'Stay the fuck away from me! I broke the bond. I can't feel them anymore. There is nothing that can stop me from going berserk again.' Ina looked at her trembling hands, afraid she would see the destructive flames of chaos burning out of control.

'Calm down. You had control over your magic before you met them, and you are in control now, so stop fretting over it. It may be just temporary, anyway. Maybe it is just overload and exhaustion. I will bring Mirena. She might know.' Velka turned on her heel and ran to find the healer, while Ina tried to calm her racing thoughts as she walked to the nearest tree.

'Leshy, please help me. Whatever happens, help me reverse it. I may be in control now, but how long will it last? I don't want to harm anyone. I did all you asked of me. Please help me because, with the chaos regalia and nothing to hold me back, it won't take long before I descend into madness.'

(at the same time)

Mar stood behind the king's chair, helplessly clenching his fists. He couldn't believe he'd agreed to let Ina face Marzanna's curse whilst he stood here like some glorified fairytale monster used to keep naughty children from misbehaving. In his distraction, he barely listened to the proposed peace treaty, offers, counteroffers, and veiled threats bandied around the room by the various nobles on either side.

When Tobias, Verdante's latest ruler, arrived at the meeting, everyone had been on edge, with Kaian refusing to leave Rewan's side for fear of another assassination attempt. It was clear both sides expected the worst, but Rewan surprised everyone by asking his counterpart directly why he kept sending assassins to his court. When Verdante's king threw down evidence of the assassins Rewan had sent, it soon became clear something wasn't right. It was Kaian who noticed the emblem on the letter, the wheatsheaf motif eliciting a stifled curse from his lips, and when Tobias accused Cornovii of cursing their lands, Rewan looked at his lover and frowned.

From that moment on, it had become more tense, with each leader arguing over who did what and whose assassins went where until, begrudgingly, both monarchs conceded that they'd been misled and neither had attempted to take the other's life.

Once that issue was concluded, or at least put aside, Rewan told the Verdantian king about Marzanna's curse and the steps being taken to resolve it, keeping the details vague to avoid further arguments.

Tobias had given his counterpart a deep, searching look before turning to his advisors and beginning a long, whispered conversation. After several minutes, even Rewan was fidgeting, but after an angry denial from a young noble in the Verdante group, Tobias turned to Rewan and spoke.

'I propose an alliance cemented by our two nations' blood. My sister, Łyna, is of age. You shall marry and produce an heir so that these… *little misunderstandings* shall never be repeated.'

This statement shocked Mar out of his stupor, and he looked down as Rewan nearly leapt from his seat before replying. 'We both know I already have a partner I love. Why would you propose this, knowing your sister won't find happiness in my kingdom?'

'Yes, I realise Master Kaian is not here only as his king's protection, but we both know you need an heir. Łyna may be young, but she is not stupid and is well-versed in the world. As long as she has the respect and power of her position, she won't complain or interfere with who you have in your bed, and she will give your heir a legitimacy that will ensure peace for years to come.'

'Are you seriously trying to marry your sister off in the name of peace? We are both seated here facing each other, and rather than make a deal we're both happy with, you'd rather force your sister into a loveless marriage far from everyone who cares about her? Kaian is more than a casual affair, and while I'm not expecting much happiness as king, in this regard, I deserve some.'

Rewan stood up and paced in the small space, and Mar could see the conflict in the king's heart.

'We will kindly accept this offer, and our future queen will receive the respect and protection she deserves.' Kaian's voice broke the temporary silence, and at his statement, the king's head snapped around to look at his lover.

'You forget yourself, Lord Kaian. My private matters are not for you to decide.' The pain in Rewan's voice softened his harsh words, but when the spymaster stood up and approached the king, Rewan sagged under his gentle touch.

'Cornovii needs a queen and an heir. I love you enough to spare you that grief and strife, so if the lady Łyna consents, knowing all the facts about this strange arrangement, we will make it work, my love,' he said, and as the last word passed his lips, the ground beneath their feet trembled, nearly knocking the two men off their feet.

'What was that?' Tobias looked around, fear and suspicion on his face, but soon noticed everyone was just as ignorant as he was. Mar instinctively reached for the bond, assuming Ina would be involved in such a strange phenomenon and that there must be trouble if it was felt this far away.

There was nothing there; no thread, no feelings, no sense of Ina of any sort. Panic washed over him when Mar realised he could no longer feel his woman, and in the centre of his being was a dark, empty void. Ina was gone. The racing heart trying to burst from his chest left him entirely at the mercy of the dragon as it clawed its way into the light, scales forming like a wave across his body.

Sunlight blinded everyone as the tent was opened, and a panting squire ran in, shouting, 'My lords, spring is… Spring has come.'

In moments, the tent was empty, each person stumbling to a halt at the sight before them. As far as the eye could see, lush green growth covered the earth where minutes ago had been muddy, lifeless fields.

Mar was at his wit's end, struggling to focus, even as he realised Ina had broken the curse. But no matter what he thought, his instincts were telling him to transform and find his mate. He didn't notice when a young mage ran up to the king, bloody tears running down his face.

'Your Majesty, dire news. Mage Rurik has torn the veil of Veles… to beg… for help. The witch has been betrayed… they are pursued….' Before he could utter another word, the young necromancer collapsed, unconscious, the spell's cost too much for his unprepared mind.

The deafening roar of a dragon staggered everyone, Mar's form exploding outwards in a blinding flash of light as pain tore open his heart, burning away all reason. A raging beast emerged, ready to rip apart any who would hurt his love.

Rewan turned, quaking in fear and pointed to the skies, shouting. 'Go, find her and keep her safe!'

Mar didn't care what the human said, but something in his tone reached the beast's mind, helping him focus before he leapt into the sky. Northwards, he flew, unsure of his destination but knowing which direction. A fleeing speck caught his eye, and, unable to resist, the dragon dived, claws reaching out. About to grasp his prey, Mar veered off, landing heavily as he recognised the figure he'd chased.

Ren held onto his rearing horse, keeping his seat, even as a large bundle fell to the floor behind him. After calming his mount, he turned towards the dragon, angry and ready to chastise such stupid behaviour when Mar spoke.

'Ina was betrayed, and I can't feel her bond. Tell me you can!'

Ren shook his head but pointed to the squirming bundle on the ground. 'No, I felt the bond disappear and knew something was wrong. I knew this bastard prince would know something, so I grabbed him.' Kicking the prince in the middle, Ren swore and looked up at the dragon. 'He says he doesn't know what happened, but when I mentioned the temple, he knew what I meant. I gave him a choice, life as a eunuch or showing me the way.'

Mar shook his head, trying to suppress his fear of losing Ina, and roared. 'Forget the fucking horse, Ren, drag that whoreson onto my back and let's go to her.'

Ren's visage was more a promise of death than the expression of a man as he grabbed his burden by the scruff and climbed onto the dragon's back, tying the helpless prince to a spine between Mar's wings and pressing a knife to Wawrzyniec's throat.

With a curse, Mar realised he couldn't talk to his friend as they flew and reluctantly linked their minds before launching himself, once more, into the sky.

Do you know what could have happened? Why can't we feel her anymore? he asked, the sensation of talking to Ren strangely intimate and intrusive.

An overwhelming wave of anger washed through his mind as Ren replied. *No, but I will skin the bastard alive.* The two men's emotions swept back and forth—fear, anger, and guilt—till Mar roared for it to stop. In reply, Ren shook his head. *Is this our fault? Did we cause this by forcing her to choose? Did the bond disappear because I kept my distance? Or because you...?*

Did I tell her to sideline you? No, your friendship means the world to her, and if that were the reason, I would still feel her. I may have many flaws, Ren, but I wouldn't let her be harmed or sad because of my jealousy.

He could feel a hint of amused regret when Ren answered. *Many flaws? Dragons are very possessive. I'm not sure what you think we have, but Ina gave me the sense of family I thought forever lost.*

387

I want to be there when she needs me. I want to be her moonlight guardian to repay her for that gift. If you loved her any less, I would have killed you, and right now, I'm terrified I will never see her again.

Mar shivered at the flood of emotion from their connection. *Ren, you know I can sense what you are feeling now. It's still hard knowing how much you love Ina, even as friends, so please try not to share so much.*

CHAPTER TWENTY-SEVEN

Ina wasn't sure how long she'd spent searching for her bonds, but when Velka returned with Daro and Mirena, the witch was at the end of her tether. Could she remake the bond?

Mar was as good as dead the first time it happened, and she almost died with him before chaos forged the connection, healing his body. It had felt easier with Ren, but they both went through tremendous pain and nearly died. Ina knew both men would volunteer to repeat the experience without hesitation, but there was always a risk the change in her magic was permanent, and she won't be able to re-establish the connection. Without it and the chaos healing, they would die, and their life was not something with which she was willing to gamble. While the witch frantically considered her options, Rurik stood beside her, awkwardly patting her shoulder in silence. She could feel his concern, but he didn't offer false platitudes, for which the witch was grateful.

One look at her face and Daro took charge, taking her to the makeshift camp outside the town. Ina noticed that with the curse gone, the eyes of the townsfolk were no longer lifeless and dull, but wide open in fear and confusion. She tried to convince herself that the long-awaited spring and saving the province was worth it. That losing the anchors that allowed her to use her magic safely didn't mean she was going to break the world, but deep down, she knew it wasn't working, and Ina felt she had awakened these people from their nightmare, only to descend into her own.

Daro sat the two women next to the fire, gesturing for Rurik to join them, ordering him to stand guard while he took the soldiers to hunt enough food to feed everyone. Ina felt unwanted tears pool in her eyes as she rested her head on Velka's shoulder. While too tired to even talk, they watched Mirena brew another potion over the small fire.

The healer was soon finished and knelt in front of the two friends. 'Drink this and rest here while I check on the villagers. Using so much magic must have been draining, especially for you, Ina,' she said, passing them cups filled with a lavender-scented concoction. 'It was quite the experience, feeling the ground shake as spring growth rolled over the land like a tidal wave.' Mirena looked them in the eyes before smiling sadly. 'Bottoms up. Do not argue with the healer and finish it all.' Ina returned her smile, feeling empty as her aunt pulled her hood up and walked over to the villagers.

The drink was too sweet and smelled strongly of magic and herbs. Something in the back of her mind protested, but Ina was too tired to care. She sipped it slowly, trusting her aunt, careful not to burn her tongue on the honeyed sludge, feeling an overwhelming numbness and weariness spread throughout her body. The sensation was so rapid and unusual that Ina shook her head, trying to clear her vision. *Did Mirena give me a sleeping potion again? I don't mind a good sleep, but some warning would be appreciated.*

When the rustling hedge to her left caught her wavering attention, she attempted to stand, intending to investigate, only to fall back as a wave of dizziness overcame her. Ina watched in disbelief as the foliage disgorged several brigands, staring at the woman with evident hostility. Their leader's face was familiar, and that impression intensified when he spoke.

'We meet again, my lady, but now my patron wants you to go with us. She said you would be as weak as a lamb, and I'd prefer not to knock you about, so if you'd come along peacefully, we have a carriage nearby for your convenience.'

'Weak? As a lamb... I think not?' Ina slurred, confused and, as the brigand said, weak and helpless, her limbs failing to follow the simplest instructions. As she looked at Velka, hoping her friend could escape, she saw the pregnant mage unconscious and looked instead for Rurik and Daro. The orc was nowhere to be seen, and with the brigand's intentions, the witch worried about Mirena. Thankfully, she eventually caught sight of Rurik, standing and confronting the bandit leader.

'Who gave you that order? No one touches them without their consent unless you want to taste the living death.' Rurik's angry voice brought Ina's bitter smile, especially when the air shimmered with a necromancy spell.

'Step aside, death master. Lady Mirena gave the order, and she made sure those two won't be able to fight, but if you wish, you can keep the blond one. We are only here for the chaos mage.'

Ina tried, once again, to stand up, grab a sword, or even concentrate enough to call her magic, but nothing happened. All she could think about as the world tilted alarmingly were the brigand's words. Her aunt ordered this? *Fuck! Her potions—*

What have I been drinking? What did she do? I... A wave of nausea interrupted her thoughts, and the witch groaned. *I knew Rurik's arrival was too convenient.*

It was all Ina could do not to pass out, and if not for the necromancer's quick response, she would have fallen, face first, into the fire.

'Whatever she's paying you, I can offer more...' Rurik tried to bargain, but a burst of laughter interrupted his words.

'She said you were too soft, and we came prepared. Last warning, Death Master....'

Ina's vision narrowed, darkness closing in, but she still saw Rurik raise a hand, black lightning streaking into the chest of the nearest bandit, the spell stopping his heart instantly. After a single lurching step, the now-dead man turned to his former colleagues and tore into them wordlessly.

A flash of light made her turn her head, squeezing her eyes shut, and when it faded, Rurik was on the ground, his hands being tied by the brigands, his minion lying dead beside him. For a moment, Ina wondered if the absence of Daro meant he'd been killed or was trapped somewhere, but a flash of grey distracted her. Zjawa, claws exposed and rearing, was attacking the bandits, trying to reach her.

Ina cursed as rough hands grabbed her from behind, efficiently binding her wrists. Hoping her mount understood, the witch shouted, 'Zjawa! Get help!' before a sharp pain to the back of her head sent her into oblivion.

392

The sudden burst of light blinded him and dispersed his magic. He was too weak to fight anyone, especially veteran warriors like these. *What in Nawia is my mother doing now?* It wasn't the first time he'd felt helpless. Most of his childhood had been that way, but it had been years since he'd faced the bitter taste of impotence. Now, for whatever reason, Mirena had strayed from their plans and drugged the two women, rendering them defenceless. If she were hoping to recruit Ina, this would never work, but seeing how tightly the brigand tied the ropes on Ina's wrists, Rurik didn't think that was the intention.

The bandit leader looked down at the necromancer before turning to one of his men. 'Why do they always have to fight? Fetch Lady Mirena from the temple ruins. I need to talk to her.' The man grumbled something under his breath before nodding and walking away while his boss tried to make the women as comfortable as possible, tied up as they were, before helping Rurik sit up next to the fire.

The necromancer stewed in his frustration until a voice behind made him turn his head angrily. 'Stop being so sentimental and load Ina onto the carriage.' Filled with disapproval, his mother's words made no sense to him, and he unsuccessfully tried to stop the men from taking the women.

'Why are you doing this? She removed the curse and subdued the southern rebellion. She is already a force to be reckoned with, even without the full regalia. We need to change our plans. The new king already listens to her, and the rest will follow his example. I gained their trust and friendship, and although you ruined it all, we can still salvage the pieces, but you have to leave now. The last thing Ina saw was me defending her. Take your men and run, mother. I will contact you when things are settled.'

'One taste of friendship from a pretty woman, and you lose your way. You still harbour feelings for Velka but never understood Ina, just as you never understood me. I don't want Cornovii to thrive. I want to wipe my shame away with the ashes of their destruction. Removing the connection she had with her men should have turned her into a maelstrom of death, but that stubborn witch survived. I don't need your schemes and political manoeuvring any more. Cornovii is powerless without its little protector, and when I'm finished, there'll be nothing left but blood and tears.'

'Are you mad? We never planned to destroy it. I didn't even want to rule. We just needed to weaken them, to leave Cornovii as vulnerable as Arknay and Verdante, so they'd acknowledge their failure and turn to the mages for help. Then we could step in and force the changes required to prevent our tragedy from happening to someone else. Was that what you intended all this time? To wipe them out? I should never have listened to you.' Rurik looked at his mother, seeing her fanaticism clearly for the first time. He knew her suffering had robbed them of their chance to be a proper family, but he hoped, deep down, that there was still a bond between them.

That hope died when she looked down at him, her expression full of disgust, and spoke. 'That was your plan, my son. Idealistic foolishness, but useful for furthering my revenge. The monarchs of Warenga would never listen to a mage, powerful or otherwise. This kingdom is lost and will pay dearly for what that scum, Roda, did to me.' He saw her vicious smile, transforming the mother he thought he knew into a creature of savage cruelty. 'Cornovii is seen now as a country that only survives thanks to one flawed mage, one that's now in my possession, and with that news reaching the ears of the Iron Emperor in the North, well, let's just say he is not a man to look a gift horse in the mouth. As we speak, his armada is on its way. She will make a fine tool in his arsenal, and I will rejoice at seeing them brought to heel with blood and fire.'

Rurik felt his blood turn to ice. The Iron Empire was everything in the world he detested. They were ruled by a tyrant, crushing everything and everyone who couldn't stand against their military power. Even the Eastern Dragon Emperor seemed docile compared to the northerners. Cornovii declined any contact, avoiding even trading with them, and his mother's scheme had brought this plague here. 'Why?' His voice sounded small, but he felt like a fool who thought he had a golden egg, only to find lead beneath the gilded paint.

'Why? You, of all people, ask me why?' His mother stepped towards him with eyes narrowed in anger. 'Maybe you should call the corpse of the former king and ask why he raped me, why, in his debauchery, he passed me around his companions like I was less than nothing and when he found out I was pregnant, married me off to that weakling in House Thorn. I had to pretend to be the perfect little wife while that lecherous old spider tormented and controlled me all these years, but now I will take my revenge, and you will help me.'

'You said Roda loved you,' Rurik murmured, repelled by Mirena's words. 'What he did is horrifying, evil, deserving of terrible revenge, but the Iron Empire, Mother? They will kill thousands and enslave the rest. How can you condemn more people to the evils we suffered? What insanity prompted you to contact those monsters?' Rurik's pale face and tight lips didn't escape Mirena's attention, and she cautiously approached her son.

'Their rule won't last long, and they will be your unifying force, bringing the disparate nations together to repel the common enemy. It would even allow you to be the hero you desired. Ina is a small price to pay, especially knowing her ability to cause trouble. If we had her magic under our control, we could rule them all.'

'Ina won't use her magic without the bond to anchor her. She is terrified of becoming another Sowenna. If you force her, this insanity will kill us all. Just go, Mother. I will fix this somehow.'

'You think you know everything. The sacrifice spell can work both ways, and I'm sure the emperor won't have any qualms about ordering a mage to perform a sacrifice spell to control his new pet,' she said, attempting to stroke his face, but Rurik withdrew, flinching away from her touch.

'What on Veles's arse is going on here?' Daro's furious question interrupted Rurik's pleading. The small hunting party had returned, and the captain stood before the shocking scene, the sight of his wife's unconscious body in the carriage shocking him into anger. 'What have you done to my wife, you bastards?' This time, Daro wasn't shouting, his voice full of deadly, calm menace as he reached out for the bandit leader.

A shimmering barrier appeared as the leader turned his panicked glance towards Mirena, stopping the orc. The next moment, axes and swords were drawn as the captain and his men fought to break through and rescue the women.

With only a few soldiers to fight, the brigands quickly gained the upper hand, overpowering the inexperienced guards and dispatching them mercilessly, but Daro fought as one possessed, trying to reach his wife's side with brutal, deadly efficiency, killing or wounding everyone who came within reach. His opponents sheltered behind the barrier and picked up their bows, taking aim and calmly shooting the orc until he collapsed.

Struggling to breathe, still trying to move towards Velka, Daro was forced to stop when Mirena kicked him back, a vicious sneer on her lips.

'Barbarian fool, you fight against your betters and expected to win? Should I let you live to watch your wife die at the hands of these ruffians? Oh, but not to worry, my burly friend, your little wife has value to me. As long as Ina lives, she will be safe because nothing will keep that unnatural mutt in line more than the life of her dearest friend. Unfortunately, that means you are a surplus to our requirements.' Mirena pulled a dagger out to deal the final blow when a blast of black magic knocked her to the side, and the crack of a whip caused the carriage to lurch forward down the muddy road. Mirena screamed, abandoning her dagger and running towards the horses, shouting at her men.

'Catch that bloody witch! One hundred gold for the one who brings me the crimson witch alive, and if my idiot son resists, kill him.'

Despite straining his wings, Mar felt like time stood still, tormenting him. Once they passed Alsia, Mar impatiently nudged Ren's mind. *Find out where to go now.* With a bit of prodding, Wawrzyniec pointed towards the forest, and after an hour, his directions led them to the ruins of a ramshackle settlement, overgrown and silent.

The village was deserted with no sign of life, and Mar would have sworn no one had lived there in years, but as he looked around, he saw a pattern to the growth, a series of circles spreading out from the very centre of town and dived, landing clumsily in the lush growth. As soon as Ren was down and the prince thrown to the ground, the dragon transformed, and the two men searched for Ina until Mar caught the smell of burning.

Following the scent, it didn't take long to find the still-warm ashes of the fire, and Ren found the bodies of House Thorn's soldiers with a trail of blood leading to the side.

Their worry for Ina's safety grew, and the two men raced forward, coming across another pile of bodies, this one surrounding their friend, Daro, with several arrows protruding from his torso. With tears running down his face, Mar cursed and knelt beside the orc, only to see him take a shallow, shuddering breath, his eyes flickering open and blood spraying into the air when he tried to talk.

'Necromancer took them. Mirena… betrayed us and did something to them… Save my wife….' His eyes rolled to the back of his head as Mar tried to make sense of his words.

Ren looked at Mar with determination, then stripped back Daro's armour, pulling supplies from pockets the dragon hadn't even seen, trying to save their friend's life.

Both men set to work, trying to staunch the blood flowing from the orc's body. Then Mar turned to the fire and began rebuilding it before trying to use his dragon fire to light it. After several attempts, he created enough flame to start the fire, but an angry braying startled him as he turned back to his companions.

Ina's orein rushed towards Mar, snapping her fangs in front of his face, then biting and grabbing his arm, pulling him away.

'They headed north?' he asked, and the orein whickered, pulling him again.

Ren looked up as he kneeled beside Daro, slowly pulling an arrow from the orc's shoulder. 'We need to take him to a healer first, and then we can search. Ina has a lot of friends, not only among humans. Someone will help us find her.'

Mar looked at Ren and knelt beside him to help. 'I am going to kill whoever did this, but first, we help Daro. Then they die!'

Nodding as he worked, Ren agreed. 'Yes, they will die.'

Glossary

Baba Yaga – (Slavic mythology) is, in Slavic folklore, the wild old woman, the witch, mistress of magic and a mythical creature.

Bi chamd hairtai - I love you (Yanwo dialect) – actually Mongolian (from Google translate, but I love it)

Botchling – a lesser monster, a small creature resembling a highly deformed foetus - created from the improper burial of unwanted, stillborn infants - preys on pregnant women.

Boruta – (Slavic mythology) a forest demon who is often considered an avatar of Leshy.

Chram - (Slavic mythology) – the most sacred place, a temple for the Slavic deity associated with specific rituals, prophecies and miracles. Chram could be a building, a forest, a swamp, or any natural setting.

Cornovii – Merchant kingdom between the Black Forest and Grey Mountains. Because of the geographical position multiracial centre of trading.

Daro – "dark power" Steppe Orc, the rebellious son of a tribe thane drafted into the King's Guards, a known womaniser until he married Velka.

Domowik - In the Slavic religious tradition, Domowik is the household spirit of given kin. They are deified progenitors, the kin's fountainhead ancestors.

Gruff – "the rock" Rock troll, owner of Drunken Wizard and spymaster of Osterad.

Gamayun - Gamayun is a mythological creature with a bird's body and a beautiful woman's head. They derive from Slavic and Old Russian folklore and are described as mythical beings that can mesmerise humans with their enchanting voices. Their role is to be a messenger of gods.

Hela, also called the "Two-Faced Terror," is a goddess of the dead, especially those who drown in the sea.

Imp – a lesser demon. Imps are often shown as small and not very attractive creatures. Their behaviour is described as being wild and uncontrollable. Imps were fond of pranks and misleading people.

Inanuan – "beautiful destruction." Also known as Ina or Inanuan Zoria Thornsen. High-born lady of the principal ducal house of Cornovii and the first pure Chaos mage born in a generation. Sometimes referred to as Striga by friends and Autumn's Child by older races.

Jarylo/Jaryło - god of vegetation, fertility and springtime.

Jorge – "supreme knowledge". Arche-mage of pure Order. He can foresee the future by applying his order magic to the reality patterns.

Kaian – "strong warrior". Scion of the primal ducal house of Cornovii, the House of the Water Horse. Also head of the Assassin Guild. The lover of king Rewan.

Kings's Guards – also called the second son's company. Unit designed strictly to guard the palace and investigate issues related to high-born nobles or state affairs.

Kobold – member of the kobold race. Cruel and proficient warriors and metalworkers living in the mines and tunnels in the

Grey Mountains. Shorter than humans, often seen in bulky black metal armour. Their race has zealous adherence to oaths, pacts, or customs.

Lada/Łada (Slavic mythology) - a goddess of love, Spring and Nature's rebirth, patron of weddings and matriarchy, and protector of families and ancestors who passed away.

Lady Midday/Południca – a mid-class demon who makes herself evident in the middle of hot summer days, takes the form of whirling dust clouds and carries a scythe, sickle or shears. She may appear as an old hag, a beautiful woman, or a 12-year-old girl. It is dangerous at midday when she can attack workers, cut their heads off, or send sudden illness.

Leshy – (Slavic mythology) a God of wild animals and forests. He protects the animals and birds in the forest and tells them when to migrate. He is a shapeshifter who can appear in many forms and sizes but is usually a tree, wolf, cat, or hairy man. His fickle Nature causes him to help one he deems worthy and punish those who mean wrong to the forest.

Liander – "flower of pride". Half-elve, the strongest psychic mage Int the count. Also, the court mage after Ina's departure.

Liath - dukedom of Cornovii associated with the House of Liath. It is a mountain region on the west defending the Grey Mountains, known for its military power and dragon-blood origins.

Litha or Kupala night - a midsummer solstice celebration dedicated to love, fertility, and water. Young people jump over the flames of bonfires in a ritual test of bravery and faith. The failure of a couple in love to complete the jump while holding hands signifies their destined separation.

Marcach – "wind rider." Also known as Mar or the Scion of Liath. The oldest son of the principal dukedom house of Cornovii. A war veteran and former Captain of the King's Guards, currently holding the title of Royal Dragon and Lord Marshall of Cornovii.

Marika –"kitten" Were-cat from Grey Mountains clan and Inanuan housekeeper.

Morena/Morane/Marzanna (Slavic mythology) – also known as Winter's Death. A personification of the repetitive cycles regulating life on earth, the changing seasons, and a master of both life and death. As Morena symbolises death on the battlefield. In folklore the death of Marzanna symbolises the rebirth of the world.

Morganatic marriage – a marriage where a high-born woman marries the commoner losing her status.

Meridian -The meridian system is a concept in traditional Chinese medicine adapted for this series. Meridians are paths through which the life energy is known as "qi" or Chaos flows. In the book, meridians are an energetic highway that distributes life energy/raw Chaos along the body.

Nawia – (Slavic mythology), an afterlife, is also used as a name for an underworld over which Veles exercises custody

Nerissa – grand -duchess of the house of Thorn. Arch-healer of Cornovii and Inanuan grand-aunt.

Osterad – The capital of Cornovii. Started as a simple river port with time, grew in riches and became the centre of human magic on the continent.

Orein – mountain spirit in the shape of a horse, often with a grey or black coat with sharp lynx-like fangs and lynx paws instead of hooves. However, it can curl the paw into a hoof shape and disguise itself as a horse. Mischievous and, by preference, carnivorous. They are called the blessing of the mountain because they often came to aid travellers they found worthy.

Phoenix –Immortal bird, a good omen, that dies in flame to rise from the ashes

Rewan – "the cunning one". Cunning but fairly current ruler of Cornovii.

Roda – "the nest", womaniser and drunkard. King of Cornovii, also known under the "Limp Dick Roda" moniker after Ina's outburst.

Sa'Ren Gerel – "son of a moonlight". The native name of Ren, for his martial skills and calm demeanour, knows as the Ghost. Ina's best friend and guardian, the current general of Cornovii's forces.

Senad – the bastard child of a high house, lesser noble. Second in command of King's guard and Marcach's friend.(deceased)

Skarbnik – Mountain spirit/ god called the Guardian of the Mountains. Depictured mostly as an old man but can shapeshift in any given form. Guards minerals and ores from greedy miners and helps lost travellers on the path. Often mischievous and unpredictable. He lives in self-imposed isolation.

Sophia – "the white gem". – Princess of Cornovii, sister of King Rewan, renowned for her beauty. After an unsuccessful coup, she was killed by the king's order.

Striga/Strzyga (Slavic mythology) – is a female creature who feeds on human blood. Their origins are connected to the belief in the duality of souls. A common explanation was that a human born with two souls could become a *strzyga* after death. Such people were easy to recognise, born with two rows of teeth, two hearts, or other similar anomalies. They could die only partially – one of the souls is leaving to the outer world, but the second one is getting trapped inside the dead body, losing many aspects of humanity. *Strzyga*'s appearance can resemble an average person with a mean character. The longer they live as a *strzyga*, the more they change. They are often presented with bird-like features: claws, eyes, and feathers growing off the back.

Swaróg/Swarożyc- god of fire, blacksmithing and creation, pictured as an old but powerful man with white hair and a hammer. Often believed to be the creator of the world.

Truthseeker – a branch of mind magic associated with Order. A psychic mage that can connect with another person's brain to trace patterns of lies and, if needed, dissect memories looking for the truth.

Tomb hag/ Grave hags are territorial creatures. Their lairs resemble caricatures of human homes and are built near burial sites. They venture out at night to hunt, stalking straggling travellers or mourners too lost in their grief to notice the sun's setting.

University of High Magical Arts/ The Magica Council – School and the highest authority for practising mages, witches and warlocks that have supreme jurisdiction over the magic of Cornovii

Volkhv – high-rank priest of Slavic religion

Veles – (Slavic mythology) a major Slavic god of earth, waters, livestock, and the underworld. A shepherd and the judge of the dead that rules Nawia. Associated with swamps, oxes and magic.

Velka Powoj– lesser noble. Gifted Nature with a strong association with trees and flowers. Also, Ina's best friend.

Vyvern - was a large winged lizard, distantly related to the dragon, with a poisonous stinging tail and sharp teeth.

Shifter tribes – shapeshifters with the ability to change into three forms, human, animal and were-form, that contain both aspects of their soul.

Wyraj – (Slavic mythology) part of Nawia, an equivalent of heaven

Yanwo – far east land, ruled by the Dragon Emperor and trading silks, spices and gems with Cornovii. Polygamy is widely practised there as dragon lords believe in the survival of the fittest, pitting their offspring against each other to strengthen the bloodline. (yup, I took this from the ottoman empire and the rules of the sultanate)

Zhrets – low-rank priests in the pagan religion. A man who performs the sacrifices.

Zmij – (based on Slavic mythology) a winged serpent with fangs dripping with venom and breathing fire. He was a ferocious and dangerous creature and a mighty protector of those he found worthy.

About the Author

Olena Nikitin is the pen name of a writing power couple who share a love of fantasy, paranormal romance, rich, vivid worlds and exciting storylines. In their books and out, they love down-to-earth humour, a visceral approach to life, striving to write realistic romances filled with the passion and steam people always dream of experiencing. Meet the two halves of this Truro UK-based dynamic duo!

Olga, a Polish woman, has a wicked sense of humour with a dash of Slavic pessimism. She's been writing since she was a small child, but life led her to work as an emergency physician. While this work means she always has stories to share, it often means she's too busy to actually write. She's proud to be a crazy cat lady, and together with Mark, they have five cats.

Mark, a typical English gentleman, radiates charm, sophistication, and an undeniable sex appeal. At least, he's reasonably certain that's what convinced Olga to fly across the sea into his arms. He's an incredibly intelligent man with a knack for fixing things, including Polish syntax in English writing. If you give him good whiskey, he might even regale you with his Gulf War story of how he got shot.

Olena Nikitin loves hearing from their fans and critics alike and welcomes communication via any platform!

- ALL-IN -ONE Social Link - https://linktr.ee/olenanikitinauthor
- NEWSLETTER Please sign up if you wish to receive free books, updates and giveaways - https://dashboard.mailerlite.com/forms/126534/76567309713409971/share
- WEBSITE - https://olenanikitin.uk/
- Also, consider following us on Amazon to be notified about new releases, discounts and more.

Also By

411

and dark desires, creating an intense rivalry between the warriors over a woman who despises any commitment. Saddled with unwilling guardians, with bodies piling up in the sewers of Osterad, Ina must solve a mystery to clear her name, knowing her failure will devastate the kingdom, while the heart she so fiercely guarded reluctantly yields to the men she never wanted.

Immerse yourself in Season's War series and learn about the kingdom of Cornovii, where passion is mixed with cruelty, and the unwilling hero with world-shattering power has to make impossible choices. Dark Fantasy with mature themes - reader caution advised.

WINTER DRAGON– SECOND BOOK FROM SEASON'S WAR SERIES

Buy Now on: https://geni.us/WinterDragon
"When a Chaos mage fights, only blood and scorched earth remain."
Mage War Chronicles

Some victories are more costly than others, and Ina was the one that paid the price. Determined to rescue her dragon, the newly appointed royal witch embarks on a gruelling journey through the wintery Grey Mountains. The weather is not her only obstacle, as the enemy forces gathered in the kobold mines have only one goal. To capture the Chaos mage and deliver her to the heart of the mountain. With the help of Sa'Ren, Ina arrives at Castle Liath almost unscathed, but her joy is short-lived, as its granite walls hide a shocking revelation. With blossoming love shattered by a possessive dragon's claim and an impossible mission to fulfil, will the mysterious Blessing of the Mountain help or hinder her efforts to protect Cornovii?

Immerse yourself in the second book of Season's War, where passion mix with cruelty and the world-changing power is buried deep in the ancient tomb guarded by the stern Mountain God.

Printed in Dunstable, United Kingdom

63327673R00251